A Touch of
TREACHERY

A SECTION 47 BOOK

JENNIFER ESTEP

A TOUCH OF TREACHERY

 To sign up for Jennifer's newsletter, scan the QR code or visit https://bit.ly/41AGJvn

*To all the readers who wanted more
Section 47 books—this one is for you.*

To my mom—for everything.

*The cover-up is always worse than the initial crime,
especially at Section 47."*

—Jack Locke, Section 47 cleaner

*"Keep everyone close, friends and enemies alike, because you
never know when one might turn into another."*

—General Jethro Percy,
head of the Section 47 board of directors

ONE

CHARLOTTE

You could always tell the thieves by their props.

A watering can and a pair of gardening gloves. A waiter's tray and a notepad. A gold watch and a briefcase.

At first glance, thieves always looked like they belonged in their surroundings, and they blended into the background like paint on a wall. But thieves had their tells, just like players in a poker game, and if you looked closely enough, you could spot the subtle signs they weren't what they appeared.

A woman kneeling by a flower bed but not actually dousing the blossoms with her watering can or digging her gloved hands into the dirt. A man leaning against a table that held an empty tray and a notepad but not actually waiting on anyone or scribbling down orders. Another man sitting in a chair, checking his imitation-gold watch and fiddling with the black leather briefcase on his lap but not actually opening the container and drawing out any papers.

So far, I'd clocked three thieves in the lobby, all situated at different points around the perimeter like a lopsided triangle.

The woman with the watering can was close to the entrance, where rows of trees, hedges, and flowers formed a large garden. The waiter was next to a gray marble column beside the café that dominated the left side of the lobby, while the business-man was in a chair close to the reception desk at the center of the back wall.

The three thieves maintained their positions and pretenses while scores of people pushed through the revolving doors at the front of the lobby, strode past the garden, and then either veered into the café or headed toward the left or right bank of elevators. A few folks stopped at the reception desk to ask for directions.

Like many buildings on the outskirts of Washington, D.C., this structure housed a variety of businesses, everything from dentists and lawyers to accountants and acupuncturists. One elevator car after another dinged out its arrival, while the café's espresso machines hissed, burped, and spewed out one beverage after another, creating a pleasant symphony of sound. The dark, rich scent of a dozen different coffees curled through the air, along with a yeasty whiff of fresh-baked cinnamon rolls that made my stomach rumble with longing.

Too bad Section 47 spies didn't get coffee breaks.

I angled my phone left and right, using the screen to watch the thieves scattered around the lobby. This crew was more subtle and disciplined than most, but they all looked tense and wary, and they were all turned so that they had a clear view of their target—me.

Just like the thieves, I too was wearing a disguise—a bright royal-blue pantsuit that stood out like an unwanted ink stain amid the bland gray furniture. I hadn't bothered with a watch or any jewelry, and instead of the expected heels, dark gray sneakers covered my feet. The scuffed shoes were my tell, but I didn't care about blending in with everyone else. Comfort had always been much more important than fashion to me, since you never knew when things might go wrong, and you might have to run for your life as a spy. Something that happened far too frequently for my peace of mind.

I put my phone away and stared through the glass wall at the street outside. Traffic flowed at a steady pace, accompanied by the impatient honk of horns, and no cars were idling at the curb, waiting to whisk the thieves away after they'd finished their heist.

In addition to the front wall, two side walls were also made of glass, and the bright sunlight streaming inside made the silver flecks in the floor shimmer like minnows swimming through the gray marble. Off to the right, the garden greenery clustered around a wooden bridge that stretched over a stream of bubbling water that widened into a round stone pool filled with glimmering coins.

A sea of worn couches spread across the center of the lobby before giving way to black wrought-iron tables and chairs that perched around the café on the left wall. A corner escalator rose to the second floor, which featured a glassed-in terrace that served as overflow seating for the café.

Chandeliers dangled from the ceiling, each one with long, skinny, stiff white paper strands that made them look like giant dandelion puffs about to be blown away by the aggressive heating system. Black security cameras also dangled from the ceiling and swiveled back and forth like oblong spiders swinging from thin strands.

I stared up at the closest camera. Gia Chan and Diego Benito, my colleagues at Section 47, were no doubt viewing the live footage right now. They were stationed in a building down the block, along with a strike team, just waiting to rush in and apprehend the thieves when they finally decided to make a move. But I couldn't help but wonder who else might be peering through the cameras—and what their plans were for me.

I resisted snapping off a cheeky salute to my silent watchers, Section 47 and otherwise, and dropped my gaze back down to the lobby.

Everyone looked perfectly normal, but I kept glancing around, trying to figure out whether I'd missed spotting any more thieves. Hard to tell, given the dozens of people coming and going, but maybe I could fix that.

I stretched my hand out and drummed my fingers on the briefcase perched on the cushion beside me, as though I was growing bored waiting to be seen. All three thieves tensed, and the woman with the watering can dug her knees into the dirt like she wanted to leap up, sprint forward, and brain me with the metal container.

Given how fidgety she had been since I'd entered the lobby ten minutes ago, I was willing to bet the gardener-thief was a paramortal, someone with special magical abilities. Most likely, she was an enduro with incredible stamina, someone who could fight, run, or stay awake for days on end. Many enduros felt a constant need to burn off the amazing amount of energy pumping through their bodies, and this woman kept shifting on her knees and curling and uncurling her fingers around the watering can.

As for the waiter-thief and the businessman-thief, they were most likely paramortals too, although I couldn't tell what powers the two men might have. They could be enduros like the woman—or something even more dangerous.

I kept drumming my fingers on the briefcase, which was the same bright blue as my suit, as though I were a peacock preening my feathers to attract maximum attention. The three thieves were the only ones who reacted to the motion, but I couldn't shake the nagging feeling that someone else was watching me, so I drew in a breath and reached for my magic.

Just like the three thieves, I too was a paramortal. My ability? A magical form of synesthesia that let me see mistakes, typos, and errors in whatever document, spreadsheet, or contract I was reviewing, something that helped me track rogue paramortals as a spy-slash-analyst for Section 47. But my synesthesia took other forms as well, including a highly tuned sense of danger and an inner voice that whispered of threats—

A bit of pink flared off to my left. I tensed, but the pink flare was centered on a puddle of spilled coffee. My synesthesia might be useful in sensing true mortal danger, like an assassin who wanted to shoot me, but it often bombarded me with bright, colorful lights, even when it was just pointing out a minor hazard like a slick floor. I grimaced and looked away before the neon-pink flare sparked a headache.

"Excuse me, Ms. Locke," a light, feminine voice called out.

Heels clacked on the floor, and a woman came out from behind the reception desk and stopped beside me. Her pantsuit was the same light silver as her short, wavy hair, and she blended into the background even better than the thieves did. The woman looked to be in her fifties, with rosy skin and pretty features schooled into a polite expression.

"I'm Iris Berriston." The woman smiled and held out her hand. "I'm the agent on-site and will be handling the transfer of assets."

I leaned forward, shook her hand, and returned her smile with one of my own. "Thank you, Iris. And please, call me Charlotte. People only call me Ms. Locke when there is some sort of trouble at Section 47."

Iris's light brown eyes twinkled with amusement. "Isn't there always some sort of trouble at Section 47?"

I snorted. That was an understatement.

To most folks, Section 47 was a bland moniker, a nondescript name for a corporation that did important yet vague things for the government like so many other businesses in Washington, D.C. In reality, Section 47 was a super-secret spy organization devoted to gathering intelligence and analyzing information to thwart crimes, mass-casualty events, and terrorist activities. Only instead of chasing regular villains, Section 47 was tasked with tracking, apprehending, and policing dangerous para-mortals.

Section 47 took its name from a specific, extra bit of DNA that supposedly imbued paramortals with all their amazing abilities. At least, that was the commonly accepted scientific theory, although most paramortals just called their abilities magic.

As an analyst for Section 47, I monitored and tracked the worst of the worst—criminals, terrorists, and other rogue para-mortals who used their magical abilities and enhanced weapons to commit horrific atrocities. Like Henrika Hyde, a weapons maker I had been chasing for the last few months who had morphed into my personal nemesis.

Iris's smile melted away, and her face turned serious. "I'm just waiting to receive a final confirmation and some paperwork from headquarters, and then I can take you down to the Vault. It should only be a few more minutes."

Section 47 was all about hiding in plain sight. Several decades ago, this building had been a bank, and over the years, the Section higher-ups had quietly repurposed the lowest level, turning it into a storage facility for illegal biomagical drugs, weapons, money, and other items that were confiscated during raids. Hence the nickname the Vault.

Iris gestured at the café. "Can I get you anything while you wait? Water? Juice? Coffee?"

"No, I'm fine. Thank you."

She nodded, then returned to the reception desk. Iris reached for the landline phone, but her hand trembled, and the receiver squirted out of her grasp and landed with a loud clatter. She winced and scooped up the receiver.

Thwack.

The wet slap of a mop hitting the floor drew my attention. Off to the left, a janitor nudged a yellow cart forward and swiped his mop back and forth, cleaning up the spilled coffee my synesthesia had pointed out.

His dark blue coveralls outlined his broad shoulders and lean, muscled body, while black boots encased his feet. A blue baseball hat topped his head, covering most of his dark blond hair and casting a shadow over his tan skin, along with the golden stubble that clung to his strong jaw.

The janitor bent down over the mop, hunching his shoulders and making himself seem much shorter than his six-foot height.

"Don't ogle me too much, Numbers." A low, teasing voice with a hint of an Australian accent echoed through my earbud. "You don't want to blow my cover."

Desmond Percy was always worth ogling, even if he was wearing drab coveralls instead of the sleek business suits he preferred. I grabbed my phone and held it up to my ear, pretending to talk to someone.

"I'm just surprised to see a Section 47 cleaner actually cleaning something up, Crocodile Dundee," I replied, my soft Southern accent adding an extra drawl to my voice.

When I'd first met Desmond, I'd dubbed him Crocodile Dundee because of his Australian accent, while he'd called me Numbers because of the calculations he said were always going on in my mind. At first, I'd despised the nickname, but now I loved the extra connection between the two of us.

"Usually, all you cleaners do is make a bloody mess—in every sense of the word," I continued.

Desmond chuckled at my black humor. As an analyst, my job was to track rogue paramortals, but as a cleaner, Desmond's job was to eliminate them—permanently. He was one of Section 47's top assassins and a powerful galvanist, someone who could control and manipulate different forms of energy, from the electricity humming through the chandeliers to the steam spewing out of the café's espresso machines to the battery charge in my phone.

"At least you get to be the anonymous worker bee today instead of me." I sighed. "Although those coveralls look a lot more comfortable than the nutcracker outfit I had to wear at Christmas."

"Are you still holding a grudge about that?" he teased again.

A few weeks ago, Desmond and I had gone undercover during a Christmas Eve party at Tannenbaum Castle in Germany. Desmond had attended as Desmond Macfarlane, his undercover alias as a notorious arms dealer. Me? I'd been stuck pretending to be a waiter, and given the party's holiday theme, I'd been forced to dress up like a toy soldier from *The Nutcracker* ballet, complete with an itchy black brimmed hat, a stiff button-up jacket, and knee-high boots that had pinched my feet.

"You would hold a grudge too if you'd had to wear that awful costume," I muttered.

Desmond chuckled again. "Well, I thought you looked amazing. Then again, you always look amazing."

The low, husky note in his voice made me shiver. Desmond and I had been together for a few months, and so far, things had been wonderful between us, despite the trouble we'd run into in Germany. The couple that spies together stays together. At least for now. I didn't know what kind of future Desmond and I might have, but I was eager to find out.

At their respective positions, all three thieves suddenly snapped to attention. The gardener surged to her feet and looked at the businessman, who'd been checking his watch. He stood up and nodded to her, as well as to the waiter. Then all three of them headed in my direction. Whatever they had been waiting for had finally happened, and now they were ready to get down to business.

I glanced over at Desmond. "Here we go. Wish me luck."

A smile crooked the corner of his mouth. "You don't need luck, Charlotte, but I'll wish it for you anyway, and I'll be watching your back, just like always."

Desmond pulled a *Caution* sign out of the janitor's cart and stuck it on the damp floor. Then he slid the mop into the bucket and pushed the cart away, whistling a soft tune. Desmond strode right by the fake waiter, but the other man didn't give him a second look.

Over at the reception desk, Iris murmured something into the landline phone, then set the receiver down. She stared at it a few seconds, then raised her head and gestured at me.

I slid my phone into my pocket, then reached for the briefcase. My fingers curled around the handle, and I blew out a tense breath, got to my feet, and headed toward the other agent.

Time to see if the thieves took the bait.

TWO

CHARLOTTE

The three thieves kept heading toward me. I turned my back and strode away as though I hadn't noticed them at all, much less the fact that they were focused on me like heat-seeking missiles streaking toward a target.

I reached the reception desk, and Iris stretched her arm out to the side. "This way, Charlotte."

By this point, most folks had come in to work for the day, and the lobby was empty, except for some stragglers in line at the café. Good. Section 47 kept a tight lid on magical activities, so the general public had no idea paramortals and their powers even existed. I wanted to keep it that way, although I had a sinking feeling that things were going to get messy with the thieves. Then again, everything involving Henrika Hyde always got messy—and bloody—in the end.

I fell in step beside Iris. Maybe it was my synesthesia surging up and messing with my senses or just knowing the thieves were behind me, but the scuffing of my sneakers on the floor morphed into a squeaky, disjointed mantra in my mind.

Dan-ger, dan-ger, dan-ger . . .

I ground my teeth and ignored the unwanted noise. I glanced out of the corners of my eyes, looking for shadows coming up on the floor behind me, as well as listening for the quick slap of footsteps . . .

Nothing happened. No shadows, no footsteps, no rough hands yanking the briefcase away.

Iris led me over to the elevator bank on the left side of the lobby and swiped a white keycard over a reader embedded in the wall. A light flashed green, and the door slid back. The two of us stepped into the elevator and turned around, facing out toward the lobby.

I tensed, my fingers curling even tighter around the briefcase handle. Any second now, the thieves were going to storm into the elevator and try to wrest the case away from me . . .

But once again, nothing happened.

Iris hesitated, then swiped her keycard over the elevator panel. A light flashed green, and the door slid shut.

What was going on? Why hadn't the thieves rushed forward and tried to take the briefcase? Had I done something to spook them?

I frowned at my reflection in the mirrored door. Auburn hair, blue eyes, pale skin, bright blue suit, matching briefcase. Everything about me was the same as when I'd left Section 47 headquarters, and I'd followed the mission plan to the letter. Enter the lobby, sit down, and let the thieves approach me.

But the thieves hadn't made a move, which meant they had some *other* plan to steal the briefcase. What was I missing?

I pulled out my phone to ask Desmond what was happening in the lobby, but a message on the screen warned that I didn't have a signal. Even more alarming was the faint buzz of static crackling through my earbud. My stomach clenched. Someone was jamming our comms.

Iris let out a loud, raspy exhale, and a puff of warm, sour air wafted across my neck. I looked at the other agent out of the corners of my eyes. She stabbed a button to take us to the lower Vault level, but her hand trembled, just as it had earlier when she'd been reaching for the landline phone on her desk.

My heart sank right along with the elevator, but I turned toward her. "How did Henrika Hyde get to you?"

Iris blinked. "What?"

"How did Henrika convince you to try to steal this?" I jiggled the briefcase in my hand. "Did she blackmail you? Threaten your family? Or did you just take the money she offered?"

I didn't bother keeping the disgust out of my voice, and Iris flinched at my harsh tone. "I don't know what you're talking about. I've never heard of Henrika Hyde."

Lie, my inner voice whispered. In addition to pointing out hazards and dangers, my synesthesia also told me whenever someone was lying, whether it was a small, harmless fib (*of course your new haircut looks great*) to an outright whopper (*of course I didn't eat the last cookie*).

Even without the telltale whisper, I still would have known Iris wasn't telling the truth. Everyone at Section 47 had heard of Henrika Hyde, thanks to Desmond and me and our run-ins with the weapons maker over the last few months.

I looked at Iris, who stared right back at me. Her tongue swiped out over her lips, and a pink light flared around her body. The seconds ticked by in soft, charged silence, and the pink light intensified, morphing into a bloody red I knew all too well.

"Dammit," Iris muttered.

She slapped a button on the panel, and the elevator screeched to a halt. The abrupt motion tossed me to the side, and my right shoulder banged against the side of the car. I lost my grip on the briefcase, which tumbled to the floor.

I cursed and reached for the briefcase, but Iris yanked a small gun out of the pocket of her suit jacket.

"Stop right there!" she growled.

I stopped, even as my synesthesia surged up, outlining the gun in an even brighter, bloodier red than it had Iris. I ground my teeth again. Sometimes I thought my paramortal power was total overkill, since I could clearly see the other woman aiming the weapon at my chest, and I already knew *exactly* how much danger I was in.

"Pick up the briefcase," Iris growled again. "Slowly."

I crouched down. My fingers curled around the handle, and I thought about snapping my arm up and using the briefcase as a weapon, but I resisted the urge.

I slowly rose to my feet. "You didn't answer my question."

"What question?"

"How did Henrika get her hooks into you? Blackmail, threats, or money?"

Iris's dark brown eyes narrowed. "Money, not that it's any of *your* business."

I jerked my chin at the gun in her hand. "You've made it *my* business."

She scoffed. "You wouldn't understand. A Legacy like you will *always* have a place at Section, but people like me don't have the same luxury."

Legacy was Section 47's term for folks with other family members who also worked for the spy organization, either currently or in the past. If your family members did well and climbed up the leadership ranks, then being a Legacy could greatly aid your standing at Section. But if your family members screwed up, well, being a Legacy could be more of a hindrance than a help.

I'd always fallen more on the hindrance side of the Legacy equation, thanks to my father, Jack Locke, a cleaner who had died under mysterious circumstances on a Section mission roughly fifteen years ago.

"People like you?" I asked.

Iris shrugged. "Paramortals without amazing abilities.

Technically, I'm a transmuter, although the only thing I've ever been able to do with my magic is make things sparkle."

A silver glow flickered around her fingers, and the gun in her hand gleamed brightly in response, as though she had just polished it. Strong transmuters could change the physical properties of objects, like turning water into ice, but Iris was right about her limited magic.

"I *dreamed* about being a Section field agent, but my weak, useless power got me a weak, useless job." Iris sneered. "I'm nothing but a glorified elevator operator, taking people down to the Vault, and it's long past time I made a career change."

"So you took the money."

"Absolutely. Now, shut up and stand still."

Iris took a little better aim at me with her gun. I tensed and tightened my grip on the briefcase, ready to snap up the container and put it between me and any bullets that came my way.

The other agent stared at me a second longer, then hit a button on the panel. Instead of descending toward the Vault, the elevator rose and climbed up past the lobby.

"Where are we going?" I asked, worry making my stomach swell like a balloon in my body.

Iris's lips pulled back into a sly smile. "You'll figure it out soon enough, Charlotte. But for right now, just enjoy the ride."

A few seconds later, the elevator stopped and dinged out its arrival on the fifth floor. The door slid back, revealing a glass wall running the length of a corridor. On the opposite side of the glass, low white plastic walls partitioned off the space beyond like a giant tic-tac-toe board. The cubicles were empty, although landline phones, headsets, and wires crisscrossed the floor like a nest of black snakes.

According to the building blueprints I'd reviewed, the call center had recently gone bankrupt, leaving this floor empty of people. A lone security camera dangled from the ceiling, but it didn't swivel around, and I couldn't tell if it was monitoring us—or if Gia, Diego, and the other Section agents stationed outside the building realized just how much trouble I was in.

Iris waggled her gun. "Move."

I stepped out of the elevator. She followed and gestured for me to stop beside a high wooden table against the glass wall. "Put the briefcase down."

I did as ordered, although I kept my hand curled around the handle.

Iris backed away a few steps, pulled her phone out of her jacket pocket, and held it up to her ear. "Package secure."

"Get the goods and get out of there," a male voice murmured through the phone.

"Roger that," she replied, then waggled the gun again. "Open the briefcase."

"Why do you want the case? There's nothing in it."

A low, ugly laugh trilled out of her mouth. "Please. I might be a glorified elevator operator, but I get a list of all the items brought to the Vault for storage, so I know you're carrying the Grunglass Necklace. Henrika wants her property back, Charlotte."

A few months ago, Henrika Hyde had tried to steal the Grunglass Necklace from the Halstead Hotel in Washington, D.C. The necklace had belonged to Hiram Halstead, Henrika's father, who had promised it to her mother, Natasha, as payment for being his longtime mistress. But Hiram's other daughter, Petra Halstead, had kept her half sister from getting the necklace. A furious Henrika had bombed one of Hiram's hotels, killing her father and forcing Petra into hiding.

"Open the briefcase," Iris repeated. "Now."

"Why? So you can kill me a second later?" I shook my head.

"No way. If you want the necklace, come over here and get it yourself."

The other agent rolled her eyes. "Killing you isn't part of the plan, Charlotte. I'm here to get the necklace and get paid. Nothing more, nothing less."

I waited, but my synesthesia was silent. Iris was telling the truth. She either didn't want to or didn't have orders to kill me. Why not?

During the Tannenbaum mission in Germany, Desmond and I had battled a group of thieves who wanted to steal the Nutcracker Ruby, a ring worth millions of dollars. Katarina Tanetsa, the group's leader, had claimed that Henrika had promised her a bonus for eliminating me. So why would Henrika let me live now? What had changed?

A soft beep sounded. Iris checked her phone again. "Time's up. Open the case. Or I'll start putting bullets in your body until you change your mind."

"Okay, okay. You win."

I keyed in a code on the electronic panel embedded in the blue leather. The lock clicked, and the lid lifted. I spun the briefcase around on the table so that the open side was facing Iris.

"Raise it up," she ordered.

I slowly lifted the lid, revealing a large gold chandelier necklace on a bed of pale green velvet. The stunning necklace was studded with large teardrop-shaped emeralds and smaller princess-cut white diamonds, and all the jewels sparked and flashed with a vibrant inner fire.

Iris let out a low, appreciative whistle, then lifted her phone to her ear again. "Secondary objective secure. Heading toward the exit."

"Roger that." Once again, a man's voice echoed out of her phone.

I frowned. Henrika was obsessed with the Grunglass

Necklace, and the whole point of this mission had been to leak the fact that I was bringing it to the Vault for safekeeping. I'd expected Henrika to make a play for the necklace, and I'd been planning to use the thieves to try to discover where she was hiding. So why would Iris refer to the necklace as a secondary objective? And why hadn't the three thieves come here to help her?

Unless . . . the thieves were busy stealing *something else*.

A chill swept down my spine, and my stomach churned with worry. Henrika never did anything halfway, and if she had ordered the thieves to target another item at the Vault, then their primary objective had to be something big. What could be worth more to Henrika than the necklace she had coveted since childhood?

Iris slid her phone into her pocket, although she kept her gun aimed at my chest. "Close the case and hand it to me. No tricks, or I'll shoot you."

I closed the briefcase lid and stepped forward.

"Stop!" Iris barked out. "Stay where you are, and push the case over to me."

I grabbed hold of the briefcase and shoved it forward like I was a bartender sliding a drink over to a thirsty customer. The case slid to a stop at Iris's end of the table.

She picked it up, then grinned. "A pleasure doing business with you, Charlotte."

"It's not business. Not to me. Henrika made it personal."

Iris shrugged. "Well, that's between you and her. Me? I'm planning to retire to a nice little tropical island."

I shook my head. "You're not going anywhere."

She laughed. "In case you haven't noticed, *I m* the one with the gun."

"Oh, I knew someone would have a gun." I grinned. "So I brought a few toys of my own."

Iris's forehead creased with confusion, and her gaze flicked up and down my body, trying to spot whatever weapons I might have tucked away in my clothes.

"Execute Command Jewelry Box," I called out in a loud voice.

Iris flinched, and her entire body tensed.

One second ticked by. Then two, three, four, five . . .

Nothing happened.

Iris's body relaxed, although her face twisted into an ugly sneer. "I don't know what you're playing at, Charlotte—"

Bang!

An explosion sounded, and a cloud of bright green smoke spewed out of the briefcase.

THREE

DESMOND

I pushed the janitor's cart toward the café exit, where the spout of a water cooler hanging off the side of a table was dripping onto the floor. I turned the spout fully to the off position, then pulled my mop out of its bucket and slapped it against the gray marble, cleaning up this latest spill.

I kept my shoulders hunched, but my gaze remained on Charlotte. Even if we hadn't been on a mission, I still would have been watching her, since Charlotte Locke was the most beautiful woman I'd ever seen, especially when it came to her aura.

People constantly gave off energy, just like all the phones, tablets, and laptops they used. As a galvanist, I could see and feel that energy the same way I could sense the light and heat from a glowing bulb. People's auras usually appeared as shimmering colors, although I occasionally sensed ripples of emotion instead. Charlotte's aura was a deep, brilliant blue, more vivid than any sapphire, and most of the time, she radiated a sense of cool calm that was like a balm soothing my heart.

Charlotte joined Iris Berriston at the reception desk. Iris's dark green aura flickered over and over like a bulb about to short-circuit, indicating she was more nervous than she appeared. As the Section agent on-site, Iris was responsible for overseeing, cataloging, and protecting all the dangerous, valuable objects stored in the Vault. That was enough to make anyone nervous.

The two women went down the corridor on the left side of the lobby, heading toward the elevators.

Our plan was simple. Charlotte would let the thieves approach and try to steal the briefcase. While the thieves were focused on her, I would come up from behind and subdue them.

The three thieves picked up their pace, crossing the lobby and following along behind Charlotte and Iris. Their auras were a swirling miasma of rusty red, sickly yellow, and putrid orange that reflected their raw nerves and ill intentions.

The thieves quickened their pace. My fingers tightened around the mop, and I stepped out from behind the janitor's cart, ready to sprint forward to help Charlotte . . .

At the last instant, the three thieves veered away from Charlotte and rounded the right side of the reception desk.

I froze mid-step, and one of my boots slipped on the wet patch of floor I'd mopped. By the time I steadied myself, the thieves had entered the corridor on the right side of the lobby and vanished from view.

Worry dripped off me faster than the water sluicing out of the mop. Why had the thieves moved away from Charlotte? Had they realized I was watching them? But if that was the case, why go deeper into the lobby? Why not head toward the exit?

A flash of movement caught my eye, along with the murmur of a low baritone voice. I looked to the right just in time to see a man wearing a dark business suit cross the wooden bridge over the stream of water and step behind a tree in the garden section of the lobby.

I'd only seen the man for a moment, but something about him seemed strangely familiar. I peered in that direction, but I only got glimpses of the man moving back and forth through the trees, as though he was pacing while he took a call.

I shrugged off my unease. The mystery man didn't matter. Protecting Charlotte did.

I glanced at the left side of the lobby. Charlotte and Iris stepped into the elevator, and the door closed behind them. The thieves hadn't even tried to get close to the two agents, which increased my confusion. If the thieves weren't after Charlotte, what were they doing here?

I stowed my mop in its bucket and pushed the janitor's cart toward the right side of the lobby where the thieves had gone.

"Charlotte?" I murmured. "Charlotte, can you hear me?"

A faint whine erupted in my earbud, along with crackling static. I pulled my phone out of my pocket, but I didn't have a signal. Someone was jamming our comms, which meant Charlotte and I had no way to talk to each other.

I glanced up at the nearest security camera, but it was no longer sweeping back and forth. Looked like it had been disabled too, which meant our Section backup was most likely blind to what was happening. Fuck.

I shoved my phone back into my pocket. My steps slowed, and I wavered, torn between checking on Charlotte and tracking the thieves. But Charlotte could take care of herself, something she'd proven time and time again, including a few months ago here in D.C., when we'd been trying to ferret out Henrika Hyde's moles inside Section 47, and a few weeks ago in Germany, when we'd been separated at Tannenbaum Castle.

I trusted Charlotte to do her job the same way she trusted me to do mine. Right now, my job was apprehending the thieves, so I pushed the janitor's cart forward again.

I parked my cart beside the reception desk, then plucked the mop out of its bucket and glanced around the corner into the right corridor. The three thieves were standing beside an elevator. The man in the business suit pulled a white keycard out of his pocket and waved it over the reader on the wall. A light turned green, a loud *ding* sounded, and a green arrow pointing downward appeared over the elevator. Somehow the thieves had gotten a keycard that let them access the Section elevator that went down to the Vault, which meant they could still ambush Charlotte on the lower level.

The thieves stepped into the elevator. Still clutching the mop, I abandoned all pretense of stealth and rushed forward, but I was too slow, and the door closed before I was halfway down the corridor.

I didn't have time to wait for another elevator, so I hurried over to a door in the corner topped by a sign that read *Emergency Exit Only*. Even Section 47 had to follow fire and safety codes, so I knew the door led down to the Vault.

I slapped my hand up against the card reader embedded in the wall and reached out with my galvanism. In an instant, I could feel the current running through the reader, and I twisted the electricity around and around like I was turning a key in a lock. In a way, that was exactly what I was doing.

Beep!

The light on the reader turned green, and the door buzzed open. Still holding the mop, I yanked the door open the rest of the way and stepped through to the other side. A light clicked on above my head, revealing a concrete staircase. I pulled the door shut behind me and hurried forward.

I had to reach the Vault—and Charlotte—before the thieves did.

I sprinted down the stairs, my footsteps banging out a loud, frantic rhythm that rattled off the walls like I was beating a drum in the enclosed space.

"Charlotte?" I called out. "Charlotte?"

Once again, the only response I got was the crackle of static in my earbud. Comms were still down.

Thirty seconds later, I reached a metal door at the bottom of the stairs. It too was locked with a keycard reader, but a surge of my galvanism took care of that.

The door buzzed open. I hooked my fingers around the frame, cracked it open a little wider, and peered through to the other side.

A dark gray marble corridor stretched out in front of me. In the distance, the soft echoes of footsteps sounded, along with the faint murmur of voices. The thieves had beaten me here, which meant they could already be creeping up on Charlotte.

I stepped into the corridor. I'd had a gun hidden among the cleaning supplies in the janitor's cart, and I'd foolishly left it behind in my rush. But that was okay. As a cleaner, I had been trained to kill with whatever I could get my hands on, and the mop I was currently holding would make an excellent weapon, as would the pocket watch with its long, attached silver chain in the front flap of my coveralls. And I could always use my galvanism to take down an enemy by stopping the electrical charge that powered their heart.

I quickened my pace, keeping my steps soft and silent. I reached the end of the corridor and peeked around the corner. The next corridor was much longer, with thick metal doors set into the walls like lockers in a school.

The three thieves were about halfway down the corridor, clustered around a door that was wider than most of the others. To my surprise, Charlotte was nowhere in sight.

The woman who'd been pretending to be a gardener looked at the man who'd been masquerading as a waiter. Small name tags on their clothes marked her as Bonnie and him as Woody.

"Are you *sure* this is the right locker?" Bonnie asked.

"Of course I'm sure," Woody replied, then gestured at the fake businessman. "Hey, Arnold, hand me the codebreaker."

Arnold reached into a flap on the side of his briefcase and pulled out a device that looked like a small black phone. Woody plucked a cord out of his pants pocket and used it to attach the codebreaker to the keypad on the wall beside the locker door. He hit some buttons, and a series of numbers flashed on the device, the six-digit combinations zipping by too fast to follow.

"You're sure the evidence is stored in *this* locker?" Bonnie repeated her earlier question. "Because we don't have time for you to be wrong."

"Yes," Woody muttered, his gaze on the codebreaker. "The manifest said all the German evidence is stored in *this* locker."

My ears pricked up. German evidence? They had to be talking about the Tannenbaum mission where Charlotte and I had stopped a group of mercenaries from stealing the Nutcracker Ruby. The valuable ring belonged to Elsa Eisen, who had used her ancestral castle as a storage facility for paramortal criminals to hide their ill-gotten goods. Elsa's brother, Peter, had foolishly embezzled money from Henrika Hyde, a longtime Eisen family client, and Henrika had retaliated by killing Peter and trying to steal the Nutcracker Ruby from Elsa.

I frowned. Elsa had been allowed to keep the ring as part of the deal she'd made to secretly feed information on her clients to Section 47, and the Nutcracker Ruby was safely locked away in the depths of Tannenbaum Castle. If the thieves had a manifest of the locker's contents, then they knew the ring wasn't here. So what were they after? The only other thing Charlotte and I had found at the castle that was truly valuable had been . . .

The Redburn explosive.

Henrika Hyde had created dozens of nasty weapons over the

years. Poisons that targeted specific individuals and bloodlines, chemicals that would freeze people's lungs seconds after being inhaled, even drugs that would give regular people short-lived paramortal powers and melt their insides at the same time. But Redburn was perhaps the deadliest, most powerful formula Henrika had ever concocted, and it was designed to kill even the strongest paramortal.

Something I had discovered the hard way on the Blacksea mission.

My chest tightened, my heart squeezed, and my gut twisted with a sickening wrench. The dim underground corridor vanished, replaced by a bright, sunny beach on an island off the coast of Australia. I blinked, and suddenly, I was standing in the sand, feeling the loose grit shift under my boots. In the distance, one bomb after another blew up in slow motion, each explosion a little closer, louder, and more violent than the last.

Fire, heat, force, and fury rolled toward me in an unstoppable red-orange wave. Dimly, I could hear Graham Walker, my best friend and fellow Section cleaner, yelling at me to run, get back, get down. I flinched as Graham crashed into me, driving my body deep down into the sand and shielding me as best he could. The powerful explosions blasted over us both, the intense, burning heat searing off one layer of my skin after another and scorching all the way down into my bones—

Beep.

The codebreaker finished its work, shattering my memory. The beach vanished, and the corridor snapped back into focus, although cold sweat beaded on my forehead, and my heart pounded in my too-tight chest.

A light on the keypad turned green, and the locker door opened. Woody unhooked the codebreaker and handed it to Arnold, who slid it back into the flap on his briefcase.

Bonnie grinned. "Well, that was easier than expected."

"I told you it would work," Woody crowed. "Now, let's get what we came for, while Bryce takes care of the primary objective."

Primary objective? If breaking into this locker was merely a side mission, then what was the thieves' most important purpose? Stealing the Grunglass Necklace from Charlotte? Or something else?

The three thieves entered the locker. They left the door open behind them, and clangs, clanks, and bangs sounded as they searched through the contents.

"Charlotte?" I whispered. "Charlotte?"

Still no answer, only static. Whatever the thieves were after, it was up to me to stop them. Then I could find Charlotte, and we could figure out what was really going on.

I waited a few more seconds, giving the thieves enough time to wade deep into the locker, then eased around the corner, tiptoed over to the open door, and peered inside.

A long metal table stood in the center of the storage space, and metal shelves lined all three walls. The thieves were in the very back, pulling out one plastic bin after another, tearing off the lids, and rifling through the contents.

"Where is it?" Bonnie muttered.

"Keep looking," Arnold replied. "Maybe the Section 47 evidence techs didn't realize what the vials were and labeled them wrong."

Vials? Once again, that sandy beach loomed up in my mind, blotting out everything else. I swiped the cold sweat off my forehead with a shaking hand. Anger erupted in my chest, and I seized onto the red-hot emotion, letting it ground me in the here and now. The phantom beach melted away, replaced by the storage locker.

After I'd killed some of the mercenaries at Tannenbaum Castle, I'd found several vials of bloodred liquid among the mercs' supplies. In addition to stealing the Nutcracker Ruby,

Henrika had wanted to blow Elsa Eisen to smithereens, along with her ancestral castle.

I drew in a breath, and the remembered stench of the Redburn explosive flooded my nose—sweet, sticky honey mixed with rotten eggs. My nostrils flared in disgust, and more anger erupted in my chest.

Given my own horrific experience with the explosive, I'd swiped the vials from the castle, and Charlotte and I had agreed to hide them from everyone. The Redburn formula was simply too dangerous to entrust to anyone, especially the Section 47 leaders, who would try to reverse engineer the formula. If they succeeded, then more people would suffer the same agonizing fate as Graham.

I couldn't let that happen. Not again. Not to anyone. Not even an enemy.

I tightened my grip on the mop in my hand and stepped into the locker. I'd deal with the thieves, then find Charlotte.

Squeak.

My damp boot squelched against the floor. The thieves whirled around. For a heartbeat, we all stood there staring at each other. Then Woody cursed, as did Bonnie and Arnold.

I sprinted forward and twirled the mop around in my hand, holding it out in front of me like a spear. Arnold, the fake businessman, was the closest, and I jabbed the blunt tip of the mop into his stomach. He let out a muffled cry and staggered back, gasping for air.

I spun toward Woody, but the fake waiter chopped the mop out of my hand, then rammed his shoulder into my chest. The thief was definitely an enduro, strong and fast, and the hard blow sent me stumbling back out through the open door.

Woody growled, sprinted forward, and dug his hands into the front of my coveralls. Then he churned his legs, drove me all the way across the corridor, and slammed me into the opposite wall.

Pain exploded in my back, even as an answering surge of power spiked through my body. As a galvanist, I had the ability to control and manipulate all the energy around me, even if that energy was a physical blow to my own body. I snarled, grabbed onto that painful spike of power, and drove my fist into the thief's jaw.

Woody let out a brief, muffled snort. His dark eyes rolled up into the back of his head, and he dropped to the floor unconscious.

"Bloody Section spies," Bonnie spat out.

The female thief stepped out of the storage locker and yanked a gun out of her pocket. I was too far away to tackle her, so I plucked the silver pocket watch out of the front flap of my coveralls. I gripped the watch in my hand, then lunged toward her and snapped the long, attached chain forward like a whip.

The chain slapped against Bonnie's hand, and the razor-sharp edge sliced a deep gash across her fingers. She yelped and lowered her gun, giving me enough time to cross the distance between us and knock the weapon out of her hand.

The gun hit the floor and skidded back into the locker. Bonnie scrambled after the weapon. I followed her, slammed my hand into her back, and used the resulting momentum, along with her own forward motion, to ram her body into the closest shelf.

Bonnie's head banged into a metal corner with a loud, meaty *thwack*, and she too dropped to the floor. Blood gushed out of the ugly cut on her head, and I couldn't tell if she was unconscious or dead. I didn't much care either way, so long as she stayed down.

Arnold, the thief I'd attacked with the mop, was still wheezing, but he scooped up Bonnie's gun and aimed it at me. I lashed out with the watch chain again. The silver links wrapped around his wrist and tore into his skin, making him yelp.

I tightened my grip on the watch and yanked it back, along with the attached chain. The sharp motion jerked Arnold off-balance and sent him staggering in my direction. I drew my arm back, then stepped forward and slammed my fist into his face.

Crack!

Arnold's nose broke, and he slumped to the floor.

I stood there, breathing hard, but none of the thieves stirred. I bent down, unwrapped the silver chain from around Arnold's wrist, and slid the watch back into the front flap on my coveralls. Then I moved from one thief to another, searching them, but they only had burner phones in their pockets.

I pressed Woody's thumb onto his phone, unlocking it, since he had seemed to be the leader. The thieves might have been blocking Section comms, but his device had a signal, so I quickly keyed in a number and sent a text.

Code name BRIEFCASE. Mission compromised. Three thieves subdued on Vault level. More hostiles might be in the building. D.

A few seconds later, the phone chimed with a message. *Understood. Strike team will move in. G.*

G was Gia Chan, my immediate supervisor and the head of the Section cleaners in the D.C. station.

Charlotte and I hadn't wanted to scare off the thieves by having a bunch of undercover Section agents camped out in the lobby, so we'd entered the Vault building by ourselves. Gia was stationed nearby, monitoring the lobby's security feed in case we needed backup, although the thieves had most likely disrupted the cameras, just like they had done with Charlotte's and my comms.

I scanned Woody's texts, but the phone only contained generic messages like *In position* and *Waiting.* But the surprising thing was that Woody was reporting to someone else, which meant he wasn't the leader after all.

Frustrated, I shoved the burner phone into my pocket, then grabbed Woody's ankles and dragged him into the storage locker with Arnold and Bonnie. I shut the door behind me, and the keypad light flicked to red. That should hold the unconscious thieves until more Section agents arrived.

In my pocket, Woody's phone buzzed with a new text. *Primary objective almost complete. Grab what you can and meet me at the rendezvous point.*

Once again, the vague message didn't tell me who had sent it or where they were. Whoever was in charge was smart, and so far, they had been one step ahead of Charlotte and me.

Now, let's get what we came for, while Bryce takes care of the primary objective, Woody's voice whispered through my mind. I hadn't paid much attention to his words at the time, but now they were all I could think about.

Bryce . . . Bryce . . . Bryce . . .

The name echoed in my mind like a hated song I couldn't ignore, no matter how hard I tried. I knew a Bryce, although I hadn't seen or heard from him in years. He couldn't be the leader of this crew . . . could he?

My gut twisted with a sinking sense of certainty. Knocking out enemy comms, sending cryptic messages, playing a shell game with mission personnel and objectives. Those moves were all straight out of Bryce's playbook.

I sprinted away from the locker and raced back toward the emergency stairs. I didn't know what Bryce was doing here, but I had to find Charlotte and warn her that the mission had gone sideways—and that we were dealing with an unexpected and extremely dangerous enemy.

FOUR

CHARLOTTE

ris shrieked and flung the smoking briefcase away. It landed on the floor and skidded in my direction. Smoke continued to spew out of the booby-trapped case, but the green clouds were harmless, so I bent down and slammed the lid shut. Then I scooped up the briefcase and swung it at Iris's gun.

Smack!

The briefcase banged into the gun, knocking it out of her hand. It too clattered to the floor. Iris lunged toward the weapon, but I drew the briefcase back, then swung it forward again, this time aiming for her right arm.

Crack!

Iris's arm broke with a loud, sickening sound. She shrieked again and staggered back, her arm now hanging limply by her side. Not only was the briefcase booby-trapped, but it was also lined with lead, which made it an excellent battering ram. A handy little toy from the Section 47 armory.

Iris lunged to her left, trying to spin past me, but I swept my leg out, tripping her, and she tumbled down onto her knees. The other agent cursed, then lunged forward. Her left hand closed around the gun, and she spun around on her knees and raised the weapon.

I wrapped both hands around the briefcase, stepped up, and slammed it into her face. Iris's head snapped back, and she crumpled to the floor without another sound. I loomed over her, breathing hard and still clutching the case.

"Update," a male voice demanded, startling me. "Everyone, check in."

I whirled around, thinking someone had entered this level, but the corridor was empty.

"Status update." The male voice sounded again, more demanding and annoyed than before.

During our fight, Iris's phone had slid out of her pocket and landed on the floor. I picked it up. The screen was unlocked and open to a comms channel with a single name at the top of the screen: *Bryce*.

Who was that? One of the male thieves I'd spotted in the lobby? Or someone else?

"Status update," the male voice—Bryce—asked for a third time.

I remained silent, and no other voices joined the conversation. Several *clickety-clack-clacks* sounded, along with a steady hissing sound. What were those noises?

A few more seconds passed, then Bryce muttered a curse. "If you can hear this, I'm almost done with the primary objective. Get to the rendezvous point or get left behind."

He cut the connection, and the phone went silent.

Iris had said stealing the Grunglass Necklace was a *secondary* objective, something Bryce had confirmed by referring to whatever he was doing as the *primary* objective. My stomach clenched with worry. The thieves had something else in mind than just swiping the necklace.

I needed to find the mysterious Bryce, but how? He could be anywhere in the building, as could the other thieves—and Desmond too.

A knot of dread lodged in my throat, but I swallowed it. Desmond Percy was one of the best cleaners in Section 47, and he could eliminate any threat that crossed his path. I believed in Desmond's skills as much as I believed in my own, and right now I needed to stop worrying about him and figure out where Bryce was.

I stared at the phone, and I thought of the background noises that had echoed out of the device while Bryce had been demanding updates. Those *clickety-clack-clacks* had sounded like . . . typing on a keyboard, while the hisses reminded me of . . . the espresso machines in the café.

Bryce was in the lobby, and so was his primary objective, whatever it was.

I crouched down beside Iris, who was still unconscious. I rifled through her pockets, but the only thing she was carrying was a white keycard. I grabbed it, along with her gun, then picked up the briefcase. I swiped the keycard across the elevator reader, opening the door. Then I shoved the keycard into my pocket, stepped inside, and punched the lobby button.

The elevator door closed, and I once again found myself staring at my reflection in the mirrored surface. My shoulder-length auburn hair was a tangled mess, my blue suit was wrinkled, and my hands were stained a sickly pea-green from the smoke bomb that had been hidden inside the briefcase.

I grimaced. As a spy, I was used to things going wrong, but I couldn't shake the feeling that everything was going *exactly* the way Henrika Hyde wanted—and that I was already too late to stop her master plan.

The elevator floated down to the ground level. I was still clutching Iris's gun in my right hand, and I dropped the weapon to my side, hiding it from sight as best I could, even as I tightened my grip on the briefcase in my left hand.

The door slid back, and I cautiously stuck my head outside. The corridor was empty, so I stepped out of the elevator and headed toward the lobby.

"Desmond?" I said in a low voice. "Desmond, do you copy?"

More static crackled through my earbud. Our comms were still being jammed, which meant I couldn't warn Desmond about what was going on. I growled with frustration and walked on.

I stopped at the end of the corridor and peered out into the lobby. It was after ten o'clock, so the rush of people going to work and appointments had vanished, and the area was largely empty, except for some folks working on laptops at the café.

I walked slowly, approaching first one person and then another and sneaking glances at their screens. I concentrated on the men, but I studied all the women as well, since I had no idea who might be working for Bryce.

No one gave me a second glance, and everyone remained focused on their screens, which featured everything from work documents to spreadsheets to word games. I even spotted some super-cute photos of a cat named Kitty Boodle.

The longer I looked at the laptops, the more my synesthesia surged, and the more colors bloomed like flowers on the screens. Grays mostly, indicating typos and other small mistakes, although a few pinks flickered on some of the spreadsheets, indicating more serious mathematical errors. One college-age guy's screen was a veritable sea of red, which indicated knowing, outright, deliberate fraud. Someone was plagiarizing a paper.

I finished my winding route and stopped at the café exit. Frustration bubbled in my chest. Bryce was here *somewhere*, and the steady hiss from the espresso machines sounded like a chiding chorus, chastising me for not spotting him yet.

I examined everyone again, from the folks in the café to a woman reading a comic book in the middle of the lobby to the people walking past the glass wall that fronted the building. Nothing was out of the ordinary, but I had the nagging feeling I was missing something . . .

Or, rather, *not* missing something.

My gaze zoomed over to the reception desk. Instead of it being empty, since Iris Berriston was unconscious on the fifth floor, a man was sitting in her chair, typing on her laptop. He looked to be in his mid-thirties, the same age as Desmond and me, and was quite handsome, with thick, wavy dark brown hair, tan skin, and a strong, square jaw. A scar slashed a jagged white line through his bushy left eyebrow and zigzagged down into his cheek.

My gaze snagged on his suit. The man's jacket, tie, and shirt were all the exact same charcoal-gray. Nothing terribly unusual—except for the fact that dark, monochromatic suits were practically the uniform of Section cleaners.

You could always tell the assassins by their suits.

The man must have sensed my stare because he looked up. His gaze locked with mine, and his dark brown eyes narrowed. He clearly recognized me, which meant he was the mysterious Bryce. Everything about him, from his tall posture to his calm demeanor to his snazzy suit, screamed alpha leader.

In the distance, footsteps pounded out a fast, furious rhythm, drawing my attention. Desmond sprinted out of the corridor on the right side of the lobby and skidded to a stop. His gaze flicked to me, and I jerked my head to the side. Desmond spun in that direction and spotted Bryce behind the reception desk.

The two men stared at each other for a long, tense moment. Bryce's eyes narrowed a bit more, while anger sparked in Desmond's gaze. They definitely knew each other, and no love was lost on either side.

"Bryce!" Desmond yelled. "Stop right there!"

Bryce stabbed a final key on the laptop, then plucked a silver flash drive out of the device. He tucked the flash drive into his jacket pocket, then stood up. His gaze zipped over to me before zooming back to Desmond. Another long, tense moment passed.

Then both men started moving at once.

Desmond charged at Bryce, who grabbed a clear glass vase filled with white orchids off the corner of the reception desk. Bryce threw the vase at Desmond, who stopped and crossed his arms in front of his chest, forming a crude shield.

Smack!

The vase bounced off Desmond's arms and dropped to the floor. The vase shattered, spewing glass, water, and flowers everywhere. The blow knocked Desmond back. One of his boots slipped on the floor, and he lurched to the side, landing awkwardly on his right knee.

Bryce smirked at Desmond, then braced a hand on the reception desk and vaulted over the top. He landed on his feet as nimbly as a cat, then cut diagonally across the lobby, running toward the garden. He was *fast*—supernaturally fast—indicating he was an enduro.

I snapped up the gun still in my right hand, but Bryce stepped behind a tree before I could shoot. I lowered the gun and sprinted in that direction.

"Charlotte! Charlotte, wait!" Desmond's voice rang out. "You don't know who you're dealing with!"

I had a pretty good idea, but Bryce being an enduro and a possible assassin wasn't going to stop me from trying to stop him.

I sucked in a breath and picked up my pace. Over the past few months, Desmond and I had been training together, sharpening our skills and pushing our bodies—and our respective magics—to their limits. I despised running, but all the cardio Desmond and I had done together was paying off now. I sprinted across the lobby with ease and plunged into the garden.

I stepped onto a red-brick path that wound past several trees, along with evergreen hedges and flower beds filled with bright blossoms. I forced myself to stop and peer through the thick screens of leaves. The revolving doors at the front of the lobby were still, which meant Bryce hadn't left the building and was in the garden . . . somewhere.

I looked and listened, but I didn't spot Bryce, and the only sound was my raspy breathing, along with the gurgling stream flowing under the wooden bridge. I raised the gun in my right hand and crept forward. The briefcase was still dangling from my left hand.

I followed the winding path past one clump of greenery after another, but I didn't spy Bryce anywhere.

Crack!

A branch snapped off to my left, and I spun in that direction. Bryce stepped out from behind a tree. He raised his hand and waggled a long, skinny silver object. I tensed, thinking it was a gun, but Bryce smirked and lifted it a little higher. My eyes widened in horror, even as my synesthesia outlined the device in a bright, bloody red.

Not a gun—a grenade.

Bryce pulled out the pin on the side and tossed the grenade toward me. It hit the brick path with a loud *tink* and skittered in my direction. I dropped the gun in my hand and snapped up the briefcase, holding it out in front of me with both hands like a shield, even as I backpedaled, trying to get out of the blast radius—

BANG!

The grenade exploded, the sound as loud as a shotgun blaring in my ears, but instead of a scorching fireball, acrid gray smoke spewed out. The smoke blasted over me, stinging my eyes and making me cough. I stumbled around. My synesthesia painted the thick, billowing clouds a brilliant red, and I couldn't figure out how to escape from the smoke and the haze of scarlet flooding my vision . . .

"Charlotte! It's okay! I've got you!" Desmond's voice rang out, and a hand clamped around my right wrist.

I followed his lead, letting him pull me out of the stinging, choking clouds and back into the open lobby. Above our heads, lights flashed, and a loud, distinctive clanging rang out. Someone had pulled a fire alarm.

I sucked in one breath after another, trying to clear the acrid smoke out of my lungs. Desmond's concerned face swam into view, and he gently wiped away the tears streaming down my cheeks.

"Charlotte! Are you okay?" he asked, worry rippling through his voice and making his Australian accent more pronounced.

"Fine . . ." I wheezed. "Just . . . inhaled . . . some . . . smoke."

Some of Desmond's concern melted away, replaced by an angry glower. "Let's get him."

I wiped away a few more tears. Together, we plunged back into the garden. I grabbed the gun from where I had dropped it, then Desmond and I spread out, keeping each other in sight through the curling clouds of smoke while we searched for Bryce.

A few seconds later, Desmond muttered a vicious curse. I hurried over to his position. A manhole cover was lying on the ground next to a round black hole at one end of the wooden bridge. The rusty metal cover was at least three inches thick, and only someone with paramortal strength could have removed it without help.

"Bryce must have gone down into the sewer system." Desmond pulled a phone out of his pocket, turned on the flashlight, and angled it into the hole, revealing a metal ladder.

He started to go down into the hole, but I grabbed his arm, stopping him. "No, Bryce might have booby-trapped the passageway. We can't follow him. It's too risky."

Frustration filled Desmond's face, but he nodded. Together, we stood there staring down into the hole.

Bryce was gone, along with whatever he'd stolen.

FIVE

CHARLOTTE

esmond and I were still staring down into the manhole when a couple of black vans screeched to a stop in front of the building. The doors slid back, and several men and women wearing black tactical clothes and helmets and sporting an assortment of weapons jumped out. The Section 47 strike team had finally arrived.

The strike team members ran up to the building, pushed through the revolving doors, and streamed into the lobby. Once it became apparent the danger was over, they quickly lowered their weapons.

The fire alarm had cut off several seconds ago, but instead of exiting the building, most people had stayed in the lobby. Several folks were looking around, clearly confused, while others had their phones out, filming everything that was happening.

The strike team leader hurried over to Desmond and me. We told her what had happened, and she stabbed her finger in first one direction, then another, ordering her agents to secure the scene and set up a perimeter around the open manhole.

"Come on," Desmond said. "There's nothing else we can do here."

I sighed, then followed him out of the garden, across the lobby, and over to the reception desk.

Footsteps clacked against the floor, and a sixty-something woman wearing a scarlet pantsuit and black stilettoes entered the lobby. Her short black hair was styled in an attractive pixie cut, and her body was lean and muscled. A small gold pendant shaped like the letter *G* glimmered against her golden skin, and a pair of red reading glasses was tucked into the front pocket on her jacket.

Gia Chan was the cleaner supervisor, which made her one of the most powerful people in Section 47. She was also one of the few folks who knew Desmond and I had been assigned to track down Henrika Hyde.

Gia's dark brown gaze flicked around the lobby, moving from the strike team members to the milling crowd before finally landing on Desmond and me. Her mouth flattened out into a thin line, and she strode over to us.

"Well, this certainly went wrong in a hurry," she said. "I've already gotten three calls from members of the board of directors, wondering why there was such a public incident at what is supposed to be a secure, discreet Section facility."

I winced. "I'm sorry. I thought my plan would work. This is all my fault."

Gia shrugged, neither agreeing nor disagreeing. "Perhaps. But all we can do now is manage the fallout and spin the story."

She snapped her fingers, and a woman in a gray pantsuit who'd entered the lobby with the strike team members turned around. Gia tilted her head to the side, where a large group of people had gathered by the café. The woman nodded, then went over to the curious onlookers, flashed a badge at them, held up her hands, and started speaking.

". . . an unfortunate prank . . . disgruntled worker . . . no property or other damage . . ."

She recited the usual Section 47 disinformation, and warm ripples of magic flowed off her body right along with her calm, soothing voice. The woman was a charmer, someone with magical charisma that could be used to subtly manipulate people's emotions, like easing an anxious crowd. After a few seconds, all the people started nodding in time to her words.

The charmer would spin the same lies to the mortal authorities when they arrived. In addition to tracking down criminals, another one of Section 47's missions was to make sure the general public never realized that people with magical abilities were living among them.

Most paramortals wisely hid their powers, so as not to be ostracized, targeted, used, abused, or exploited, but others weren't so cautious, and plenty of videos were floating around the Internet that showed combustos liquefying metal or transmuters turning concrete blocks into piles of dust with their bare hands. Still, despite all that damning footage, most folks didn't believe paramortals existed, and they chalked up such displays to magic tricks, deepfakes, or artificial intelligence.

The charmer kept talking, although many folks got bored and either headed toward the elevators to return to their offices or stepped into the café to get another coffee.

Sneakers scuffed on the floor, and a thirty-something man wearing a green button-down shirt over neatly pressed khakis came over to us. His short brown hair and bronze skin gleamed under the lights. Square black glasses perched on his nose, and he was carrying a padded laptop case in the crook of his elbow.

Diego Benito, one of Section 47's tech geniuses, nodded at Gia, then focused on Desmond and me. His dark brown gaze lingered on the green stains on my hands before flicking over to the similarly stained briefcase, which I'd set on the reception desk. Diego's nose twitched, as though he'd gotten a whiff of the acrid smoke that was still clinging to the case, and me too.

Gia stabbed her finger at the laptop Bryce had used. "I want to see the security footage. Everything that happened after Charlotte left the lobby with Agent Berriston and Desmond followed the other thieves down to the Vault."

"That's when our comms went out," I said.

Gia nodded. "That's when we lost eyes on you too. One second, I was watching you both through the lobby cameras. The next . . ." Her voice trailed off, and she flicked her fingers. "*Poof!* No more security footage."

"I tried my best, but someone locked us out of the system," Diego muttered. "That won't happen again."

Anger sparked in his eyes. The computer whiz had been stationed with Gia and the strike team, and he didn't like being beaten at his own game.

Diego pulled a laptop out of his padded case, sat down, and connected his device to the reception desk computer. His fingers flew over the keyboard in a quick, graceful rhythm, and he quickly pulled up the security footage. Gia, Desmond, and I crowded into the space behind Diego, and the four of us studied the different feeds and camera angles.

Everything played out just as it had earlier. Me heading toward the elevator on the left side of the lobby with Iris Berriston. The other three thieves accessing the elevator on the right side. Desmond ambushing the thieves on the lower Vault level, neutralizing them, and leaving them in the storage locker. My own fight with Iris on the deserted fifth floor. Then both Desmond and me hurrying back to the lobby.

Gia stabbed her finger at the screen again. "Focus on the lobby this time. I want to see everything that happened here at the reception desk."

Diego rewound the footage, this time showing only the lobby. For several seconds, nothing happened. Then a shadow fell over the smooth, shiny counter, and a man stepped forward and dropped into the empty chair.

Gia blinked a few times, then bent down, her chin hovering over Diego's shoulder. "Is that . . ."

"Bryce Finkley," Desmond growled.

"Who is he?" Diego asked.

Gia drew back. Her lips puckered as though she'd just bitten into something rotten. "A former Section cleaner."

On the footage, Bryce sat down, fished a flash drive out of his pocket, and plugged it into Iris's laptop. He also slid a comms device into his right ear. Bryce bent forward and started typing. The security camera angle wasn't quite right, but I could still see lines of code streaming across the laptop screen.

A few minutes passed. Bryce kept working, his lips moving every once in a while as he communicated with the other thieves. The former cleaner played his part perfectly, smiling at everyone who approached the desk and even pausing his typing long enough to answer questions from passersby.

Another minute passed. The lines of code vanished, replaced by a status bar, as though Bryce was uploading something onto the flash drive. His fingers tapped out an impatient rhythm on the desk, then abruptly stopped.

"That's when I came back into the lobby and spotted him," I said.

Once again, everything played out as it had earlier, with Bryce vaulting over the counter, plunging into the garden, and escaping through the manhole.

"Bryce never left the lobby," Gia said in a thoughtful voice. "He didn't even try to access the Vault level with the other thieves."

"Which means whatever he wanted was on *this* computer," Desmond growled again.

"Diego, can you tell what Bryce was doing?" I asked.

"Give me a second . . ." Diego's voice trailed off, and his fingers flew over the keys again. "Looks like he—"

Diego's fingers stilled. His head jerked back, and he blinked several times. "The flash drive he plugged into the laptop contained some serious decryption software."

A few weeks ago, Diego had given me a flash drive loaded with similar software, which I'd used to hack into Elsa Eisen's laptop during the Tannenbaum mission. If Bryce had done something like that here . . . well, today's mission was even more of a disaster.

Diego clicked through several screens, following a trail of electronic breadcrumbs only he could see and understand. He stopped and let out a low whistle, although I couldn't tell if it was one of admiration, concern, or both. "The decryption software breached several Section firewalls. He got into our servers."

Gia tensed. "Can you tell what information Bryce accessed?"

Diego shook his head. "It was a sophisticated attack, and he pulled up hundreds of thousands of files. I'll have to examine the decryption software and sort through everything before I can pinpoint what he was really after."

Gia pinched the bridge of her nose. "All right. Pack it up and return to headquarters. I want an update in two hours."

Diego nodded, got to his feet, and unplugged the compromised laptop.

Gia went over to the Section charmer. The other agent had calmed the onlookers and was now talking to the mortal cops and firefighters who had responded to the scene.

I picked up the smoke-stained briefcase, which felt as heavy as an anvil. I thought I was being clever by dangling the Grunglass Necklace in front of Henrika, but it had turned into a giant albatross hanging around my own neck.

Desmond laid a hand on my shoulder. "You can't blame yourself for this, Charlotte."

"Of course I can, and I absolutely should," I muttered. "This was *my* plan, *my* mission. I should have realized Henrika would see this as an opportunity to steal more than just the Grunglass Necklace—that she would target Section secrets. After all, the more she knows about Section, the easier it is for her to stay three steps ahead of us."

Desmond's hand dropped from my shoulder, and he shifted on his feet. "Henrika wasn't just after Section secrets—she was after ours too."

"What do you mean?"

He glanced around, but the other agents were busy, and no one was paying attention to us. "The thieves who went down to the Vault were looking for the evidence from the Tannenbaum mission. Something they thought the Section techs might have mislabeled or overlooked."

I tensed. "The vials of Redburn?"

Desmond nodded. "Yes."

Twin arrows of worry and dread shot through my body. I'd been so certain Henrika would send someone after the Grunglass Necklace it hadn't occurred to me that she might target something *else* stored in the Vault. Of course she would want to recover the vials from the Tannenbaum mission. She wouldn't want Section 47 to have any samples of Redburn, lest our scientists find a way to neutralize the formula—or, worse, reverse engineer it.

Desmond's shoulders slumped, and he kept shifting on his feet, his gaze fixed on the floor. Henrika had wanted to prove how deadly her explosive was to Adrian Anatoly, a paramortal terrorist, so she'd used Desmond and Graham Walker as her own personal lab rats and blown up an entire beach in hopes of killing the two cleaners. Even though Desmond had survived the explosions and his body had healed, he still bore deep, ugly scars from the attack on his heart.

My own heart squeezed tight with guilt. Desmond had already suffered so much because of the Redburn formula, and I'd failed him today. "I'm so sorry," I rasped. "This is all my fault."

Desmond lifted his gaze from the floor, although he still didn't look at me. "No. Don't blame yourself, Charlotte. We both know how smart, clever, and dangerous Henrika is."

My heart squeezed tight again, this time with shame. I'd been so caught up in my own vendetta against Henrika that I'd forgotten how much Desmond was still hurting. And him *not* blaming me for my mistakes . . . well, that made me feel worse than anything else.

"I need to talk to Gia," Desmond said. "See what she wants to do about Bryce."

I opened my mouth to ask who Bryce Finkley was and why Desmond despised the former cleaner so much, but he spun around and walked away. He went over to Gia, and the two of them started speaking in low voices.

I looked around the lobby again. Several strike team members eyed me in return, their gazes more than a little hostile. They knew just how spectacularly my mission had failed. One of the strike team members strode out of the garden carrying a plastic evidence bag that contained the splintered remains of the smoke grenade Bryce had used. I grimaced and looked away.

By this point, the clouds of gray smoke had curled all the way up to the high ceiling and had dissipated into faint wisps, but the sight made even more anger, frustration, guilt, and shame crackle in my chest, like a violent thunderstorm about to spit out jagged forks of lightning.

Once again, Henrika Hyde had gotten the better of me. Even worse, I had no idea what she had stolen from the Section 47 servers—or how she was going to weaponize the information.

SIX

DESMOND

There was nothing else we could do here, so Charlotte and I left the lobby, got into a van with Gia and Diego, and went to the main headquarters of Section 47, which was only a few miles away.

Gia pushed through the revolving doors at the front of the building. Diego followed her, carrying his laptop, along with the one he'd taken from Agent Berriston's desk. Charlotte and I brought up the rear.

Section 47 was housed in an old three-story train station that took up an entire city block and had been converted into an upscale shopping center. The first floor featured restaurants, bakeries, and coffee shops, along with a cafeteria that was also named Section 47. Escalators in the center of the enormous open space led to the upper two levels, along with stone stairs tucked into all four corners.

Low glass walls topped with silver handrails cordoned off the upper levels, which boasted shops selling luxury clothing, organic teas, artisanal chocolates, and more. Black wrought-iron chandeliers dangled from the high ceiling, bathing the storefronts in soft white light.

Even though it was the middle of a workday, a steady stream of people flowed from one shop and level to the next, and the din of conversation filled the air, along with an occasional sharp *cha-ching!* as someone used a phone app to pay for their pricey goods.

Gia and Diego kept going, but I stopped and jerked my thumb over at the cafeteria. "You want a smoothie? My treat."

Charlotte had been quiet ever since we had left the Vault building. I knew she was still beating herself up for the mission failure, but I'd been there too, and it was just as much my fault as hers that things had gone wrong.

Charlotte arched an eyebrow at me. "If by smoothie you mean hot chocolate brimming with marshmallows, whipped cream, and chocolate shavings, then yes, I would very much like a smoothie."

I huffed. "I've said it before, and I'll say it again—"

"All that sugar will be the death of me." Charlotte finished my thought. "I know. Hot chocolate isn't exactly healthy, but it sure would be comforting right now."

Charlotte and I had radically different ideas about food. She loved anything that was deep-fried, was crusted with sugar, or came with a dipping sauce, whereas I tried to eat as clean, natural, and organic as possible, which included smoothies packed with fruits, veggies, and spices.

Some of the tension eased out of Charlotte's shoulders. "But thank you for trying to cheer me up."

"Was I that obvious?"

Her blue eyes softened with warmth. "Yes."

She threaded her arm through mine, and I relished the feel of her body next to mine. When we had first met at headquarters a few months ago, we had gotten off to a rocky start, and I had promised never to touch Charlotte without her permission. Of course, she had given me that permission long ago, but I never forgot that being with her was a privilege, even when it was something as simple as walking arm in arm.

"Let's go," Charlotte said. "Gia and Diego have already checked in with Evelyn."

Charlotte and I went over to a raised, round dais where a sixty-something woman was ensconced behind a curved marble counter.

The woman was wearing a bright fuchsia pantsuit that highlighted her cropped black hair and ebony skin. A row of monitors mounted in front of her showed different views of the three floors and cast a bluish glow onto her silver glasses and dark brown eyes. A keycard reader and a metal turnstile were positioned a few feet away, although no mortal shoppers were going near that area.

Evelyn Hawkes looked up as Charlotte and I approached. Most Section 47 agents thought Evelyn was merely a receptionist, someone who passed out travel brochures to lost tourists and steered mortals away from the main entrance. But she was actually Maestro, the code name for the head of the Washington, D.C., station, and one of the most powerful people in the spy organization. The Section leaders were all about compartmentalizing information to protect the agency as a whole, and not even my father, General Jethro Percy, knew Maestro's real identity.

Charlotte had figured out who Evelyn was a few months ago, after realizing that the older woman kept pushing us to work together to ferret out some moles in the D.C. station. Evelyn's subterfuge still impressed me. Sitting out here in the open as though she was just a gatekeeper was an inspired way to pick up gossip and other information Section agents would keep to themselves whenever they were around senior officers.

I nodded respectfully at Evelyn, who returned the gesture. Her dark gaze flicked over to Charlotte. "I'm sorry the mission didn't go as planned."

"Me too," Charlotte muttered.

Evelyn nodded, then cleared her throat. "A mission debriefing has already been scheduled. You two have been ordered to report immediately. Level-five conference room."

That was odd. Back at the Vault building, Gia had said she wanted an update in two hours, not as soon as we returned to headquarters.

I turned to ask Gia if she had moved up the timetable, but she was already waving her keycard over the reader, pushing through the turnstile, and heading for the Section elevators. Diego juggled the two laptops from one arm to the other, scrambling to swipe his own card, shove through the turnstile, and keep up with her.

Charlotte eyed Evelyn. "Anything else you'd like to tell us?"

Evelyn tapped her index finger on her mouse, making the monitors flicker in front of her. "I just got the message a minute ago. I'll see you both down there. I should know more then."

Charlotte nodded. The two of us waved our keycards over the reader, then moved through the turnstile. Diego held the elevator for us, and the door closed with a whisper.

"What's going on?" Charlotte asked, her voice sharp with worry. "Why the sudden rush to debrief?"

Gia scrolled through screens on her phone. "That's what I'm trying to figure out."

The elevator dropped, and my gut along with it. Urgent, unexpected debriefings were never a good thing, especially after a mission gone wrong. Someone was not happy with our failure.

The elevator kept going down, down, down. The old train station had seven underground levels, all serving a different purpose and facet of Section 47. The accounting department was on level one, followed by the IT hub on level two. Analysts like Charlotte usually worked on level three, along with charmers, although both analysts and charmers could be assigned to different departments and work on different levels as needed.

Level four was reserved for the offices of the Section leaders, including Evelyn as Maestro, along with holding cells for prisoners until they could be sent to a black site for further interrogation. Level six housed the armory, which was filled with weapons, clothing, and other supplies, while level seven served as a parking garage for Section surveillance vans and vehicles.

The elevator floated to a stop at level five, which was where cleaners like me worked, along with our liaisons, Section agents who made sure we assassins had everything we needed to find, track, and eliminate targets. Most of the mission briefings and debriefings were also held on this level.

The elevator door slid back. Gia strode forward, her nose still buried in her phone. Diego juggled the two laptops again and followed her. Charlotte and I also stepped out of the elevator.

"Does this feel as wrong to you as it does to me?" I murmured.

"Yep." Charlotte blew out a tense breath. "But we've been summoned by someone, so we might as well get it over with. Right?"

"Right," I echoed, although my voice was just as wary as hers.

Charlotte smiled, but her expression quickly twisted into a grimace, and she trailed after Gia and Diego. I fell in step beside her.

Something was most definitely wrong, and I had a sinking feeling that Charlotte and I were in much more trouble than simply botching a mission.

I followed the others down a long corridor with light gray walls and matching carpet. Gia waved her keycard over another reader, and a set of bullet- and magic-resistant doors buzzed open, revealing the level-five bullpen. Clear plastic cubicles took up most of the space, and a wide walkway running down the center led to some glassed-in offices and a large conference room set into the back wall.

Cleaners sat on the left side of the main aisle, while their liaisons were situated on the right side. Even assassins had to do paperwork, and several cleaners were dutifully typing away on keyboards. Some of the liaisons were also typing away, while others murmured into phones. Every time I entered the bullpen, it always struck me how it seemed like an ordinary office—except for the fact that we killed people.

Gia and Diego went to the conference room, but Charlotte headed over to her assigned desk, which was in the back row of cubicles, directly across the aisle from my own desk. She slung down the green-stained briefcase, then plopped into a chair, flipped on a monitor, and powered up her laptop. She was clearly still trying to find out who had called the sudden debriefing.

I headed over to my own desk to do the same. Forewarned and forearmed and all that.

I was just about to sit down when I realized that all the cleaners and liaisons had turned their heads to stare at me. They all had the same stiff posture—high shoulders, squinty eyes, pinched lips—and the air practically crackled with tension. If I touched someone right now, my galvanism would give me a violent static shock from all the nervous, pent-up energy.

Charlotte stopped typing and looked at me, her eyebrows raised in a silent question. I wondered if her synesthesia was whispering that we were in danger, but I couldn't ask with everyone staring at me.

Why were they staring at me? Sure, my mission with Charlotte had been a failure, but this level of scrutiny bordered on disturbing.

"Ahem." Someone cleared her throat.

The woman sitting at the desk in front of Charlotte swiveled around in her chair. She had long black hair, light blue eyes, and rosy skin. Like everyone else in the bullpen, she was wearing a pantsuit, although hers was a cheerful sky-blue instead of the somber blacks, navy blues, and dark grays the other agents were sporting.

Joan Samson was my closest friend at Section 47, and she had been my liaison on dozens of missions. She was a powerful transmuter, someone who was able to transform the physical properties of an element or object, like shifting glass to sand or reducing a wooden block to splinters. Joan was also a Legacy, and several of her relatives had worked at Section 47, although her family name didn't garner the same notoriety as being a Locke or a Percy did. I envied my friend her distinguished reputation, along with that of her family.

Joan had also been involved with Graham. With his dying words, Graham had told me how much he loved Joan, and he'd begged me to watch out for her. Joan had never revealed how she'd truly felt about Graham, but the ice-blue aura around her heart always dimmed whenever she said his name, indicating she felt his loss as keenly as I did.

"I heard about the mission, Dez," Joan murmured. "Sorry it didn't go as planned."

I shrugged. "These things happen."

Joan's cool gaze flicked over to Charlotte. "Yes, things always seem to go off the rails whenever *she's* involved."

An accusatory note colored her voice. Charlotte rolled her eyes in response.

Gia and Evelyn had tasked Charlotte and me with discreetly tracking down Henrika Hyde, at least until we could make sure Henrika didn't have any more moles inside the D.C. station, but I suspected Joan had figured out what we were doing. She was one of the smartest people I knew, right up there with

Charlotte, and she had dropped several hints that she would be happy to help me with the mission, but so far, I'd played dumb. I didn't want Joan to get caught in the crossfire of the dangerous game Charlotte and I were playing with Henrika.

Joan kept staring at me, as though waiting for me to say something. Most of the other cleaners and liaisons returned to their work, although a few kept glancing over their shoulders at me.

That uneasy feeling swept over me again. "What's going on?"

"You haven't heard?" Joan asked.

"About what? The emergency debriefing? Yeah, I know about that." I frowned again. "Wait. Is something *else* going on?"

Sympathy crinkled Joan's face, which only added to my unease. She opened her mouth, but before she could answer me, a door buzzed open in the distance. Everyone in the bullpen straightened in their seats, as though guns had just been shoved against their spines. Charlotte stopped her typing, once again picking up on the sudden tension.

In the distance, footsteps sounded. Even though they were muffled by the carpet, my chin immediately lifted, and my shoulders squared, as though I was a soldier called to attention. I'd been hearing those swift, heavy footsteps my entire life, both inside and outside Section 47, and they always filled me with a sense of weary, wary dread.

Everyone froze, still maintaining their impossibly stiff postures. No one moved, no one whispered, no one fidgeted. I don't think some people even bloody *breathed.*

The footsteps stopped, but a familiar presence loomed behind me like a dark storm cloud. I slowly turned around.

A sixty-something man was standing in the middle of the aisle. He was roughly my height, six feet tall, although his body was broader and stockier than mine. His wavy silver hair had been brushed back from his forehead, and his skin had the deep, permanent tan of someone who had spent years outdoors. Lines grooved into the skin around his light blue eyes, and the matching aura pulsing over his heart was such a pale blue it was almost translucent.

He was wearing a navy jacket over a matching shirt and tie. To him, it wasn't a suit but just another uniform, and it was as neat, crisp, and sharply creased as any military garb he'd worn over the years.

General Jethro Percy, the head of the board of directors, one of the most powerful people at Section 47—and my father.

SEVEN

CHARLOTTE

esmond's face remained smooth, but his hands fisted at his sides, his knuckles standing out in stark white contrast against his tan skin.

The two Percys stood there, facing off, with the cleaners and liaisons gathered around like moviegoers watching an intense scene on the big screen. Forget hearing a pin drop. It was so deathly quiet I could have heard a feather float down to the floor.

General Jethro Percy tipped his head the tiniest bit to his son. "Desmond."

"General." Desmond returned his father's greeting in a flat, toneless voice.

General, not *Father* or *Dad* or *Pops*. Desmond almost always referred to the older Percy by his Section 47 title. Over the past few months, Desmond had told me more than once how strained his relationship was with his father, but this exchange was frostier on both sides than I'd expected.

Two men stepped into the bullpen behind the General. From the rumors I'd heard, Percy always had at least a few bodyguards in tow.

Years ago, Jethro Percy had been the head of the cleaners in Washington, D.C., although these days, he traveled all over the world, moving from one Section 47 station to another, making sure everything ran smoothly in the spy organization and cutting off crises before they even arose. General Percy had a reputation for being smart, ruthless, and efficient when it came to problem-solving, which made me even more concerned about why he'd made this sudden, surprise appearance.

"What are you doing here?" Desmond asked, suspicion creeping into his voice. "Did you call the mission debriefing?"

"Of course I did," the General replied in a deep baritone that wasn't softened in the slightest by his faint Southern drawl. "In my experience, it's always best to own up to one's mistakes as soon as possible."

A muscle twitched in Desmond's jaw, and the two men continued their staring contest. The captive audience of cleaners and liaisons remained frozen in their seats, except for Joan, who shot Desmond a sympathetic look. The two bodyguards standing behind the General seemed bored, as though they'd seen this show a dozen times before.

I didn't want Desmond to face his father alone, especially since the Vault mission had been my idea—and my failure. I slid my chair back, got to my feet, and stepped into the aisle so that I was standing shoulder to shoulder with Desmond.

General Percy's gaze flicked over to me. His features were hard, stern, and utterly devoid of the easy, charming warmth his son exuded, and I felt like I was staring into the craggy face of an iceberg that was about to slam into and crush me.

"Charlotte Locke, I presume." A loud note of disgust curled through General Percy's voice.

No surprise there. Once upon a time, Jethro Percy had been a Section cleaner, an enduro with incredible stamina, just like my father, Jack Locke. The General was also a Legacy, and his father, Percival Percy, had been one of the founding members of Section 47, while my father's mother, my grandma Jane, had also worked for the spy organization.

But that's where the similarities ended. General Percy had deftly played all the political games and climbed up the ranks, but my father had eschewed such maneuvers and remained a cleaner for his entire career, right up to the day he died.

To say that Jethro Percy and Jack Locke didn't get along would be like saying the surface of the sun was a tad toasty. The two men had actively, openly, thoroughly *despised* each other, and my father had constantly complained about the General putting his own ambitions before the agents he was supposed to lead, support, and protect.

I didn't know everything that had happened between the two men, but I'd always found it highly suspicious that General Percy had overseen my father's last mission. *The Mexico mission*, as it was known in Section circles, was notorious for being a colossal fuckup.

Roughly fifteen years ago, Jack Locke had led a group of cleaners to Mexico to assassinate Feliciano Salvador, a cartel leader who was selling drugs that gave regular people paramortal powers. At least, until they started bleeding out of their eyeballs and dropped dead. Rumor had it that Salvador had hired a new biomagical scientist who was going to concoct even more dangerous drugs, hence the reason for the kill mission. My father had always been exceptionally devoted to his work, and he'd prepped for the mission for weeks, especially since he thought that Salvador was connected to the Syndicate.

The Syndicate was a shadowy, mysterious group of criminals, terrorists, and other rogue paramortals who occasionally worked together to pull jobs, trade secrets, and more. Most folks in the paramortal intelligence community thought the Syndicate was a myth, an urban legend run amok, but my father had firmly believed in its existence, and he'd been determined to figure out who belonged to the group.

My father and the other cleaners had easily infiltrated Salvador's seaside compound. But after that . . . well, no one seemed to know exactly what had happened. All the other cleaners had been killed, but my father had been captured, and Salvador had demanded three million dollars for his return.

Section 47 didn't negotiate with anyone, so the higher-ups had refused to pay the ransom, but Grandma Jane had borrowed the money from Leon Chase, a family friend and another Section cleaner who was part of the support staff for the Mexico mission.

Leon had delivered the money, but General Percy had secretly sent another team of cleaners to the ransom exchange to eliminate Salvador. Once again, no one seemed to know exactly what had happened, just that Salvador had escaped, and my father had been killed. The three-million-dollar ransom had also vanished. The Section cleaners hadn't recovered it, but Salvador hadn't gotten it either.

That was the official story, but I was determined to uncover the *unofficial* story—no matter how dark, dangerous, and ugly the truth might be.

I thought I'd put all the unanswered questions about my father's death behind me, but that had changed a few months ago when Desmond and I had confronted Henrika Hyde at the Halstead Hotel.

Henrika had claimed it was an honor to meet the daughter of the infamous Jack Locke. She'd also said my father had gotten closer to taking her down than anyone else. And then she'd dropped the biggest bombshell of all.

And what would you know about Mexico? My own harsh voice floated through my mind, along with Henrika's smug answer. *Everything.*

Henrika's cryptic words had reopened all those old wounds. Ever since that night, I'd been reviewing everything related to the Mexico mission, but so far, I hadn't come up with any new leads. Which was why I needed to track down Henrika and squeeze the answers out of her.

General Percy crossed his arms over his chest, and a faint outline flared around his body. At first, the light was a dull gray, but it quickly brightened to a nauseating pink and then morphed into that burning bloodred that signaled a serious threat. My synesthesia kicked into high gear, and a little voice muttered in the back of my mind.

Danger-danger-danger.

My breath caught in my throat, and I had to bite my tongue to keep from flinching. I didn't normally get such a stark, vivid warning unless someone was about to shoot, stab, punch, or otherwise physically harm me, and the fact that I'd gotten such a strong vibe off General Percy right now . . . well, nothing good could come from it.

Oh, Jethro Percy wouldn't whip out a gun and shoot me in the bullpen. But grudges never died at Section 47, and I wouldn't put it past the General to slyly undercut or even openly sabotage me . . . or whatever he had done that had contributed to my father's death.

Desmond shifted closer to me. I longed to grab his hand and feel his warm, strong fingers wrapping around my own, but I remained still. General Percy would see such a public display of affection as a weakness.

Percy looked at Desmond, then back at me. I didn't think it was possible, but his face grew even colder, like frost sweeping across a windowpane. He didn't like whatever conclusions he had drawn about his son and me.

"Debriefing. Conference room. Now." General Percy arched a silvery eyebrow at me. "Unless you plan on wasting more of my time, along with Section resources?"

I bit my tongue to keep from sniping back and gave the General a blank look, as though his barbed words and snide tone had no impact on me.

His eyebrow arched a little higher at my silence. "I see you're as stubborn and obstinate as your father, Ms. Locke. What a pity you've inherited his worst traits."

Percy shook his head, then strode forward. Desmond and I whipped to opposite sides of the aisle. General Percy marched right in between us, opened the door to the conference room, and went inside. The two bodyguards followed him.

I blinked a few times, but the outline of General Percy's body continued to burn a bright, bloody red in my eyes, like a camera flash firing over and over. My inner voice also kept up its *danger-danger-danger* chorus, but this time, the threat was my own roiling emotions.

Even with all my questions about the Mexico mission, I'd thought I'd made a tenuous peace with my father's death, along with his blind devotion to Section 47, but General Percy's stinging criticism of us Lockes brought all my old anger and disgust roaring back to the surface.

Anger at my father for getting himself killed and leaving Grandma Jane millions of dollars in debt. Anger at General Percy and the other Section higher-ups for not doing more to save my father and then blaming him for everything that had gone wrong after the fact. Disgust at my father for always— *always*—putting Section 47 above everything else, even me, his own daughter.

Jack Locke had been gone for more days of my life than he'd been present in it, and yet I still couldn't shake the knowledge that I had *never* been the most important thing in my father's world. And most of all, disgust at myself for still caring so damn much about him and what really happened in Mexico and all the rest of it.

Now that the big boss had stepped away, the tension in the bullpen eased, although the other agents kept sneaking looks at Desmond and me.

Desmond's fingers flexed as though he wanted to reach for

my hand, but just like me, he stopped himself. He couldn't afford to look weak either.

"Ahem." Joan cleared her throat again, stood up, and grabbed some folders off her desk. "You heard the General. Time for the debriefing."

Joan didn't particularly like me, but for once, her tone was neutral, and I could have sworn a bit of sympathy flickered across her face. She hoisted the folders a little higher in her arms and headed toward the conference room.

Worry creased Desmond's forehead. "Charlotte, are you okay?"

"Of course," I replied, grateful my voice remained calm and steady, unlike the sea of bitter, messy emotions still sloshing around in my chest.

I thought I'd been ready for any tricks Henrika Hyde might pull trying to steal the Grunglass Necklace, but I'd been no match for her cleverness, and I had a nagging feeling I was playing a similar losing game with the General. Jethro Percy being here wasn't good for Desmond, but my synesthesia kept whispering that the General's appearance was going to be even worse for me.

I grabbed a notepad from my desk, along with a pen and the smoke-stained briefcase, and followed Desmond into the conference room. I was about to close the door when I spotted Evelyn hurrying in this direction, also carrying a notepad and a pen. In addition to her guise as a receptionist, Evelyn also played the part of an assistant, and she often took notes during debriefings.

I waited until she had entered the room, then shut the door, which locked with a soft click. A moment later, a buzz sounded, indicating that the room had also been soundproofed.

The two bodyguards took up positions beside the door, but instead of watching the bullpen, they both faced the conference room. Even more disconcerting, one of the men kept his gaze fixed on me, as though he thought I was a physical threat. Please. General Jethro Percy was a strong enduro and a ruthless assassin with years of combat experience. He could kill me with a paper clip before I could so much as brandish my pen at him.

"If everyone would find their seats, we can finally proceed," Percy said.

The remark was directed at me, so I set my things down and took my usual chair.

General Percy was sitting at one end of the long, rectangular table, with several empty seats between the two of us. I was near the middle, with Desmond right beside me. Gia was at the other end of the table, Evelyn on her right side, then Diego and Joan on her left.

Percy made a couple of circles with his right index finger, a clear signal to get this spy show on the road, as the old saying went.

Diego started typing on one of his laptops. The overhead lights dimmed, and a large film screen dropped down from the ceiling and covered one of the walls. Diego hit some more buttons, and the security footage from this morning's botched Vault mission started playing. Far more cameras had captured the action than I'd realized, so everyone got bird's-eye and close-up views of just how badly things had gone, in high definition with crystal-clear color and sound to boot. Hurray for technology.

We watched the footage in silence. When it finished, Diego hit some more buttons. The lights brightened to a normal level, but the film screen remained in place. Diego had frozen the security feed on Bryce right before he lobbed the smoke grenade at me.

"As some of you know, this is Bryce Finkley, a former Section cleaner," Diego said. "He was suspected of stealing drugs, cash, and weapons from raids, although nothing was ever proven. He left Section several years ago."

Below the tabletop, out of sight of the others, Desmond's hands clenched into fists.

"Bryce now runs a private contracting firm," Diego continued. "But really, it's just a semi-legitimate cover for a group of highly trained mercenaries. In the years since he left Section, Bryce has done jobs all over the world—kidnappings, political assassinations, even a few heists."

"And now he's working for Henrika Hyde." Gia took over the briefing. "Bryce commanded the crew of thieves who infiltrated the Vault."

General Percy drummed his fingers on the table. "Where are the other thieves?"

Gia checked her phone. "The strike team delivered the thieves to headquarters a few minutes ago. They are currently being interrogated on level four."

Desmond glared at the frozen image of Bryce on the screen. "The thieves won't know anything. Bryce will have told them just enough to do their jobs. Nothing more."

Gia nodded again. "Agreed. So far, all the thieves have said is that Bryce paid them a large sum of money. Iris Berriston, the Section agent, is telling a similar story. She was to get Charlotte alone and steal the Grunglass Necklace."

Gia gestured at me, and I opened the briefcase, revealing the glittering gold, emerald, and diamond necklace nestled inside the velvet compartment.

General Percy studied the sparkling stones. "Please tell me you didn't take the *actual* necklace on your doomed mission."

"Of course not," Gia replied in a smooth voice. "This is just a copy. The real Grunglass Necklace is safely locked away in the armory."

I blinked at her lie. This wasn't a copy—it was the *real* necklace. Henrika would have told the thieves to be on the lookout for a fake, which was why I'd lobbied to take the genuine necklace on the mission. Gia had agreed, although the cleaner leader had insisted that we add a tracker to the necklace in the shape of a small extra diamond just in case the thieves snatched it after all. But I didn't blame Gia for claiming the necklace was a fake. She was just trying to cover her ass and save mine in the process.

"Well, at least you showed a modicum of common sense about that," Percy said.

Desmond remained stone-faced, but Evelyn, Gia, Diego, and Joan all winced at his harsh tone. I shut the briefcase lid with far more force than was necessary.

Gia cleared her throat. "In addition to stealing the necklace from Charlotte, the thieves were also told to break into a storage locker, although we don't know exactly what they were looking for."

Desmond and I both tensed. We couldn't reveal that the thieves had been after the vials of Redburn from the Tannenbaum mission. I hated lying to Gia and Evelyn, but if they knew Desmond and I had samples of the explosive, they might one day be forced to turn them over to General Percy, something Desmond vehemently opposed. Me too, especially after meeting the General.

Percy waved his hand. "The necklace and the storage locker were just smokescreens. Bryce was the one with the true objective. How did he escape?"

Diego hit some more buttons on his laptop, and photos of the open manhole appeared.

"Bryce accessed a manhole in the garden section of the lobby," Gia said. "From there, he dropped into the sewer system. By the time the strike team checked the area for booby traps, he was gone."

"Bryce had to come out of the sewers somewhere," Joan chimed in. "As soon as we pinpoint his exit location, we can start tracking him."

Diego nodded, his fingers flexing over his laptop. "I've already started scrubbing traffic cameras from the surrounding area."

"But you haven't found him yet, so you've got *nothing*," Percy growled, that disgusted note creeping into his voice again. "No leads on Bryce and no idea what information he accessed."

Diego's fingers plummeted to the keyboard. He shrank down into his seat like a turtle pulling its tender body back inside its protective shell, but Joan lifted her chin and met the General's cold gaze with a steady stare of her own. Despite our uneasy relationship, I admired the liaison for standing her ground.

"Not yet," Joan replied. "But it's just a matter of time. Diego has several programs running to determine what Bryce was after—"

Percy waved his hand again, cutting her off. "Spare me the technobabble. Just figure out what he accessed and make sure nothing like this ever happens again."

Joan and Diego both nodded. "Yes, sir," they said in unison, although Joan's voice was louder and harsher than Diego's soft, apologetic murmur.

General Percy rocked back in his seat, and his fingers drummed on the tabletop in an ominous chorus of impending doom. His gaze skimmed right over Evelyn, who was still taking notes. He glanced at Joan and Diego, then turned his attention to Gia, Desmond, and me, studying the three of us with obvious displeasure.

"Let me recap today's events," General Percy said in an icy tone. "You three hatched a harebrained scheme and leaked information that Ms. Locke was transporting the Grunglass Necklace to the Vault storage facility in hopes of catching some unimportant, low-level thieves. Only the thieves were a diversion for someone smarter to come along and break into our system, putting valuable information at risk. Is that right?"

Everyone at the table froze.

"Is that right?" Percy repeated, his tone louder and sharper than before.

"Yes, sir," Gia admitted in a low, reluctant voice.

"Today's mission is just the latest in a string of failures. Starting with the night when not one but *two* moles were discovered here. Moles who had been feeding information to Henrika Hyde for who knows how long." General Percy shook his head. "Maestro isn't doing a very good job of overseeing the D.C. station. It's been one disaster after another over the last few months."

Evelyn's face remained calm, but the tip of her pen dug into her notepad hard enough to rip the top piece of paper. Joan also noticed the motion, and her gaze lingered on the other woman.

"Then again, I suppose it's easy to get away with failing when no one holds you accountable," Percy continued.

"Sir, you know the identities of station chiefs are often classified, even kept from you and the other members of the board of directors, for security reasons," Gia said.

The General sliced his hand through the air. "Bah! An antiquated, useless tactic. As if I and the other board members couldn't find out such information if we really wanted to. It's long past time for Section chiefs like Maestro to step out into the light and face the consequences of their actions."

As the head of the board of directors, Jethro Percy was one of the few public faces of Section 47, and he often liaised with mortal authorities and smoothed things over so that regular paramortals could stay under the radar and spies like us could keep operating in the shadows. Legacy families also chipped in to help cover Section's budget, with the Percy family being one of the organization's main benefactors.

"But really, Maestro and their secret identity isn't the problem. We are talking about yet another failure because of one person: Charlotte Locke." Percy stabbed his finger at me. "Because *she* thought this mission was a good use of Section time, resources, and manpower."

I bristled. I'd been expecting the personal attack, especially given the General's obvious, immediate dislike of me, but I hadn't thought he would be quite so blunt. Percy was looking for someone to blame, though, and that someone was going to be me.

"Charlotte is the best analyst at Section," Desmond said, anger seeping into his voice. "She knows more about Henrika Hyde than anyone, and she was right about today's mission. Henrika *did* try to steal the Grunglass Necklace."

"Yes, Henrika just didn't do it in person, which means she is still free and plotting against Section," Percy replied, his cold voice a sharp contrast to his son's hot tone. "That alone would have made today's mission a failure, but now it's been compounded by the fact that Bryce Finkley breached our servers. Henrika is probably reviewing Section secrets at this very moment."

A tense silence fell over the conference room. As much as I hated to admit it, he was right. Henrika had seen through my trap, and even worse, she'd turned it around and beaten me at my own spy game.

Desmond opened his mouth to keep defending me, but I touched his arm under the table out of sight of the others. Desmond hissed out a breath, and some of the tension trickled out of his body. Arguing with the General wouldn't do him or me any good.

"As of this moment, I will be spearheading the efforts to find Henrika and make sure she pays for her many crimes against Section 47," General Percy said, his voice booming out like thunder.

He looked at me, his pale blue eyes even frostier than before. "Ms. Locke will no longer have an active role in any missions regarding Henrika and her associates."

His words slapped me across the face, but all I could do was sit there and take the brutal blow.

General Percy regarded me in stony silence. My heart dropped with every long, slow second, but I met his gaze with a steady one of my own and resisted the urge to wipe my cold, clammy palms on my legs.

"Ms. Locke will return to her previous duties as an analyst on level three," Percy said. "She will forward any information related to the Hyde investigation to Ms. Samson, who will be Desmond's liaison going forward."

Being banished to level three was a clear, harsh demotion, like I was a broken, defective doll being stuffed back into a box and returned to the store. Frustration pounded through me at losing access to all the Section intelligence regarding Henrika, much of which I had painstakingly gathered myself, but I held my tongue. General Percy might use my arguing as an excuse to fire me outright.

Everyone stared at me. No one spoke, although Joan winced the faintest bit, as if she didn't like this new development any more than I did. Curious. She should have been *thrilled* to be Desmond's liaison, especially since she had wanted the plum job all along. Given her relationship with Graham Walker, Joan had just as many reasons to want Henrika captured—or killed—as Desmond and I did. Being demoted was a bitter pill to swallow, but at least Joan would watch Desmond's back.

"Do you understand your new assignment, Ms. Locke?" Percy asked in that same booming voice.

"Yes, sir," I replied, careful to keep my tone calm and neutral.

My father had been one of the best cleaners Section ever had, and he had lost almost all his battles with the General. I might not be as deadly as the infamous Jack Locke, but I knew better than to repeat his mistakes.

Jethro Percy was not the kind of person you took on unless you were absolutely certain you could succeed. I would sacrifice this battle—and a large chunk of my pride—if it meant winning a long-term war, even if I still wasn't exactly sure why the General had me in his crosshairs.

Percy must have thought I'd been sufficiently cowed because he snapped his fingers at Diego. "I want to know the second you figure out what Bryce Finkley accessed in our system. Then we can determine how to best mitigate the damage from this disastrous mission. That is all. Dismissed."

Desmond, Evelyn, Gia, Diego, and Joan looked at me. Even General Percy stared at me, and his two bodyguards drifted forward, as if they thought I might throw myself along the length of the conference table and try to choke the life out of their boss with my bare hands. As difficult as it was, I squashed the tempting urge. I couldn't outbrawn Percy, much less his bodyguards, so I would have to outthink them, even though my mind felt like it was mired in quicksand right now.

Several seconds ticked by. When it became apparent that I wasn't going to make a scene, the others pushed their chairs back from the table and gathered up their things. I should have done the same, but I was frozen in place, as though a transmuter had turned the blood in my veins to ice and then glued my ass to my chair for good measure.

Beside me, Desmond got to his feet. He skimmed his fingers along my jacket sleeve, only touching the fabric and not my skin, but the small show of support cracked through the ice that encased my body.

I pushed my own chair back and slowly stood up. With every motion, more of that ice cracked away, replaced by hot, pounding fury.

General Percy wanted to demote me? Fine. I would return

to level three like a good little analyst, put my head down, and get to work. But one way or another, I *was* going to find Henrika Hyde, and then she was going to pay for everything she'd done to me, and especially to Desmond.

No one was getting in the way of my mission, not even General Jethro Percy.

EIGHT

DESMOND

Beside me, Charlotte got to her feet. Her face was calm, serene even, but her aura exploded with color, burning like a sapphire sun over her heart. The light was so intense and bright it made me wince, and sensations burst off her one after another—red-hot anger, rock-hard stubbornness, and most of all, a razor-sharp spike of determination that slammed into my own chest like a spear.

Despite the General's orders, Charlotte wasn't giving up her quest to track down Henrika. Pride rippled through me, along with more than a little admiration. Most people folded in on themselves like a paper bag rather than go up against my father, but not Charlotte. Her inner strength was one of the things I respected about her the most.

Well, I wasn't giving up either. I'd promised Graham to take down everyone responsible for his death, along with the other agents who had been killed on the Blacksea mission, and I would do anything to keep that vow, even defy my own father.

Then again, this would hardly be the first time I'd done that.

More like the latest rebellious act in the never-ending game of tug-of-war between my father and me.

The General was practically vibrating with cold fury. Well, I was just as pissed. He might be one of the leaders of Section 47, but he had no right to speak to Charlotte that way. I'd gone on the mission too, and it was just as much my fault as it was Charlotte's that we had failed, but my father had deliberately humiliated and demoted Charlotte in front of the others. He'd been nothing but a giant, egotistical bastard. The Jethro Percy special, in other words.

As far as I knew, my father had never met Charlotte before, and I was willing to bet his harshness had more to do with his dislike of Jack Locke than with Charlotte's supposed failure.

Sometimes I thought the true legacy of Section 47 was all the anger, scorn, disgust, and derision we spies heaped on each other with our family feuds and old, deep-seated grudges.

"Desmond, with me," the General barked out, getting to his feet and tugging down his suit jacket, even though it was already perfectly straight.

The last thing I wanted was to talk to my father, but he was my superior officer, and I had no choice but to do as commanded.

I looked at Charlotte. "I'll see you later. At the diner. Okay?"

In addition to being an analyst, Charlotte also worked as a waitress at the Moondust Diner, which was a few blocks from Section 47 headquarters. She had originally taken the job to help with her grandmother's massive medical bills, although those bills had been paid off a few months ago when Charlotte had drained the bank accounts of Trevor Donnelly and Miriam Lancaster, the Section moles who had been feeding information to Henrika.

Despite being debt-free, Charlotte had kept working at the diner, claiming she did some of her best thinking there. Plus, she loved the food, especially the desserts.

"Charlotte?" I asked again.

She blinked. The burning aura around her heart dimmed, as did her blazing emotions. "Okay. We'll talk later."

Her gaze skipped past me and landed on the General. Power surged off her, and magic flickered in her dark blue eyes. I didn't know what Charlotte saw when she looked at my father with her synesthesia, but I doubted it was anything good.

Even more telling was the way her eyes narrowed ever so slightly. I knew *that* look. Charlotte was already doing those beautiful mental gymnastics in her mind, trying to figure out a way to thwart my father. I'd been attempting that feat for years and had never even come close, but if anyone could succeed, it was Charlotte.

She stared at the General a few seconds longer, then nodded to me and strode out of the conference room.

Diego scooped up his laptops and followed her, as did Evelyn and Joan. Gia went next door to her office.

I spun around on my heel and marched out of the conference room. Charlotte had already vanished from the bullpen to return to level three, but I headed over to my desk. I needed a few seconds to brace myself for my upcoming meeting with the General.

Joan had already sat down at her own desk across the aisle. She stared at her screen, but the corner of her mouth moved. "Sorry, Dez," she murmured. "I know that didn't go the way you wanted."

That was an understatement, although I appreciated her sympathy. Given our long-standing friendship, Joan knew all about my difficulties with my father.

Those familiar, heavy footsteps scuffed on the carpet, making my spine stiffen.

"Desmond, with me." The General repeated his earlier command.

He strode by my desk, followed by his two bodyguards. The

other cleaners and liaisons looked at me out of the corners of their eyes, and their auras pulsed with interest and speculation.

"Good luck," Joan murmured, her gaze still on her laptop.

I nodded at her, then headed after my father, bracing myself for a tense, angry confrontation. The Percy family special, in other words.

I stepped inside an elevator with the General and his bodyguards. One of the men punched the button, and the elevator rose. I leaned against a wall and studied the other two men, both of whom stood at rigid attention while my father scrolled through screens on his phone.

I hadn't seen either man before, but they were clearly Section cleaners like me. Enduros, most likely. My father always employed the best of the best, and he wouldn't trust his life to anyone he found lacking, especially when it came to their paramortal powers.

The elevator stopped, and the door slid open. The two guards stepped out first, making sure the corridor was clear. I held back a derisive snort. As if my father couldn't take care of himself. He too was an enduro, and he hadn't risen through the Section ranks by being anything other than exceptionally deadly and completely ruthless. Perhaps that was the reason the General and Jack Locke had been such bitter enemies. Charlotte's father had been one of the few people who could go toe-to-toe with the General.

One of the bodyguards waved his hand in an all-clear signal. My father put his phone away and left the elevator. I trailed along behind him.

Many of the Section levels had a similar layout of a long corridor that led to a central bullpen, but level four was different.

The corridor here split in two directions. The interrogation rooms and holding cells were off to the left, while the offices of the Section leaders were to the right.

I trailed my father and the guards down the right corridor, which opened into an enormous round space, like a circle inside a square. The gray walls and carpet were the same as in the level-five bullpen, although someone had spruced things up here with floral-printed couches. Fresh-cut flowers perched in crystal vases on the high tables along the walls, next to a few potted trees. The faint, perfumy aroma of the flowers, along with the hushed atmosphere, reminded me of a funeral home. My nose crinkled with disgust.

No security cameras were embedded in the ceiling, and I didn't sense the telltale hum of any electronic listening devices. The big bosses might like to spy on all the analysts, charmers, liaisons, and cleaners, but they didn't want anyone monitoring their own questionable actions.

Thick wooden doors were set into the wall, along with glass windows that revealed offices and a large conference room. A gleaming brass nameplate on a door read *Maestro*, but the office inside was spartan, with only a closed laptop sitting on a desk, and it revealed no hints about Evelyn Hawkes's true identity.

The other offices were similarly furnished, but no one was toiling away inside. Like my father, most of the other Section leaders either worked remotely from home or moved from one station to another, handling crises around the world.

The General went over to a door directly opposite Maestro's office and punched in a code on a keypad. The door buzzed open, and he moved through to the other side. One of the guards gestured for me to follow my father, then stepped forward and pulled the door shut behind me. Through the window, I watched the two men take up positions on either side of the door, still protecting my father, even though the fourth level was one of the most secure places inside Section headquarters.

The General strode forward. His wing tips barely made a whisper on the gray carpet, which was much thicker and nicer than what was in the waiting area outside. Somehow the faint scuffs made his footsteps even more ominous than usual.

He stepped behind a wooden desk that stretched along the back wall. The General sank into a black leather chair, and the padding let out a soft sigh, indicating just how luxe and comfortable it was. In contrast, the two chairs squatting in front of the desk were plain metal frames that looked like they belonged in an interrogation room.

Metal bookcases bristling with history, military, and other nonfiction books stood along one wall, opposite a gray couch and a mini fridge on another wall. A high wooden table covered with gleaming liquor bottles and crystal glasses stood in the back corner, and a shiny black metal filing cabinet was in the other corner.

An open door led to a gray tile bathroom. Folded white towels were stacked up on a long counter, while travel-size soaps and shampoos ringed the sink. This space looked more like a hotel suite than an office, and it was cold, functional, and sterile, just like my father so often was.

The only things out of place were the cardboard boxes piled on the couch and a smaller, battered, open box sitting on the desk.

"Moving in?" I drawled, leaning a shoulder against a bookcase.

My father shrugged. "I completed my review of the Section station in Vienna last week. I thought it was high time to return to D.C., especially given all the problems here over the last few months."

As the head of the board of directors, my father was always moving from one Section station to another, like a shark gobbling up all the missions and problems in his wake, large and small, important and trivial. Basically, the General was a CEO, only he dealt in secrets, lies, and super-spies instead of cars, computers, and assembly-line workers.

I might be his son, but as a Section cleaner, I rarely saw my father, since I too was always traveling from one mission and one part of the world to another. At least before I had settled in D.C. But that arrangement had suited me just fine, especially after the Blacksea mission.

Even though Graham and several other agents had been killed, the General hadn't sent anyone after Adrian Anatoly, the terrorist responsible for planting the bombs on the beach and ambushing the Section support staff in Australia. My father had claimed someone would kill Anatoly sooner or later and that going after the terrorist wasn't a good use of my time and skills.

Despite our issues over the years, his lack of support had stunned me. Eventually, my shock had turned to anger, and I'd decided to go after Anatoly myself, which had eventually led me to Charlotte.

But right now, my anger was tempered by wariness. The General never did anything without a reason, which made me even more curious about what he was doing here. What person or mission had caught his attention at the D.C. station?

My father reached into the open cardboard box and pulled out a silver picture frame, which he positioned on the corner of the desk so that it was facing toward him. In the photo, my mother, Iylena, relaxed on a beach towel. A floppy hat covered most of her strawberry-blond hair and protected her pale, freckled skin from the sun, but her hazel eyes sparkled with warmth and merriment as she grinned at the camera.

My father was American, but Iylena had been born in Australia, and I had spent a lot of time there during my childhood, hence my accent. My mother had suffered from a rare type of blood cancer that only struck paramortals, and later this year would mark the fifteenth anniversary of her death. I'd always been close to my mother, and seeing her smiling face made the sharp ache of her loss hit me all over again.

My father trailed his fingers down the glass as if he was caressing Iylena's face. Despite his faults, he had truly loved my mother, who had been a kind, gentle, wonderful woman. Our mutual respect for her was just about the only thing the two of us had in common these days.

"Iylena would have loved seeing you establishing yourself here in the D.C. station," the General said in a low, gruff voice. "She was always so proud of you, Desmond."

I swallowed the knot of emotion in my throat. "Yes, she was."

My father caressed her photo a moment longer, then hit a red button on the desktop. A familiar buzz rang out, indicating that he had soundproofed the office.

The General lifted his gaze to mine. The warmth drained out of his eyes like water leaking through a sieve, and he squared his shoulders, as if bracing for the unpleasant but familiar task of dealing with me, his disappointing son. "I suppose you want to talk about the analyst. Plead your case for how Ms. Locke should be allowed to continue working on the Hyde mission."

His cold, flat tone punched the softness out of me, and I lifted my chin and squared my shoulders right back at him. "I don't have to *plead* anything. Charlotte is the best analyst here, in all of Section, actually, and she knows more about Henrika than anyone else. Sidelining her is a mistake."

My father arched an eyebrow. "So you said in the debriefing, but I remain unconvinced." He gestured over at a pile of cardboard boxes stacked on the couch. "I've reviewed Ms. Locke's work regarding Henrika. Her information-gathering skills and analytical deductions are average at best."

I scoffed. "That's bullshit, and we both know it. Besides, Charlotte was the one who figured out that Trevor Donnelly and Miriam Lancaster were moles."

The General's eyes narrowed. "My question is why didn't *you* figure it out? You and Trevor were friends. You went on dozens of missions together, and yet you never noticed that Trevor wasn't as committed to Section as he pretended to be."

Anger surged through me, and my jaw clenched so hard I thought I might crack a tooth. My father had been here all of an hour, and he was already pointing out my many flaws. But the thing that annoyed me the most was that in this case he was *right*.

Trevor Donnelly had been one of my closest friends, and he, Graham, and I had jokingly referred to ourselves as the Three Musketeers. I'd had no idea Trevor was involved with Miriam Lancaster, one of the charmers he was supervising, much less that they had both been feeding information to Henrika Hyde.

Not only had Trevor betrayed Section 47, but he'd also betrayed *me*. Trevor had leaked information to Adrian Anatoly that had resulted in Graham's death, along with those of the other agents assigned to the doomed Blacksea mission.

I was the only one who had survived, and when I'd come to Washington, D.C., to track down the mole, Trevor had doubled down on his treachery. First, he'd sent several cleaners to kill Charlotte, who was getting closer to the truth than she'd realized. Then Trevor had sent more cleaners to try to kill us both with a car bomb.

And perhaps worst of all, after Charlotte had outed him as a mole, Trevor had admitted how jealous he was of me. How he hated the fact that I was a Legacy and he wasn't, and how my father had handed everything to me on a silver platter. That was the first time I'd seen Trevor's true colors, and the knowledge had stunned, saddened, and angered me. The two of us had fought in the level-three bullpen, and I'd killed Trevor by using my galvanism to stop his heart.

Sometimes I thought all I did was go around killing my friends.

"Well?" the General demanded. "Why didn't you discover the truth about Trevor yourself? Instead of being so blind to his actions? I taught you better than that, Desmond. I taught you to keep *everyone* close, friends and enemies alike, because—"

"Because you never know when one might turn into the other," I muttered, finishing his saying, which I'd heard more than once, along with similar pearls of pernicious wisdom.

The General had taught me a lot of things, most of which involved manipulating, hurting, and killing other people, whether it was emotionally, mentally, or physically. He'd been giving me a master class in deceit, treachery, and power mongering my entire life. I didn't know whether to be grateful or hate him for it. The General's lessons had saved me more than once, but they had also deeply scarred my soul, something I hadn't even realized until I'd met Charlotte.

"Trevor's dead, so he doesn't matter anymore," I lied, trying to ignore the anger and hurt pounding through my chest. "We were talking about Charlotte and her skills. In addition to ferreting out the moles, she also figured out that Henrika would attack the Christmas Eve party at Tannenbaum Castle to try to steal the Nutcracker Ruby. No other Section analyst made that connection—just Charlotte."

My father arched his eyebrow again. "Listen to you sing her praises. I would almost think you genuinely admire her analytical skills."

"But?" I challenged.

"But you're sleeping with her." A disgusted note crept into his voice.

Of course my father would boil it down to that. What I felt for Charlotte went far beyond the physical, but I wasn't about to confess my feelings. He would just use my emotions against me, the way I'd seen him do to countless agents. The General never met a heartstring he wouldn't tug, twist, or tear to get what he wanted.

I forced myself to give a nonchalant shrug. "So what if I am? Fraternizing isn't against Section rules. Besides, it's not like I meet a lot of people in our line of work. Just criminals, terrorists, and assassins."

"Yes, but you should know better than to get involved with a bloody *Locke*." My father snarled the name like it was a vile curse. "All that family has ever done is cause problems. That's their true legacy at Section 47. Out of all the women in this building, you just had to get involved with *her*. Sometimes I think you do these things to deliberately annoy me, Desmond."

"You've never cared who I'm involved with as long as I got the job done on whatever mission you assigned—and I *always* get the job done," I growled.

To my surprise, the General tipped his head, acknowledging my point. "You do have the second-highest kill rate in Section history."

A subtle barb. To my father, *second-highest* was the equivalent of saying *not-the-best*.

"Yes, well, we both know who has the highest kill rate in Section history: Jack Locke."

The General flinched at the cleaner's name, and petty satisfaction sparked in my chest at annoying him for a change.

"Exactly how much of your dislike of Charlotte has to do with her father?" I asked. "Because I remember *exactly* how much you despised Jack Locke."

Growing up, I'd overheard dozens of heated phone calls between the General and the Section cleaner, and my father had constantly complained to my mother and his friends about the other man. I'd never been able to figure out exactly why the General disliked Jack Locke so much, other than the fact that Locke was one of the few people brave—or foolish—enough to stand up to him. Then again, for General Jethro Percy, that was reason enough. If you weren't an ally, then you were an enemy, and he would neutralize you—one way or another.

Anger flared in my father's eyes, and his pale blue aura prickled with the hot emotion. "Jack Locke was an arrogant fool. He didn't understand how the spy world works, how Section 47 truly works." He waved his hand in a short, dismissive motion. "Jack Locke was always more concerned with upholding his precious *ideals* than anything else."

"Funny how people with no ideals, rules, or limits see those things as failings in others," I drawled again.

My father sighed and looked upward, as if asking some higher power for the strength and patience to deal with me. More petty satisfaction sparked in my chest. I took great pride in exasperating him as much as he exasperated me. It was the only battle I could ever win between us.

The General dropped his gaze back down to me, and his aura cooled and congealed into an icy ring around his heart that only my mother had ever been able to breach. "Do us both a favor, Desmond, and don't try my patience any more than you already have. And stay away from Charlotte Locke."

"Or what?" I asked, hearing the underlying threat loud and clear.

"Or I'll fire her, and the only thing she'll be analyzing is the menu at that low-rent diner where she moonlights."

Dread flooded my veins like an ocean of ice. The General never made idle threats. Charlotte loved being an analyst, but my father would take that away from her in a second if he thought it would further his own agenda.

My hands clenched into fists. "You are *impossible*."

"And you are as impertinent, reckless, and emotional as ever," my father snapped right back. "You might not realize it, but I'm doing this for your own good, Desmond. Go say your goodbyes to Charlotte tonight at that seedy diner, if you must."

"But?" I challenged.

"But from this moment forward, you are not to share *any* information regarding Henrika Hyde with Charlotte Locke. Not the smallest scrap of intel, not the faintest whispered rumor, not the most tenuous lead. I will *not* let another Locke screw up my mission. The stakes are too high."

My father shrugged. "But if you choose to defy me, as you so often do, then I'll make sure Ms. Locke pays the price for your actions. Are we clear?"

It took me a moment to unlock my jaw. "Crystal."

The General clearly heard the anger and disgust in my voice, but he waved his hand again, brushing aside my feelings and opinions the way he always did. "Dismissed. Get back to work. I want an update on where Henrika might be hiding by the end of the day."

"Yes, sir." I raised my hand and snapped off a mock salute.

My father frowned, but I spun away, yanked the door open, and stormed out of his office.

NINE

CHARLOTTE

After the debriefing ended, I stalked back to the desk I had been using on level five. My feelings seesawed from anger to determination and back again, with a fair amount of frustration, disgust, and bitterness mixed in, and my mind spun from the emotional vertigo.

Under the watchful eyes of the liaisons and cleaners, I quickly gathered up my things, including my laptop, several folders, and the smoke-stained briefcase I was still carrying around like a child with a stuffed animal. The instant I left the bullpen, whispers sprang up behind me. Spies loved to gossip, and news of my demotion would be all over the building within minutes. Terrific.

I trudged along the corridor and stepped into an elevator. I stared at my own murky reflection in the metal door as the car rose.

By the time the elevator floated to a stop on the third level, my internal seesaw had landed on determination, and I was marginally calmer. I had no choice but to keep my placid mask locked in place. You never knew who was watching at Section

47, and I wouldn't put it past General Percy to be studying me through a security camera. My having a meltdown and throwing a tantrum would probably please him to no end.

I went down a corridor and swiped my keycard over a reader. The door buzzed open, and I stepped into the level-three bullpen. In many ways, it was a mirror image of the fifth level where the cleaners and liaisons worked. A long, wide aisle running past cubicles cordoned off with clear plastic walls. A couple of glassed-in offices and a conference room along the back wall. People of all ages, shapes, sizes, and ethnicities typing on laptops or murmuring into phones.

Yes, in many ways, this area was exactly like level five, but I'd always thought the analysts and charmers had far more personality and flair than the cleaners and liaisons, at least when it came to their workspaces. Family photos, movie posters, and calendars featuring cute animals doing yoga decorated many of the cubicle walls, while everything from crocheted superheroes to autographed footballs to snow globes adorned the desks.

Grandma Jane always said you could learn a lot just by studying how people decorated their personal spaces, and I'd used her advice more than once to figure out something someone didn't want me to know.

At the sound of my footsteps, several folks peered past their laptop screens. A few surprised hums sounded, and a couple of folks started typing on their keyboards, no doubt emailing their friends about my stunning fall from grace. Everyone knew my returning to the third level could only mean I had been demoted.

I tightened my grip on my belongings, lifted my chin, and marched down the center aisle.

A few folks waved at me, including Ronaldo and Helga, who were analysts like me, tasked with using their own unique forms of synesthesia to study reports from Section agents, looking for patterns and actionable intelligence.

I returned the waves, ignored the curious looks and snide whispers, and walked to the back of the bullpen. Even though I'd been working on level five for the last few months, no one had claimed my old desk, and it was empty, except for the standard office equipment—a monitor, a mouse, a keyboard, a landline phone, and a place to plug in my Section-issued laptop.

I dumped my things on the desk, then reached into my pocket and drew out a small crystal mockingbird. The beautiful keepsake had been a gift from Grandma Jane the day I had started working at Section 47, and it was always on my desk, no matter where that desk happened to be. Grandma Jane had meant the figurine to be a visual reminder that people could sing more than one tune, just like a mockingbird could mimic the songs of other birds, and that folks in the spy world were often not what they seemed.

Jethro Percy certainly fell into that category. On the surface, he seemed like your usual blustering leader, blowing into town certain he could right the company ship that was in danger of sinking. But Desmond and I had been tracking Henrika Hyde for months, so why had Percy shown up now?

I didn't know, but I was going to find out why Percy had suddenly taken such a keen interest and a starring role in my and Desmond's mission. And it was still *our* mission. I didn't care what Percy said, did, or threatened. I was going to find Henrika and make her tell me everything she knew about my father's doomed mission. Then she was going to pay for everything she'd done to Desmond.

I plugged in my laptop, then sorted through the folders and other items I'd brought from the fifth level.

The twenty-something woman in the neighboring cubicle swiveled her chair toward me. She was on the petite side, with dark brown eyes, dark brown skin, and black hair that was pulled back in a ponytail. She was wearing a dark blue pantsuit, although a T-shirt for a popular local rock band peeked out from beneath her jacket. Ticket stubs from concerts were sitting in a glass cup on her desk, flanked by toy guitars and pianos. A classical tune drifted out of the headphones hooked around her neck.

"Hey, Charlotte." Mika Doleni smiled at me.

Mika was a linguist, aka a lingo, someone who could read, write, speak, and understand any language. Something that came in handy when transcribing chatter from paramortal villains and trying to figure out the code words they used to communicate.

My synesthesia surged. My vision flickered, and Mika melted away, replaced by a woman with long red hair and rosy skin sitting in that same chair and smiling at me. Miriam Lancaster, the charmer I'd thought had been my friend but who had really been a mole.

My gaze zipped over to the front of the bullpen and landed on the spot where Miriam's body had fallen after Desmond had shot her to save me. My vision flickered again, and suddenly, I could see Miriam lying on the floor, blood oozing out of the bullet wound in her head, her hazel eyes already glassy with death.

I shivered and looked away from the phantom image. Even though Miriam had been responsible for the deaths of other agents and had been willing to kill me to escape, part of me still missed the charmer, missed the part of her that had been my friend—if that part had even existed at all and hadn't been just another illusion that Miriam had projected with her paramortal charisma.

Mika cleared her throat, drawing my attention.

"I'm sorry. What did you say?"

She gestured at the folders on my desk. "Are you back here now? As a . . . level-three analyst?"

She was asking if I'd been demoted. Mika was kinder about

it than most folks would have been, but I still had to resist the urge to throw something.

"Yep. My assignment on the fifth level ended, and I'm back here full-time again."

Mika flashed me another smile. "Well, I'm glad you're here, Charlotte. In fact, I was wondering if you could help me with something . . ."

The lingo showed me a transcript she had been working on. Some paramortal criminals she was tracking were planning to meet up, which was pretty unusual, given their territorial disputes. Had I ever run into a situation like this? Should she pass it along to the analyst supervisor? Or wait for more information?

Mika's questions washed over me one after another, but I only listened with half an ear. Mostly, I was still thinking about General Percy showing up out of the blue. Why had he come to Section headquarters? And why was he suddenly so eager to track down Henrika Hyde?

I didn't need my synesthesia to know something about this whole situation was rotten, and I couldn't help but wonder just how much worse things were going to get.

I pushed General Percy out of my mind and answered Mika's questions. Satisfied, she slipped her headphones back on, cranked up her classical music, and returned to work.

I opened my laptop. An automated email reminded me to complete my after-action report about today's mission as soon as possible. I huffed. The last thing I wanted to do was dissect my failure yet again, but it was better to get it over with, so I filled out the necessary forms and paperwork. I also emailed the armory, and a tech came to my desk and picked up the stained briefcase, along with the Grunglass Necklace, and whisked them away for cleaning and repairs.

The rest of the afternoon dragged on. I checked on the other criminals, terrorists, and assorted rogue paramortals I was tracking, but there were no imminent threats or actionable intelligence to pass along. Even villains took time off for the holidays, and January was often a quiet month, as everyone ramped back up to their normal levels and schedules of mischief, mayhem, and murder.

Every time the door buzzed open, my gaze snapped to the front of the bullpen, hoping it was Desmond, but he didn't appear, and he didn't text me either. Unease simmered in my stomach, but Desmond had his own work to do, as well as dealing with the sudden appearance of his father. Desmond had promised to find me at the diner later, so I'd just have to wait to get answers.

Desmond didn't show up, but someone else from level five did: Joan Samson.

The liaison appeared just before six o'clock, right as I was packing up my things. Mika had already left, along with the other analysts and charmers, so the bullpen was deserted except for me. Joan walked over to my cubicle and scanned the barren wasteland of my desk with a curious gaze.

Before Grandma Jane had gotten sick, my desk had been filled with my favorite things, just like everyone else's. Family photos, several fantasy and sci-fi figurines in their original boxes, even a few vintage comic books in protective cases. But one by one, I'd sold them all to help pay for Grandma Jane's medical care.

I didn't regret my actions, although I missed my treasures from time to time, especially my first-edition *Karma Girl* comic book. That one had been particularly difficult to part with. The art had been so bright and colorful and whimsical and fun, and it had really cheered up my drab cubicle.

Joan gestured at the crystal mockingbird, the lone personal item on my desk. "May I?"

"Sure."

She picked up the mockingbird, admiring the sparkle of the clear crystal and the winking black facets that made up the creature's eyes. "It's beautiful. Vintage crystal. Very old, very rare, and very expensive. And it's in perfect condition."

"Thank you." I gave the polite, automatic response, then frowned. "How do you know it's vintage?"

A small smile played across her lips, and she returned the crystal bird to its perch on my desk. "A little quirk of my transmuter magic. I can often tell how old something is just by touching it, along with the quality of materials used and the level of craftsmanship. It's just a sort of extra sense I have."

Her smile vanished, and her gaze met mine. "Kind of like the extra senses you have with your synesthesia, Charlotte."

I waited, expecting a derogatory comment, but it didn't come. Synths were fairly common, and many paramortals looked down their noses at us, thinking synesthesia was one of the weakest forms of magic. Shortsighted idiots.

Oh, synesthesia might not be an offensive power like Joan's transmuter ability to reduce a marble column to dust with a wave of her hand, but synesthesia had its uses, and my magic often told me everything I needed to know about someone. And right now, my synesthesia was whispering that this was far from a casual visit. Or maybe that was just my own healthy paranoia. Hard to tell, since they were often one and the same.

"What can I do for you, Joan?"

She fiddled with a silver brooch pinned to her suit jacket. Joan noticed me tracking the movement, and she abruptly released the brooch, which was shaped like a tiny sword. White diamonds glittered along the sword's blade, which was pointed down and in, as though it was about to prick her heart.

"What a beautiful brooch," I said. "Is it vintage too?"

"Thank you. And yes, it is vintage." Joan cleared her throat and held out some manila folders. "You left these behind."

I'd been in such a hurry to escape from General Percy's scorn that I'd forgotten to check all my desk drawers. A sloppy, rookie mistake, just like all the others I'd made today.

"Thank you." I took the folders and added them to the piles on my desk.

Joan rolled her shoulders back and down, as though mustering up some courage. "I also wanted to apologize, Charlotte. It's no secret I lobbied hard to be Desmond's liaison when he came to the D.C. station a few months ago, but I never wanted to get the job like this."

I shrugged. "I appreciate the apology, but it's not your fault. From what I know of General Percy, he does whatever he wants whenever he wants to whomever he wants, and damn the consequences."

Joan laughed, but it was a dry, bitter sound. "You have no idea. Some of the things Graham told me . . ." Her voice trailed off, and sorrow pinched her face.

"I'm sorry about Graham," I replied in a serious voice. "Desmond told me how many missions you worked on with Graham. How . . . close the two of you were."

Another laugh rasped out of Joan's mouth, and she fiddled with the diamond sword brooch on her jacket again. "Yeah, *close*. That's one way of putting it." She dropped her hand and gave me a knowing look. "Just like you and Desmond are *close* now."

Desmond and I hadn't kept our relationship a secret, but I wasn't about to discuss it with Joan like a girl giggling over a crush at a slumber party. Apologies were nice, but in the end, they were just words, and I had no idea if I could trust the liaison. Just like with General Percy, there was a lot more to Joan Samson than met the eye.

"Don't worry about Desmond," Joan said, breaking the

awkward silence. "I've worked with him several times. More important, he's a friend. I'll keep an eye on him and make sure he doesn't go rushing into danger." A wry grin curved her lips. "At least not without the proper equipment."

That was all I could ask of any liaison, so I nodded. "I appreciate that."

Joan nodded back, then left the bullpen. I watched her go, unease simmering in my stomach. She hadn't said anything remotely threatening, and I hadn't gotten the smallest whiff of danger from her, but I still felt like she was hiding something.

Just like everyone else at Section 47.

TEN

CHARLOTTE

I slung my tote bag onto my shoulder and grabbed my purse. Then I left the bullpen and rode the elevator up to the lobby.

A few people were still browsing through the shops in the pedestrian mall, but Evelyn wasn't sitting on the dais. Her coffee mug was gone, the monitors were turned off, and her chair was pushed up to her desk. Maestro had left the building.

I wondered what she thought of General Percy taking over her station, but I doubted she would tell me. Evelyn never revealed anything she didn't have to, and she was the kind of person whose secrets had secrets. I also wondered if General Percy would figure out she was Maestro—and what he might do with the information.

But those weren't my problems, at least not anymore. Another wave of sour anger washed over me, and I shoved through the revolving doors and stepped outside. The evening air was bitterly cold, even for mid-January, and the winter wind whistled against my body like a pack of wolves trying to tear through my clothes with their sharp, icy teeth. I shivered, tucked my chin down, and walked faster.

A few minutes later, I reached my building and went up to my apartment, which I'd inherited from Grandma Jane. I eyed the lock, but no scratches marred the metal, and I didn't sense any threats lurking inside with my synesthesia, so I opened the door. I slapped on the lights, punched in the code for the alarm system, and slung my things down on the kitchen island.

At the front of the apartment was a sizable kitchen, along with an even larger living room and a fireplace. The entire space used to be filled with comfortable furniture, cozy blankets, and cute knickknacks, but I'd literally sold everything that wasn't nailed down to help pay Grandma Jane's medical bills. A few months ago, when I'd exposed the Section moles, I'd seen a chance to finally get out from under that crushing debt, so I'd accessed the agents' secret bank accounts and stolen all the bribe money they had accepted from Henrika Hyde.

After paying off my debt, I'd still had a nice chunk of change left, and I'd splurged and replaced some of the items I'd been forced to sell. A couch, a TV, a new yoga mat, a set of dishes to eat on instead of a single, mismatched plate and bowl. But my favorite purchase had been the blue recliner sitting by the windows.

I went over and stroked my fingers over the soft, plush fabric. I'd bought the exact same chair Grandma Jane had had, and rocking in it always made me feel close to her. A crystal mockingbird that matched the figurine on my desk at work was perched on the nearby windowsill.

The apartment would still look like an empty shell to a normal person, but I liked the open, minimalist feel. If nothing else, Grandma Jane's illness had taught me that stuff was just stuff in the end, and I could do without a lot of things I'd once thought essential. A hard lesson in heartache, loss, and humility, but I could see the value of it now, and it had made me stronger.

I dropped my hand from the recliner, went into my bedroom,

stripped off the borrowed Section pantsuit, and hung it on a rack to return to the armory. Then I changed into my uniform for the rest of the day: a short-sleeved powder-blue shirt with an oversize white collar, round white plastic buttons, and a matching knee-length pleated skirt.

Given the blustery weather, I pulled on a thick pair of white tights and slid my feet into white sneakers. I also shrugged into a dark blue fleece coat and shoved my hands into a pair of gloves. Then I returned to the living room, grabbed my purse off the kitchen island, and left the apartment.

Once again, the bitter cold motivated me to walk fast, and a few blocks later, I reached an old metal train car squatting at the back of a parking lot filled with cracked black asphalt and potholes deep enough to swim in. Over the train car's front door, a sign burned like a neon-blue beacon, highlighting the many dents in the battered metal. The words *Moondust Diner* lit up one bright cursive letter at a time, along with a white half-moon and several pulsing stars. In the windows, smaller neon signs shaped like burgers, fries, and milkshakes glowed atomic red, adding more cheery pops of color to the dark evening.

I went up the steps and tugged the front door open, and a small silver bell chimed out my arrival. A few months ago, everything inside the diner had been threadbare, bordering on falling apart, but after some massive remodeling over the holidays, the interior now sparkled with a brand-new air, from the chrome booths with red cushions that lined the windows to the long counter with matching chrome stools, also topped with red cushions. Even the cutesy glass salt and pepper shakers shaped like half-moons and stars glimmered.

I stepped around the end of the dining counter and moved past the cash register, the coffee pots, napkin holders, and tubs of silverware spaced along the back counter. I slid my purse onto a shelf below the counter, then exchanged my coat and gloves for a white apron I tied on over my uniform.

"Hey, boss lady," a deep voice murmured. "It's about time you showed up."

A twenty-something guy grinned at me through the open service window in the wall. A white chef's hat topped his head, hiding most of his thick black hair, although his bronze skin gleamed against his white chef's jacket.

"Hey, Pablo. What's on the menu tonight?"

His grin widened, and his dark brown eyes crinkled with amusement. "Why don't you tell me?"

I drew in a deep breath, tasting the scents in the air. My mouth watered, and my stomach rumbled in anticipation. "Pot roast with carrots and onions, along with some cheesy potato thing."

"Cheesy potato thing?" Pablo clutched a hand to his heart in mock outrage. "That's my potatoes au gratin with not one, not two, but three kinds of cheese."

Like me, Pablo Suarez had been in desperate need of a paycheck, and he'd started working at the Moondust Diner several months ago to put himself through culinary school. Pablo had a real gift for cooking, and the first thing I'd done after I'd bought the joint was give him a hefty raise and make him the head chef.

I'd also made Pablo the face of the diner. The other chefs and waitresses thought Pablo was the owner and that I was just another employee, the same as them. My father's enemies had targeted me more than once over the years, and I hadn't wanted my own work at Section 47 to put anyone at risk, so I'd kept my ownership of the diner as quiet as possible.

A few days after Thanksgiving, Zeeta Kowalski had in-formed the staff she was finally selling the diner and going to live with her daughter Penny in Florida. I'd had to restrain myself to keep from jumping with joy. Zeeta had been a seventy-something piece of work, and she hated me with a passion, criticizing every little thing I did, but I'd given her enough cash to persuade her to sell me the diner. I'd also promised to keep the interior largely the same. Zeeta might have been a battle-ax of a boss, but she had a surprising sentimental streak when it came to the diner, which she had opened with her late husband Mel decades ago.

I liked the old-fashioned look of the diner, so restoring the space to its former glory hadn't been a chore, although I was far less enthused about wearing the same old waitress uniform. But Zeeta got what Zeeta wanted, and after some serious haggling, we'd come to terms.

Along with the remodel, I'd also upgraded all the appliances, with lots of input from Pablo and the other chefs. Word about the diner was spreading, and it was already turning a healthy profit.

I still wasn't sure why I'd bought the diner, especially since I used to *hate* coming here. Having to get a second job had felt like a huge failure, like I hadn't been smart enough to figure out a way to take care of Grandma Jane without falling so deeply into debt. Plus, Zeeta barking out orders every time I walked by hadn't helped matters.

But as soon as I'd heard the diner was for sale, I had to have it. Maybe I had just wanted something of my own, something that wasn't tied to being a Locke or Section 47 or anything else related to the spy world. Maybe I had just wanted to create my *own* legacy, however small it might be, and have a bit of distance and freedom from my father's mistakes. Although given General Percy's disdain, I might be working full-time at the diner soon, especially if I couldn't figure out Henrika Hyde's next move.

"Charlotte?" Pablo asked. "Are you okay?"

Thinking about General Percy and Henrika soured my mood, but it didn't diminish my appetite. "I'm sure the potatoes au gratin will be wonderful. But let's talk about the most important thing: What's for dessert?"

Pablo shook his head, still grinning. "I should have known you would want dessert first. You always do."

He gestured at a glass cake stand on the back counter. "A three-layer chocolate cake with a whipped strawberry filling and drizzled with a dark chocolate ganache."

The cake looked wonderful, and I had to close my mouth to keep a bit of drool from escaping. "You had me at three-layer."

Pablo laughed. We chatted back and forth through the service window while he and the other chefs cooked and dished up food. I took orders and carried the finished plates over to customers, with the other waitresses who were working tonight.

Despite the cold, a steady stream of customers came and went, scarfing down pot roast, along with burgers, fries, patty melts, and other diner classics. Pablo had taken control of the menu, and he had elevated every dish with quality ingredients and unique flavor combinations, like the BLT, which featured thick, crispy strips of brown-sugar-glazed bacon, microgreens tossed in a zesty lemon vinaigrette, fried green tomatoes, and onion jam.

I worked for more than an hour, dealing with the dinner rush, before I was finally able to take a break and eat my own dinner. Pablo's fork-tender pot roast melted in my mouth, while the roasted carrots and onions added sweet and tangy notes to the dish, and the potatoes au gratin were just as cheesy as Pablo had promised. I had just cut myself a hunk of the chocolate-strawberry cake when the front door opened, the bell chimed, and a familiar presence filled the air, like a shadow sliding across the floor.

I smiled, put my piece of cake on a plate, and cut another generous slice. I grabbed both plates, then turned around. "Perfect timing. I was just about to have cake."

A muscled man who was a couple of inches over six feet leaned his elbows down on the counter, although the motion didn't make him look any shorter. His short black hair gleamed under the lights, as did his light brown eyes. He was dressed in black, from his leather jacket to his cashmere sweater to his corduroy pants. People say clothes make the man, but not in this case. This guy exuded the supreme confidence of someone who knew he was a total badass.

Gabriel Chase, a former Section cleaner, grinned, his white teeth flashing against his ebony skin. "You know I'm more of a pie guy myself."

I rolled my eyes. Gabriel and I had known each other since we were kids, and we'd had this debate many times before, especially since I'd started working at the diner. "And *you* know *I* think pie is inferior to cake. Most pies are all crust and not enough filling. If I want to eat crust, I'll eat a piece of bread."

"Hey!" Pablo called out through the service window. "Not *my* pies. They have the perfect ratio of crust and filling!"

"Agreed. Your pies are excellent. That lemon-blueberry pie last week?" I blew him a chef's kiss. "Scrumptious perfection."

Pablo grinned, his ego placated, but I'd only spoken the truth. His pies were excellent, but excellent pies were few and far between in my experience.

I held out one of the plates to Gabriel. "A cake is all soft, fluffy goodness, often filled and covered with even more melty, fruity, chocolaty goodness. That makes cake *infinitely* superior to pie."

Gabriel rolled his eyes right back at me. "Has anyone ever mentioned you take food *way* too seriously, Char?"

"You have. Multiple times. It's one of your many character flaws." I pulled the plate away from him. "But if you don't want any cake . . ."

Gabriel straightened up and snatched the plate from me with quick, effortless grace. "I didn't say that."

He took his plate, along with mine, to our usual booth in the back corner. I poured Gabriel a cup of coffee, grabbed a glass of water for myself, and joined him.

I glanced up at a neon sign shaped like a freestanding carton of fries hanging in the window beside the booth. The sign was glowing a bright, steady red, except for three small dark red tubes tucked in with the other fries that looked as though their lights had burned out. They weren't really lights at all but rather the vials of Redburn that Desmond had found during the Tannenbaum mission.

I'd thought hiding the vials in plain sight was the safest, smartest thing to do. Even Desmond didn't know exactly where they were in the diner. Just as I didn't know exactly where he'd hidden the other vials of Redburn in his safe-house apartment.

Gabriel didn't even glance at the vials nestled in the sign. Instead, he sliced a fork through his dessert and shoved the big bite into his mouth. "Mmm-mmm-mmm! Maybe your crazy cake theory is right. At least when it comes to *this* cake."

I dug my fork into my own piece. It was *amazing*. The chocolate cake was light and moist, while the strawberry filling offered a perfect pop of tart, sweet creaminess, and the dark chocolate ganache added a layer of rich, gooey decadence. Mmm-mmm-mmm, indeed!

Gabriel and I didn't speak for a few minutes, both of us too busy enjoying our cake. I slid the last bite into my mouth, then sighed with happiness. My sugar rush was on, and I was going to enjoy every second of it.

Gabriel picked up his coffee cup and toasted Pablo, who was still standing in the service window. Pablo tipped his chef's hat, then disappeared into the kitchen.

"So," Gabriel said. "Why did you text and ask me to swing by?"

"What can you tell me about Bryce Finkley?"

Gabriel eyed me over the rim of his cup. "Why are you asking about Finkley?"

"I ran into him today, and I didn't particularly enjoy the experience."

I filled Gabriel in on the botched Vault mission and how Finkley had accessed the Section 47 servers and made off with potential valuable—and damaging—info.

Gabriel let out a low whistle. "Strolling into a Section facility, even one that's just used for storage, is pretty bold, even for someone like Finkley."

"Someone like Finkley?"

Gabriel nodded. "Yeah, Bryce used to be a cleaner, the same as me. We went on a few missions together. He's a smart, tough guy who has the big three enduro traits: strength, speed, and stamina. Bryce was also willing to do whatever it took to eliminate our targets, no matter the potential paramortal powers exposure or collateral damage to innocent people."

"Do you know why he left Section? Supposedly, he was accused of stealing drugs, weapons, and money from raids."

Gabriel shrugged. "No clue, but the Section higher-ups will definitely axe you for stealing. Happened about five years ago. I heard all the usual rumors but nothing concrete. It was the same bullshit people said about me, so I didn't put any stock in it."

His mouth flattened out, and his fingers curled around the coffee cup like he wanted to crush it with his bare hands. *Danger-danger-danger*, my synesthesia warned, but I ignored the whispers. I didn't have many friends, but Gabriel was one of them, and he would never hurt me.

A few years ago, Gabriel had gotten embroiled in a scandal involving the daughter of a Section general. Officially, he'd been booted out of the spy organization, but I knew that Gabriel had used some sort of blackmail to force his way out, although he'd never told me exactly what had happened to sour him on being a cleaner.

After that, Gabriel had founded Chase Industries, his own private contracting firm, and he had built a reputation for being professional, effective, and invisible. Protection details, kidnapping rescues, witness protection. Gabriel and his crew did all that and more, and he'd made a fortune using his Section skills in the private sector.

An image of General Percy dressing me down filled my mind. Today was definitely one of those days when I envied Gabriel's ability to be his own boss and choose the missions he wanted, instead of being yanked around like a dog on a leash the way I so often was.

"What does Bryce Finkley have to do with that sour look on your face?" Gabriel asked.

"It's not Finkley so much as who showed up after the mission. Jethro Percy."

Gabriel's eyebrows shot up his forehead, and he let out another low whistle. "The big boss was at headquarters?"

"Yeah, and he was none too pleased with me."

I recapped Percy booting me off the Hyde mission, along with my demotion to level three with the other analysts.

Gabriel winced. "That sucks. I'm sorry, Char."

"It is what it is. You know how much my father hated General Percy. Well, the feeling is definitely mutual."

"That's the legacy of Section 47," Gabriel said in a sardonic tone. "Grudges galore."

I snorted. "More like a legacy of lies."

We both fell silent, thinking about all the ways Section 47 had used us—and abused us—over the years.

I looked at Gabriel again. "Speaking of lies, are you finally ready to tell me what you were really doing at Tannenbaum Castle?"

He jerked back in his seat, and his startled gaze snapped up to mine. Gabriel opened his mouth, but I held up my right index finger in warning, then pointed at my ear.

"Lest you forget, I *always* know when you're telling the truth—or lying to my face."

"You and that damn synesthesia," Gabriel muttered. "Sometimes I wish I had your magic instead of my own phasing power."

Gabriel had the ability to move his body through any solid object, from the metal side of the diner car to a marble wall to a steel vault. One second, his body was whole. The next, it was like a shadow sinking into whatever surface it touched.

Even among paramortals, phasing was an unusual power, which Gabriel put to good use. He'd told me more than one story of how he'd rescued a kidnapping victim simply by walking through whatever obstacles stood between him and the person he'd been hired to save.

"Nah," I replied. "Being able to walk through walls is way cooler than hearing lies and seeing shades of danger."

Gabriel grinned. "You're right. Walking through walls is *way* cooler."

I crossed my arms over my chest and looked at Gabriel, who stared right back at me. Several seconds ticked by, and the only sounds were the scraping of knives on plates and the gurgling of the coffee pots.

Gabriel's smile twisted into a scowl. "Has anyone ever mentioned you have an excellent death stare?" he groused. "Like you are calmly plotting the most vicious and painful way to murder me with my own fork. It's disturbing."

"It's not a death stare. It's an *I've-had-a-really-shitty-day* stare. So do us both a favor and come clean about Germany. You've been hemming and hawing and trying to bring it up for weeks anyway."

Gabriel sighed. "How did you figure it out?"

"For starters, I wondered why you told Desmond that Elsa Eisen invited you to her castle, but you never told me that."

He scowled again. "Because you would have heard it was a lie. Damn synesthesia."

I shot my thumb and forefinger at him. "*Exactly.* Why

wouldn't you fill me in like you did Desmond? That was one of the things that made me suspicious."

Gabriel arched an eyebrow. "*One* of the things? What were the others?"

"You didn't text me that you were coming to the Christmas Eve party, you showed up at the very last minute, and you weren't on the official guest list." I ticked off the points on my fingers. "Plus, as far as I knew, you had never had any dealings with Elsa Eisen, so why would she invite you to such an important shindig? If Elsa had really been interested in hiring your company for protection, she would have done it *before* the party, not during."

I crossed my arms over my chest again. "Everything indicated you came to the party of your own accord. Now, are you going to tell me why? Or do I have to start digging into you like you're the latest criminal I'm tracking?"

Gabriel gave me a rueful grin. "How long would it take you to figure out my route to Germany?"

"Maybe a day or two. Depending on how discreet and careful you were with your travel arrangements, rental cars, and hotels. Everything leaves some sort of paper or electronic trail, especially a spur-of-the-moment holiday trip to a remote German castle."

He shook his head. "Have I ever mentioned you think *way* too much, Char?"

"Frequently. Now, quit stalling and answer my questions."

Gabriel stared down at the tabletop for a moment, then looked up at me again. "First of all, I want you to know that I didn't mean to or want to lie to you. Things just happened so fast."

Truth, my inner voice whispered.

"But you're right. Elsa Eisen didn't invite me to her Christmas Eve party." He drew in a breath, then let it out. "Nemesis did."

Shock jolted through me. "Who the fuck is Nemesis?"

I'd thought Gabriel had come to the castle to watch my back, which would have been thoughtful, if annoying. I hadn't realized another player was involved.

Gabriel told me he had been in Frankfurt, Germany, wrapping up an assignment, when he'd gotten an anonymous call from a woman calling herself Nemesis who said that Desmond and I were going undercover at Tannenbaum Castle and that we might need Gabriel's help.

"I thought I could find my mystery woman on my own, but no luck so far," he finished. "I've had my best folks trying to trace her texts and calls, but they've come up empty. Nemesis knows what she's doing."

"And you're sure the voice on the other end of the line wasn't Henrika Hyde?" I asked.

Gabriel shook his head. "I had the same thought after Katarina Tanetsa and her mercenaries tried to rob the guests—that Henrika was playing some sick game with me, you, and Desmond. But I've listened to a dozen voice clips of Henrika online. She's definitely *not* Nemesis. Besides, why would Henrika send me to help you and Desmond stop the mercenaries she'd hired to steal the Nutcracker Ruby? It doesn't make any sense."

No, it didn't, especially since Katarina had claimed that Henrika put a bounty on my head. Henrika had wanted me to die in Germany, so she hadn't sent Gabriel to come to Desmond's and my rescue.

I tapped my fingers on the tabletop, my mind spinning in a dozen different directions. Gabriel's tech gurus were top-notch, and if they hadn't been able to find the mystery woman, then I had my work cut out. But maybe texts and calls weren't the only clues she had left behind.

My fingers stilled. "Why Nemesis?"

"What do you mean?" Gabriel asked.

"Why choose that as her alias?"

"Who knows? Because she didn't want to call herself the Sugar Plum Fairy?"

I huffed at his sarcasm. "We both know how important code names are, especially to spies. Nemesis has *some* special meaning to this woman. If we figure out what that meaning is, then we'll be one step closer to tracking her down."

Gabriel shrugged. "She did say she wanted revenge, although she didn't say against whom."

"Well, it probably wasn't me, you, or Desmond, since she sent you to help us. And I doubt she wanted revenge against Elsa Eisen either, since helping Desmond and me also helped Elsa." I frowned, another thought occurring to me. "How did she even know Desmond and I were going to Tannenbaum Castle? Gia and Evelyn were the only people in Section 47 who knew that."

Gabriel groaned and massaged his temples. "You're giving me a headache. Is this what analysts do all day? Look for hidden motives in every single word, thought, deed, and action?"

"Absolutely," I murmured in an absent voice.

I plucked the pen and the notepad out of my apron pocket and started jotting down ideas about how I could discover Nemesis's identity. "I want everything you have on her. All the texts, the party invitation, and everything your techs have done to try to find her."

Gabriel snorted. "You're *enjoying* this. Then again, you always did love puzzles, even when we were kids. Remember all those logic games our dads would give us? You would solve yours in about three minutes, and it would take me three hours."

Gabriel's father, Leon Chase, had also been a cleaner for Section 47. Leon had been friends with my father, and they had often gotten together on the weekends to do extra training—and dragged a reluctant Gabriel and an even more reluctant me along for the ride.

"True. But when our dads would make us go outside for

survivalist training, you would find food and water in less than an hour, and I would tromp through the woods all day before you would take pity on me."

Gabriel grinned. "I always put extra chocolate bars in my backpack just for you, Char." His grin faded away. "I just hope you can forgive me for not telling you the truth sooner."

Part of me was annoyed he hadn't told me everything back at the castle, but Gabriel hadn't withheld the full truth with malicious intent. And if Nemesis hadn't told him about the Tannenbaum mission, then the outcome might have been very, very different. Gabriel had helped Desmond kill the mercenaries who were holding a ballroom full of innocent people hostage. Those folks owed their lives to Gabriel, as did Desmond and I.

"Of course I forgive you." I paused. "Just don't make a habit out of lying to me."

Gabriel drew an *X* over his heart with his index finger. "Never will I ever."

Satisfied, I nodded and looked over my scribbled notes, adding a few more ideas and avenues of attack. One way or another, I was going to find Nemesis—and ask exactly why she had dragged my friend into a dangerous Section mission.

Gabriel scrolled through his messages while I kept brainstorming. By this point, it was after nine o'clock, and the diner had largely emptied out.

The door opened, the bell chimed, and another familiar presence filled the air, like the electrical charge before a thunderstorm. Soft footsteps sounded, and a hand skimmed along the right sleeve of my waitress uniform. Desmond stopped beside the booth. He was still wearing the janitor's uniform from this morning's mission, under a thick blue coat.

"Sorry I'm late," he said.

A hundred questions burned on my tongue, but I swallowed them. "No worries."

I scooted over, and Desmond slid into the booth beside me. I held my breath, wondering if he might notice the three vials of Redburn hidden in the red French fries sign, but, just like Gabriel, Desmond didn't even glance at the window. Seemed my hiding place was a good one.

Desmond nodded at Gabriel. "Gaby."

"Hello, Slick," Gabriel replied.

"Aw, your budding bromance is so cute," I drawled. "The two of you are already at the nicknames stage."

The two men gave me sour glares, but I just grinned in return. When they had first met at the diner a few months ago, Desmond and Gabriel had immediately disliked each other. That tended to happen when you put two alpha cleaners together. But the two of them had worked together and saved each other's life during the Tannenbaum mission, and each cleaner now had a grudging, mutual respect for the other, although neither one of them would ever admit it.

Pablo came over and set a glass filled with bright yellow-orange liquid in front of Desmond, then poured more coffee for Gabriel and handed me a plate with another piece of cake.

"Remind me to give you a raise," I murmured.

Pablo winked at me. "Sure thing, boss lady."

Desmond and Gabriel knew I owned the diner now, so they didn't bat an eye at the chef's words.

Pablo gave an elegant flourish with his hand. "And for your gentleman friend, a mango-lime smoothie with a dash of turmeric and a hint of cumin."

Desmond stuck a straw into the liquid and took a sip. "Mmm! You'll have to give me the recipe. It's delicious."

Pablo grinned. A few months ago, he'd learned Desmond

loved smoothies, and he had been trying new recipes out on the cleaner ever since. He'd even added some of the recipes to the menu, including a strawberry-vanilla concoction that tasted like a decadent cheesecake.

One of the chefs signaled Pablo, and he left me with Desmond and Gabriel.

I downed a few more bites of cake, but even the delectable treat couldn't drown out my questions, so I pushed my plate away. "How was your meeting with your father?"

A disgusted look filled Desmond's face. "Lots of blustering by the General, along with several threats, demands, and angry accusations."

Desmond shrugged, as though his strained relationship with his father didn't bother him, but I could see how much it did.

"Par for the course for the two of us. We've never really gotten along, and today went exactly as I expected." He scrubbed a hand through his hair, rumpling the dark blond locks. "After our meeting, I went back to the bullpen. Joan, Diego, and I worked the rest of the afternoon, trying to track down Bryce, along with Henrika."

I started to ask if they had any leads, but I held my tongue. I didn't want to put Desmond in an even more awkward position than he already was in. Besides, my selfish pride wanted me to find Henrika on my own and prove to General Percy that I was as good an analyst as I claimed.

Desmond gestured at my notepad. "What are you doing?"

"Trying to track down a new nemesis."

"A *new* nemesis? Did I miss something?"

"Don't you always, Slick?" Gabriel drawled.

Desmond glowered at the other man, but Gabriel gave him a sunny smile in return.

"I don't miss things any more than you do, Gaby," Desmond drawled right back. "But we all know Charlotte is by far the smartest person at this table."

"At last, something we can agree on," Gabriel replied.

I rolled my eyes. "Come on, fellas. Let's focus on the task at hand."

"Which is?" Desmond asked.

I gestured at my notepad. "Tracking down Nemesis."

I gave Gabriel a pointed look. He grumbled, but he told Desmond about being contacted by Nemesis.

Desmond leaned back and crossed his arms over his chest, his right index finger tapping out a quick rhythm on his left elbow. "And you have no idea who this person was? You just *assumed* she was telling the truth and came to Tannenbaum Castle on a whim?"

"I wanted to make sure Charlotte was okay. Besides, a holiday party at a swanky castle sounded like fun." Gabriel popped up the collar of his jacket. "Plus, we all know how good I look in a tuxedo."

I snorted. "Only you would think battling a castle full of mercenaries was the epitome of a good time."

Gabriel grinned again. "I'm special that way."

I snorted again, then looked at Desmond. "Does the name Nemesis mean anything to you?"

He shook his head. "No. I don't remember any missions with that name. No targets or informants either."

My heart sank with disappointment. I'd known it wouldn't be that easy, but I'd still hoped Desmond might have some sort of clue and an inkling of whether Nemesis was a true friend or another enemy waiting in the wings.

Gabriel polished off his coffee, then got to his feet, pulled out his wallet, and laid a hundred-dollar bill on the table.

"You don't have to do that—"

He waved off my protest. "I'm happy to pay for my cake and eat it too. Give it to Pablo as a tip. I'll keep digging into Nemesis and Bryce Finkley."

Gabriel winked at me, tipped his head to Desmond, and left

the diner. A black SUV cruised into the parking lot, avoiding the many potholes. Gabriel opened a door and slid into the back of the vehicle, which whisked him away.

"He really is cool as a cucumber, isn't he?" Desmond murmured.

"Is that a note of admiration I hear?"

He gave me the same grumpy look Gabriel had earlier. "As much as it pains me to admit it, the man knows how to make an exit. And an entrance too. You should have seen him strut into the ballroom during the holiday party. He walked into Tannenbaum Castle like he owned it."

I laughed. "Yeah, that sounds exactly like Gabriel."

Desmond chuckled too, but his amusement quickly vanished. "I'm sorry I didn't text you this afternoon. There was a lot going on. Can I walk you home?"

My stomach clenched at his serious tone. "Sure. Just let me make sure Pablo has everything he needs."

Desmond slid out of the booth so that I could get up, then sat back down. He took another sip of his mango-lime smoothie, then pushed it away. Normally, Desmond gulped down Pablo's smoothies, but his lack of appetite spoke volumes about how his day had been—just as tough and shitty as mine.

I left Desmond sitting in the booth and headed toward the kitchen. No one was threatening me, and my synesthesia was still and silent, but for some reason, I felt like this was just the beginning of our troubles.

ELEVEN

DESMOND

Charlotte helped Pablo while I finished my smoothie. It truly was delicious, but I had too much weighing on my mind to properly enjoy it. Pablo promised to close the diner for Charlotte, so she grabbed her coat and her purse, and the two of us left.

We walked for about two blocks before Charlotte broke the silence. "How was your meeting with your father?"

"You already asked me that."

"How was the meeting with your father *really*?"

I huffed. "I suppose I have to tell you the truth, no matter how ugly it is. You'll know if I don't."

She slipped her hand into mine. "I want you to tell me the truth because you *want* to. Not because I can magically hear it with my synesthesia. But if you don't want to talk about it, I understand. I have plenty of issues with my own father."

"Yes, we are certainly a matched pair in that regard," I murmured.

In some ways, Charlotte and I had the exact same problem with our fathers in that the two of us had never factored much into their decisions. Jack Locke had been devoted to Section 47, while Jethro Percy was devoted to himself.

I shook my head. "I *do* want to talk about it with you."

"But?" Charlotte asked.

I sighed. "But talking about it won't change anything. The General will *never* change. I've had thirty-six years to come to terms with that fact, and yet I keep hoping that someday things will be different between us—that *he'll* be different."

"I felt the same way about my father," Charlotte confessed in a low voice. "I always hoped when Jack returned from his latest Section mission that he would finally decide he'd had enough blood, death, and danger. That he would cut back, stay home, and spend more time with Grandma Jane and me instead of immediately taking another assignment. But he never did."

She rasped out the last few words, and the blue aura around her heart flickered and dimmed with hurt and sorrow.

I squeezed her fingers. "Perhaps the saddest thing is that my father *used* to be different. Well, not *different*, but a slightly *better* version of himself. At least until my mother died."

Charlotte eyed me. "You don't talk about your mother very much. I don't think you ever even told me how she died."

I drew in a breath, then let it out. "Iylena died of a rare form of blood cancer that only strikes paramortals. I haven't mentioned it because I didn't want to dredge up bad memories of your grandmother's illness."

This time, Charlotte squeezed my fingers. "You can talk about anything you want to, Desmond. I'm always here for you."

Her aura burned bright and steady, and I tightened my grip on her fingers.

"That means more to me than you know. As for my mother, well, Iylena was the glue that held our family together. She was one of the few things my father and I had in common, and she kept the peace between us." I paused, trying not to drown in all the good, bad, and painful memories of the past. "Although I have to give my father credit. When my mother got sick, he cut back on his Section duties and spent as much time with her as possible. The General attacked her illness like he did everything else. New therapies, experimental medicines, clinical trials. He got her all that and more, but in the end, it just wasn't enough."

I had to stop and clear a hard knot of emotion out of my throat. "He really did love her."

Charlotte didn't say anything, but we kept holding hands, and we walked for the better part of a block in silence. I drew in one breath after another, just absorbing the calm, soothing blue of her aura.

"But enough about my mother. You asked about my meeting with my father. It was a bit more . . . unpleasant than usual."

I told Charlotte all about my talk with the General, including his threat to fire her.

Charlotte's face remained calm, but her aura sizzled with anger, the emotion hot enough to warm my cheeks, despite the chilly night air. An answering amount of anger filled me. Why did my father have to be such an egotistical jackass? Why couldn't he simply admit Charlotte was an excellent analyst and that we never would have gotten this far without her expertise?

"I wanted to tell him to fuck off, but I didn't," I confessed in a low voice. "I didn't want him to make things even more difficult for you. It's bad enough he banished you to the third level."

"It's okay. I got the impression during the debriefing that arguing with General Jethro Percy is a losing proposition."

I laughed, but it was a hollow, bitter sound. "You have no idea." I rubbed my pounding head. "And if the day wasn't miserable enough, Joan, Diego, and I reviewed all the security footage from the Vault building and the surrounding area, but we didn't find anything new on Bryce or Henrika."

Charlotte's eyebrows lifted. "I thought you weren't supposed to tell me anything about Henrika."

"I don't care what the General says. You're the best chance we have of tracking down Henrika. You'll find her, Charlotte. I know you will."

A pleased blush pinkened her cheeks. Every word I'd said was true, and I believed in Charlotte more than I believed in anyone else.

"What about Iris Berriston?" Charlotte asked. "What is she saying?"

"Nothing useful. She was contacted through anonymous channels and told to get you alone and steal the Grunglass Necklace. Iris thought the other thieves were there to back her up. She claims she didn't know they were going to break into one of the Vault storage lockers, much less hack into the Section servers."

Charlotte's eyes narrowed in thought. "Did the three thieves who broke into the locker say what they were after?"

"The thieves claimed they were told to steal any weapons related to the Tannenbaum mission. Guns, explosives, and the like. They didn't mention Redburn by name." I paused. "They were also told to plant a bomb in the locker to destroy any weapons they couldn't take with them."

Charlotte tensed, her fingers gripping mine a little more tightly. "Did the thieves have any vials of Redburn with them?"

"No. Although Arnold, the fake businessman, had a brick of C4 hidden in the lining of his briefcase. The plan was to leave the bomb in the locker, shut the door, and detonate it."

"So Bryce didn't tell the thieves what they were really after, and he wanted to make sure all the Tannenbaum evidence—especially any vials of Redburn—was destroyed," Charlotte said.

I nodded. "That's my conclusion too."

Charlotte's eyes narrowed a little more, and I could see

those mental gymnastics going on in the depths of her gaze. "What's so special about Redburn that Henrika was willing to risk sending thieves into a Section facility to neutralize any samples of it?"

"I don't know."

"What about your friend?" Charlotte asked. "The paramortal scientist studying Redburn?"

I'd taken seven vials of Redburn from Tannenbaum Castle. I'd given three to Charlotte for safekeeping, which were currently stashed somewhere inside the Moondust Diner. Three other vials were stored at my safe-house apartment, which was located above an art gallery close to Section headquarters.

Last week, I'd sent part of the seventh vial to a scientist friend so she could analyze the formula, although I hadn't told her what it was. Letting someone else examine even a small sample of a Redburn was a risk, but we needed to know more about it.

"My friend identified a few chemicals commonly found in other explosives, but there was one main component she couldn't identify. Based on her analysis, the mystery component is what makes the formula so much more powerful than other explosives."

More frustration pounded through me. I'd hoped by finding out what was in the formula, we could either neutralize it or at least come up with a way to defend ourselves against it.

"Tell me about Bryce Finkley," Charlotte said.

I grimaced at the change in subject.

"I saw how you reacted in the lobby at the Vault building. You *know* him. And you were very familiar with his tactics during the debriefing."

"What did Gabriel tell you? He knows Bryce too, although not as well as me." I muttered the last few words.

Charlotte shrugged. "Just that Bryce was a Section cleaner who would do whatever it took to get the job done and wasn't concerned about pesky things like collateral damage or exposing paramortal powers."

I nodded. "That's about right. Bryce came up through the ranks with me, Graham, and Trevor Donnelly, although I didn't work with him as much as I did with Graham and Trevor."

"What happened?" Charlotte asked.

I raked a hand through my hair, trying to slough off the memories flickering through my mind. "Bryce and I were on a mission in Malta. We'd been assigned to eliminate a guy named Ellis, a paramortal terrorist who bombed an art museum and swiped a fortune in jewels to further fund his activities. We tracked Ellis to a rented villa and infiltrated it. We must have tripped an alarm, because Ellis figured out we were there and took a hostage, a private chef he'd hired to cook his meals. He was using the woman as a human shield when Bryce and I cornered him in the kitchen. I was standing down, trying to reason with Ellis, but Bryce didn't follow my lead."

"What happened?" Charlotte asked.

"Bryce fired a shot with no warning. He put a bullet through the hostage's neck to get her out of the way. The hostage dropped, and then Bryce dropped Ellis with another shot."

Charlotte blanched. "And the hostage?"

It took me a moment to unclench my jaw. "She died too."

Charlotte blanched again, disgust and anger crinkling her face. "Bryce killed an innocent woman?"

My head jerked in a short, sharp nod. "Yes. Like it was *nothing*."

Even now, all these years later, I could still hear the sharp *crack* of Bryce's shot and the woman's muffled scream of pain, along with the heavy *thump* of her body hitting the floor. I could still smell the coppery tang of her blood and feel the hot, sticky liquid gushing over my hands as I tried and failed to keep her from bleeding out . . .

I blinked, forcing myself to focus on Charlotte. "Bryce said it was no big loss. That the woman was taking Ellis's money, so that made her just as dirty as he was. I lost it. I threw myself at Bryce and started punching him. He tried to fight back, but even with his enduro magic, I was still faster, stronger, and angrier. I got Bryce down on the floor. Broke his nose, broke his jaw, split his lips."

Charlotte eyed me. "You gave Bryce the scar through his left eyebrow and on his cheek."

I gave a short, sharp nod. "Yes. I was still punching him when the Section support team arrived. I would have killed Bryce if the other agents hadn't dragged me off him."

Once again, the coppery scent of blood flooded my nose, and the *thwack-thwack-thwacks* of my fists slamming into Bryce's face banged in my ears like a drum, punctuated by his pain-filled groans. That long-ago rage bubbled up and sizzled through my veins like an acidic poison corrupting every part of me it touched.

Charlotte stepped closer and threaded her arm through mine. Once again, I drew in one breath after another, just drinking in the blue of her. Slowly, my rage faded away, although the ugly memories remained, like pictures stuck on the wall of my mind.

"Bryce filed a complaint against me, but the General pulled some strings and had it dismissed. After that, Bryce and I went on a few more missions together, but he hated me, and I hated him. On our last mission, some weapons and cash went missing."

"Do you think Bryce stole them?"

"I don't know. No one could ever prove anything, but Bryce was forced to resign from Section a few weeks later."

Another bitter laugh burst from my lips. "First Bryce Finkley and then Trevor Donnelly. Two cleaners I worked with for years. Bryce killed an innocent hostage, and Trevor set me up to be murdered multiple times. I'm really shitty at picking friends, aren't I?"

Charlotte shook her head. "Bryce shooting the hostage wasn't your fault. *He* made that choice, not you, Desmond."

"I know that, but I still feel responsible. Just like I do for Graham's death." I let out a tense breath. "And *I* made the choice to attack Bryce. I also broke Section's rules of engagement, and that's entirely on me."

We both fell silent, and we reached Charlotte's apartment building a few minutes later. She stopped under a streetlight, the glow bringing out the warm highlights in her auburn hair.

I cupped her cheeks in my hands and stroked my thumbs over her smooth, silky skin. "I'm sorry you had such a terrible day. And I'm especially sorry my father is such an overbearing jackass."

She covered my hands with her own. "Right back at you, Dundee. Although sadly, I think overbearing jackasses are the norm in the spy world."

I smiled a little at her joke, then leaned down and kissed her. Charlotte's lips were chilled from our walk, as were mine, but the heat of her body washed over my own, and I sank into her welcoming warmth.

Right now, for this moment, there was no Section 47, no overbearing father, no mysterious new nemesis. Just Charlotte and me and the way we felt about each other.

I tilted my head and pulled her closer, and her tongue darted out to stroke against mine. Charlotte tasted like the cake she'd eaten, rich chocolate and bright strawberry. I relished the heady mix of flavors, along with her scent, which always reminded me of sugar and limes swirled together. On Charlotte, it was the perfect sweet-tart perfume.

Then again, just about everything about Charlotte was perfect, from the way her body molded against mine to her soft gasps to the bright crackle of her aura, which was sparking with the same desire zinging through my own body.

A minute later, we broke apart, both of us breathing hard.

"You should come inside," she whispered, digging her fingers into my coat. "We haven't properly broken in some of my new furniture yet."

Temptation surged through me, and I smoothed a lock of hair back over her shoulder. "I want to, more than you know. But right now, it's better if I keep my distance. The General will have his own spies watching everything we do inside Section. Maybe outside too. He'll be looking for an excuse to get rid of you, and I'm not going to give it to him. I know how important being an analyst is to you, and I would never do anything to jeopardize that."

Charlotte drew back, a stubborn look filling her face. "Don't worry about me. Your father might have demoted me to level three, but I'll keep poking around. Between the two of us, we're bound to find Henrika sooner or later."

"Well, let's hope for all our sakes it's sooner. And that my father will leave on another mission the minute Henrika is captured."

Charlotte's stubbornness melted into sympathy, and the same emotion pulsed off her aura, once again acting like a soothing balm to my own soul. Charlotte had issues with her father too, and we both had hidden wounds and deep, aching scars from our work for the spy agency. Such things were just part of the Section legacies we carried with us, for better or worse.

I kissed Charlotte again, then forced myself to step back. "I'll see you tomorrow at headquarters. Good night, Numbers."

"Good night, Dundee."

I gave Charlotte a small, tight smile, then turned up the collar of my coat to ward off the cold, spun around, and walked away. I didn't look back, but I wondered at all the pieces of my heart I was leaving behind—far more than I realized Charlotte had accumulated in our time together.

TWELVE

CHARLOTTE

I didn't get much sleep that night.

Thoughts rattled around in my mind. The Vault mission failure. General Percy's appearance. My demotion. Our lack of progress in identifying the dangerous mystery component in the Redburn formula. Bryce Finkley's cruelty. Desmond's pain over the hostage's death.

I tossed and turned for hours before I finally drifted off, and I woke early the next morning feeling tired and cranky. Even spending some time on my yoga mat breathing, stretching, and flowing through cat, cow, tree, gate, and other poses didn't soothe me.

I took a hot shower, then donned a sweater, cargo pants, and sneakers, all in varying shades of blue. I shrugged into my winter gear, grabbed my purse and tote bag, and left my apartment.

This morning was even colder than last night, and a few flakes of snow drifted down from the gunmetal-gray sky and stung my cheeks. Normally, I loved snow, but today it only made me harrumph in annoyance.

A few minutes later, I reached Section headquarters and veered into the cafeteria. I emerged with two cups, one of which I placed on the counter above Evelyn's desk.

Evelyn scooped up the cup, removed the lid, and drew in a deep, appreciative breath. "Ahhh. Peppermint hot chocolate. Thank you, Charlotte."

I toasted her with my own cup, and we both sipped our drinks, which were the perfect mix of rich, dark chocolate and sharp, sweet peppermint.

Evelyn peered at me through her glasses. "What's the bribe for?"

I clutched a hand to my chest in mock outrage. "*Me?* Try to bribe *you*? *Never.*"

Evelyn's eyebrows rose in a chiding look.

"Okay, fine. I was wondering if you'd heard what Bryce Finkley accessed in the Section servers."

She shook her head. "Nothing yet. Diego and some other techs worked on it most of the night, so we should have an answer soon."

"And General Percy? Why do you think he really came to the D.C. station?"

Evelyn's lips puckered in thought. "I'm not sure, but that is one of many things I intend to discover."

I waited, but she didn't say anything else. Evelyn and I might be friends, but she was still my boss, and she would keep information to herself until she thought I needed to know it.

"And before you ask, Percy hasn't sussed out my real identity as Maestro yet."

I grinned and drew an *X* over my heart. "I'll never tell."

Evelyn grinned. "I know you won't. Now, get to work, Charlotte. That's an order."

I saluted her with my hot chocolate. "Yes, ma'am."

I waved my keycard over the reader, pushed through the

metal turnstile, and stepped into an elevator. I rode down to the third level and headed into the bullpen.

It wasn't even eight o'clock, so no analysts and charmers were in their cubicles yet. I went to my own cubicle in the very back, sat down, plugged in my laptop, and got to work.

I did my usual checks on my assigned rogue paramortals, reviewing their online posts, travel histories, bank records, and more, seeing if anything important had changed overnight. But there was no unusual activity, so I turned my attention to Henrika, reached out with my synesthesia, and studied every scrap of recent information relating to her, along with Bryce Finkley.

Despite being on the run from Section 47, Henrika maintained an active online presence, although her posts and photos were all carefully worded and cropped to show harmless things, like a meal she was eating or the outfit she was wearing, instead of giving any specific, tangible hints to her current location.

Bryce Finkley had zero online presence, other than a bare-bones website for his contracting firm, which was owned by a string of shell companies that ultimately led nowhere. I also couldn't find any credit cards, utilities, properties, or bank accounts in his name. The former Section cleaner was a ghost, and he wouldn't be found until he wanted to be found.

Thirty minutes later, I rocked back in my chair, frustrated by my lack of progress. I released my grip on my synesthesia and massaged my throbbing temples. Using and focusing my magic for such an extended amount of time almost always gave me a headache. Right now, I felt like someone was jangling a tambourine in my skull, and the words *failure-failure-failure* jingled through my brain in a steady, depressing chorus.

I plucked the crystal mockingbird off my desk and turned it around and around, watching the facets sparkle and gleam. An idea occurred to me, and I set the figurine down, exited the Section system, and pulled up a fresh login screen. Instead of my name, I typed in the word *Mockingbird*, along with the appropriate password.

Every time I logged in to the Section system, a record was made of everything I accessed, but Mockingbird was Grandma Jane's back door to access highly classified files. Mockingbird was how she had kept track of the negotiations about my father's ransom after General Percy and the other Section higher-ups had frozen her out of the briefings about the Mexico mission.

A few months ago, I'd used Mockingbird to dig up info on Desmond when he'd come to D.C., since I didn't know who he was or what he wanted. The program had also helped me track down—and empty—Miriam Lancaster's and Trevor Donnelly's secret bank accounts.

My finger hovered over the *Enter* key. Then I let out an annoyed huff, deleted the Mockingbird password and login, and accessed the system under my usual *CLocke* credentials.

Grandma Jane had told me to use the Mockingbird program only in emergencies, and getting booted off the hunt for Henrika Hyde wasn't an emergency so much as it was a blow to my pride. Besides, Gia and Evelyn had given me access to every file on Henrika, so the Mockingbird login wouldn't tell me anything new. And I didn't want the program to become a crutch I always relied on, instead of doing the work myself. My pride as an analyst wouldn't allow that either, so I returned to my regular methods of sleuthing.

I worked for another thirty minutes, but I still came up with nothing. I took a break to stand up and stretch and check my phone, but I didn't have any messages from either Desmond or Gabriel. They were probably hitting the same dead ends I was.

The steady *squeak-squeak-squeak* of wheels sounded, and a mailroom clerk pulled an envelope out of his cart and set it on my desk. I murmured my thanks, and he nodded and pushed his cart onward.

Like many agents, I got my mail delivered to Section

headquarters. Intercepting mail was an excellent way to gather all sorts of intelligence, from how many credit cards someone used to how many sports channels they watched to how many treats they ordered for their pets. Spoiler alert: some criminals spent more on dog treats and cat toys than I made in a month.

Plus, the fewer people who knew my home address, the safer I was. I had no desire for someone to break into my apartment and rifle through my things—or worse, try to murder me in my own kitchen.

I plopped back down into my chair and picked up the brown manila envelope. My name was printed in a standard black font, as was the sender, a company called Seashell Imports, with a logo of a pretty scalloped clamshell with a pearl inside. I snorted. I might be a spy, but even I couldn't hide from junk-mailers who wanted to sell me overpriced life insurance or buy my apartment for pennies on the dollar.

But distracting myself with the junk mail would give my brain a break, so I opened the manila envelope and upended it. A thicker, smaller cream-colored envelope slipped out and landed on my desk. Weird. I frowned and picked it up.

Charlotte Locke. My name was written in beautiful black calligraphy on the cream envelope, which was made of expensive paper that was as smooth as velvet between my fingertips. The junk-mail folks were really upping their game with the fancy trappings—

I froze. My gaze locked onto my name, and I traced my right index finger along the elegant flowing script. My dread rose. I'd know those cursive loops anywhere, along with the extra, distinctive flourishes in the *C* and the *L*.

This was Henrika Hyde's handwriting.

All the air whooshed out of my lungs, and I stared at the envelope with wide eyes. Then my mind kicked back into gear, and I carefully laid the cream envelope on the desk. My heart throbbed as worry flooded my body. Had Henrika coated the envelope with some undetectable toxin the mailroom scanners had missed? Was the poison already circulating through my system? Was I going to die sitting at my desk?

What a shitty way to go, especially for a spy.

Ten seconds passed. Twenty . . . thirty . . . forty-five . . .

The other analysts and charmers kept typing on their keyboards and murmuring into their phones, completely oblivious to my fear and paralysis. Even Mika in the cubicle next door was focused on her work, bobbing her head and waving her index finger in time to the classical music drifting out of her headphones as though she was conducting the orchestra herself.

Sixty seconds . . . seventy-five . . . ninety . . .

At the three-minute mark, I wiped the cold sweat off my forehead with a shaking hand. The envelope wasn't poisoned. Otherwise, I would be dead by now.

I exhaled, steadying my nerves, then fished a box of plastic blue gloves out of a desk drawer. I yanked the gloves onto my hands so I wouldn't further contaminate anything, then picked up the cream envelope again.

Charlotte Locke.

I tilted the envelope back and forth and let the light play across the surface, just in case a microdot or some other message was hidden in the calligraphy. But no secrets were embedded in the black ink, so I opened the envelope and plucked out the cream-colored card inside, which also had fancy calligraphy in black ink. I read the message:

My dearest Charlotte,

Since my previous auction at the Halstead Hotel was so rudely interrupted, I am holding a new event.

You are cordially invited to attend the annual Winter-fest charity event at my Glittertop Resort. Special guests such as yourself will have the opportunity to bid on my

Redburn formula, in addition to taking part in other festivities throughout the weekend.

Please arrive by 5 p.m. this evening for the kickoff event. Bring all the toys you want, but this invitation is limited to you and your plus-one. I'm just dying to see Desmond again.

Toodles for now,
Henrika

I sat there, completely dumbfounded, for the better part of a minute. Then my shock wore off, my eyes narrowed, and I read the invitation again—and again and again, parsing every single sentence, word, and syllable.

Henrika was telling me *exactly* where she was going to be. The spider was inviting the fly into her parlor, which meant it had to be a trap. But the longer I stared at the invitation, the more determined I was to crawl into Henrika's web and strangle her with the strands.

My gaze slid over to the clock in the bottom-right corner of my monitor. Just after nine a.m. Henrika hadn't given me much time to get to her resort.

Footsteps scuffed across the carpet, and a shadow fell over my body. I glanced up to find Joan Samson standing beside my desk.

"You need to come with me, Charlotte," Joan said in a tense voice. "Right now."

My stomach clenched with dread. "Why?"

Her lips pinched together into a tight line. "We received a message from Henrika Hyde."

Still clutching the invitation, I grabbed the cream-colored

envelope with my name, then followed Joan out of the level-three bullpen and into the elevator.

"What happened?" I asked.

Joan shook her head, making her long black hair swish around her shoulders. "I'm not entirely sure, but Henrika contacted someone at Section, and now it's all hands on deck. Gia told me to bring you to the fifth-level conference room. That's all I know."

Truth, my inner voice whispered. Joan was in the dark, but I knew—*I knew*—this had something to do with the invitation in my hand. What sick game was Henrika playing now?

The elevator stopped, and we hurried down the corridor and entered the level-five bullpen. The cleaners and liaisons sitting at their desks eyed me as I followed Joan down the center aisle. I looked past her, but Desmond wasn't at his desk. Surely he would be involved in any meeting about Henrika. So where was he?

Joan stopped at her own desk and sorted through some folders. I awkwardly hovered beside her, all too aware of the eyes on me. Desperate for something else to focus on, I scanned her cubicle.

Just like my space on the third level, Joan's was largely devoid of toys and knickknacks. Several mugs held a variety of expensive pens, but the only truly personal item was a picture on the corner of the desk. Curious, I picked up the silver frame.

In the photo, Joan was smiling wide, with one hand flung out at a beautiful sunset over some old ruins. The gorgeous image was drenched in color, from the hazy pink rays that streaked the sky to the dark gray of the stone ruins to the deep blue sea in the background. A bit of silver winked on Joan's chest right over her heart, matching the glitter of her pale eyes.

"What a lovely photo. Where was it taken?"

Joan jerked back as though I had startled her, and she hesitated before answering. "Greece. On vacation."

Truth, my inner voice whispered.

"How fun," I murmured.

Joan's fingers clenched around the folders in her hands. She obviously didn't like me touching her stuff. Couldn't blame her for that. I studied the photo another moment, committing it to memory, then set the frame down.

"Let's go," Joan said in a curt voice.

I followed her into the conference room in the back of the bullpen. Evelyn, Gia, and Diego were already sitting in the same spots as yesterday. Evelyn and Gia both had grim looks on their faces, and Diego swallowed hard as though he was about to be sick.

"What's wrong? What's happened? Where's Desmond?" I asked, my voice growing louder and sharper with each question.

Evelyn shook her head, but she didn't answer me. Gia's face remained grim, and Diego shoved his black glasses farther up his nose.

Joan skirted around the table and took her usual seat next to Diego, leaving me to drop into the same chair as yesterday.

We sat in silence for the better part of two minutes. Then several sets of footsteps scuffed on the carpet, quickly growing closer and louder. Desmond entered the conference room and sat down beside me.

Relief rushed through me. I opened my mouth to ask him what was going on, but General Percy entered the room, along with his two bodyguards.

One of the bodyguards shut the door, and the familiar buzz of the soundproofing rang out. General Percy slapped a stack of folders onto the table, then took his own seat, his posture ramrod-stiff. His gaze met mine, his blue eyes as cold as ice. I didn't need my synesthesia to know something was very, very wrong—and that the General blamed me for it.

"Show it to them," Percy commanded in a stern voice.

Diego swallowed again and hit some buttons on his laptop.

The film screen dropped down to cover the wall, and a video started playing.

Henrika Hyde's face popped up onto the screen. She was forty-something, with light brown hair, green eyes, and flawless pale skin free of wrinkles thanks to the many beauty serums and creams she had invented. Henrika was a lovely woman, but the sight of her wide, mocking smile made me flinch.

"Greetings, Jethro," she said in a low, silky voice. "I trust you and the other members of Section 47 are doing well."

General Percy glared at the video as though he wanted to reach inside the screen and throttle the weapons maker.

"You're probably wondering why I'm contacting you," Henrika continued. "I wanted to extend a personal invitation to my Winterfest charity extravaganza, which is being held at my Glittertop Resort. I'm sure you're familiar with both the event and my property."

Several photos flashed by on the screen, showing a beautiful resort sprawling across a mountain, along with people skiing, ice skating, tubing, snowboarding, and even jumping into a frigid-looking lake.

"During Winterfest, hundreds of guests flock to my Glittertop Resort to enjoy a weekend of luxury amenities, gourmet food, and a variety of games." Henrika's voice played over the photo montage. "All the proceeds benefit cancer research. Such a worthy cause, wouldn't you agree? Especially given how many Section members have lost friends and family members to such awful diseases."

My hands clenched into fists on my lap. She was talking about Grandma Jane.

The photos vanished, and Henrika appeared again. "I will also hold an auction for my Redburn formula at the resort. Two designated representatives from Section 47 are invited to come and bid on my marvelous creation, along with other special guests."

More photos appeared on the screen. I recognized the faces, and my stomach clenched with fresh dread. Henrika was giving some of the most dangerous paramortal criminals and terrorists in the world a chance to acquire her deadly explosive.

The images vanished, and Henrika appeared again.

"Now, Jethro, I imagine you will get some rather unpleasant ideas about crashing my party, so before you do anything rash, I wanted to let you know *exactly* what my associate stole from your storage facility yesterday." Henrika leaned a little closer to the camera, her green eyes glittering in her face. "A list of all Section 47 agents currently undercover around the world."

I stiffened in my chair. Beside me, Desmond also stiffened. Joan sucked in a startled breath, and Evelyn tapped her pen on her notepad. Gia muttered a curse and glanced over at Diego, who gave a reluctant nod of confirmation.

Bryce Finkley had stolen the undercover—UC—list, which meant Henrika had access to every agent's real name, along with their aliases and mission objectives, and she could expose them to their enemies at any time.

A fist of guilt wrapped around my heart and squeezed it tight. Henrika had the UC list because of my failure on the Vault mission. All these agents were in danger because of *me* and my stupid pride and selfish desire to beat Henrika at her own game. My stomach roiled.

"Now that I have your attention, let's get down to details," Henrika said, leaning away from the camera. "Section 47 wants my Redburn formula, and I want to conduct my business safely without the constant threat of arrest and imprisonment, so come to my auction. If you win, Section gets the formula *and* the UC list. If you don't win, well, you don't want that to happen."

Henrika's eyes gleamed with triumph. She held all the cards, and she knew it.

"I've left some further instructions with Charlotte Locke.

Follow them exactly, and Charlotte and her plus-one will be allowed into the auction." Henrika's gaze bored into the camera. "Deviate from my directions in any way, and you will be severely punished, along with your undercover agents and all the innocent bystanders at my resort. Toodles for now, darling."

Henrika raised her hand to her red lips and blew a cheeky kiss at the camera. A few seconds later, the video ended.

"I received this message thirty minutes ago in my private email account," General Percy said, his voice cold, clipped, and furious.

No one said anything. Everyone, including me, was still trying to digest all the threats and implications in Henrika's message.

General Percy stabbed his finger at me. "What did Henrika mean when she said she sent you further instructions?"

I told them about the envelope I'd received, then laid the invitation on the table. Everyone leaned forward and studied the handwritten note.

"Why would Henrika want *you* to attend her weapons auction, Ms. Locke?" General Percy said. "Is there something you're not telling us?"

I bristled at his snide implication. "I am *not* working with Henrika. I would *never* betray Section 47 like that."

I would never betray Desmond like that. The words dangled on the end of my tongue, but I held them back. Reminding the General that I was involved with his son would not help my case.

General Percy kept glaring at me, suspicion stamped in every line in his wrinkled face. "Perhaps all the times Henrika has tried to kill you are just a clever cover. Your father was quite adept at such deceptions, and I have no doubt he passed those skills down to you, Ms. Locke, along with his many insubordinate tendences."

Anger flared in my chest, and I opened my mouth to give him a piece of my mind, but Gia cut me off.

"Don't be ridiculous, Jethro," the cleaner supervisor snapped. "We all know Charlotte isn't involved with Henrika. You're just pissed because Henrika wormed her way into your private email."

A muscle twitched in the General's jaw, but he didn't deny her accusation.

"The real question is what are we going to do about the situation?" Gia's dark gaze flicked to me. "Charlotte, are you familiar with the Winterfest event?"

"Yes, I did a deep dive into the charity and its finances last year when I first started tracking Henrika. Winterfest is exactly what she said—a weekend of games, activities, and events at the Glittertop Resort in southwest Virginia. The resort is one of the crown jewels of Henrika's empire, and it has ski slopes, a luxury spa, gourmet restaurants, a golf course, and other attractions."

Diego hit some keys on his laptop, and more photos of the resort appeared on the screen. "The resort covers several thousand acres in the Appalachian Mountains. Not much else is around it. Lots of dirt roads and hiking trails, although the area is riddled with abandoned coal mines."

"And the Winterfest event itself?" Joan asked in a skeptical voice. "Does it really raise money for charity?"

I nodded. "Yes. Every penny raised during the weekend goes to fund cancer research at legitimate companies, including Henrika's. She even donates some of her own money."

"Why would she do that?" Desmond asked.

I shrugged. "Henrika gets a lot of good press and a hefty tax write-off out of the event. Winterfest has become a hot ticket among the rich and wealthy, both mortal and paramortal."

Evelyn tapped her pen on her notepad again. "And now Henrika is going to use all those people as cover to conduct her weapons auction," she murmured, breaking out of her assistant role to make a rare comment. "You have to admire her audacity."

"I don't have to admire anything about that woman," General Percy growled. "Now that we know where she'll be, we'll send in a strike team to capture her. The only thing Henrika will be enjoying this weekend are the dark confines of a Section black site."

Gia shook her head. "You heard what Henrika said. If you go after her at the resort, she'll turn on the guests. We all know about the horrific biomagical weapons Henrika has developed. If she has a big enough stockpile, especially of the Redburn explosive, she could kill every person at the resort."

"She could do that anyway, just for spite," General Percy growled again.

"Yes, she could," I replied. "But Henrika also loves to play games. She is literally a genius, and one of her main pleasures in life is proving how smart she is and beating people at their own games. In this case, she's decided to turn her attention to Section 47."

"Are you suggesting we actually go along with her demands, Ms. Locke?" Percy turned his icy glower back to me.

"This is the closest we've been to Henrika in *months*," I replied, struggling to keep my own voice calm in the face of his frosty anger. "She's giving us a chance to play her game for a change. We can't win if we don't even sit down at the table."

General Percy kept glaring at me, while everyone else glanced back and forth between us.

"Charlotte's right," Desmond chimed in. "Henrika blames Charlotte and me for keeping the Grunglass Necklace from her at the Halstead Hotel last year. And now she wants to get her revenge on us, along with the rest of Section 47."

"But?" Percy demanded.

Desmond looked at his father. "But if there's even the smallest chance we can recover the UC list before Henrika leaks it, then we have to take it. The lives of hundreds of Section agents are at stake, along with all the innocent civilians at the resort."

Desmond glanced over at the film screen where Henrika's face had been. Anger flared in his eyes, making them flash a bright silver-blue. "If Henrika wants to play a game, then I say we show her just how formidable Section 47 really is."

"For Graham," Joan added in a soft voice, her hand drifting up to the sword brooch pinned to her suit jacket.

Desmond nodded back at the liaison. "For Graham and all the other agents who died on the Blacksea mission."

He looked over at his father. So did everyone else. General Percy drummed his fingers on the tabletop for several seconds, then his hand abruptly stilled and curled into a tight fist.

"Fine," he growled again. "We'll play her game—for now. But the second we get the chance, we're taking down Henrika, along with everyone else who shows up for her auction."

THIRTEEN

DESMOND

We spent the next thirty minutes setting up mission parameters, reviewing procedures, and theorizing potential pitfalls. It was just before ten o'clock, which meant we had roughly seven hours to prep for the mission, pack our gear, and reach the resort. Henrika was putting us in scramble mode right from the beginning.

Gia did most of the talking, while my father sat back in his chair, his arms crossed over his chest, glowering at nothing in particular. The General hated being outmaneuvered, and so far, Henrika was dancing around him like he was standing still.

"Joan, you'll also be going to the resort," Gia said. "Diego, see if you can hack into the reservation system and book Joan a room, along with an invitation to Winterfest. Be sure to use a brand-new alias since the UC list has been compromised."

Joan nodded, while Diego's fingers started flying over his keyboard.

"What about Henrika's warning that only Charlotte and I can attend the auction?" I asked.

Gia shrugged. "You and Charlotte will attend the auction,

but I want someone on-site watching your backs. Henrika should be so focused on the two of you that she doesn't notice Joan. Plus, Joan can nose around and keep an eye on the other paramortals. I want as much information as possible about everyone who shows up for the auction."

We discussed a few more things. Once we had the rough outlines in place, everyone split up.

The General returned to his office to coordinate with the strike team, while Joan headed down to the level-six armory to start gathering gear. Evelyn, Gia, and Diego kept working in the conference room, reviewing satellite photos of the Glittertop Resort, while Charlotte and I returned to our desks.

Charlotte tilted her head to the right, and I followed her out of the bullpen and down the corridor. She veered away from the elevators, stepped behind some concrete columns, and slipped into a shadowy alcove. No security cameras or listening devices were planted in this area, and it was a rare surveillance dead zone inside headquarters where we could speak freely.

"How are you holding up?" Charlotte asked. "It must have been hard seeing Henrika again, and especially hearing what she wanted. She is forcing us into an impossible situation. If any of the criminals she's invited to the auction figure out who we really are, or if Henrika tells them, then the other paramortals will stop at nothing to kill us."

I shrugged. "I'm used to the danger, and I'll march into Henrika's viper's nest like a good little soldier."

"But?"

I scrubbed my hands over my face. "But I don't like the thought of you being in danger. Henrika sent that invitation to *you*, Charlotte. That means she wants something from *you*, something she can only get in person. In some ways, that's worse than her simply wanting to kill you."

"You're right. Henrika *does* want something from me, or

you, or Section, or maybe even all of us. Although right now, I can't imagine what it might be." A thoughtful look filled Charlotte's face, and her eyes narrowed as she once again did those complex mental calculations, trying to determine Henrika's motives.

I didn't care about Henrika's motives. I just wanted her dead for everything she'd done to me, Graham, and the other agents who'd died on the Blacksea mission.

Charlotte reached out and squeezed my hand as if she knew exactly what I was thinking. "We'll find a way to take Henrika down. No matter how many tricks she has planned or how many guards and vials of Redburn she has."

"Yes, we will," I echoed her promise.

Charlotte stepped forward, wrapped her arms around my waist, and rested her head on my shoulder. I buried my face in her auburn hair and drank in her sweet, sharp, sugar-lime scent.

The thought of suffering through another Redburn explosion—or worse, Charlotte being exposed to the deadly formula—made my chest tighten and cold sweat break out on the back of my neck, but I shrugged off the uncomfortable sensations and tightened my arms around her. No matter what happened, keeping Charlotte safe was my main objective, and I would do anything—*anything*—to complete that mission.

My phone chirped, interrupting our quiet, private bubble. I dropped my arms from around Charlotte and pulled the device out of my pocket.

"The General wants to see me in his office." I sighed. "No doubts he has some thoughts about the mission he wants to share."

Sympathy filled Charlotte's face, although her aura flickered with guilt. "I'm so sorry Henrika put you in this situation. I should have found some way to track her down before now. Maybe if I had, we could have confronted her and gotten our answers without General Percy ever getting involved."

I shook my head. "It's not your fault. It was only a matter of time before my father showed up. For better or worse, the General is *always* at the center of whatever drama is currently happening inside Section, and right now, there is no bigger drama or greater danger than Henrika Hyde."

Charlotte's phone also chirped, and she made a face at the screen. "Joan wants to meet in the armory so we can gear up for the mission."

"I'll meet you there after I talk to the General."

Charlotte nodded, then leaned forward and brushed her lips against mine. I wound my hand into her hair and pulled her closer, deepening the kiss—

This time, both our phones chirped with messages. I didn't want to let Charlotte go, but as with so many things at Section, I didn't have a choice.

I dropped my hands, stepped back, and forced myself to wink at her with confidence that I didn't feel. "See you soon, Numbers."

Charlotte returned to the conference room to check in with Evelyn, Gia, and Diego before heading to the armory. I rode the elevator up to the fourth level. I ignored the guards flanking my father's office and knocked on the door. The General buzzed me inside, and I stepped into the office.

My father was sitting at his desk watching the video of Henrika. He paused the feed, and her frozen face smirked at us on the monitor.

Anger shimmered in the General's eyes. "I can't believe she had the audacity to send me this video. The sheer, unmitigated *arrogance*. As if Section couldn't crush her any time we wanted."

I got the impression he was talking more about himself than Section 47, but I didn't ask any questions. The General only told his version of the truth, and never the whole of it, and he wouldn't answer anything I asked unless it fit into his plans.

"You wanted to see me?"

The General finally tore his gaze away from the monitor. "I have no interest in capturing Henrika. I want her eliminated."

I hesitated. "Does Gia know this?"

Back in the conference room, Gia had ordered Charlotte and me to gather intelligence about the other auction guests and to figure out if Henrika had a biomagical lab on the resort grounds where she might be storing samples of Redburn and other weapons. But our primary objective was to recover the UC list, then capture Henrika so a Section strike team could swoop in and abduct her. With Henrika out of the way, the threat of her selling the Redburn formula would be neutralized. Although no one had any idea how we might accomplish those goals, given the legions of guards Henrika was sure to have at her disposal.

My father waved his hand, brushing off my concern. "Gia Chan might oversee the cleaners, but I'm the head of the board of directors, which means I outrank her. Gia might not like it, but there's nothing she can do about it. You are to eliminate Henrika as soon as possible. That's an order, Desmond."

The General speared me with a hard gaze, his eyes glittering like chips of ice. My father was primarily a political animal, always weighing and measuring actions and reactions. Such maneuvers had enabled him to climb to the top of the Section ranks, but for once, he didn't seem to care about any fallout from his orders. Odd.

"Is there a problem?" the General asked. "I thought you would relish this opportunity. After all, your being so desperate to kill Henrika Hyde and Adrian Anatoly is what got us into this mess in the first place."

I stiffened at the verbal barbs. "No. I don't have any problem eliminating Henrika."

And I didn't. My personal hatred and vendetta aside, I had killed people who had committed far fewer and much less atrocious crimes than Henrika and not thought twice about it. In some ways, Henrika Hyde was the most dangerous, vicious enemy I'd ever encountered, and it would be a pleasure to finally make her pay for everything she'd done. All the undercover agents she was currently threatening, all the lives she had already taken, all the pain, misery, and suffering she had visited upon the families of the Section agents who'd been killed on the Blacksea mission.

The only thing that made me hesitate was Charlotte. Henrika couldn't answer questions if she was dead, and Charlotte deserved to know what had really happened to her father all those years ago.

The General nodded, mistaking my silence for obedience. "Good. I'm also giving you another objective."

I bit back a tired sigh. Of course he was. The General never just asked for one thing when he could ask for two, or three, or a dozen. "What?"

He pulled a photo out of a folder and slid it across the desk. The image showed a glass vial with a thick red liquid inside.

In an instant, the office melted away, and I was back on the beach in Australia, my body burning with agony, even as I watched the light die in Graham's eyes and took his remaining energy, his life, to save myself like the bloody coward I truly was . . .

"I'm sure you can guess what that is." The General's eager voice snapped me back to the here and now.

"Redburn," I muttered. "How did you get a picture of it?"

A sly smile curved his lips. "Given the D.C. station's lack of progress over the past few months, I planted a few of my own spies in Henrika's organization. One of them sent me this photo earlier today, which they took in a secret lab at the resort. I was plotting the best course of action to find and retrieve the vial when I received the video."

My gaze snapped up to his. "You've confirmed Henrika has a weapons lab *and* samples of Redburn at the resort?"

The General nodded, leaned back, and steepled his fingers together. "Yes. Obviously, the threat of unleashing Redburn is one of her contingency plans to keep Section agents at bay, so Henrika *has* to be storing a supply of the explosive at the resort, although my spy hasn't been able to pinpoint the exact location yet."

A sick, sinking sensation flooded my stomach. "What do you want me to do?"

My father stared at me, his eyes even colder than before. "We can't allow any samples of Redburn to fall into enemy hands."

I nodded, working hard to hide the relief crashing through my body. "So you want me to find Henrika's lab and destroy any samples?"

The General let out a deep, hearty chuckle, as though I'd just made a marvelous joke. "Of course not. I want you to bring me all the samples of Redburn, along with any other weapons Henrika might have on-site."

Back in Germany, when I'd confiscated the vials of Redburn the mercenaries were going to use to blow up Tannenbaum Castle, I'd told Charlotte that the Section leaders, including my father—*especially* my father—would want to reverse engineer the explosive for their own purposes. And now the General was confirming my worst fears.

As a cleaner, I could see why he wanted Redburn so badly. Paramortals could be difficult to kill, and a weapon like that would give Section 47 a huge tactical advantage. But I didn't want anyone to suffer the way Graham and I had suffered on the beach. The force, fire, and fury of the explosions blasting over me was something I would never, ever forget. I still woke up sweating and screaming in the middle of the night, clawing at the phantom burning sensation in my skin as though I had been doused in boiling honey. In my own way, I could be as ruthless as the General, but I wouldn't wish that searing, unending agony on my worst enemy—except for Henrika, for creating such a horrid weapon.

Section 47 might keep the public safe from rogue para-mortals, but not everyone in the spy organization had pure, good, noble intentions. It wouldn't be long before Redburn was used in a personal vendetta rather than in a strategic mission, and innocent people might get caught in the crossfire, subjected to horrible pain and certain death just because they happened to be in the wrong place at the wrong time.

I couldn't let that happen.

"Do you understand what I'm saying, son?" the General asked, once again jerking me back to the here and now.

Son. My father only called me that when he wanted to drive home a point—and remind me exactly who was in charge.

I nodded again, even though every fiber in my body rebelled at the small, acquiescing motion. "Yes, sir. I'm to bring in as many samples of Redburn as possible and eliminate the rest, along with Henrika."

"Good. I'm glad we understand each other." My father speared me with another hard look. "This is strictly between the two of us, Desmond. Understand? Gia doesn't need to know about this either. Neither does Charlotte."

I nodded yet again, still trying to think through the remembered pain skittering through my skin like a live electrical current scorching everything it touched.

"Good," he repeated. "Go prep for the mission. I'll find you later. Dismissed."

I spun around and left the office. My father had given me a mission, but for the first time in my life, I wasn't going to complete it. I *couldn't*—not if I wanted to be able to live with my own conscience.

The General wanted me to eliminate Henrika? Okay. As soon as Charlotte got her answers from the other woman, then I would follow his orders and kill Henrika. But I was going to destroy every single sample of Redburn that I found before the formula could fall into the wrong hands—including my father's.

FOURTEEN

DESMOND

till plotting how I could keep the General or anyone else from getting their hands on any samples of Redburn, I rode the elevator down to the sixth level.

The armory always reminded me of a massive department store that carried everything a spy could ever need. Shelf after shelf of weapons, tech, gadgets, and clothes stretched out as far as I could see, and the entire floor was divided into large squares cordoned off with clear bullet- and magic-resistant glass walls to keep any stray weapons fire, smoke bombs, or explosions from escaping and hitting anyone walking past.

Joan was in a square close to the elevator, plucking guns, knives, and ammunition out of an open metal locker and laying them on a table. Charlotte's arms were crossed over her chest, and she was watching Joan with a wary expression. Diego was also here, swiping through screens on his tablet and cataloging the weapons and ammo.

Joan waved her hand over the table like a magician unveiling a trick. "I got all your favorites, Dez."

I nodded at the assortment of weapons. "An impressive spread, as always."

Joan jerked her thumb over at some suitcases on the floor. "Your suitcases have the usual secret lead-lined compartments. Henrika will no doubt have her security team search your luggage, but she did say you could bring all the toys you wanted."

"Yes, I suppose it's no fun if the prey you invite into your death trap isn't armed to the teeth," I muttered.

Joan shrugged, then gestured over at a single gun on another table. "Are you sure you don't want to take more weapons, Charlotte? You never know what might happen."

"I'm not a cleaner, so I'm not nearly as deadly as Desmond," Charlotte replied. "If I can't think my way out of a situation, then using a weapon will be a last resort."

Joan shook her head. "Your loss."

Diego grinned at the liaison. "You love this, don't you? Picking out just the right gear for the mission."

Joan returned his grin with an even wider one of her own, and the ice-blue aura around her heart pulsed with happiness. It had been a long time since I'd seen her look so relaxed, and her good mood lightened my own.

"Absolutely! It's like being a personal shopper for a bunch of badasses who have access to the best toys money can buy." Joan waggled her eyebrows. "Speaking of toys . . ."

She moved away from the weapons locker, opened a glass door in the wall, and stepped into the next square. Charlotte, Diego, and I followed her. This area was filled with racks of clothes in different colors, sizes, and styles, from luxurious cashmere sweaters to classic black tuxedos to glittering sequined gowns.

Joan looked at Diego. "What's the weather supposed to be like?"

The tech guru hit some buttons on his tablet. "Cold and

blustery. A big storm is supposed to move in tomorrow, Saturday afternoon. The forecasters are predicting a foot of snow, maybe more."

Charlotte grimaced. "That sounds like the Tannenbaum mission."

It had snowed quite heavily during the Christmas Eve party, which had been great for the mercenaries, as it had cut off easy access to Tannenbaum Castle, and bad for Charlotte and me because it had taken so long for help to arrive.

"We survived that storm," I said. "We'll survive this one too."

Charlotte smiled, but her eyes remained dark and troubled, and the aura around her heart dimmed with doubt.

Armed with the weather forecast, Joan plucked one garment after another off the racks and laid them on two separate tables, along with shoes, jewelry, and other accessories.

"I've reviewed the Winterfest schedule posted on the website," Joan said. "The daytime events are all casual, but there's a formal themed party each night."

"Of course there is," Charlotte muttered.

I nudged her with my elbow. "Aw, what's the matter? You don't want to get dressed up?"

Charlotte stabbed her finger at a pair of silver stilettoes on the table. "Not when getting dressed up includes wearing shoes that will lead to my death. Those stilettoes will rub blisters on my feet in minutes, and I can't possibly run in them. Why can't I have practical shoes, like the ones you picked out for Desmond?" She pointed at a pair of hiking boots that were squatting next to some gloves.

Joan rolled her eyes. "Relax. This isn't my first mission, and I'm packing a variety of shoes for you and Desmond. You aren't the first Section agent to ever bemoan wearing heels, Charlotte. Trust me. The stilettoes are way more comfortable than they look. Even better, they contain a few surprises."

The liaison picked up the stilettoes and clicked the heels together. *Snick-snick*. Three small, sharp spikes jutted out of the pointed steel toe of each shoe. "Just in case you want to climb up a wall or kick someone while they're down."

Charlotte harrumphed. Joan rolled her eyes again, then set the stilettoes down and moved on to the other items.

"The top buttons on your coats are equipped with small but powerful flashlights. Twist the button to one side, and the light activates. Twist it to the other side, and the light vanishes." Joan demonstrated with one of the buttons, then set it aside.

"Your necklaces, watches, and other jewelry contain standard comms equipment so the two of you will be able to hear and talk to each other." The liaison gestured over at a couple of sparkling snowflake brooches. "Cameras are also hidden in the jewelry, so I, Diego, Gia, and everyone else can see what you're seeing. The comms equipment will also let us hear and talk to you, as well as track your locations."

Charlotte shot a sour glance at the jewelry. Me too. I had never particularly liked other agents listening in on everything I said and did. It might be necessary to maintain mission safety and security, but it also felt extremely invasive at times.

Joan plucked a long shoestring with two fluffy black pom-poms off the side of a woman's boot and dangled it at us like a cat toy. "Since you didn't want a lot of weapons, I added some extra accessories to your gear, Charlotte. A little something I came up with myself. Both pom-poms are packed with explosives. Just dig through the fabric until you find the button, hit it, and then ten seconds later, *boom!*"

Pride rippled through her voice. In addition to packing gear for agents, Joan also dreamed up new gadgets, and several of her inventions were housed in the armory.

Charlotte blanched. "You want me to wear explosives pom-poms on my boots?"

"Absolutely!" Joan replied in an enthusiastic voice. "They're also attached to your gloves and hats. All your purses are also lined with explosives."

Charlotte blanched again.

Joan set the pom-poms down. She hesitated a moment, then cracked open a large green velvet box, revealing the Grunglass Necklace. Or at least a copy of it, according to the white identification tag.

"You should take this too," Joan said, nudging the case over to Charlotte. "Maybe you can fool Henrika into thinking it's the real necklace and use it as a bargaining chip."

Charlotte's forehead crinkled at Joan's words, as though the liaison had said something wrong, but she trailed her fingers over the glittering jewels. Charlotte blinked a few times, then stared at Joan.

"What an excellent fake," Charlotte murmured. "Why, it's so good it looks like the real thing. But I'm no expert in vintage jewelry. Not like *you* are, Joan."

The liaison bristled, and the two women stared at each other, having some silent conversation I didn't understand. I looked at Diego, who shrugged in confusion.

Joan stared at Charlotte a few more seconds, then spun around on her heel and opened another glass door. Charlotte, Diego, and I trailed the liaison.

If the first square had been a weapons locker and the second square a designer closet, this third square was a drugstore with shelves full of seemingly ordinary, everyday items, from keychains to lotions to a pack of playing cards with colorful suits and numbers.

Joan's face brightened, and she rubbed her hands together in glee. "And now, the *really* fun stuff—gadgets and gizmos galore!"

The liaison grabbed several items off the shelves and laid them on a table, but she also rejected just as many, examining the items for a few seconds before shaking her head in disapproval and returning them to their original spots.

Joan held up a silver lipstick tube. "You're already familiar with this, Charlotte. Standard Section issue." She hit a button on the side, and a small hypodermic needle popped out of the bottom of the tube. "Jab this into someone, and it's lights out in five seconds."

She hit the button again, retracting the needle, then removed the top and twisted up the lipstick. "And this plum color will look terrific on you."

"Great," Charlotte drawled. "Because I *have* to wear just the right lipstick when walking into a trap."

Joan ignored the sarcasm and showed us the rest of the items. A toothbrush with a ceramic knife hidden in the hilt. An acidic deodorant that would eat through metal locks. A fountain pen that shot out a surprisingly long length of wire in case we needed to tie someone up—or garotte them.

"What does this do?" I asked, picking up a rectangular gray box that was about as long as my index finger and twice as wide.

"That old thing? It's a recorder with a tiny cassette tape," Joan replied. "It uses batteries. Completely analog. An antique from spy days gone by."

"Cool." I set the recorder down.

Joan planted her hands on her hips, then made another round of additions and subtractions from the items she had picked out. Diego followed her, marking the selections in the armory database.

Charlotte wandered along behind them. Her eyes narrowed, as though she was seeing far more uses for the gadgets with her synesthesia than what Joan had suggested.

I too stared out over the sea of seemingly innocuous items. Joan was making sure we had everything we needed, but dread still twisted my gut into knots. No matter how well equipped Charlotte and I were, something completely unexpected would inevitably come up.

I just hoped the unexpected thing wouldn't be the death of us.

FIFTEEN

CHARLOTTE

Joan gave Desmond and me each a set of clothes to put on, along with the appropriate accessories, then shooed us out of the armory so she could finish packing our gear. Diego stayed with her, still cataloging everything.

Desmond and I returned to level five. He veered into the bullpen to check in with Evelyn and Gia, while I headed into the locker room to get changed.

I stripped off my clothes and donned a powder-blue cashmere sweater, along with black leggings lined with microfleece. Wool socks and sturdy yet fashionable black boots completed the ensemble.

Next, I hooked a silver necklace with a sapphire pendant around my neck and pinned a silver snowflake brooch studded with white crystals to my sweater. I rubbed my finger over the sparkling crystals, which reminded me of the diamonds in Joan's sword brooch.

I studied my reflection in the floor-length mirror on the wall. I looked like a skier ready to hit the slopes. I made a face. Not my usual super-comfortable, super-low-key style, but the luxe look would let me blend in with the rich resort guests. Sometimes I thought the worst part of being a spy was the unfamiliar wardrobes. Donning a disguise didn't help me get in character and make me feel like the person I was supposed to be—more like a kid playing dress-up who was desperate not to be discovered.

I made another face in the mirror, then left the changing room and shoved my regular clothes into a locker. Behind me, the door creaked open.

I grinned and turned around. "Are you finally ready to put on your ski suit—"

My words died on my lips. Desmond hadn't entered the locker room—General Percy had.

He stopped a few feet away and crossed his arms over his chest. "Ms. Locke."

"General."

Percy's gaze trailed over my outfit and comms jewelry. He did a double take at the fluffy black pom-poms attached to my boots, but other than that, his face remained unreadable. For once, even my synesthesia was quiet, and I couldn't tell what he was thinking.

"I'm giving you a second chance with this mission, Ms. Locke," Percy said. "Do us both a favor, and don't screw it up."

My tongue itched with the urge to remind Percy that he hadn't given me anything. If the General had his way, Joan would have been going on the mission with Desmond. But Henrika had singled me out, forcing Percy to go along with her request.

Once again, I wondered why—*why* had she done that? Why was Henrika so eager for Desmond and me to come to the resort? She'd tried to kill us multiple times in the past, but now here she was, letting us stroll into her lair. Henrika could want to murder us in person, face-to-face, but Section agents would move in the instant Desmond and I were dead, and Henrika was too smart to risk getting captured just to enact some petty revenge on us.

Desmond was right. Henrika wanted something from the two of us, something she could only get if we were alive and right in front of her. But what could that be? What was Henrika's goal?

I might be a synth analyst, but this was a rare occasion when I just couldn't figure out what someone truly *wanted*. And I desperately needed to figure it out, since Desmond's and my lives depended on the answer.

"As difficult as it might be, you would do well to put your instincts aside and *not* follow in your father's footsteps on this mission, Ms. Locke," General Percy continued.

My eyebrows shot up at his snide tone. "What does that mean?"

"Jack Locke was one of the most reckless cleaners Section 47 ever employed. He had a patent disregard for authority, along with rules and regulations that are designed to keep agents safe." Percy shrugged. "You reap what you sow, and eventually, that blatant disregard got him killed."

Anger exploded in my chest, and words poured out of my mouth before I could stop them. "And here I thought my father died because you jumped the gun on the Mexico mission. *You're* the one who sent in a second squad of cleaners to try to kill Feliciano Salvador before the ransom exchange was complete and my father was freed."

I finally managed to stop talking, although I silently cursed my loose lips. Grandma Jane had taught me never to reveal any information I didn't have to, but everything about General Jethro Percy rubbed me the wrong way. Pompous, arrogant, overbearing jackass.

Percy's eyes narrowed. "How do you know that? Have you been accessing classified information, Ms. Locke?"

"As you said, Section has rules and regulations." I side-stepped his question. "Analysts are supposed to stick to their own work, targets, and assignments, not go poking around in other people's files."

Even before I had met Desmond, I would always bend a few rules if it meant getting more dirt on the criminals I was tracking. Such regulations certainly weren't going to stop me now, especially when I was going to be face-to-face with someone who might finally be able to shed some light on my father's death.

"But?" General Percy snapped.

"But people talk, even Section agents who should know better, and I've had numerous conversations with people about the infamous Mexico mission. Why, Henrika Hyde even claimed to know something about my father's death, if you can believe that."

It was a wild, reckless jab on my part, but to my surprise, the blow landed. A shadow passed over Percy's face, and he grimaced, as though he was worried about something. But what could that be? Jack Locke had been dead for fifteen years. My father couldn't interfere with Percy's plans anymore, and I was certainly no threat to someone so powerful inside Section 47.

But my first swing had connected, so I decided to keep punching. "Maybe I'll ask Henrika what she knows about the Mexico mission. Maybe she'll indulge me with a secret or two while she's playing all her other games with Desmond and me this weekend."

General Percy shrugged off my words. "As you said, Henrika loves to play games. I wouldn't believe a word she says, especially about a years-old Section mission that had nothing to do with her."

LIE, LIE, LIE!

My inner voice shrieked, and my entire vision exploded with red, as though I was drowning in a river of blood. The sensation was so strong it rocked me back on my heels, and I had to blindly clutch a locker to keep from falling on my ass.

Through the haze of red, I saw Percy frown. I gritted my teeth and blinked and blinked. Slowly, the red faded from my vision, although my head kept pounding from the sheer, raw force of Percy's blatant lie.

The General's eyes narrowed again. "What's wrong with you?" he demanded in a sharp, suspicious voice.

"Nothing," I muttered. "These stupid boots are just pinching my feet."

Percy frowned again. He clearly didn't believe my excuse.

The locker room door opened, and Desmond stepped inside, clutching a duffel bag. He stopped short when he saw me facing off with his father.

"Something wrong?" Desmond asked in a sharp, suspicious voice that was an eerie echo of his father's tone.

"Of course not," I lied, releasing my white-knuckle grip on the locker. "Your father was just wishing us good luck on the mission. Isn't that right, General?"

"Of course," Percy replied in a smooth voice. "A little luck never hurt anyone."

Desmond arched a chiding eyebrow at his father. "You don't believe in *luck*. Only information, preparation, and training."

The General ran a hand down his suit jacket. "Yes, well, perhaps I'm mellowing in my old age."

Desmond snorted in disbelief. Me too. If I had to use one word to describe General Jethro Percy, it would not be *mellow*. Controlling. Secretive. Dangerous. Duplicitous. But never, ever *mellow*.

Desmond hefted the duffel bag in his hand. "I need to get changed so Charlotte and I can get on the road."

The General's left eye twitched at the curt dismissal in his son's voice. "Very well. I need to check on a few final things. I'll see you in the garage."

Desmond turned his back to his father and moved over to one of the wooden benches between the rows of lockers. He placed his duffel bag on the bench, then sat down and tugged off his shoes. Desmond ignored Percy, who stared at his son with a strange mix of pride, wariness, and something I could have sworn was a touch of fear.

The General noticed me watching him watch Desmond, and his chin jutted up, even as he peered down his nose at me.

Danger-danger-danger, my synesthesia whispered.

General Percy wasn't doing anything threatening, but the longer he looked at me, the more I could have sworn he was plotting the best way to get rid of me as soon as possible.

SIXTEEN

DESMOND

My father hovered behind me for a few more seconds, then wrenched open the door and strode away.

I waited until the door had shut behind him, then looked over at Charlotte. "What were you and my father really talking about?"

When I'd stepped into the locker room, the two of them had been glaring at each other, and anger had sparked, sizzled, and crackled like fireworks in their auras. A small part of me had hoped the General would set aside his animus toward Jack Locke, judge Charlotte on her own merits, and realize just how amazing she was. But no one could hold a grudge like Jethro Percy, even against someone he'd never met before for crimes she hadn't even committed.

Charlotte stared at the closed door, a thoughtful look on her face. "He told me to ignore everything my father ever taught me, along with every single instinct I have as an analyst. In other words, be a good little spy, don't ask questions, and follow his orders to the letter."

I sighed. "The General always thinks he knows what's best

for everyone. I'm sorry he cornered you."

Charlotte shrugged. "I'm used to people underestimating me. Now, let's get you ready for the mission."

She reached into my duffel bag, pulled out a blue winter hat topped by a fuzzy pom-pom, and plopped it onto my head.

"Hey! Careful with that. That pom-pom contains a highly concentrated explosive." I removed the hat from my head and placed it on the bench.

"Yes, I know," Charlotte drawled, pointing at the black pom-poms attached to her boots. "I just *love* wearing explosives on my feet. Makes me feel all warm and cozy."

I grabbed her waist and pulled her closer. "You know what makes me feel all warm and cozy? You."

Charlotte arched an eyebrow. "Warm and cozy? Is that code for something else?"

I grinned. "It can be code for whatever you want it to be."

Her face split into a wide, happy smile, and she put her hands on my shoulders, leaned down, and brushed her lips across mine. I drew in a breath, drinking in her scent, along with her deep blue aura.

"We still have a few minutes before we're supposed to be down in the garage." I waggled my eyebrows in a suggestive manner.

Charlotte gave me another quick kiss. "As much as I would enjoy that, we're on a tight schedule. Besides, your father would probably have a stroke if he came in here and saw us fooling around."

"Well, that would be one way to get rid of him."

Charlotte laughed at my black humor and drew back. "Come on, Dundee. Hurry up and get dressed before I decide you have to wear explosive pom-poms after all."

I quickly donned the clothes Joan had picked out: a dark blue suit jacket and pants, with a light blue shirt and tie and a matching vest with a paisley pattern. I nestled my silver watch into the vest pocket and slid my feet into black wing tips, sans pom-poms.

Fifteen minutes later, Charlotte and I got off the elevator on level seven, which was a massive parking garage of dull gray concrete that housed a fleet of Section surveillance vans and other vehicles.

Gia and Evelyn were talking with Joan and Diego, who were loading laptops, monitors, and other equipment into a van. My father was standing a few feet away, barking orders at the strike team. I couldn't hear everything the General was saying, but the strike team members stood stiffly at attention and gave him sharp, crisp nods. My father was good at motivating others to do what he wanted the instant he wanted it done. Plus, no one wanted to get on the bad side of the head of the board of directors.

Except Charlotte. Every time she looked at my father, those mental calculations filled her eyes, as though she was trying to figure out his ulterior motives. I wished her luck, but I had given up understanding the General's reasoning long ago.

Gia waved us over and handed me the keys to a black sedan parked next to the surveillance van. "The sedan is equipped with all the usual protective gear. Bullet- and magic-proof windows, run-flat tires, dashboard buttons that will let you drop spikes and smoke bombs out of the undercarriage."

Charlotte went over to talk to Evelyn, Joan, and Diego, but Gia stepped closer to me, a serious look on her face.

"I know how difficult this is for you, Desmond, and how much you want justice for Graham and the other agents who died on the Blacksea mission, but don't let Henrika get in your head. Find a way to recover the UC agent list, then neutralize Henrika and any Redburn on site. I don't care what Henrika threatens you or Charlotte with. If you need backup, you call in the strike team. I am *not* losing any more agents to her. Understood?"

I nodded. "Understood."

Unlike my father, Gia didn't bark out orders, something that made me respect the former cleaner much more as a leader.

"Be careful, and come back alive," Gia said. "That's an order."

I grinned. "Yes, ma'am."

Gia went back over to the others, who were still clustered around the surveillance van.

Footsteps tapped out a quick rhythm on the floor, and my father strode over to me. He looked at the others a moment, his gaze lingering on Charlotte, then faced me.

"Remember your orders," the General said in a low voice. "I want Henrika dead and a sample of the Redburn explosive in my hands before the weekend is through. Understood?"

Just like the strike team members, I couldn't stop my spine from stiffening at his brisk, commanding tone. "Yes, sir."

My father hesitated, then clapped me on the shoulder, which was his version of a hug. "Be safe, son."

Despite all the years of simmering anger and hostilities between us, I had to swallow a hard knot of emotion in my throat before I could answer. "Yes, sir."

My father hesitated again, like he wanted to say something else, but the moment passed. He gave me a short, curt nod, then spun around and returned to the strike team members. He didn't look back.

I headed over to Charlotte. I didn't look back either.

Joan checked our gear one more time, then Charlotte and I got into the sedan. I steered the car up several long, curving ramps, then through a tunnel that rose to the ground level. The tunnel ended in a locked metal gate, which slid back at our approach. I drove the sedan through the opening, turned onto a street, and left Section headquarters.

I concentrated on the surrounding traffic and making sure no one was tailing us, while Charlotte swiped through screens on her tablet, reviewing information about the Winterfest event, the Glittertop Resort, and more.

A few hours later, I exited the interstate and navigated a series of narrow, curving, two-lane roads that wound deeper and deeper into the mountainous countryside of southwest Virginia. I had never been to this region before, and the lovely, woodsy scenery was a welcome contrast to the miles and miles of city streets and office buildings that surrounded Section headquarters.

"It's prettier than I expected," I said.

Charlotte stared out the windshield, a wistful look on her face. "I've always thought the Appalachian Mountains were particularly beautiful. Being in this area is like coming home."

"What do you mean?"

"My father owned a cabin in this region. He would often bring me here on the weekends."

"To relax?"

"Jack Locke, take a few days off to relax? *Never.*" Charlotte scoffed. "My father brought me here to train. Sometimes Gabriel and his dad would join us too, and we would spend the whole weekend playing war games."

"You don't sound too happy about that."

"It was usually the only quality time I got to spend with my father between his Section missions, but even then, he was never really *here* in the moment with me. Instead of swimming, biking, or walking in the woods, my father would chase me around with a paintball gun, yelling that I needed to run faster if I didn't want to get mock-killed." Charlotte rubbed her left shoulder. "Those paintballs *hurt*. They also ruined my clothes and stained my skin for days afterward."

"What did Gabriel think about your fathers' war games?"

"He loved them, right up to when my father persuaded his father to blindfold Gabriel and me, take us deep into a cavern, and force us to find our way out."

I winced. "How old were you?"

"Fifteen," she muttered. "It's a good thing Gabriel is a phaser who can walk through walls, or we never would have gotten out of that stupid cavern."

Her face darkened like a thundercloud, and her aura pulsed with hurt and anger, so I changed the subject.

"Did you tell Gabriel about the Winterfest mission?"

"Yeah, I texted him after we left the armory, and he was really cryptic about it." She frowned. "At least more so than usual."

Cryptic was one way to describe Gabriel Chase, and even his smoky gray aura didn't reveal much about what he was thinking or feeling. The former cleaner marched to the beat of his own drum, and I envied how he had told the Section leaders to shove it, walked away from the spy world, and forged his own path. More than once, I'd thought about doing the same thing, but I'd never quite had the courage to go through with it. Perhaps Gabriel was right when he claimed that he was the better, stronger man.

I steered around a hairpin curve. The dense pine trees that lined the road vanished, the land flattened out, and a parking lot appeared, running alongside a lake. We'd made excellent time, and it was just after four o'clock.

I took a few extra seconds to back into a spot near the end of the lot, just in case we had to leap into the car and leave in a hurry. Small things like making your escape as quick and easy as possible were often the keys to surviving a mission. Although if Charlotte and I were running for our lives, we'd be lucky to get out of the hotel, much less make it back to our vehicle.

I turned off the engine and looked at Charlotte. "No matter what happens, all I care about is making sure we both live through this. Just you and me from here on out, Numbers. That's the most important thing."

Charlotte's aura burned a bright, steady blue over her heart, and she grabbed my fingers and gave them a gentle squeeze. "Just you and me, Dundee—no matter what."

We stared at each other a heartbeat longer, our mutual promise lingering in the air. Then we opened the doors and got out of the sedan.

I grabbed our luggage while Charlotte checked her phone. "Diego is set up in the surveillance van on the other side of the lake, and Gia says that strike teams have been positioned all around the area, ready to move in when we give the signal."

I fiddled with the sapphire pin in the center of my tie. "Comms check."

"Comms are live, and the signal is good." Gia's voice sounded in my ear. "You two be careful."

Charlotte snorted. "Sure thing, Mom."

Gia's laughter filled my ear.

Charlotte took her suitcase from me, and together we fell in with the stream of people heading toward the far end of the parking lot. Most were dressed in either expensive winter gear or even more expensive suits, just like Charlotte and I were, while the workers sported puffy green jackets bearing Henrika Hyde's personal logo: two large, swooping, interlocking Hs stitched over their hearts in white thread.

Several folks were taking golf carts to the resort, but Charlotte and I trailed after the people walking across a wide stone bridge. Excited chatter filled the air, along with the pleasant buzz of people's auras.

". . . can't wait to try the new desserts in the restaurant . . ."

". . . got to win my money back from last year's casino night . . ."

". . . can't believe these idiots are paying to do a polar-bear plunge for charity when they could jump in the lake for free . . ."

Charlotte and I reached the other end of the bridge, where more golf carts were waiting to whisk folks to their destinations.

The sprawling Glittertop Resort was about halfway up the steep slope and overlooked the lake that curved around this side of the mountain like a dark blue crescent moon. The resort's hotel was made of gleaming gray stone, dark wood, and acres of glass windows. Walkways led from the central hotel to similar buildings up and down the mountainside like a spider's legs jutting out every which way.

Wide, flat terraces had been carved into the slope and featured everything from restaurants to pools to hot tubs with steam that wisped up into the chilly air. A chairlift churned up the incline, hauling skiers and snowboarders to the top of the mountain, where snow sparkled like a carpet of white diamonds.

According to Section files, the resort used to be a small, family-owned business, until Henrika had swooped in about ten years ago, bought out the family, and spent an obscene amount of money expanding and renovating the guest rooms, ski shops, and more.

Charlotte and I rolled our suitcases up a cobblestone drive-way to the nine-story hotel, which glowed like a gray pearl in the late-afternoon sun. Floor-to-ceiling windows ringed the bottom floor, while crenellated balconies adorned with snarling gargoyles jutted out from the upper levels. The interlocking double-H logo had been carved into one side of the hotel, stretching up more than three stories.

"Henrika's not very subtle, is she?" I murmured as we headed toward the entrance.

Charlotte snorted with derision. "If you looked up the word *ostentatious* in the dictionary, a smiling picture of Henrika would be right next to it."

Glass doors whooshed open at our approach, and Charlotte and I stepped into the lobby. The double-H logo stretched across most of the gray marble floor, while more Hs were stamped into the square columns that supported the ceiling. My steps quickened. I was already tired of seeing that symbol, and I was more than ready to get on with the business of confronting—and killing—Henrika Hyde.

Charlotte and I stepped up to the check-in counter.

"Name, please?" the clerk asked.

"Desmond Macfarlane," I replied.

Since Henrika was auctioning off her Redburn formula, Gia had decided that I should use my most common alias, Desmond Macfarlane, a paramortal arms dealer who bought, sold, and delivered weapons to shady groups and individuals around the world, as well as used them in his own criminal enterprises.

"And you, miss?" the clerk asked.

"Charlotte Locke," she replied in a cool voice.

Charlotte had decided not to use an alias, arguing it was pointless since Henrika already knew exactly who we were. I agreed with her logic, but I still found it hard to abandon my undercover identity.

The clerk tapped a few more keys, then looked up and gave us a wide smile. "Ah, yes! Mr. Macfarlane and Ms. Locke." He practically cooed our names, much friendlier than before. "Ms. Hyde requested that you be put in our most luxurious honeymoon suite."

"Did she, now?" Charlotte said, her voice even cooler than before. "How thoughtful of her."

The clerk wilted a little under her icy glower, but he handed us both keycards stamped with the room number. He snapped his fingers at a nearby bellman, who scurried forward. "Your luggage will be taken to your suite. You are just in time for the cocktail hour Ms. Hyde is hosting for her special guests."

Cocktail hour? Murder party was more like it.

The clerk gestured to the right. "Those guards will escort you to the penthouse."

Two men wearing dark suits stood in front of an elevator tucked into the back corner of the lobby. Each man sported an earbud with a white wire trailing down the back of his neck, and the guns holstered to their belts were clearly visible beneath their open jackets.

The two men were almost as wide as they were tall, with thick, blocky bodies packed with muscle, and bright yellow auras pulsed over their hearts, indicating that they were both paramortals. Enduros, if I had to guess. Henrika seemed to have an endless supply of them.

Charlotte and I handed our luggage off to the bellman, although she kept her purse, which hung off her shoulder. Then we headed over to the guards. One of the men punched a button with a beefy finger, and the elevator opened with a whisper. The other guard jerked his thumb, silently ordering us to step inside. Charlotte and I did as commanded, putting our backs to the wall.

The two guards stepped inside the car, one to the right and one to the left. The first man punched a button, the door slid shut, and the elevator started to rise.

Charlotte and I eyed the two guards, who returned our hostile looks with suspicious stares of their own. The mortal hotel workers might think Charlotte and I were honeymooners, but these two men knew exactly who we were, and they were prepared to attack us—kill us—for the slightest offense.

But nothing happened, and the elevator floated to a stop on the top floor. The door opened, and the two guards backed out, keeping their eyes on us. Charlotte and I followed them.

We stepped into a large foyer. One of the guards gestured

toward the open double doors at the far end, and Charlotte and I headed in that direction. None of us had spoken a word the entire time, and I saw no reason to start now. These men were just pawns Henrika had set on her game board, and sooner or later, I would knock them down to get to the queen.

Charlotte and I stepped through the double doors into a living room. The instant I crossed the threshold, a strong electrical current swept over my body, making the back of my neck tingle. A faint, high-pitched whine also filled my ears.

Charlotte grimaced and rubbed her temples, as though she had a sudden headache. She'd sensed the electrical field too.

I reached out with my galvanism. My phone still had power, but I was willing to bet the signal was being jammed. And my comms were completely dead with no current or charge. The electrical field must have fried the devices. With no energy in those devices for me to manipulate, I couldn't make my comms functionable again. Frustration rippled through me.

Henrika had realized we would be wearing comms and cameras, and she'd taken countermeasures to bug-proof the penthouse so that Gia, Joan, Diego, and the General wouldn't be able to see into her inner sanctum. Section 47 tech was hard to beat, but Henrika had managed it, probably with Bryce's help.

One of the guards moved over to the right and knocked on a set of closed double doors. A muffled voice told him to enter. The guard twisted the handles and threw the doors open.

Together, Charlotte and I moved forward.

The doors led to a massive library that took up most of the penthouse. Gold chandeliers dangled from the high ceiling, and thick rugs in shades of gray and green covered the hardwood floor. Similarly colored leather couches and cushioned chairs were scattered throughout the room. Stained-glass lamps perched on wooden end tables, casting warm pools of colored light down onto crystal bowls filled with pinecones that perfumed the air with a sharp, tangy scent.

Smaller gray marble versions of the snarling gargoyle statues on the outside of the resort flanked a fireplace, and tables filled with food and drinks were set up in the corner. A few books perched on the shelves that marched down one wall, but most of the space was taken up by glass cases filled with rings, necklaces, and bracelets that sparkled and shimmered on colored velvet backdrops. Even some tiaras glittered among the impressive jewelry collection.

A desk holding a laptop, monitor, keyboard, and mouse was situated in front of glass doors that led out to a balcony. A second, even larger desk in the far corner was covered with beakers, burners, test tubes, and other lab equipment, making it look like a mad scientist's workstation.

Anger flooded my veins, and my fingers clenched into fists. I wanted to charge across the room and smash every single beaker and vial to smithereens. Charlotte sidled closer, as if she knew what I was thinking. I breathed in the cool, soothing blue of her aura and steadied myself.

A man and a woman were speaking in soft voices by the glass doors. They broke off their conversation to look at Charlotte and me.

The man was wearing a navy suit that was almost identical to my own, right down to the paisley-patterned vest. My gaze traced over his familiar features—dark brown hair, dark brown eyes, tan skin, and a white scar that slashed through his left eyebrow and down into his cheek.

Bryce Finkley smirked at me, but I ignored him and focused on his boss.

The woman was in her mid-forties, about ten years older than Charlotte and me, and her wide, satisfied smile mirrored Bryce's smirk. Her light brown hair had been pulled up into a high bun, with a couple of pieces left loose to frame her face and draw attention to her pale, luminous skin.

The woman's dark green turtleneck sweater accentuated

the matching color of her eyes, while her pants were a lighter mint green. An old-fashioned gold skeleton key with a square emerald set into the hilt hung from a thick braided gold chain around her neck, as though she was the keeper of a castle. Despite her elegant façade, black flecks swirled through her dark green aura, indicating just how dangerous she was.

We'd finally reached the venomous spider in the center of this gilded web: Henrika Hyde.

SEVENTEEN

CHARLOTTE

Henrika looked Desmond up and down, as though he was a tempting dessert she wanted to sink her teeth into. After a few seconds, she turned and gave me the same slow, appreciative once-over.

"Charlotte," she purred in a light, feminine voice. "I'm so delighted you accepted my invitation. And especially that you brought your plus-one. How lovely to see you again, Desmond."

A muscle twitched in Desmond's jaw, and his fists clenched even tighter. As much as I wanted to reach out and comfort him, I kept my hands to myself. Now was not the time to show any emotion. Henrika had brought us here for a reason, and we needed to survive this initial confrontation, lest our mission end before it truly began.

In the distance, the soft *ding* of the elevator rang out, followed by several sets of footsteps.

Henrika's grin widened. "And the rest of our party has arrived. Excellent! I love it when people show up early. It indicates just how eager they are to acquire my products. I think you'll both find the guest list quite exclusive—and extremely interesting."

Desmond and I moved to the side so that we could see the people entering the library and still keep an eye on Henrika and Bryce.

The first person was a curvy, petite woman with straight black hair that ended in a severe line right above her shoulders. Black shadow highlighted her dark brown eyes, while crimson lipstick did the same for her golden skin. She wore a bright red sweater with black leggings and knee-high boots.

I recognized her from Henrika's video and from Section intelligence reports. Oriana Luzzo, the leader of a Paris-based paramortal gang who dealt in black-market antiques. A strong combusto who liked to use her magic to restore corroded art to its original glory—and liquefy the bones of her enemies. Oriana wasn't carrying any obvious weapons, but she didn't need to, given her magic.

Two men followed her into the library, then split off from each other.

The first man was on the short side with a square, stocky body. His thin brown hair was brushed back from his forehead, while his silver glasses made his blue eyes look even larger and paler than they really were. He was dressed in a thick blue sweater, black pants, and black boots.

Niles Perran, a biomagical chemist from right here in Virginia who specialized in concocting unique poisons to kill paramortals in the most painful ways possible. Rumored to be an enduro with an exceptionally high IQ. No obvious weapons on him either.

The other man was more than a foot taller than Niles, with ice-blue eyes, ruddy skin, and pale blond hair spiked up across his forehead. A thick, dark blue plaid shirt stretched across his wide shoulders, along with a light blue vest that looked like something a hunter would wear. Black cargo pants and hiking boots finished off his ensemble, and a large knife gleamed in a loop on his black leather belt.

Steig Helseth, a Norwegian assassin who enjoyed stalking and terrorizing his victims before he killed them. Another enduro with incredible stamina, speed, and strength.

The two guards who had ushered Desmond and me into the elevator followed Steig into the library and took up positions on either side of the open doors.

Beside me, Desmond's body practically vibrated with worry and wariness. He knew the same uncomfortable truth I did: that the two of us were essentially trapped in this hotel with some of the world's most dangerous paramortals.

Several seconds ticked by in tense, frigid silence as we all sized one another up, searching for weapons—and especially any weaknesses.

Henrika clapped her hands together, and everyone flinched, including Bryce and the two guards. "Silly me! Let's have a round of introductions to break the ice."

She gestured at first one person, then another, including Bryce, saying their names, although she didn't mention their criminal affiliations or paramortal powers.

Finally, Henrika gestured at Desmond and me. "This is Desmond Macfarlane and his better half, Charlotte . . ." Her voice trailed off, and she gave me a challenging look.

"Locke," I replied. "Charlotte Locke."

A smile played across Henrika's lips. My using my real name instead of an alias amused her.

"Charlotte Locke," she finished, then clapped her hands together again. "Now, let's have some fun. Or at the very least, copious amounts of chocolate and alcohol."

She moved over to the chairs and couches in front of the fireplace. Flames crackled behind the black iron grate, adding some much-needed warmth to the drafty library. Silver platters brimming with fresh fruits, cheeses, and other treats were situated on tables along the wall, while champagne flutes and crystal liquor decanters perched on another table.

"Eat, drink," Henrika said. "Have a seat, relax, and warm up by the fire. It's quite cozy, and I'm sure you all must be tired after your long journeys."

"Forget the pleasantries," Niles said, pushing his glasses farther up his nose. "When do we get to see this new weapon that's so deadly? I'm here for it, not to wine and dine and chit-chat with the competition."

Oriana murmured her agreement, while Steig nodded and crossed his arms over his muscled chest. Desmond and I remained still and silent. Bryce shifted forward, putting himself between his boss and her guests, while the two guards by the doors flexed their hands over the guns on their belts. Henrika might have invited the other paramortals here, but this tête-à-tête could still go wrong a dozen different ways.

Henrika plastered another smile on her face, but her green eyes were cold as she looked at Niles. "We might be old acquaintances, but I'm the one hosting this little get-together, so you would do well to remember you are on *my* timeline, Niles."

Everyone glanced back and forth between them, and you could have cut the tension in the air with a spoon.

My research into Henrika over the last few months had extended to all her *old acquaintances*. She and Niles had been in each other's orbit since graduate school, back when they were both getting degrees in everything from biochemistry to engineering to genetics. Over the years, Niles had become one of Henrika's main rivals when it came to creating biomagical weapons, and the two of them were always competing to see how quickly and gruesomely they could kill people with their latest inventions.

Henrika kept staring at Niles, her eyes still cold and hard. Niles looked right back at her, his own gaze sharp and shrewd.

A few more seconds ticked by, then he shrugged. "I was just trying to be efficient."

Niles grabbed a glass of champagne and chugged it down. He exchanged his empty glass for a full one, then started placing food on a plate.

Oriana also took a glass of champagne, then positioned herself in the chair closest to the fireplace.

Steig gripped the massive hunting knife on his belt. His gaze flicked from my throat to my chest to my legs, as though he was thinking about the fastest way to skin me like a rabbit.

Danger-danger-danger, my synesthesia whispered an urgent, unnecessary warning. Revulsion pulsed through me, and I had to grind my teeth to keep from shuddering.

Steig gave Desmond the same serial-killer perusal. Then he frowned. "You look familiar. Have we met before?" he asked, his voice featuring a hint of a Norwegian accent.

"Possibly. I've sold weapons to people all over the world." Desmond jerked his chin at the knife on Steig's belt. "Although I'm guessing you like to take care of your problems the old-fashioned way."

Steig grinned and patted the knife, which had a blade that was longer than my hand. "Sometimes the old ways are the best ways. Clean and simple." He reached up and drew his right index finger across his throat, as if we all didn't understand exactly what he meant.

"But the new, improved ways are so much more *fun*," Henrika chimed in. "Let's have a drink."

She threaded her arm through Steig's and walked him over to the refreshment tables. Desmond and I also drifted in that direction.

The others took their sweet time getting food and drinks, but finally, it was our turn. My stomach was in knots, but I filled a plate with fruits, cheeses, crackers, and some delectable-looking chocolate truffles, although I opted for water instead of champagne. Desmond mirrored my selections, then we both sat on an overstuffed love seat off to the side of the fireplace.

The others had already arranged themselves in a loose semicircle, although everyone maintained a healthy distance from their neighbors.

Niles and Steig gobbled down their food, along with several rounds of champagne, while Oriana eschewed the snacks and delicately sipped from a single glass.

Desmond raised his eyebrows in a silent question, and I nodded. Thanks to my synesthesia, I could tell the food and drinks were not poisoned. Desmond quickly drank his water and polished off his food.

My father had always told me to eat, drink, and sleep whenever possible because I might not get another chance until a mission was over. Even something as simple as downing a glass of water now might keep me alive later, so I forced myself to clean my plate, even though everything tasted like ash and landed like bricks in my stomach.

Henrika nibbled on some strawberries, then picked up her own glass of champagne and stood in front of the fireplace like a queen holding court. "Now, isn't this so much nicer than getting straight down to business? It's so rare I get to entertain these days."

"Yes, I heard you had been having some trouble," Oriana piped up in a snide tone. "That you were running across Europe trying to escape some enemy."

Henrika let out a merry, mocking laugh. "Don't we all have troubles from time to time? It was nothing serious, and the situation will soon be resolved."

She smirked at me over the rim of her glass. My hands

tightened around the plate on my lap, and I resisted the urge to chuck the expensive crystal at her head. Nothing had been *resolved*, and the only reason the Section strike teams hadn't moved in was because Henrika was holding the undercover agent list like a sword over our heads.

"Troubles? How odd, Henny. I thought your mysterious benefactor took care of all your problems," Niles piped up, his voice even more snide than Oriana's.

"Benefactor?" Steig asked in a sharp, suspicious voice. "What benefactor? I thought you were the only one involved in this transaction."

Henrika shrugged off his question. "Redburn is entirely my creation."

Truth, my inner voice whispered.

"Aw, there's no need to be ashamed, Henny," Niles said. "It's okay to admit you've accepted help from others. You took full advantage of your big break way back when, and look at everything you've accomplished since then."

He waved his champagne glass around at the luxe library, although his lips curled back with disgust. I got the sense Niles was wishing he'd gotten that big break instead of Henrika. And who was the mysterious benefactor he kept mentioning?

One of the things I grudgingly admired about Henrika was how she'd used her brains, skills, and determination to pull herself out of poverty and build a pharmaceutical empire, even if a large part of that empire was devoted to hurting others. In all my months of research, I'd never come across anyone giving Henrika money for anything, other than the weapons she invented, but Niles made it sound like someone *else* was responsible for her initial success. Curious.

Henrika's fingers tightened around her glass like she wanted to toss the champagne in Niles's face, but she kept her expression neutral. "You'll have to forgive Niles. The two of us are old friends, and we've competed for several of the same contracts.

I just happen to have been more successful in securing them. Then again, I don't skimp on ingredients, cut down processing times, and hire lackluster talent."

An angry flush stained Niles's cheeks, and he threw back the rest of his drink.

"This is quite a group of bidders you've assembled," Oriana chimed in. "But I'm curious about one thing: Why is *she* here? Because I've never heard of Charlotte Locke."

She looked at me, a clear challenge in her dark eyes. Niles and Steig also stared at me. Henrika watched the proceedings with obvious amusement, as did Bryce. Beside me, Desmond tensed again.

I gave Oriana a flat stare. "I handle Desmond's money. That's all you need to know."

"Oh, yes," Henrika murmured. "Charlotte is quite good with numbers."

She said the words calmly, as though they were a fact that was not up for debate, but something about her tone bothered me. It almost sounded like Henrika *wanted* me to be good with numbers for some reason.

"First, some ground rules," Henrika said. "We're all para-mortals, and each of us is dangerous in his or her own way. But this is my resort, which is currently hosting more than a thousand guests and workers for my annual charity fund-raiser. So no using your abilities where the regular humans can see them—and absolutely no using the humans to amuse yourselves."

She stabbed her finger at Steig. "That is especially true for you, Mr. Helseth. My resort is *not* your latest hunting ground."

Steig let out an aggravated huff. "I suppose I can dial back my expectations for the weekend."

Henrika kept staring at him.

After a few seconds, he harrumphed. "Fine, fine. No hunting humans."

Lie, my inner voice whispered, but I didn't need my synesthesia to know that Steig would go after whoever caught his eye, just like a predator stalking its prey. I held back another shudder.

"And the Redburn formula?" Niles asked, an excited note creeping into his voice. "When do we get to see it in action?"

"I have a few final details to sort out, but everything will be ready tomorrow," Henrika replied. "Everyone will meet in the lobby at eight a.m. to go to the demonstration site."

All three paramortals grumbled at the delay, but Henrika ignored their discontent and gave everyone a bright smile.

"For the moment, you are free to do as you please. Explore the resort, go skiing, get a massage. But I expect you all at my party tonight. Eight o'clock sharp in the grand ballroom. The theme is Casino Night, so wear formal attire and be prepared to play a few games of chance."

Henrika glanced at first one person, then another. All the paramortals gave reluctant nods, including Desmond and me. "Mr. Finkley will show you out. I have work to do."

She drained her champagne, set the empty glass on the fireplace mantel, went to her desk, and sat down. Henrika hit a few keys on her laptop and focused on the monitor, ignoring us.

Oriana left the library without a backward glance, as did Steig. Niles stared at the worktable full of beakers and burners, his gaze flicking from one thing to the next as though he was cataloging the items to concoct his own formula. Then he too left.

Bryce stepped forward, along with the two guards, forming a wall between Desmond and me and Henrika. All three men put their hands on their guns, and Desmond and I couldn't get to the other woman without getting shot.

Frustration surged through me, but I climbed to my feet, as did Desmond. He eyed Bryce like he wanted to try his luck and tackle the other man, but I cleared my throat. This was just the start of the weekend's games, and it wasn't time to make a move against Henrika.

Desmond stared at Bryce a moment longer, then turned his back to the former cleaner and held out his arm to me. Together, the two of us walked out of Henrika's library, leaving our enemies behind—for now.

EIGHTEEN

DESMOND

The two guards followed Charlotte and me out of the library and watched while we got into the elevator. The car glided down and deposited us in the lobby.

"We need to check in with Joan," I murmured. "Fancy a walk outside?"

Now that we had left Henrika's penthouse, we were free of the electrical field that had disrupted our comms, but I doubted the devices were working, since I didn't hear Joan, Gia, or anyone else asking for an update. But I could clearly see the black domes of several security cameras in the lobby, and I had no doubt Bryce had someone watching us.

"Of course, darling," Charlotte replied, raising her voice for the benefit of anyone who might be listening. "Let's take in the sights."

Arm in arm, we ambled through the lobby as though we were just another couple seeing everything the resort had to offer. We did a lap of the first floor, peering into the shops and restaurants. I made a mental note of all the corridors, as well as the entrances and exits. Charlotte glanced around, doing the same thing.

Next, we went outside. This part of the hotel featured several wide stone terraces that stepped down the slope and ended in a lawn that rolled all the way down to the lake. Tennis courts were situated off to the right, as was a golf course, although no one was playing, given the brisk January wind. Copses of trees dotted the lawn before spreading out and forming dense woods that flanked the hotel like armies of tall pine soldiers.

Even though it was just after five o'clock, the Winterfest charity event was already in full swing. Hundreds of people roamed around the terraces, eating, laughing, drinking, and talking. Dozens of game, food, and vendor booths had been set up on the lawn, and people were tossing rings onto bottles, eating cotton candy, and browsing through displays of soaps, lotions, and jewelry.

Charlotte and I stopped on the topmost terrace and looked out over the crowd.

"These people have no idea they're giving their money to a monster," she murmured.

"I thought you said this was a legitimate event to raise money for cancer research."

"It is, which makes me even more curious about why Henrika is hosting it. The tax write-off is nice, but we both know she's not going to all this trouble out of the goodness of her heart."

I snorted. "Henrika doesn't have a heart. Just a cold black diamond where it should be."

A bright glint of glass caught my eye, and I spotted Joan sitting at a table on the terrace below us. A steaming cup was at her elbow, and she was staring into a silver compact as though she was powdering her nose. She tilted the compact to the side so that the glass glinted at me again.

"I see Joan."

Charlotte nodded, but she didn't look in that direction. "Find out if she has any new intel from Gia and Diego. I'm going to study the resort grounds and try to figure out where Henrika might be storing the formula."

"Meet back here in thirty minutes?"

She nodded again, then slipped her arm out of mine and moved away.

I didn't see Oriana, Niles, or Steig on the terraces, but I was sure they would be exploring the resort just like Charlotte and I were. The other paramortals might ostensibly be here to bid on the Redburn formula, but they would also be trying to figure out where Henrika was hiding it, so they could steal a sample instead of coughing up the cash to buy the explosive outright.

I set off at a slow, ambling pace, as though I was enjoying the crisp winter day and the beautiful scenery. A passing waiter offered me a hot chocolate, which I took, although I didn't sample the sugary drink. I wound my way down a set of steps at the far end of the terrace, then strolled back to the center where Joan was sitting. She'd put her compact away and now had her phone held up to her mouth, as though she was talking to someone.

I took a seat at the table beside Joan, although I kept my back to her. Then I set my hot chocolate aside and pulled out my own phone. Now that I was away from Henrika's library, the device was working normally, and I held it up to my ear as though I was also talking to someone.

"Can you hear me?" I asked in a low voice.

"Your actual voice here and now? Yes," Joan replied. "But Charlotte's and your comms got fried the second you stepped into Henrika's penthouse, and they haven't come back online. No picture, no sound, nothing. Diego is trying to find a work-around, but no luck so far."

Frying our comms was an expected move on Henrika's part, although I'd been hoping Diego's cleverness would win out.

"What room are you in? Henrika put us in the honeymoon suite. Eighth floor. Room four."

Joan huffed. "Cute. You've got to admit she's got a twisted sense of humor."

"Lucky us," I muttered.

Joan murmured her room number, which I committed to memory. I also told her about Henrika's orders for Charlotte and me to attend Casino Night and report to the lobby at eight a.m. tomorrow for the Redburn demonstration.

"What have you found so far?" I asked.

"Lots of rich, important, influential folks here, paramortal and otherwise," Joan said. "My comms and cameras are still working, so I've been sitting here getting shots of all the guests so that Diego can run them through facial recognition."

"I've got some names to add to his list: Oriana Luzzo, Niles Perran, and Steig Helseth. They showed up, just like Henrika said they would in her video message."

Joan let out a low whistle. "Those are some heavy hitters."

"Yes, they are. Bryce Finkley is here too."

"He's still working for Henrika?"

"Apparently so," I muttered again. "Looks like he is her current head of security."

Joan let out another low whistle. "No wonder Henrika was able to disable your comms. Bryce has probably told her everything he knows about Section 47 tech, weapons, and procedures."

Anger filled me, but Bryce Finkley wasn't the first cleaner to leave Section 47 and sell his services to the highest bidder. Over the years, I'd been sent to eliminate more rogue cleaners than I cared to remember, and if I got the chance, I would take Bryce down too. Not just for selling out Section but for killing that innocent hostage all those years ago.

"I'm not nearly as worried about Bryce as I am about Oriana, Niles, and Steig. They all have the resources to bid millions of dollars for the Redburn formula—and the magic to kill the competition to get their hands on it."

"You don't think everyone is going to play nice?" Joan asked.

"Nope. Oriana, Niles, and Steig are probably looking for the formula right now. Even if they don't find it, all bets are off once the demonstration takes place tomorrow morning. After that, it will be a free-for-all. Everyone will be trying to get the weapon, and the other paramortals will kill anyone who gets in their way, including Charlotte and me."

"I'm surprised Henrika didn't blow your cover already," Joan replied.

Me too. I'd been expecting Henrika to gleefully announce who Charlotte and I really were the second the other paramortals had entered the penthouse. Henrika would have taken great pleasure in watching us battle the other paramortals, but she'd kept quiet. So had Bryce. No doubt Henrika was saving the information about our true identities to use when it would benefit her and endanger Charlotte and me the most.

I scrubbed a hand through my hair. "Charlotte was right. Henrika is playing a game with us, but damned if I know what it is. She's playing it with Oriana, Niles, and Steig too, and we're all just her bloody puppets."

Joan fell silent, although I could hear her texting, sending the names to Diego. "I'll see if I can figure out if the other paramortals want the formula for themselves or if they're bidding on behalf of someone else."

More worry shot through me. "You think one of them might be working for the Syndicate?"

Like most folks, I'd thought the Syndicate was a myth until a few months ago. Miriam Lancaster had claimed to have information about the shadowy group, although that info had died when I'd shot the charmer to save Charlotte. Learning more about the Syndicate was another one of her father's causes Charlotte had taken up and another mystery she was determined to solve.

"No idea," Joan replied. "I didn't think the Syndicate even existed, but you and Charlotte have convinced me. Either way, Henrika is here right now, and we need to take her out."

Joan paused, and when she spoke again, her voice was pitched much lower than before. "We *have* to take her out, Dez. For Graham."

"For Graham," I replied in a soft voice, although I had to force out the words through the knot of guilt lodged in my throat.

I thought back to all the smug looks Henrika had given Charlotte and me in the penthouse. Red-hot anger hit me again, and my hand curled around my phone hard enough to make the plastic creak in protest. If Charlotte hadn't been in the penthouse, I would have thrown caution to the wind and gone after Henrika, no matter how many guards were between us.

"Can you go quiet for a moment?" I asked.

"Sure." Joan typed a few buttons on her phone. "My comms are offline. Go ahead."

I drew in a breath, then let it out, along with my confession. "The General has ordered me to kill Henrika the first chance I get."

Even though I couldn't see her, I could still feel Joan's aura pulsing with surprise. "That's not listed in the official mission file."

"You know my father is too smart to put an order like that in the mission file."

Joan snorted her agreement.

"I'm not sure . . ." My voice trailed off, but once again, I forced out the words. "I'm not sure I can kill Henrika. At least, not right away."

"Why not?" Joan growled.

"Killing Henrika might trigger some doomsday protocol she has in place to release the undercover agent list, or blow the resort sky-high, or both. As much as I want to avenge Graham,

I don't want to get anyone else killed, and I couldn't live with myself if the UC list fell into the wrong hands." I let out a bitter laugh. "I can barely live with myself as it is right now."

"What happened to Graham was *not* your fault, Dez," Joan said in a low, fierce voice. "He loved you like a brother, and he wanted you to live, even if he couldn't. That's why he told you to use your galvanism to take his strength and save yourself. I knew Graham better than anyone, so I know he wouldn't blame you for *any* of this. Not one little *bit* of it "

"I know," I replied, my own voice thick and raspy with emotion. "If Graham were here, he'd clap me on the back and tell me I did the right thing. But knowing that doesn't make what I did to him any easier to bear."

We both fell silent. Even though I wasn't facing Joan, I could still feel her aura pulsing with the same cold sorrow that was coursing through my own veins, as though they were filled with a sluggish river of ice instead of warm blood.

I cleared my throat. "I'll do my best to get justice for Graham. As soon as Charlotte and I get any sort of leverage on Henrika, we'll use it to get her to turn over the UC list. Once she does that, we can start planning how to take her down."

"I know you'll do your best, Dez," Joan replied in a low, strained voice. "That's all any of us can do."

Once again, that cold, heavy, sorrow-filled silence dropped over the two of us.

Joan scooted her chair back, making the metal scrape against the stone. "Someone's approaching Charlotte. Topmost terrace, on your three o'clock."

I turned my head to the side so I could see Charlotte, who was leaning against the stone railing almost directly above me. To everyone else, she probably looked like she was admiring the view, but her eyes flicked back and forth, indicating that she was analyzing and cataloging everything around her.

For a moment, I didn't see who Joan was talking about. Then

a group of people stepped aside, and I spotted Niles Perran making a beeline toward Charlotte, two champagne glasses clutched in his hands.

"That's Perran," I muttered.

"What do you think he wants with Charlotte?" Joan asked.

"Nothing good."

"Be careful, Dez," Joan muttered out of the side of her mouth, then got to her feet and strode away.

"You too, Joan."

I stood up and slid my phone back into my pocket as though I had finished my call. Then I headed for the nearest set of steps. I needed to reach Charlotte before Niles Perran did.

NINETEEN

CHARLOTTE

Desmond wandered down to a lower terrace to meet with Joan, who looked like every other rich person at the resort, right down to her expensive clothes, designer purse, and the vaguely bored, disdainful look on her face.

My estimation of the liaison went up several notches. Not only could Joan pick out disguises for others, but she could inhabit them as well as any undercover agent. If I hadn't known Joan was a Section spy, I never would have given her a second glance.

While Desmond sat down, fiddled with his phone, and pretended not to talk to Joan, I strolled along the topmost terrace, comparing the resort grounds to all the photos, maps, and blueprints I'd crammed into my brain over the past few hours ever since the Winterfest mission had been greenlit.

The terraces, lawn, tennis courts, and golf course looked exactly the same as they did in the pictures, only more brown and barren in the January cold. I peered at the woods in the distance, but I only saw trees, trees, and more trees. No flashing signs magically appeared that said *Top-secret biomagical weapon hidden here!*

I sighed. Sometimes I thought my synesthesia only worked when it wanted to, rather than me controlling it. My magic spent far more time highlighting mundane dangers, like the uneven terrace steps, than showing truly important things, like where Henrika was storing the Redburn formula.

Another thing I grudgingly admired about Henrika was her work ethic. She had labs at Hyde Engineering facilities around the U.S., as well as in other countries, and I was certain she had one tucked away here too. My gaze strayed back toward the woods, which would be a great place to hide a lab from prying eyes.

The resort sprawled across several thousand acres, much of it heavily wooded. Section satellite scans hadn't picked up any suspicious structures in the rugged terrain, but nothing was foolproof, and Henrika might have found a way to camouflage her lab. Or maybe I was wrong, and Henrika didn't have a lab on-site. Maybe her evil lair was hidden at the bottom of a tropical ocean or inside a dormant volcano or on a deserted island. Maybe I was wasting my time trying to find it when I should be figuring out how to get the undercover agent list.

"We have to stop meeting like this," a low, familiar voice drawled. "Or your boy Slick might get jealous."

I kept my body facing out toward the woods, even as my gaze slid to the right.

Gabriel was standing a few feet away, his hand on the low wall, as though he too was admiring the view. Even for a cleaner, Gabriel was exceptionally stealthy, and I hadn't even heard his footsteps on the stone. If I'd been one of his targets, I would have already been on the ground bleeding out while he strolled away whistling.

"When I texted you about the mission earlier, I didn't think you would show up in person," I drawled right back at him. "First Germany and now here. I'm starting to think you don't like to take vacations by yourself."

Gabriel chuckled, although I was the only one close enough to hear his laughter. "I couldn't let you and Slick have all the fun of taking down Henrika. Besides, if this goes anything like the Tannenbaum mission did, the two of you are going to need my help."

He was probably right about that. We'd been here less than two hours, and my synesthesia kept muttering that Desmond and I were in serious danger, not just from Henrika but also from the other paramortals.

"How did you get onto the resort grounds? I thought Winterfest was invitation only." A thought occurred to me. "Wait a second. Is this your mystery woman at work again? Did Nemesis send you here?"

Gabriel held up his phone and pretended to take a photo of the gorgeous view. "Nope. I haven't heard a peep from Nemesis since Christmas Day, just like I told you at the diner last night. And I got here the usual way—I called in a favor. One of my clients had some extra tickets. He mentioned them a few weeks ago. He and his wife couldn't make it, so I came in their place."

"And Henrika's guards just let you waltz into the lobby?"

A wry grin curved the corner of Gabriel's mouth. "My fake ID might have helped matters, along with the generous tips I've been doling out to every worker who so much as looks at me."

I rolled my eyes. You could take the cleaner out of Section 47, but you couldn't separate him from his fake IDs. Even if the guards had stopped him, Gabriel still would have found some way to sneak in. And once on the grounds, he could go anywhere he wanted, thanks to his phasing ability.

"Things must be pretty boring in the private sector for you to crash another spy mission."

"Absolutely," Gabriel agreed. "I might have hated Section rules and regulations, but hearing my clients whine about the smallest, most inane things is even worse." He closed his eyes and tilted his face up to the winter sun. "Besides, it will be good for me to get out of the office for a while. Get some fresh air, commune with nature, indulge in a massage or three."

I stared out over the terraces, wrestling with the guilt that had taken up residence in the pit of my stomach. I'd done my homework on Henrika, and I was willing to bet she'd done the same on me, which meant she probably knew exactly who Gabriel was and how much I cared about him.

I hated that Gabriel had come here and put himself in danger, but he was loyal to a fault, and nothing I said would persuade my friend to leave so long as he thought Desmond and I were in trouble. And Desmond and I *were* in trouble, surrounded by enemies on all sides and with no idea what Henrika was really plotting.

Maybe it was cold and calculating of me, but Gabriel was here, so I might as well let him watch our backs. Besides, I trusted Gabriel, and the same could *not* be said for Jethro Percy. The General was probably monitoring drone and satellite footage of the resort right now, just itching to send in the Section strike teams as soon as possible. Despite the innocent civilians on-site, Percy wouldn't hesitate to storm the resort if it meant killing Henrika and getting his hands on the Redburn formula.

Gabriel opened his eyes and pretended to take another photo with his phone. "Who's that with your boy Slick?"

My gaze drifted down to the terrace below us. "Joan Samson, a Section liaison. She's worked with Desmond before. Graham Walker too, before he was killed. Joan and Graham were . . . close."

"Do you trust her?" Gabriel asked.

"Desmond trusts her."

He snorted. "That's not an answer, Char. Unless the answer is no."

Gabriel was right. I didn't trust Joan. I didn't *not* trust her either, but something about her nagged at me. Some little thing Joan had said or done over the past two days was pinballing around in my mind, although I couldn't nail down what it was and why it was so important.

I pretended to pick a loose thread off my sweater. "After I figured out Miriam Lancaster and Trevor Donnelly were moles, I did a deep dive into everyone at Section headquarters. From what I can tell, Joan Samson is clean as a whistle, but I thought Miriam was clean too. So I'll trust Joan, but I'll also watch her, just in case she tries to stab me in the back like Miriam did."

"Might not be a bad idea for me to keep an eye on her too," Gabriel suggested. More than a little interest sparked in his light brown eyes.

I groaned. "Oh, no. You want to keep an eye on Joan because she is precisely your type."

"And what, exactly, is *my type*?"

"Smart, clever, strong, attractive, and, most important of all, unattainable. Joan is by the book, and you are not, and we both know you love the thrill of the chase."

Gabriel grinned. "Unattainable? Clearly, you haven't been paying attention to my many charms."

I snorted. "Oh, I've seen your *charms* up close and personal, especially the messy aftermath they leave behind. I distinctly remember you dating my high school and college friends like they were different flavors of candy you were sampling."

Gabriel's grin widened. "What can I say? I'm just irresistible to some folks."

Somehow I bit back another groan. Gabriel practically oozed confidence, although I thought Joan would be far more resistant to his so-called charms than he realized, especially since she was still mourning Graham Walker.

"While you're keeping an eye on Joan, do me a favor. Nose around, and see if you can find anything that might tell us where Henrika's lab is. Desmond and I need to get our hands on any samples of Redburn she might have here. Maybe we can trade the samples for the UC list and avert at least one catastrophe this weekend."

Gabriel nodded. "I'll see what I can do. Might be harder than you think, though. Even with my phasing ability, this place is huge and crawling with guards."

He was right. Dozens of men and women in dark suits with guns on their belts and earpieces trailing down their necks were patrolling the terraces. Henrika wasn't taking any chances with her safety, which made me wonder yet again why she'd come out of hiding and invited Desmond and me to her resort. What did she want from us?

"Incoming," Gabriel muttered. He pretended to take another photo, then wandered away.

"Ah, there you are," a voice crooned. "I've been looking for you, Charlotte."

Niles Perran strode over to me. I didn't have Desmond's galvanist ability to see and interpret auras, but something about the biomagical chemist repelled me on a deep, instinctual level. Even more telling, my synesthesia surged to life and painted his entire body a bright, bloody red, like a firecracker about to explode.

"Care for some champagne?" Niles held out a glass.

I looked at it, and a faint pink haze bloomed in the depths of the shimmering liquid. For a moment, I thought it was pink champagne, but then I realized the color was my synesthesia warning me about some hidden danger in the sparkling bubbles. Niles had definitely added a little something extra to the champagne. Maybe a truth serum to get me to spill my guts about Desmond's supposed fortune—or a poison to knock me out of the Redburn auction.

Anger flared in my chest, but I knew better than to reveal anything about my magic, so I tamped down the emotion, took the glass, and set it on the wall that cordoned off the terrace from the drop below.

"Thank you, but my thirst has been quenched for the moment."

Niles's lips flattened out into a thin line, but he didn't suggest I take a drink. He must have known that would have made me even more suspicious.

"Of course," he murmured, taking a hearty swig from his own glass. "The champagne was just an excuse to talk to you. Things were quite tense in Henrika's library, and I thought it would be nice to get to know each other better."

His pale blue gaze trailed down my body, moving from my throat to my chest to my legs just as Steig Helseth's had done earlier. But instead of gripping a knife like the assassin had, Niles wet his lips, leaned closer, and drew in a breath, as though he was trying to get a whiff of any perfume I might be wearing. More revulsion crashed over me. Niles wouldn't hunt me down like an animal the way Steig would, but he was still a dangerous predator.

"Why would you want to get to know me better?"

Niles shrugged. "I got the impression you weren't happy to be here."

"I go where Desmond and his business take me. That's my job."

"Yes, Mr. Macfarlane has *quite* the reputation. Why, if some of the gossip is to be believed, he has a special friend like you in every city around the world."

I laughed. "Is that some piss-poor attempt to make me jealous? Please. Desmond and I have an arrangement that suits us both just fine."

"A woman like you deserves an arrangement that is more than *just fine*." Niles wet his lips again, and his gaze roamed up and down my body, as if he was seeing straight through my clothes to my curves underneath. His open, lecherous perusal made my skin crawl.

Suddenly, I remembered something else I'd read about Niles Perran: the biomagical chemist had a habit of dating women who later ended up dead, usually from some severe, mysterious, and previously unknown allergic reaction. I repressed a shudder. I'd been so worried about Henrika murdering us that I hadn't given much thought to how the other paramortals might want to play with Desmond and me for their own twisted amusement.

Niles stepped even closer. His breath washed over my face in a warm, fetid wave, and I had to bite my tongue to keep from gagging. Someone had had way too many garlic crackers earlier.

"You know, Charlotte, we could always go somewhere more private and . . . talk." Niles dropped his high, nasally voice to what he probably thought was a low, husky growl, but it sounded more like a dying hyena.

"Talk about what?"

"How unhappy you are with Desmond." He cooed another wave of garlic breath into my face. "And how much happier *I* could make you. I'm *very* good at keeping women satisfied."

I blinked a few times. Despite all my Section training, I honestly did not know how to respond to his boast without laughing, cursing, or inflicting a large amount of violence on him.

Niles took my blank look for encouragement and leaned in a little more. If he got any closer, he'd be wearing my sweater like it was his own. "Since we're being so friendly, maybe you can tell me why Desmond wants the Redburn formula so badly. From what I've heard, guns and missiles are more his style, not biomagical explosives."

Niles latched onto my elbow like a cobra striking a mouse. He was quicker than he looked, and his grip was surprisingly strong. He definitely had some enduro magic to go along with his high IQ.

I tensed, contemplating the quickest—and most painful—
way to remove his hand from my body. I hadn't always enjoyed
my father's relentless training, but it was useful when dealing
with unwanted attention.

A shadow fell over Niles like a storm cloud sweeping across
a field, and a faint crackle of static electricity rubbed up against
my skin. I shivered, welcoming the sensation.

Desmond stepped up beside me and glared at Niles with
barely restrained fury. In that moment, he looked eerily similar
to General Percy. "Take your hand off Charlotte," he growled.
"Or I'll break your fingers one by one."

Niles scoffed at Desmond, completely unconcerned by the
cold menace rippling off the cleaner in palpable waves. Arrogant idiot.

Out of the corner of my eye, I noticed a couple of people
looking in our direction, sensing the brewing drama. Some of
Henrika's guards were also watching us. Well, if they wanted a
show, I was more than happy to give them one.

"It's okay, darling," I replied in a breezy tone. "I'm more
than happy to break Mr. Perran's fingers myself. In fact, I
would prefer it."

Niles's gaze swung back to me. Instead of being cowed, a
lewd smile spread across his face, and he tightened his grip.
"So you like it rough, huh? So do I."

I smiled at the disgusting creep, picked up the glass he had
given me earlier, and tossed the champagne into his face.

Niles sucked in a strangled breath and staggered back, finally releasing my arm. I watched him carefully, but his skin
didn't start blistering and burning with whatever drug he'd
slipped into the champagne. What a shame.

"You looked like you needed to cool off," I said. "If that
doesn't work, go jump in the lake until your dick shrivels up
like a raisin and your balls fall off from frostbite."

Champagne dripped off Niles's glasses and spattered onto

his clothes. An angry flush swept up his neck and stained his cheeks a bright crimson. "You bitch!" he hissed. "You're going to pay for that!"

"No, I'm not," I replied in a calm voice. "Weasels like you only target people they think are weaker than they are. And I am *not* weak, Niles. You would do well to remember that."

I turned to Desmond. "Let's head back to our room, darling. I want to take a nap."

Desmond grinned, and his eyes glowed with pride as he held out his arm. I took it, and together we left the still-sputtering Niles behind.

TWENTY

DESMOND

Charlotte and I went back into the hotel, got into an elevator, and rode up to the eighth floor, one level down from Henrika's penthouse.

We stopped in front of a door with a brass nameplate that read *Honeymoon Suite*. Charlotte studied the electronic lock, then peered at the wooden door. Her eyes glittered with magic, as did her aura. After a few seconds, she shook her head, indicating that no one had tampered with the lock and was waiting inside to surprise us.

I held up a finger, silently asking Charlotte to wait, then swiped my keycard across the reader and went in first. Bryce loved ambushing people just when they thought they were safe, and I wanted to make sure he hadn't set up any nasty surprises in our suite.

A short corridor opened into an area with a large kitchen and an even larger living room. The back wall was made of glass and offered a sweeping view of the resort grounds, and a door led out to a stone balcony with a table for two. Off to the right, an open door led to a master bedroom with an attached bathroom.

No trip wires were strung across the floor, and I didn't spot any other booby traps, either with my eyes or with my galvanism. "Clear."

Charlotte stepped into the suite and closed and locked the door. She came into the living room and glanced around, her lips curling back with disgust. "It looks like a bridal suite. Henrika is really playing up the honeymoon angle."

All the chair and couch cushions were white and accented with red heart-shaped throw pillows. A bottle of champagne was chilling in a silver bucket filled with ice on the white marble kitchen island, next to a white wicker gift basket full of chocolates. Red rose petals had been scattered over the floor leading into the bedroom, and more rose petals were strewn across the bed, looking like blood drops staining the white comforter.

"Henrika probably thinks she's being clever," I said.

Charlotte shook her head. "Henrika *is* clever—clever enough to get us here and tie our hands, waiting to see what she does next."

"Then let's untie them."

Charlotte nodded, and we went into the bedroom. Our luggage was sitting on a bench at the foot of the bed, and we unzipped our bags.

All the guns and knives were still hidden in my suitcase's secret compartment. My comms-filled watches, cufflinks, and tie pins were still in their velvet boxes, along with the innocuous-looking toiletry gadgets Joan had packed from the Section armory. Nothing was missing, but the clothes and other items were slightly jumbled, indicating that someone had pawed through the suitcase.

Charlotte let out an annoyed huff. She tilted her head, and I followed her into the living room. Charlotte opened the glass door, and we stepped outside onto the balcony. I shut the door behind us.

"Someone went through my luggage," I said. "Probably Bryce, seeing what Section toys we brought. He would recognize most of the items from his own time as a cleaner. But he didn't take or tamper with anything, and I didn't sense any cameras or listening devices in the suite with my galvanism."

Charlotte nodded. "They went through my things too, but they didn't plant any bugs. And everything in the suite is perfectly normal. Just cheesy and cliché."

"You sound worried about that."

"I am. If Bryce and his men had planted bugs, we could disable them, but Henrika doesn't seem to care about spying on us." She chewed on her lower lip. "I'm worried Henrika has something much worse in mind."

"Me too," I muttered. "And that's not our only problem."

I told Charlotte what Joan had said about our comms getting fried the moment we'd stepped into Henrika's library. "Joan can keep an eye on us whenever we're in the public areas, but she won't be able to see or hear any of our meetings with Henrika behind closed doors."

Charlotte nodded. "I expected as much, but someone might be able to help Joan with her surveillance." She paused. "Gabriel's here."

"What? How did he get here? I thought the charity event was invitation only." My eyes narrowed. "Did Nemesis send him? Like she did at Tannenbaum Castle?"

Charlotte shook her head. "No. Gabriel says he hasn't heard from Nemesis since Christmas, and I believe him." A reluctant grin spread across her face. "Apparently, Gabriel wrangled an invitation from one of his clients, and he's been tipping every worker to overlook the fact that his name isn't on the guest list."

I might not have known Gabriel Chase very long, but Charlotte's friendship meant a great deal to him. Gabriel's deep regard and concern for Charlotte was something I admired about him. The cocky, arrogant attitude not so much, especially since it was so similar to my own cleaner persona.

"Gabriel is going to nose around and see if he can figure out where Henrika might be storing the Redburn formula," Charlotte said. "With his phasing ability, Gabriel can access a lot of places we can't, especially since we have to attend Henrika's party."

My phone chirped, and I pulled it out and read the message. *Update. Now.*

"Something wrong?" Charlotte asked.

"The General wants an update."

She huffed. "Update? Please. He wants to know if you've found anything we can use as leverage against Henrika so he can send in the strike teams to take her down."

"Not exactly," I muttered.

Charlotte frowned at the sour note in my voice. I hesitated, but Charlotte was risking her life on this mission, and she deserved to know what my father really wanted. Even more than that, I wanted to tell her the truth, no matter how ugly it was.

"Before we left headquarters, the General called me into his office. A source sent him a photo confirming Henrika is storing Redburn at the resort, although the source doesn't know the location of her lab." I paused. "The General also gave me some secondary orders."

Charlotte's eyebrows shot up. "What kind of secondary orders?"

"Find and recover as many samples of Redburn as possible, then destroy the others." I drew in a breath and let it out, along with the rest of my confession. "And kill Henrika as soon as possible."

She blinked a few times, but her surprise quickly faded away. "What about the UC list?"

"The General thinks losing a few undercover agents is an

acceptable trade for getting a sample of Redburn and eliminating Henrika."

My voice was calm, but anger churned in my gut at my father for being such a power-hungry bastard and doing nothing to stop Henrika before now. But that emotion was quickly drowned out by the soul-crushing guilt I still felt over Graham's death and that I hadn't already found a way to avenge him and kill Henrika. A sharp sense of duty to protect the UC agents also throbbed in my side, like a dull knife slowly grinding deeper and deeper into my ribs.

Charlotte laid a hand on my arm. "Hey, it's okay. I wouldn't blame you if you did exactly as General Percy ordered and took out Henrika as soon as possible. I know how badly she hurt you and Graham."

Charlotte had witnessed more than a few of my recurring nightmares about the Blacksea mission. I'd woken up sweating and screaming in bed next to her more times than I cared to remember, although Charlotte always soothed me back to sleep, something I appreciated more than she knew.

I shook my head. "But if I take out Henrika, you won't get any answers about your father's death. I would never take that chance away from you."

"I know, but Henrika might not give you—or me—a choice," Charlotte replied. "If she threatens us, we might have to kill her just to survive."

A thoughtful look filled her face. "Besides, Henrika says she knows something about my father's death, but there's no telling how valuable her information is. She might think she knows more than she actually does."

"And recovering the Redburn formula?" I asked in a low voice. "We both know the General will add it to his own arsenal of weapons, and he won't hesitate to unleash it on his enemies."

Charlotte nodded. "That's exactly what General Percy will do, so you need to decide what *you* will do, Desmond. And what you can live with when it comes to your father, his orders, and how many undercover agents and other people might get hurt because of them." Her hand tightened on my arm, even as her face and aura softened with sympathy. "But no matter what happens, on this mission or any other, I'll always be right here, Dundee. Just you and me now, remember?"

My heart squeezed at her echoing my words from when we'd arrived at the resort. I stepped forward, leaned down, and rested my forehead against hers. "And I'm so glad you're here with me, Numbers."

Charlotte stroked her hand down my chest, and the heat of her fingers soaked through my vest and shirt. My breath and my body quickened at her touch, the way they always did, but for the first time, I realized just how snugly she held my heart in the palm of her hand.

Somehow, without my even realizing it, I had fallen hard and fast for Charlotte Locke.

In that moment, I reaffirmed my primary mission, one I set above all others. No matter what happened this weekend, whom I had to piss off or whom I had to kill, I would keep Charlotte safe from Henrika, Bryce, the other paramortal criminals, and, most of all, my father.

The cold chased us inside, and Charlotte and I got ready for Casino Night.

I donned a classic black tuxedo Joan had picked out, although I opted for a vest instead of the traditional cummerbund. I tucked a gun in the small of my back, strapped a knife to my left forearm, and slid my feet into shiny black wing tips with reinforced steel toes and heels that would let me break ankles and crush bones.

I tucked my silver watch with its long chain into a pocket on my vest and put on some black onyx cuff links. Each cuff link contained standard comms equipment, although I was betting Bryce would find a way to disable them again.

I tugged my sleeves into place, then went into the living room.

Charlotte was eyeing her own reflection in a mirror on the wall. She was wearing a forest-green gown with a plunging neckline that clung to her curves in all the right places. A slit up the side of the sequined fabric teased a hint of her toned leg, while silver stilettoes with steel toe tips covered her feet.

Charlotte had piled her hair on top of her head, and her smooth auburn locks gleamed underneath the lights. Smoky shadow brought out her dark blue eyes, while plum lipstick enhanced her lips.

I let out a low whistle. "You look amazing."

Charlotte smiled at me in the mirror. "So do you. Very chic and sleek, with massive James Bond vibes. Maybe I should start calling you 007."

I chuckled at her teasing, then trailed my fingers down her neck and along her collarbone. Charlotte shivered at the gentle touch, and I dropped my hand to her waist and pulled her back against my body so that I could feel her soft curves molding against me. The heat of her body soaked into mine, and my dick immediately took notice.

"I wish we could stay here for the rest of the night," I whispered.

Charlotte looked at me in the mirror again, heat shimmering in her eyes. "Me too."

I sighed with regret, then pressed a kiss to the side of Charlotte's neck and stepped back.

She turned to face me, reached up, and adjusted my bow tie. Charlotte skimmed her fingers across the stubble on my jaw, and I bent forward and lowered my lips to hers. It was a soft, gentle kiss, just a brief brush of my lips against hers, but it electrified every single cell in my body as though I was gripping a live power line.

I wanted nothing more than to keep kissing Charlotte, to sink into her touch and body and scent and aura until I didn't know where I left off and she began. But I couldn't ignore the dull knife of duty still grinding into my ribs, so I brushed my lips across hers again, then reluctantly drew back.

"Rain check?" I murmured.

"Absolutely," Charlotte whispered.

She tweaked my bow tie a final time, then grabbed her purse and threaded her arm through mine. Together, we left the suite.

We got into an elevator, rode down to the ground floor, and went to the grand ballroom. Even by the hotel's luxurious standards, the ballroom was impressive. In keeping with the Winterfest theme, white lights had been wrapped around enormous silver snowflakes that dangled from the ceiling and twirled around like disco balls. More lights wrapped around live pine trees that had been sprayed with white glitter to give them a snowy look, while ice sculptures shaped like snowflakes, trees, and skis towered on green marble columns.

Several folks were perusing the selection of food, but the main attractions were the poker tables, roulette wheels, and other gaming stations that stretched across the ballroom. Even though it was just after eight o'clock, Casino Night was already in full swing, and people in gowns and tuxedos were playing, laughing, and losing their money, while waiters fetched them round after round of drinks. The *ching-ching-ching* of slot machines filled the air, along with the occasional yelp of excitement and the tinkling of coins when someone hit a jackpot.

"How much money does Henrika usually raise for her cancer charity?" I asked.

"Last year, it was more than ten million dollars," Charlotte replied. "But given how many people are here, she could easily double that amount."

The two of us strode forward, keeping to the outskirts of the ballroom and weaving our way around the crowd.

Joan was standing at a high table and clutching a half-drunk glass of champagne. The liaison was dressed in a silver gown with long crystal strands that looked like icicles, and her black hair hung loose around her shoulders.

An older man with a bushy gray beard was also standing at the high table, talking and gesturing, but Joan ignored him and glanced over to her right. She took a sip of champagne, but the motion didn't quite hide her deep frown.

I followed her gaze and spotted Gabriel chatting with a waitress. The former cleaner noticed Joan watching him and gave her a saucy wink. Joan rolled her eyes and turned back to the bearded man who was still chatting at her.

"There's Henrika," Charlotte murmured.

She tilted her head to the side. A set of stairs in the corner led up to a second level that jutted out over the center of the ballroom. Henrika was leaning a hip against the glass railing, clutching a champagne flute, and looking out over the crowd below like a queen on a throne. She was wearing a long red-sequined gown, and an actual diamond tiara was nestled in her light brown hair, adding to the queenly illusion. A diamond choker glittered around her throat, a matching bracelet flashed on her right wrist, and rings glittered on most of her fingers.

Henrika saluted us with her glass before crooking her index finger in a clear command. I hated being at Henrika's beck and call, but we didn't have a choice, so I led Charlotte over to the stairs. The instant we reached the upper level, a familiar electrical field swept over my body, indicating that our comms had once again been fried.

"Desmond, Charlotte," Henrika crooned. "Don't you both look splendid."

Her green gaze landed on the snowflake brooch pinned to Charlotte's gown, and her crimson lips curved into a knowing smirk. "Although you must get Desmond to buy you some *real* jewels, darling, instead of those cheap crystal imitations. Such things always tend to . . . loose their luster and fritz out at the most inopportune times."

Charlotte tensed, and I had to clench my jaw to keep from sniping back. Henrika knew the brooch contained Section comms, which had once again been disabled.

"Come join us," Henrika said, although it was another clear command.

She spun around on her red stilettoes and strutted over to a poker table in the center of this level. Henrika dropped into the seat at one end of the table. Niles was sitting beside her, yanking at the collar of his ill-fitting navy tuxedo jacket. In contrast, Steig's black plaid tuxedo jacket was so tight and fitted it looked like it was about to rip open trying to cover his wide shoulders. Oriana was on the other side of Steig, wearing a pink dress with a puffy skirt that looked like a ballerina's tutu.

A dealer in a green shirt, bow tie, and tuxedo vest was perched on the other side of the table, a deck of cards in her hand.

"Would one of you care to join our game?" Henrika asked, gesturing at the empty seat directly opposite hers.

"Go ahead, darling," I said. "We both know you're the better gambler."

I kissed Charlotte's cheek and pulled out the chair. She dropped into it, and I squeezed her shoulder, letting her know I was watching her back. Then I headed over to the bar. Silver platters of food had been set out, but I ignored the spread and ordered a sparkling water.

Bryce was standing at the opposite end of the bar, and four guards were spaced along the rest of the balcony floor. All the guards were paramortals, and all were sporting at least one gun under their tuxedo jackets. Frustration pounded through me, but I couldn't make a move against them, not with hundreds of innocent bystanders milling around the ballroom below.

Bryce grabbed a glass of whiskey, then swaggered over to me. "Desmond."

"Bryce."

Each of us took a drink, eyeing each other over the rims of our glasses. Just like the other guards, Bryce was also carrying a gun under his tuxedo jacket, and I was willing to bet he had another holstered to his ankle and at least one knife tucked away somewhere, just as he had on all the Section missions we'd been on together. Old habits die hard for assassins.

I studied the energy radiating off his body, along with his aura, which was the dark, sour yellow of a rotten lemon. Bryce was as powerful as ever, and his enduro strength, speed, and stamina made him a formidable enemy. He was easily the most dangerous of Henrika's men, and I'd have to be on constant guard around him. Unlike the other paramortals, Bryce didn't need a gun, knife, poison, or explosive to kill me. He could easily beat me to death with his fists and feet.

Bryce leaned against the bar and angled his body so he could see both me and the poker table. I mimicked his relaxed posture.

"When Henrika first told me about her plan to invite you here, I didn't think you'd be stupid enough to actually show up, Dez," he said. "But I see you're still doing Daddy's dirty work, no questions asked."

"And now you're doing Henrika's. You've come down in the world since your time at Section."

"Nah. I just got smart—and rich." Bryce flashed me a wide, toothy smile. "Henrika's paying me enough for this gig to let me retire in style."

"One last job?" I snorted. "How cliché."

"Well, we can't all be a Section Legacy, and not just a mere Legacy but a Percy to boot."

I bristled. I might be a Legacy, a Percy, but I'd sweat, bled, and almost died for Section 47 too many times to count. I'd *earned* my spot as one of the spy group's top cleaners, and I wasn't about to let anyone think otherwise, especially not a piece of scum like Bryce Finkley.

"If you're so jealous of my position, then maybe you shouldn't have killed an innocent hostage, stolen Section resources, and gotten booted out on your ass."

"I eliminated an obstacle to take down a sanctioned target." Anger sparked in his dark brown eyes, and his aura pulsed with bitterness. "No one at Section would have batted an eye at my killing that hostage, except you decided to make it personal and use my face as a punching bag."

Bryce traced his index finger over the scar that slashed through his left eyebrow and down into his cheek. "*You're* the one who crossed the line, Dez. Not me. I just have to look at the result of your actions every day in the mirror."

A surprising amount of guilt churned in my gut. As much as I hated to admit it, he was right. Attacking a fellow cleaner was something you just didn't do, no matter what happened on a mission. But I'd lost control and made a deadly enemy as a result.

"*You're* the one who should have gotten booted out on your ass, but your daddy the General made it all go away." The anger in Bryce's eyes iced over into something darker and much more dangerous, and his aura shimmered with the same hateful emotion. "And for the record, I didn't steal anything from Section. Not one penny. General Percy made up that story to kick me out, all because of *you*."

I didn't have Charlotte's synesthesia, but I could see the conviction pulsing in Bryce's aura. He was telling the truth. He hadn't stolen anything, and he'd gotten kicked out of Section 47 because my father wanted to protect me. Blaming someone for something they didn't do was a classic move from the General's playbook on how to eliminate enemies.

Bryce gave me a thoughtful look. "Do you even realize you're nothing but General Percy's prize assassin? Just a weapon he points at whatever person, place, or thing he wants knocked down?" He raised his hand and shot a mocking finger gun at me.

I flinched, and Bryce smirked, knowing he'd scored a direct hit with that barb.

"Do us both a favor. Be a good little spy, and play along with Henrika, okay, Dez? Because it would be a shame for me to have to kill you before she gets what she wants."

The former cleaner drained the rest of his whiskey, then strode over and took up a position behind Henrika at the poker table.

I remained at the bar, my fingers clenched around my own glass, trying to ignore the uncomfortable truth of Bryce's words, which had punched into my chest like a hail of bullets.

TWENTY-ONE

CHARLOTTE

I laid my green sequined purse on the poker table, angling it so that the camera hidden inside the rhinestone clasp was facing the other paramortals. Given the harsh electrical tingle that had swept over me earlier, our comms had probably been fried the moment we'd stepped onto the second level, but it was worth a shot.

My back was to the glass railing and the steep drop to the first floor below. Normally, I would never put myself in such a vulnerable position, but it was the only remaining seat. Besides, Desmond was lurking at the bar, and he would cut off any potential threats.

"The game is Texas Hold'em, and the buy-in is two hundred thousand dollars. I assume that won't be a problem, Charlotte?" Henrika asked, arching a perfectly sculpted eyebrow at me.

"Not at all."

I pulled my phone out of my purse and accessed an account associated with Desmond Macfarlane that showed a three-million-dollar balance. Gia had given us some money to play with, just in case something like this came up, although she had also given Desmond and me strict instructions not to lose a penny.

The woman acting as the pit boss came over and gave me a white business card, and I followed the instructions to transfer the funds to the casino account. A loud *cha-ching!* rang out from the pit boss's phone, and the dealer pushed a stack of red chips over to my side of the table.

Henrika smiled. "Looks like we're ready to play."

The dealer shuffled the deck, then slid two cards over to Henrika, Niles, Steig, Oriana, and me. I lifted my cards. A three of hearts and a six of spades. Not a very promising start.

The dealer dealt three flop cards in the middle of the table and flipped them up so that we could all see them. A king, a jack, and a seven, all diamonds. No help for me.

Henrika started the bidding at fifty thousand dollars. Niles, Steig, and Oriana joined in, but I had nothing, so I folded. Besides, I wanted to see what the others would do and especially how they would play, since this was one instance where my magic wasn't all that helpful. Oh, if someone boasted they had a good hand when they didn't, my synesthesia would whisper that they were lying. But if someone didn't say anything specific about their cards, my magic would remain silent, and I would have no idea what kind of hand they were holding.

The dealer flipped the fourth card, the turn card. The ten of spades. Henrika bid again, even more aggressively, as did Niles, but Steig and Oriana both folded. Oriana watched Henrika and Niles with avid interest, but Steig huffed in annoyance and signaled for a drink. The assassin apparently didn't care for poker, although his gaze latched on to the waitress who deposited his beer on the table, and he tracked her all the way back to the bar.

The dealer turned over the fifth and final card, the river card, the seven of clubs. Henrika and Niles both bid again, then flipped over their cards. Henrika had a full house, three kings and two sevens, which beat Niles's two pairs of jacks and sevens.

"Sorry, darling," Henrika crooned, raking in the chips. "But you lose. Then again, you always lose to me, don't you?"

Niles shoved his glasses farther up his nose and jerked his hand at the bartender, signaling for another drink.

The dealer scooped up the cards, slid them back into the deck, and shuffled them.

Henrika looked at me. "You really need to get in the game, Charlotte. You can't win if you don't play."

I'd said something similar to General Percy and the others earlier today at Section headquarters, and I hated Henrika expressing a similar sentiment. "I prefer games that focus on skill and strategy rather than the blind luck of the turn of a card."

Henrika's eyes glittered. "Ah, but blind luck is what makes the game exciting."

Truth, my inner voice whispered.

"Why are we wasting time with this pointless charade?" Steig growled, rapping his knuckles on the table in a quick, impatient rhythm. "We came here to buy a weapon, not lose our money to you."

Niles and Oriana both murmured their agreement. Henrika's red lips pressed into a thin line. She didn't like being challenged by her guests.

"Because, unlike the rest of you, I have a normal life and identity I am quite fond of, and I need to keep up appearances," she snapped. "Redburn is my weapon, my formula, my brilliance, so *I* decide when and where and how to sell it. Anyone who doesn't like those terms is free to leave."

She gave an airy wave of her hand, then looked at Niles, Steig, and Oriana in turn. "Although I imagine none of your employers or followers will be pleased you lost out on the chance to acquire a new weapon, especially one capable of killing your paramortal rivals, just because you couldn't suffer through a game of cards."

Niles chewed on his lower lip, Steig rapped his knuckles on the table again, and even Oriana blinked. The three of them might be dangerous, but one way or another, they all answered to other people who were just as ruthless.

Desmond straightened up at the bar. His fingers curled around the glass in his hand, and his gaze flicked from one person to another, as if he was assessing who was the biggest threat and might make the first move.

Bryce and the four guards also stood at attention, their sharp gazes trained on Niles, Steig, and Oriana.

"No one wants to get up and walk away?" Henrika asked.

No one responded, and everyone remained in their seats.

"I thought not," she drawled.

Henrika signaled the dealer, and the soft rasp of cards filled the air. The other players all looked down at their cards with sour expressions, but I watched Henrika, whose green eyes gleamed with triumph. She liked this charade, as Steig had called it. She liked controlling other people and making them dance to her tune, and as much as I hated to admit it, she was masterful at it.

Henrika noticed my staring and gave a small shrug. I gave her a respectful nod, one enemy to another, then focused on my cards.

I was determined to beat Henrika at her own game.

The evening wore on.

I watched the dealer carefully, but she was dealing from the top of the deck, and she wasn't helping Henrika cheat. Given my analysis, I knew that Henrika loved winning more than anything else, but she also had an odd quirk where she wanted to win fair and square. It was a strange, unexpected bit of honor on her part.

Steig bet wildly and recklessly and had a terrible poker face, so he quickly lost all his money. He cursed viciously, then jumped to his feet, marched over to the bar, and bellowed for another beer. His gaze locked on the waitress as she handed over his drink, and his curses died down, replaced by a sharp, toothy smile. The assassin had found another game to play.

Niles was the second one to go out, after bluffing with a bad hand and losing his remaining chips to Oriana. The biomagical chemist also got up from the table and stormed over to the bar. He slugged down a bourbon and kept going, his face growing a little more flushed with every drink.

Henrika, Oriana, and I swapped chips back and forth until Oriana also tried to bluff with a bad hand, and I knocked her out. Oriana took her defeat far more gracefully than Steig and Niles, and she gave me a respectful nod. I returned the gesture, and Oriana also went to the bar to get a fresh drink.

That left me alone at the poker table with Henrika.

"It's just you and me now, Charlotte," she purred. "I'm going to enjoy taking your money. Well, what you claim is your money. We both know who it *really* belongs to."

The other paramortals pricked up their ears at her words. They probably thought Desmond was letting me gamble with his money, but Henrika knew it belonged to Section 47. She had already taken too much from me, and especially from Desmond. Maybe it was petty, but she wasn't getting the money too.

"It doesn't matter whose money it is," I replied. "Only that it's never going to be yours."

"We'll see," Henrika murmured.

We kept playing. Henrika lucked out and got three good hands in a row, raking in large stacks of my chips every time.

She had roughly eight hundred thousand dollars on her side of the table, and my own stack of chips looked puny in comparison.

The dealer dished out a new hand. Henrika grinned at her cards the way she always did, whether they were good, middling, or bad, and my synesthesia remained silent. I looked at my own cards—the queen of diamonds and queen of clubs.

The dealer flipped over the three flop cards—the three of spades, the king of hearts, and the three of clubs. Not terrible, since my pocket queens and the threes gave me two pairs.

Henrika's grin widened. "All in."

Gasps rang out as she shoved her chips forward.

"Your move, Charlotte." Henrika smirked.

For all her bluster and bravado, Henrika was smart, and she only bet high when she had a good chance of winning. I was guessing she had at least one pocket king, maybe two. Either way, Henrika was so sure she couldn't lose, she was finally going for the kill shot.

I studied my cards again, then looked at the cards on the table. My mind whirred as I thought of strategies and scenarios, but really, I had no choice. If I folded, Henrika would just take more of my chips I couldn't afford to lose. Time to make a stand and hope for a little bit of luck. Henrika had said it made the game more exciting, a theory my pounding heart and sweaty palms supported.

I also shoved my chips forward. "All in."

More gasps rang out. By this point, everyone was gathered around the table to watch this final hand. Bryce was behind Henrika, while Niles, Steig, and Oriana were standing behind their previous chairs. Desmond was hovering off to my right, watching the others the way he had been all evening. Knowing he had my back was one reason I'd been able to focus on the game instead of worrying about the other paramortals.

"All in on both sides," the dealer said. "Let's see what we've got."

She flipped over the turn card—the queen of spades.

My heart pounded, this time with excitement. At the very least, I had a queen-high full house. Maybe I could win after all.

Henrika's grin widened. "It's too bad you don't have any money left, Charlotte. I would have been happy to raise the stakes again."

My heart pounded a little harder and faster. This was the opening I'd been waiting for. I couldn't force Henrika to hand over the undercover agent list, but maybe I could persuade her to gamble it away.

"Who says we can't raise the stakes again? We both know *exactly* what I want from you."

Henrika tilted her head to the side. "What are you proposing?"

"Add the list to your bet, along with every single copy you've made."

Niles's eyes narrowed behind his silver glasses. "What list?"

"Our business doesn't concern you, Niles," I snapped. "So stay out of it."

He sucked in a breath and stabbed his finger at me, but Desmond stepped forward, putting himself between me and the other man. Desmond crossed his arms over his chest, his eyes glittering like chips of silver-blue ice in his face. Niles's finger wilted down to his side, and he swallowed whatever nasty comment he'd been about to hurl my way.

Henrika studied me for several long seconds, trying to figure out if I was bluffing. "Very well. On the off chance you win, I will hand over the list and every single copy I've made. But what do I get when *I* win?"

"Oh, I'm sure I have *something* you want." I snapped my fingers, as though a thought had just occurred to me, although the idea had been brewing in the back of my mind ever since my trip to the Section armory. "Actually, you're in luck. I have just the thing to even the stakes."

I picked up my purse, cracked open the top, and plucked out the white velvet bundle I'd stuffed inside the bag before Desmond and I had left Section headquarters.

"What's that?" Steig asked in a snide voice. "A bag of snacks?"

I placed the bundle on the table where everyone could see it. "Something a little more valuable than snacks."

I drew in a breath, then let it out and flipped open the white velvet, revealing the object inside.

The Grunglass Necklace.

A tense, heavy silence dropped over the table, and everyone blinked at the dazzling display of gleaming gold, sparkling emeralds, and winking diamonds.

Henrika laughed. "Nice try, Charlotte. Did you really think you could fool me with a fake?"

"Take a closer look."

Henrika laughed again, but she leaned forward. The longer she looked at the jewels, the more her eyes widened, and her mouth gaped. "You . . . you brought the *real* necklace," she whispered in an awed tone.

I'd been just as shocked when I'd realized Joan had given me the genuine necklace in the Section armory. Desmond frowned at me, questions flickering across his face, but I shrugged back. I still wasn't sure why Joan had let me bring the real Grunglass Necklace to the resort, but I was going to use it to my advantage.

Henrika stared at the necklace a second longer, then jerked back, as if she'd just realized that the other paramortals were watching her with avid interest. Henrika quickly smoothed out her expression, although she couldn't hide the hunger in her eyes whenever she glanced at the necklace.

She crossed her arms over her chest. "How did you manage

to persuade your employer to part with such a lovely bauble?"

Desmond shifted on his feet. We both knew she was asking how I'd removed the necklace from Section headquarters, but I didn't dare answer that question.

Niles, Steig, and Oriana looked back and forth between Henrika and me, as did Bryce and the guards, all clearly wondering what was going on.

"I came prepared," I replied, sidestepping her question. "That's my job."

"And she does it beautifully," Desmond chimed in.

I flashed him a smile, grateful for his support, then focused on Henrika again. "I'd say the stakes are more than even now. The list if I win, the necklace if you do."

It was a huge gamble, and I could easily walk away with nothing except the collective anger and wrath of Gia, Evelyn, and especially General Percy for losing the necklace. But Grandma Jane had taught me to tackle one problem at a time, and Desmond and I needed to recover the UC list before Henrika exposed the agents' identities. Everything else, including getting answers about my father's death, finding where Henrika was storing the Redburn formula, and capturing—or killing— her could wait.

Henrika looked at the four cards on the table, calculating the odds in her mind the same way I was doing. Now, more than ever, I needed some serious luck.

Henrika raised her gaze to mine. "Agreed. The list for the necklace."

A few more soft gasps sounded, although that tense, expectant silence quickly dropped over the table again. Henrika nodded to the dealer, who wet her lips and placed the final card on the table—the queen of hearts.

Once again, everyone leaned forward, staring at the river card, then at Henrika and me, wondering which one of us had won—and lost.

A triumphant smile spread across Henrika's face, and she flipped over her cards and tossed them forward. "King of diamonds, king of spades."

The dealer pulled Henrika's cards a little closer, then lifted the king of hearts, the queen of spades, and the queen of hearts out of the row of community cards. "Full house, kings and queens."

More gasps rang out, along with a smattering of applause, although the sounds swiftly faded away. Henrika's smile widened. She knew the odds as well as I did and just how hard it was to beat a king-high full house.

I dropped my head and studied my pocket cards again, as if I was hoping they were different from what they were. Then I raised my head, flipped my cards over, and tossed them forward. "The queen of diamonds and the queen of clubs."

It took a few seconds for people to do the math, but another round of gasps rang out, and the smile cracked off Henrika's face.

The dealer pulled my cards closer, then drew the queen of spades and the queen of hearts out of the row of community cards. "Four queens," the dealer said in a soft, apologetic voice. "Four queens wins the hand."

Once again, that tense, heavy silence dropped over the table, and everyone stared at Henrika, wondering how she would react to losing.

Magic flared in her green eyes, and my synesthesia surged in response, outlining her body in that familiar bloodred haze. Henrika dug her short dark red nails into the tabletop. A shower of golden sparks exploded around her fingers, and the green felt began to smoke, bubble, and burn.

My breath froze in my throat, even as my heart hammered in a quick, painful rhythm that matched the voice muttering in my mind.

Danger-danger-danger.

I knew that Henrika was a combusto, and I'd seen her use her magic at the Halstead Hotel a few months ago to melt a sheet of thick plastic like she was ripping through a paper towel. That had been a calm, controlled display, but right now Henrika was teetering on the edge of unleashing the full destructive force of her paramortal ability, and she was much more powerful than I'd realized.

Desmond slipped his silver watch out of his vest pocket and shifted closer to me. Niles, Steig, and Oriana sidled away from the table, as did the dealer, and even Bryce and the guards stepped back. Nobody wanted to get between Henrika and me if she decided to hurl her sparking combusto magic at me.

Several seconds ticked by. Down on the ballroom floor, the guests kept gambling, drinking, laughing, and talking, oblivious to the danger and drama playing out above their heads.

Henrika's nostrils flared, and her nails sank even deeper into the oozing felt. I tensed, as did Desmond, whose fingers curled a little tighter around his watch. Henrika sucked in a breath, and I dug my toes into the carpet, ready to throw myself out of my chair to get out of her line of magical fire.

Henrika exhaled, released her death grip on the table, and sat back. Her magic vanished in a shower of golden sparks, and the red haze of my synesthesia slowly dimmed around her body. The green felt kept smoking, filling the air with an acrid stench, but right now it smelled like the sweetest perfume. Better the felt than my face.

I reached out, snagged the edge of the Grunglass Necklace, and slowly drew it over to my side of the table. I lifted the necklace up, and Desmond stepped forward, took the ends from me, and fastened them at the back of my neck.

The array of gold, emeralds, and diamonds settled against my skin like a cold, heavy anvil. I might have won the game and gotten to keep the necklace, but Henrika clearly wanted to murder me with just the force of her hot, furious gaze.

I pushed my chair back from the table and got to my feet. "I'll come to your penthouse shortly. Make sure you have the list ready to hand over."

Henrika kept glaring at me, but she couldn't renege on our deal. At least, not in front of the other paramortals. She had started the game, and I'd just been lucky enough to win this round.

I looked at the pit boss and gestured at the red chips still strewn across the table. "I trust you will transfer my winnings into the appropriate account?"

The other woman looked at Henrika, who gave a barely perceptible nod.

"Yes, ma'am," the pit boss replied. "It will be done within the hour."

"Excellent." I picked up several chips and handed a couple of them to the dealer, then distributed the others to the pit boss, the bartender, and the waitress.

Everyone was still looking at me, including Henrika. I plastered a smile on my face and picked up my purse so the other paramortals wouldn't notice my trembling hands.

"Thank you for *such* a lovely evening," I drawled. "You're right, Henrika. Luck does make the game *so* much more exciting."

Henrika's eyes narrowed at my flippant tone, but I turned away and took Desmond's arm. The two of us walked past the weapons maker and headed toward the stairs.

I didn't glance back over my shoulder, but I could feel Henrika's glower stabbing into my back like a red-hot knife, and my synesthesia kept muttering of danger.

I just hoped I hadn't used up all my luck tonight.

TWENTY-TWO

DESMOND

I escorted Charlotte down the steps to the ballroom floor, then glanced up.

Henrika was standing at the second-floor railing, her hands clenched around the glass as though she wanted to melt it the way she had melted the poker table's felt. She glared down at us, then whispered something to Bryce, who nodded and moved over to speak to the guards.

I tensed, expecting Bryce and the guards to rush down the stairs after us, but they remained on the balcony.

Charlotte kept walking, her gaze straight ahead, not seeming to notice the other people in the ballroom. We went right by Joan, who was still standing at one of the high tables. Joan's gaze landed on the Grunglass Necklace sparkling around Charlotte's neck. She raised her eyebrows in a silent question, but I gave a small shake of my head. Henrika hadn't sent Bryce and the guards after us—yet—so there was no reason for Joan to blow her cover.

Charlotte and I left the ballroom and slipped past the throngs of guests milling around outside. Charlotte quickened her pace, veered around a column, and stepped into a room with dark wooden shelves filled with leather-bound books. Several long reading tables took up the center of the public library, and chairs were clustered around a fireplace at the back wall. No flames crackled behind the grate, and the air felt chilly after the heat of all the bodies in the ballroom.

Charlotte zigzagged around the furniture, then stepped into a small alcove tucked away in the back corner. No security cameras were embedded in the ceiling, and I didn't sense the telltale tingle of any electronic surveillance.

"We're clear," I said. "This area is a security dead zone. No one is watching us."

Charlotte blew out a breath, dropped her head, and braced her hand on a bookshelf. Tremors swept through her body, making the emeralds and diamonds sparkle around her neck.

After several seconds, Charlotte blew out another breath, straightened up, and released the shelf. "I am so glad that worked," she confessed in a low, raspy voice.

I frowned. "You didn't know you had the winning hand?"

She shook her head, and some more tension drained out of her body. "No. I knew Henrika had a strong hand, but I was running out of chips, and I had to make a stand. What's the old saying? Sometimes it's better to be lucky than good."

My chest tightened at just how close Charlotte had come to losing, but it was quickly drowned out by a wave of admiration for her gutsiness. "I would have done the same thing."

"Really?"

"Absolutely. The Grunglass Necklace might be valuable, but it's just a necklace, just gold and jewels strung together. Recovering the undercover list and protecting our agents is what really matters, and you played it all perfectly."

Pride surged through me, and a smile spread across my face. "Have I told you lately how brilliant you are, Numbers?"

I grabbed Charlotte around the waist, lifted her off her feet, and spun her around. A shaky laugh tumbled out of her lips, and her aura blazed a bright blue from all the adrenaline pumping through her body. I spun her around again, then set her down and gave her a quick, fierce kiss.

Charlotte let out another laugh. She smiled at me, although her lips puckered, and her eyes quickly narrowed in thought. "This gives us the perfect opportunity to divide and conquer. I'll go meet Henrika and get the UC list. She should keep most of her guards and her attention focused on me. That will give you a chance to slip out of the resort, infiltrate the woods, and see if you can find Henrika's lab."

I shook my head. "No—no way. I don't want you going anywhere near Henrika or Bryce. Not alone."

Charlotte shook her head right back at me. "I'll be fine. Henrika isn't going to kill me in her penthouse. She still wants something from me, and I think you too, although I still haven't figured out what it is." She frowned, and those mental gymnastics filled her gaze again.

I stabbed my finger at the Grunglass Necklace. "What about that? Wearing the necklace in front of Henrika is like throwing chum in the water straight at a shark."

Charlotte's hand crept up, and her fingers stroked one jewel after another. "Henrika can't kill me, and she can't take the necklace from me either. If she attacks me, then she's violating her own rules of engagement, and the other paramortals won't stand for that." She dropped her hand from the jewels. "Besides, we can cover more ground if we split up. You know I'm right."

I did know, and she was right. We'd only been at the resort a few hours, and Niles, Steig, and Oriana were already impatient that Henrika hadn't produced Redburn yet. One or, more likely, all of them might decide to take matters into their own hands and try to force Henrika to turn over the formula. Charlotte and I needed to find any Redburn samples before that happened.

"All right," I agreed in a reluctant voice. "But I want you to be extra careful around Henrika."

Charlotte used her index finger to draw an X over her heart. "I promise. Maybe by the time I leave the penthouse, you'll have located Henrika's lab, and we can call in the Section strike teams to take her down, capture the other paramortals, and end this game once and for all."

Charlotte headed to the penthouse to meet Henrika, while I returned to the honeymoon suite. I swept the area, but no one had bugged our rooms while we'd been gone.

Satisfied that no one was watching, I stripped off my tuxedo and changed into a long-sleeved black tactical shirt and matching cargo pants. I threw on a black fleece jacket and made sure I had all my usual weapons. A black knit winter hat hid my blond hair, and for a final touch, I slid my hands into a pair of thick gloves and my feet into the heavy boots Joan had picked out in the armory.

I could have left the suite, gotten into the elevator, and returned to the ground floor, but Bryce and the guards were certain to spot me on the security cameras, so I stepped out onto the balcony.

By this point, it was creeping up on midnight, and this side of the hotel was bathed in shadows. Conversation and laughter drifted up from the ballroom below, along with music. Casino Night was still going strong. Good. Chattering crowds and ambient noise were often a spy's best friends.

Each room on this side of the hotel had a similar balcony, although the ones on the floors below were much smaller, since they fronted less expensive rooms. I swung first one leg, then another, over the balcony railing, digging my toes into the two-inch stone ledge to help with balance. Then I clicked my heels together.

Snick. Snick. Snick.

Tiny spikes popped out of the toes, heels, and soles of my boots.

Next, I reached out, placed one hand on the exterior hotel wall, and tapped my thumb against the stone three times in rapid succession.

Snick. Snick. Snick.

Small hydraulic noises sounded, and tiny spikes embedded in the palm and fingertips of my glove punched into the wall, giving me a good, sturdy grip. I placed my other hand on the wall and repeated the activation process.

Snick. Snick. Snick.

More spikes punched into the stone. Now came the moment of truth. I let out a breath, slowing my racing heart, then stepped off the ledge, putting all my weight—and trust—in the spiked gloves to keep me from falling and being splattered all over the ground hundreds of feet below.

I hung in midair, the winter wind whistling around my body and whipping my legs back and forth, like I was a spider suspended on a silken strand. I grunted and dug the spikes a little deeper into the wall. A few chips of stone sprayed out and sliced across my cheeks, but I didn't dare massage away the small stings.

The wind shrieked in my ears for a few more seconds, then died down. My legs stopped swinging, and I punched the spikes on my boots into the wall, further anchoring myself to the stone.

And then I started climbing down.

I'd used the spiked gloves and boots many times before, usually to scale cliffs when a target had ensconced themselves in a mountaintop hideaway and there was no other way to reach them. But the stone was much slicker than I expected, and the wind gusted in unpredictable patterns. Hard bits of snow also battered up against my body and stung my eyes, making it hard to see.

Plus, going down was always harder than climbing up. I had to reach and step down with one hand and foot at a time without losing my grip on the wall completely. More than once, my hands and feet slipped, and I had to clench my entire body to stop my rapid slide and keep from plummeting to my death. I made a mental note to do more yoga and Pilates with Charlotte, who was always talking about being anchored in her powerhouse. Well, my powerhouse could certainly use some more anchoring right now.

It took me the better part of two minutes, but eventually, I scaled down the wall. I dropped the last few feet to the ground and landed in a low crouch behind some evergreen hedges that ran along the side of the hotel. I quickly retracted the spikes on my gloves and boots, then cupped my hands over my mouth to muffle my loud, rapid breaths, as well as the resulting clouds of frost. I also shook out my trembling arms and legs and twisted my torso from side to side to ease the burning in my abs.

The conversation, laughter, and music from the ballroom was much louder here on the ground level, although no guests were outside, given the gusty wind and increasing waves of snow. A few guards were roaming along the terraces, but they were sticking to the upper two levels, close to the hotel. Their heads were down, and they were all walking quickly, trying to stay warm.

I waited until the closest guard moved past me, then stood up, crossed the terrace, and darted behind a game booth that was part of the Winterfest event.

Keeping to the shadows, I worked my way around the perimeter of the hotel to the edge of the golf course and plastered my back up against the side of a large open-air shed where the golf carts were stored. A single security light burned above the shed, and a few more lights dotted different holes, but for the most part, the golf course was dark and deserted.

Still, the longer I looked around, the more unease filled me. I could have sworn someone else was out here, even though the closest guard was posted several hundred feet away at the hotel—

"Nice moves, Slick," a familiar voice drawled.

I whirled around, my gaze snapping left and right. Where was he?

A smoky gray shadow detached itself from the opposite end of the golf-cart shed. The shadow slinked closer, quickly solidifying into the shape of a man.

Gabriel Chase grinned, his white teeth flashing like pearls in the semidarkness. He too had traded in his tuxedo for all-black attire, along with a knit hat pulled down low over his forehead.

Gabriel leaned his shoulder against the shed wall he had just phased through. "Congratulations on not splattering your pretty self all over the main terrace. Although it was touch and go there for a while. I thought the wind was going to blow you off the side of the hotel like a bug on a windshield."

"Funny how you didn't call out and offer your assistance, Gaby," I drawled.

"Nah," Gabriel replied, grinning even wider. "It was *way* too much fun watching you crawl down the wall like some wannabe superhero."

I huffed. "What are you doing out here?"

"The same thing you are—searching for Henrika's lab. I've already checked most of the hotel, but I don't think it's in there. Otherwise, one of the guests or workers would have stumbled over it already. My guess? Henrika is hiding her biomagical toys in the woods."

His logic made sense and matched the conclusions Charlotte and I had drawn, although I would never admit it. Gabriel Chase's ego was already big enough.

The former cleaner grinned again and held his arm out to the side. "After you, Slick."

I grumbled with annoyance, but I headed toward the woods. Gabriel followed me.

We moved from one shed and outbuilding to another, keeping out of sight of the patrolling guards. Every so often, I stopped and glanced over my shoulder. I didn't know if Gabriel was using his phasing ability, but I could barely see him in the semidarkness, and I wouldn't have even realized he was behind me if I hadn't been able to sense his smoky gray aura with my galvanism.

We skirted around as much of the golf course as we could, then stopped. The next section was a wide, rolling green with nary a tree or a sand trap in sight, but we had to cross it if we wanted to search the woods beyond.

I looked at Gabriel, who nodded back. We both waited for the closest guard to turn his back. The instant that happened, I sprinted forward, with Gabriel running right beside me. The quick thumps of our boots on the grass banged like drums in my ears, along with the swish of our clothing. I strained to hear other noises, but my pounding heart drowned out everything else.

Still, the longer we ran, the bigger the smile that stretched across my face.

I might not like having to make nice with paramortal villains or watching the General gamble with agents' lives. But skulking past throngs of guards and slipping into places I wasn't supposed to be? I bloody *loved* those parts of being a spy.

Gabriel and I ran over to the tree line, then split apart. He went left and stopped behind a towering pine, while I went right and did the same thing. We both glanced behind us.

A flashlight bobbed up and down in the distance, on the other side of the golf course, but no shouts sounded, and no one seemed to have seen our mad sprint into the trees. Gabriel flashed me another grin, which I returned.

Together, the two of us moved deeper into the woods.

I went from one tree to the next, keeping my footsteps as quiet as possible. Off to my left, Gabriel did the same thing.

The whistling winter wind had finally died down, although it was snowing more heavily than before. Fat flakes fluttered down through the branches, covering the ground in an icy-white carpet. My breath steamed out in thick clouds of frost, as did Gabriel's, like we were two wolves stalking through the dark night. In a way, that's exactly what we were.

The one good thing about the snow was that it naturally brightened the landscape, so I didn't have to risk activating the button flashlight on my jacket. I stopped every few feet to scan the ground, but I didn't spot any signs that anyone had been out here recently, not so much as a stray golf ball that had sailed off the neighboring course.

"You see anything, Slick?" Gabriel murmured.

"Nope. You?"

"Nothing."

Since there were no obvious signs of a lab, I reached out with my galvanism, searching for any flickers of life or currents of energy running through the woods.

There.

A spark of electricity twinged my power, and I spun toward the energy source like a compass arrow pointing due north. A faint current hummed in the distance, although I couldn't tell what—or whom—it might belong to.

"You sense something?" Gabriel asked.

"Yeah. Let's check it out."

We hiked about half a mile deeper into the woods before the trees thinned out, revealing a large clearing. A tall, skinny security light stood at one end of the open space, its round bulb casting out a weak but steady glow like a miniature moon suspended above the trees.

No sheds or outbuildings were here, and I didn't see so much as a single footprint disturbing the freshly fallen snow. It didn't look like anyone had been in this section of the woods all day, not even a guard for a quick patrol. In the distance, I could just make out the steady slapping of the lake against the shoreline, and the fishy scent tickled my nose and made the air seem even colder and damper.

I pulled my phone out of a zippered pocket on my jacket and checked our position against the Section satellite photos, maps, and other surveillance images of the Glittertop Resort. We were at the north end of the property, where a wide swath of the lake curved around the tip of the woods. According to some reports Charlotte had found, the resort developers had deemed this terrain too rough and rocky and too far from the hotel to build anything useful, so this area was largely untouched.

I reached out with my galvanism. Once again, I sensed that faint electrical hum, a little stronger than before, so I stalked across the clearing to the security light.

I examined the metal pole from all angles, then peered up at the bulb itself, but it was just a security light, the same as dozens of others that ringed the hotel and dotted the surrounding landscape. The light didn't have a keypad or any obvious switch, which meant it was probably controlled from inside the hotel, just like all the other security lights.

"We've come to the end of the line," Gabriel said. "Quite literally. There's nothing out here but trees."

I slid my phone back into my pocket. "Let's keep searching. Maybe we're overlooking something."

We spread out, each of us scanning a different section of

the clearing. Trees, rocks, snow. Everything was exactly what it appeared to be, and nothing sinister was hidden in the surrounding woods.

Gabriel and I met in the middle of the clearing. He jerked his thumb over his shoulder. "I'll check down by the lake."

"I'll see if I can pick up any more energy sources with my galvanism."

He nodded and moved off, his steps silent despite the brittle snow underfoot.

I closed my eyes and reached out with my galvanism yet again, straining to find any energy in the vicinity, any bright flares, telltale tingles, or sharp crackles that might indicate something nearby was drawing or emitting electricity . . .

There.

A warm, sparking sensation tickled my magic like a bulb flickering in a socket. Still keeping my eyes closed, I latched on to the sensation and turned my body toward the flow of energy. I took a few careful steps forward, like a moth fluttering toward a candle flame, then opened my eyes to see . . .

The security light at the end of the clearing.

Frustration coursed through my body. I already knew the light was there, so why did my galvanism keep pointing it out? It was just a lone bulb, and it wasn't even as bright as the similar lights around the hotel—

Crunch.

A footstep broke through the snow behind me, and a new aura pinged my senses. I whirled around.

A security guard wearing a green jacket was standing about ten feet away, a gun leveled at my chest.

TWENTY-THREE

CHARLOTTE

I rode the elevator to the penthouse. By the time it stopped, I had settled my nerves and sharpened my resolve. I'd won the first round in the game Henrika was playing, and I had to be on my toes for round two.

The elevator arrived with a loud *ding* that made me flinch. The door slid back, and I stepped into the foyer. To my surprise, no guards were waiting in the space. I didn't hear a whisper of sound, and the elevator remained open behind me.

Curiosity propelled me over to the double doors that led into Henrika's penthouse, and I cautiously tried them. Locked. I glanced around, wondering if this was a test—or trap—but I didn't see any security cameras embedded in the ceiling, and my synesthesia wasn't muttering about any hidden dangers.

I bent down and took a closer look at the doors, which were locked with a numbered keypad. None of the white paint on the numbers was chipped or smudged, so I couldn't figure out the code that way. Next, I ran my fingers over the buttons, jiggling and pressing them. Three of the buttons felt looser than the others, as if they were the only ones that were ever touched.

I chewed on my lower lip, thinking about the numbers, along with everything I knew about Henrika. After a few seconds, I rolled my eyes and punched in the numbers 724—July 24, Henrika's birthday.

The light on the keypad flashed green, the lock clicked, and one of the doors popped open. I snorted. A birthday code? Seriously? That was even more obvious than Desmond using 007 as the code for the wall safe in his apartment.

I glanced back over my shoulder, but the elevator was still open and waiting. It didn't seem like a guard was going to suddenly appear, so I pulled the door open a little wider and stepped through to the other side.

The same telltale staticky tingle that had fried my comms jewelry earlier in the day swept over my body again. I shivered at the uncomfortable sensation, moved past the expensive furniture and pricey knickknacks in the front of the suite, and went over to Henrika's library. These doors were also locked, although they required an actual key instead of another code.

I plucked a small brown bobby pin out of my purse. Unlike the other hair accessories Joan had packed, it was just an ordinary bobby pin, with no knockout needles or other gadgets hidden inside. I bent the pin into the shape I wanted, then stuck it into the lock. It took me less than thirty seconds to coax it open. I stuck the bobby pin into my purse, twisted the knob, and stepped through to the other side.

Lights blazed in the library, but no one was inside, and Henrika wasn't hiding behind the furniture waiting to jump out and yell *boo!*

My heart kicked up into my throat, but I swallowed it down. My gaze flicked over to Henrika's desk. Her laptop was open, and the screen was unlocked. My fingers itched with the urge to start tapping away, but I resisted the temptation.

Henrika might have let me into her inner sanctum seemingly unsupervised, but I was willing to bet she was watching me through a security camera, and I wasn't about to fall for such an obvious trap. Besides, I doubted Henrika kept anything of importance on that laptop or the scientist's worktable in the corner. No, her real secrets would be tucked away with the Redburn formula, wherever it was stored.

I marched over to the shelves that lined one wall. Just like with a person's desk, you could tell a lot about someone by the mementoes they kept, but nothing jumped out at me. The books were classic titles bound in supple leather and stamped with foil, the kind of books people bought but never actually read, while the framed photos were posed shots of Henrika smiling and shaking hands with famous folks. The jewelry inside the glass cases was pretty, but none of the pieces was as expensive, dazzling, and ostentatious as the Grunglass Necklace I was still wearing.

Frustration pounded through me. Henrika could come here any moment, and I had nothing to show for my snooping. I spun away from the shelves and stared out over the space again. Henrika's desk, the scientist's worktable with beakers and vials filled with who knew what, the fireplace, the fancy furniture spread across the equally expensive rugs underfoot.

Once again, I didn't see anything unusual or out of place. More frustration pounded through me, so I drew in a deep breath, then slowly let it out, just like I did on my yoga mat whenever my muscles were shaking from holding a difficult pose and I needed to steady myself.

Calmer, I took another look around, and I noticed something was slightly . . . *off*.

I drew in another breath, then slowly let it out and reached for my magic just like I would lengthen my arms and legs in a yoga pose to get that tiny bit of extra stretch. I studied the library through the lens of my synesthesia, but nothing happened.

More frustration simmered in my veins, but I kept reaching

out with my magic. I wasn't looking at a document or a spread-sheet, so there were no typos or addition errors to find. I needed to shift my perspective and search for things that were . . . out of place . . . and just . . . didn't belong with the immaculate furnishings.

So I drew in a third breath, then let it out, like the others. Calmer, I turned in a slow circle, examining every single part of the library with my synesthesia, and a few muted grays flickered in my field of vision, like bulbs that couldn't quite decide whether they had enough juice to fully light up.

I focused on the first flare of gray, then another, then another, studying everything my synesthesia was pointing out. The corner of a rug that was flipped up. A long, ugly scratch on the side of a table. A cracked pane of glass on one of the lamps. I studied each imperfection in turn, then moved on to the next one.

Eventually, my gaze settled on the shelves closest to Henrika's desk, and two tiny flickers of gray caught my attention. Curious, I headed in that direction.

Two framed photos were sitting together on a shelf to the left of Henrika's desk, and both pictures were positioned so that they would be in her line of sight while she was working. My heart quickened with excitement, and I bent down and studied them.

The first photo was in a silver frame, but a crease ran down one side of the image, and the bottom right corner was torn off. My synesthesia had picked up on the flaws, but the truly unusual thing was the photo itself.

Unlike the posed shots on the other shelves, this photo showed a teenage Henrika smiling wide at the camera, her arms wrapped around another smiling teenage girl. Henrika was the picture of young, dewy health, but the other girl was obviously sick, with pale skin, sunken eyes, and a bald head. My stomach clenched, and memories of Grandma Jane floated through my mind. I was willing to bet this girl, whoever she was, had also had some form of cancer.

Besides Petra Halstead, Henrika didn't have any other known siblings, so who was this girl? A cousin, maybe? A friend from school? The girl must have been important for Henrika to still have her photo all these years later. Or maybe Henrika was playing another game, letting me think I had gotten some revealing glimpse into her psyche when the photo didn't mean anything.

I thought about it for a few more seconds, then discarded the idea. Displaying a photo of a sick kid just to mess with your enemy was a shitty thing to do, even for Henrika. Besides, my synesthesia would have warmed to a bright pink if the photo had been doctored. No, this was a real photo, and Henrika had been friends with the sick girl once upon a time.

I plucked my phone out of my purse. The device didn't have a signal, but the camera was still working, so I snapped a shot of Henrika and the sick girl. I didn't know how—or even if—the photo might help me or the mission, but it was always better to have as much information as possible, especially about an enemy.

Once that was done, I turned my attention to the second photo, which was another posed shot showing Henrika shaking hands and smiling at a man in a dark business suit. Instead of an office, the two of them were standing on a terrace with a colorful sunset and glimmering ocean in the background. I snapped a photo of it as well, then tucked my phone back into my purse. I started to turn away from the picture, but something about the man's wide, toothy smile caught my eye, so I took a closer look.

Dark brown hair and eyes, light brown skin, a nose that was slightly crooked from having been broken multiple times. Shock spiked through me, and my breath caught in my throat.

The man in the photo was Feliciano Salvador—the cartel

leader who had captured my father during the Mexico mission. Why would Henrika have a photo of *him*?

Nausea roiled in my stomach, but I examined every single inch of the photo. Henrika and Feliciano were standing on a stone terrace that overlooked sparkling waves. More nausea bubbled up in my stomach. I'd studied enough Section surveillance photos to recognize Feliciano's seaside villa.

More shock spiked through my body. Henrika wasn't lying. She really did know what had happened to my father because *she had been there*. Henrika had been in Mexico, at Feliciano's villa, when Jack Locke and the other cleaners had been sent to eliminate the cartel leader.

Once again, I reached out with my synesthesia and studied the photo. No grays appeared, no pinks, no reds, no colors of any sort. Just like the photo of the sick girl, this image was also genuine. Not only that, but the way Henrika was looking at Feliciano . . . well, it reminded me of the way I looked at Desmond.

How had I not discovered this in my research? Had Henrika and Feliciano been involved? Was that why she had been at his villa? Or had Henrika had other business with the cartel leader?

Behind me, a door creaked open. Footsteps scuffed on the rugs, and a whisper of air flowed through the library, kissing the back of my neck like an unwanted lover. I froze, still bent over the two photos.

"I was wondering where you'd run off to," a familiar voice drawled. "I should have known you would have come straight here to collect your winnings."

I straightened up and turned around. Henrika stood behind me, along with Bryce and two guards, all of whom had their hands on their guns.

TWENTY-FOUR

DESMOND

he guard grinned and took a little better aim at my chest with his gun, which featured a suppressor. He advanced toward me, crossing the snow-crusted clearing in a few quick strides. I remained by the security light, my hands loose and down by my sides. Adrenaline surged through my body, skittering through my veins like a chemical form of electricity, and I relished the natural high.

I loved this part of being a spy too.

The guard stopped a few feet away. "Bryce said you'd come out here, but I didn't think you'd be stupid enough to actually do it."

Annoyance spurted through me. Bryce had known I would search the woods for Henrika's lab, and he'd planned accordingly.

A sneer twisted the guard's face. "Bryce also said you were some big-shot assassin, but you don't look so tough to me."

I flexed my hands. "Well, if you're so tough, why don't you put that gun away, and we'll see who the deadlier man truly is?"

The guard grinned again. "Nah. I don't feel like getting your blood on my jacket. Did you know Henrika makes us buy and replace our own uniforms?" He shook his head. "That's some cheap corporate bullshit right there."

While the guard complained, I flicked my left wrist and discreetly palmed the knife I'd tucked up my sleeve earlier. I also had a gun nestled in the small of my back, but I couldn't draw it before the guard shot me. Besides, the knife would be quieter.

"We even have to replace the nametags." The guard gestured at the silver tag on his green jacket that read *FLOYD* in bold black letters. "Want to tell me what you're doing out here before I shoot you and call for backup?"

I shrugged. "Isn't it obvious? I'm looking for Henrika's lab, just like everyone else is."

Floyd snorted. "Well, you're never going to find it. Henrika doesn't tell anyone anything they don't need to know. Even the scientists who work for her are blindfolded before they're taken to the lab. Bryce is the only one who knows where it is."

The dull orange aura stayed bright and steady over his heart, indicating he was telling the truth. Disappointment flooded my body. I'd been hoping to disarm the guard and then squeeze the lab's location out of him, but he was clueless.

Floyd stepped a little closer. "Why don't you make things easier and tell me if you're wearing a bulletproof vest? If you are, I'll put a couple of rounds in your chest. Bruise a rib or two instead of winging you in the arm and getting blood everywhere."

He seemed intent on capturing instead of killing me, which made me curious about his bosses' motives. Bryce would no doubt want to torture me for as long as possible because of how I'd hurt him all those years ago, but why would Henrika want me to keep breathing? I didn't know, but trying to take me alive all by himself was a massive mistake on the guard's part.

"You said it yourself, Floyd. I'm a big-shot assassin. Don't you want to test your skills against mine? Brag to your friends about how you took me down with your bare hands?"

He laughed. "Do people really fall for that? Please. I might be an enduro just like you are, but I know better than to get within arm's reach of you." His laughter faded away, and he gave me another cruel grin. "Since you won't be a good boy and cooperate, I'll just have to put a few rounds in your arms *and* legs to put you down."

I tensed and shifted my weight into my toes. Floyd hesitated, his gun wavering, before he aimed the weapon at my left arm. The instant his finger curled back on the trigger, I whipped my left hand up, threw the knife at him, and dove to the side all in one smooth motion.

My aim was true, and the knife sank into Floyd's right shoulder. He yelped in surprise and staggered back, but he still pulled the trigger.

Pfft!

Thanks to the suppressor, the gun only made a small, muffled sound instead of a loud crack that would have made all the guards come running. Good for me. But Floyd was a better shot than I'd expected, and the bullet tore through my jacket sleeve and grazed my left arm. Bad for me.

A line of hot, stinging pain sliced across my upper arm, but I was too committed to my dive to stop, and I hit the ground hard. More pain exploded in my body at the jarring impact, but I grunted and used the momentum to roll farther away, sending up sprays of snow, dirt, and leaves in my wake.

Floyd cursed and wrenched the knife out of his shoulder. He snarled with pain, tossed the blade aside, and spun toward me.

I snatched up a rock from the ground and chucked it at him. My aim wasn't great, and the rock sailed over his head, but it still caused Floyd to instinctively duck.

I scrambled back up onto my feet and sprinted straight at the guard, who cursed and raised his gun again. I closed the distance between us and chopped down with my hand, knocking the weapon out of his fingers. Then I surged forward and punched him in the throat to keep him from yelling for help.

The blow rocked him back, but it didn't knock him down. Floyd shook his head, wheezing for air, then charged forward and lashed out with his own fists. I ducked the jab at my face, but he socked me square in the chest. Pain exploded in my ribs, and all the air whooshed out of my lungs. Floyd had a healthy amount of strength to go along with his enduro stamina.

The pain in my ribs intensified the hot, throbbing sting from where the bullet had grazed my arm, but I pushed the misery of my injuries aside and grabbed hold of the fresh energy they poured into my body. Then I drew back my fist and clocked Floyd in the jaw.

Once again, my blow rocked the guard back, but it didn't put him down. I growled with frustration. Floyd lashed out with his own fist, driving me back.

The guard raised his fists and dug his feet into the snow, firming up his fighting stance. I did the same, eyeing him warily. I also scanned the woods, but I didn't see any flashlights bobbing in this direction. None of the other guards had heard our scuffle, and the only sounds were the crunch of our boots on the snow and our raspy breaths frosting in the air.

Floyd darted in, trying to use his enduro quickness to take me by surprise, but I ignored the feint and cracked my fist across his jaw again. He staggered back, and his gaze flicked to the right. His gun was lying off to the side, looking like a lump of coal lying in the snow.

Floyd's eyes narrowed. His aura glowed an ugly orange over his heart, and he dove for his gun. He landed on his belly and slid forward like a kid playing in the snow. His hand closed around the weapon, and he flipped over onto his back and aimed the gun at my head. Despite his orders, Floyd wasn't interested in capturing me anymore.

Still channeling the pain of my injuries with my galvanism, I stepped forward and kicked Floyd in the chest as hard as I could. The force of the blow lifted him off the ground and threw him back five feet.

Crack.

The back of Floyd's head slammed into a boulder sticking up out of the ground, and his orange aura abruptly snuffed out, like a candle flame doused by a stiff wind. The gun tumbled from his fingers, his head dropped, and blood sluiced down the side of his neck and dripped onto the snow like scarlet raindrops.

Floyd was dead.

I leaned forward and put my hands on my knees, trying to get my breath back through my bruised ribs.

Footsteps crunched through the snow, heading in my direction. I straightened up, whirled around, and raised my fists . . .

Gabriel stepped out of the trees and walked over to me. He looked at the dead guard, then shook his head. "You always have to make a mess, don't you, Slick? I thought the idea was to come out here, find Henrika's lab, and sneak back into the hotel without anyone being the wiser."

He stabbed a finger at the guard's body. "I haven't been a cleaner for a while, but that is *not* what sneaking around looks like."

He was right. Section 47 prided itself on its anonymity, and cleaners were supposed to get in, eliminate their targets, and get out, all without leaving a trace of themselves behind. Snow, dirt, and leaves were scuffed all over the clearing, and Floyd had bled over everything around him.

Gabriel shook his head again. "He looks like some poor deer you gutted."

"He was a lot more dangerous than a bloody deer," I rasped.

I limped over, plucked my knife off the ground, and tucked it up my sleeve. I also grabbed Floyd's gun and slid it into my waistband. Then I knelt beside the dead guard and rifled through his pockets.

He was carrying a phone and a walkie-talkie. I used my galvanism to drain the charges out of both devices and sent those spikes of energy to my grazed arm and bruised ribs. The fresh influx of power lessened the pain of my injuries, and I sighed with relief, my breath frosting in the cold air again.

"So that's what galvanism looks like," Gabriel murmured. "Did you know your eyes glow this weird silver-blue when you're using your power?"

I rolled said silver-blue eyes. "Why the surprise? You saw me use my galvanism in Germany during the Tannenbaum mission."

"Yeah, but I didn't get an up-close-and-personal look at it. I was a little more concerned about the mercenaries attacking us than watching your eyes light up like Christmas trees." Gabriel shuddered. "Galvanism is kind of creepy if you ask me."

I slid the dead phone and the walkie-talkie back into the guard's pockets. "It's no creepier than watching your body dissolve into a smoke cloud like you're a nightmare monster."

"Nightmare monster, huh?" Gabriel grinned. "I like it. Maybe I'll use that as a code name sometime."

I huffed. "Well, Mr. Nightmare Monster, make yourself useful, and help me carry the guard's body down to the lake so we can sink him in the water. With any luck, no one will notice he's missing until morning."

"And after that?" Gabriel asked in a chiding voice. "Bryce is no fool. He'll know you killed this guy."

"Just like I know Bryce sent this guy to capture me, and we'll both pretend like nothing happened the next time we see each other. It's how the spy game is played."

Gabriel nudged the guard's leg with his boot. "Bryce wanted

this guy to *capture* you? Why not just kill you?"

"Bryce hates me. He probably has some grand dream of stringing me up like a side of beef and butchering me a piece at a time," I replied. "What about you? Did you find anything by the lake?"

Gabriel shook his head. "Nope. No sign of Henrika's lab. No guards either. I didn't even come across a couple having an ill-advised tryst in one of the boathouses."

We'd come out here and risked our lives, and we had a whole lot of nothing to show for it. The risking-my-life part came with the job, but I wanted—needed—to get back to the hotel and make sure Charlotte was okay.

I bent down and took hold of Floyd's shoulders. "Come on, Gaby. Heave-ho. Time to put all those muscles to use."

Gabriel muttered his annoyance, but he bent down and grabbed the dead guard's legs. Together, we carried the body toward the lake.

TWENTY-FIVE

CHARLOTTE

I maintained my position by the shelves, not daring to move, silently cursing my own recklessness. As soon as I realized Henrika wasn't in the library, I should have backtracked and waited in the foyer. Not waltzed right in like I owned the place and let Henrika snap her trap—or whatever this was—shut behind me.

Henrika's gaze locked onto the Grunglass Necklace around my throat. I'd known it was a risk to wear the necklace, but it was one of the few things she coveted, and I was hoping the sight of it might throw her off her game just a little bit.

Hunger creased Henrika's face, and she drew in a sharp breath. I tensed and curled my fingers around my purse a little tighter, remembering what Joan had said about the bag being lined with explosives. If Henrika ordered Bryce and the guards to take the necklace, I'd twist the rhinestone clasp, toss the purse bomb at them, and duck behind the closest table.

Henrika opened her mouth, but then her gaze flicked past the necklace and landed on the two photos on the shelf. A shadow passed over her face, but she jerked her head at Bryce and the two guards. "Leave us."

"Are you sure that's wise?" Bryce asked, his hand still on his gun. "Given who she works for? She might try something stupid."

"It's fine," Henrika replied. "Charlotte and I have an understanding, and she is far from stupid. It's one of the things I admire most about her."

Truth, my inner voice whispered, although a chill slithered down my spine at the compliment.

"I'll be right outside if you need me," Bryce said.

Henrika smiled, then reached up and cupped his cheek in her hand. "Of course, darling. You always take such good care of me."

Bryce took her hand in his and pressed a soft, gallant kiss to her knuckles, playing the part of a debonair gentleman. Henrika's smile widened. I'd thought Bryce was just a hired gun, but he and Henrika were obviously much closer than that.

Was there any genuine affection between them? Or were they just convenient lovers for each other? Hard to tell, and for once, even my synesthesia was quiet on the matter.

The two guards left the library. Bryce eyed me, then strode through the opening and shut the doors behind him.

Henrika swept past me and headed to the refreshment tables, which had been replenished since the previous meeting. She poured a flute of champagne, then gestured at an empty glass. I shook my head. Henrika slugged down that drink and poured herself another one. Then she finally faced me.

We regarded each other in silence. The seconds ticked by one after another, and the longer I stared at Henrika, the more my synesthesia flared to life, painting her in a bright, bloody red light. Oh, I didn't get the sense that she was going to physically attack me, but she seemed to know just as much about me as I knew about her, which made her a serious threat.

I had a feeling Henrika Hyde would *always* be a threat.

Henrika used her champagne flute to gesture at the photo of her and Feliciano. "That's one of my favorite pictures of the two of us."

"I didn't realize you were involved with Feliciano Salvador."

She shrugged. "It started out as a business arrangement, but it soon turned into something more, as things like that so often do. Just like you and Desmond, I imagine."

I bristled. "Desmond and I are *nothing* like you."

Her red lips flashed a small smile. "We'll see about that." Her smile vanished, and she shrugged again. "Feliciano and I kept our personal relationship very discreet. Most of the people in our inner circles didn't even know about the two of us. At least, not until after Mexico."

"This photo was taken at Feliciano's villa. You were there when the Section cleaners tried to kill Feliciano. That's why you claim to know what really happened to my father."

"Something like that."

"You could just tell me," I snapped, trying and failing to keep the emotion out of my voice.

Another small smile played across her lips. "Why would I do that? It's so much more *fun* to watch you scurry around, desperately searching for clues about what happened to dear old Dad. Bryce bet me twenty bucks you wouldn't notice the photo, but of course, I easily won that bet. Charlotte Locke is nothing if not observant."

So letting me break into the library and nose around *had* been a test. Anger simmered through my veins, but I kept my face calm and blank.

"Back at the Halstead Hotel, you claimed you didn't care what happened to your father, that Jack Locke always put Section missions before everything else, even you, his own daughter." Henrika raised her eyebrows in a questioning look.

"My father *did* put Section 47 before everything else. I always expected him to get killed on one mission or another."

The anger in my veins boiled up, the way it always did whenever I talked about my father's death. "But what really pisses me off is the mess that came *after* my father died. The worst part wasn't his death. Oh, no. It was watching my grandmother drown in debt and work her fingers to the bone trying to pay back the ransom money. How does three million dollars just disappear into thin air?"

Henrika's left eye twitched. I wondered at the small show of emotion, but she didn't respond, so I answered my own question. "It doesn't. Which means someone either screwed up the ransom exchange, or stole the money, or both."

"Mmm." Henrika made a noncommittal sound and took another sip of champagne.

My eyes narrowed. "You really do know all about it, don't you? Everything that happened in Mexico. Who screwed up and why my father died and got blamed for everything."

Henrika nodded. "Yes, I know all that and much more. But your assumptions are all wrong, Charlotte."

"What do you mean?"

"No one screwed up on either side. Everything that happened on the Mexico mission was a very deliberate act."

Truth, my inner voice whispered. Henrika wasn't lying. Oh, her information might still be wrong, or be only part of the story, but she truly believed whatever she knew. That was the tricky thing about my synesthesia. It could tell me whether someone was lying, but it couldn't always tell me exactly how correct—or not—they might be.

"What kind of *deliberate act*?"

Henrika tapped a finger on her lips, as though she was thinking of just the right description. "Arrogance, with more than a little desperate self-preservation and a touch of treachery."

"You're one to talk about acts of arrogance," I muttered.

"How so?"

I threw my hands out wide. "This whole auction for your Redburn formula. It's all just a *game*. You brought Desmond and me here, along with the other paramortals, and pitted us all against one another. Now you're just waiting to see which of us dies and who manages to live through the weekend. You do everything with more than just a touch of treachery."

She shrugged. "What can I say? It's an amusing game."

Henrika wasn't going to tell me anything. No, she preferred to dole out cryptic clues one at a time and watch me frantically race around like a mouse in search of the next morsel of cheese that was only going to lead me even deeper into her maze.

Well, it was time to squirm out of Henrika's trap and start playing my own game.

I gestured at the photo of a teenage Henrika with the sick girl. "That's one of your cousins, right?"

Henrika blinked at the abrupt change in topic. "How do you know that?"

"The two of you have the same eyes. Same shape, same size, same color green." Now that I'd had time to think about it, the research I'd done into Henrika's family tree floated through my mind. "What was her name?"

I snapped my fingers a couple of times. Henrika flinched at the sharp sounds.

The answer came to me, and I snapped my fingers a final time. "Ah! Her name was Meg. She was your first cousin. The daughter of your mother's sister."

Henrika flinched again. Then she set down her champagne, walked over, picked up the framed photo, and smoothed her hand over the glass. "Meg was the only one of my cousins who didn't look down her nose at me and my mother when my father kicked us out of his life. Meg and I were best friends— until she died."

The raw emotion in her voice surprised me, and I took another look at Meg's pale face and bald head. Of course. I could have smacked myself for not putting the pieces together sooner. "Meg is the reason you host the charity event every year. You really do care about raising money for cancer research."

Henrika returned the photo to the shelf, nudging it back into place with her index finger. "Meg is the reason I got into science, chemistry, pharmaceuticals, all of it. I didn't want anyone else to lose their best friend the way I had."

Her voice was calm, but a shadow of sorrow darkened her face, and I didn't need my synesthesia to know she was telling the truth. But the longer I looked at her, the more I thought of another image: Desmond clutching Graham Walker's body on a blackened beach, their skin burned, blistered, and a shiny, unnatural shade of red from Henrika's devastating explosive.

"And yet here you are, trying to sell a biomagical weapon to the highest bidder. Funny how your priorities have shifted over the years," I said in a snide voice.

Henrika barked out a laugh, but it was a sharp, bitter sound. She spun toward me, anger sparking in her eyes. "Do you think I started out making weapons? That I just woke up one day and began plotting the best way to hurt people? Don't be an idiot, Charlotte. I had the same grandiose dreams as everyone else."

"What *dreams*?"

Henrika gracefully raised her arms out wide, then swept her hands together and pointed at her chest. "That *I* was going to be the one to do it—to finally cure cancer, leukemia, dementia, and every other horrible disease that robs people of their loved ones far too soon, whether they are mortals or paramortals."

"What changed?"

Henrika's hands plummeted to her sides. "Unfortunately, it's a lot easier to kill people than it is to cure them." Her mouth twisted. "It pays better too."

Truth, my synesthesia whispered.

"So you started making weapons instead of medicines," I accused.

"So I started making weapons," Henrika agreed. "Turns out I was very, very good at it."

"Is that why Niles Perran is so jealous? Because you're better at making weapons than he is? Or is he still pissed that you had a benefactor and he didn't?"

Something flickered across Henrika's face, but the emotion was gone before I could put a name to it. Once again, I made a mental note to find out more about Henrika's rivalry with the other biomagical chemist and exactly who had jumpstarted her deadly career all those years ago.

Henrika huffed with annoyance. "Niles is jealous because he's just not as good as I am. Not with people, not with brokering deals, and especially not when it comes to creating new weapons." She snapped her fingers as though the most marvelous thought had just occurred to her. "Speaking of Niles, let's see what my old rival is up to."

Henrika walked behind her desk, hit some keys on the laptop, and spun the monitor around so I could see it. The screen displayed several boxes, all showing different places in and around the hotel. Henrika hit a button, and one of the boxes filled the screen.

On the security footage, Niles Perran was roaming around a conference room, holding what looked like a small metal detector. Niles waved the gadget over a pitcher of water, but he must not have liked the reading, because he glared at the pitcher and moved on.

"Niles is looking for traces of explosives, radiation, and other elements in hopes of finding my lab. Arrogant little prick." Henrika sneered. "He's always been jealous because I'm richer and more successful than he'll ever be. Smarter and more creative too. I've created a dozen new paramortal poisons over the last decade, while he's still fiddling with the same old formulas he dreamed up in grad school."

She hit another key, and a different box filled the screen.

Steig Helseth was towering over the pretty waitress from the poker game, who had her back pressed up against a column in the lobby. The assassin's eyes were fixed on the waitress's chest, and he was gesturing wildly, even though the woman was clearly trying to squirm away from him.

"At least Niles is trying to find my lab. Steig is completely ignoring my orders about not hunting mortals." A disgusted look creased Henrika's face. "Steig is hoping to lure that poor woman back to his room so he can choke the life out of her and then skin her alive with that hunting knife he carries around like a bloody trophy."

Henrika tapped another key, and another image appeared. Oriana Luzzo was standing on one of the outdoor terraces, clutching a gadget similar to Niles's metal detector. Oriana discreetly waved the device back and forth over the stone wall. A light flashed red on the device, and Oriana frowned and moved over to another section.

"Oriana is smarter than either Niles or Steig," Henrika said, shooting a sour glare at the screen. "She's looking for traces of magic in hopes of finding my Redburn formula. She even has a boat waiting on the far side of the lake to come pick her up if she manages to break into my lab."

Henrika tapped yet another key. "And then, of course, there is Desmond, who has been *much* more entertaining to watch than the others."

A bird's-eye—drone's-eye—view of the hotel appeared. Henrika fast-forwarded the footage, and the two of us watched Desmond climb down an exterior wall, drop to the ground, and vanish into the shadows.

Henrika hit another button. All the feeds vanished, and the monitor went dark. "Do you know what they all have in common, Charlotte?" She answered her own question. "None of them will *ever* find my lab."

Truth, my synesthesia whispered.

Henrika had far more cameras at her disposal than I'd realized. She might not be spying on Desmond and me in the honeymoon suite, but she was watching everything else we did.

"We're not here to talk about the others," I replied. "You have something that belongs to me: the undercover agent list."

Henrika's gaze locked onto the Grunglass Necklace again. "I could say the same thing about you, Charlotte. Then again, you got lucky, didn't you? If that last card hadn't been the queen of hearts, I would have won, and I would be wearing my necklace instead of you."

I toyed with one of the emeralds dangling from the gold band. "What was it you said? Oh, yes. Blind luck makes the game *so* much more exciting."

Henrika huffed at me throwing her own words back in her face. She raised her hand, and magic glowed on her palm like a golden ember about to burst into a raging fire. "I could march over there, rip that necklace off your throat, and turn your pretty face into putty."

Despite the distance between us, the raw, sizzling force of her combusto power blasted over me like a heat wave. Sweat broke out on the back of my neck, and my synesthesia drummed out an incessant, ominous warning.

Danger-danger-danger.

I rubbed my thumb over the purse in my hand, once again thinking about the explosives hidden inside the bag. "That wouldn't go so well for you."

Henrika scoffed. "You're an analyst with a wacky form of synesthesia. You're hardly a threat to me."

"That's what Katarina Tanetsa thought—right up to when I shoved a sword into her back."

Henrika's green eyes narrowed, glowing almost as brightly as the golden magic still pulsing in her hand.

"No matter how much you want it, you aren't going to take the necklace from me."

"Why not?" Henrika challenged.

"Because you like to *win*, not cheat. And trying to take the necklace right now would be cheating. You have a weird but pesky sense of honor about things like that."

Henrika blinked several times, as though my words surprised her, then snorted out a laugh. "I suppose you're right, Charlotte. For the moment."

The hot golden magic on her palm evaporated, and she lowered her hand to her side.

I ground my teeth to keep my relief from showing. "Enough stalling. Give me the list."

Henrika yanked open one of the desk drawers, drew out a silver flash drive, and held it up. "This drive contains your precious undercover agent list. And before you ask, no, I didn't make any copies. I didn't even open the drive. I don't care about the real identities of Section spies."

Truth, truth, truth, my inner voice whispered. She really hadn't looked at or copied the information, which had been one of Gia's and Evelyn's main worries.

Henrika tossed the drive over to me, and the slight, almost inconsequential weight shocked me. Something with the power to do so much damage to so many people should feel heavier and sturdier, like the Grunglass Necklace ringing my throat.

Relief crashed through me, but it quickly vanished, replaced by suspicion. Why hadn't Henrika at least copied the information? Why go to all the trouble of stealing the list in the first place just to hand it over so easily now?

Unless . . . the UC list had just been bait to force me to come to the resort.

My mind whirred at the implications. Henrika was enjoying taunting me with her knowledge about the Mexico mission and my father's death, but I got the impression our conversation was just a small part of a larger, more devious plot. What was Henrika's true goal?

"I'm not the only one with a twisted sense of honor, Charlotte. Yours is going to get you into trouble someday." Henrika paused. "Just like it did to Jack Locke."

I stiffened. "What does my father's honor have to do with you?"

"It's the reason he didn't kill me in Mexico when he had the chance."

Henrika's gaze strayed over to the photo of her and Feliciano Salvador. Another shadow passed over her face, and something that looked a lot like regret and longing flickered through her eyes.

Why did Henrika keep talking about my father? He had been sent to Mexico to kill Feliciano, not her. My father had avoided collateral damage at all costs, and he would have never even targeted Henrika, since she was Feliciano's lover . . .

Unless my father had thought *Henrika* was a threat.

But why would he think that? And if he had, then why hesitate? Why not go ahead and kill her?

More and more questions popped into my mind, and each one shifted my perception of the Mexico mission. I thought I'd been standing on a mountain of information, a solid foundation of facts, but it was really nothing but a pile of sand, and I was rapidly sinking into the quagmire of the unknown.

Henrika pulled her gaze away from Feliciano's photo, and her face smoothed out into its usual benign mask. "I honored my end of our bet. Your precious undercover agents are safe and will live to spy another day. Now, get out before I change my mind and liquefy your bones. I have work to do."

She sat down behind the desk, turned the monitor toward her, and started typing, her fingers stabbing into the laptop keys with far more force than was necessary. The rare show of emotion surprised me. I didn't know what memories I had dredged up, but in her own way, Henrika seemed just as haunted by the Mexico mission as I was.

I backed away from her and opened one of the library doors. Bryce was waiting outside. He shot me an icy glower, but I skirted past him, hurried through the foyer, and stepped into the waiting elevator.

The door slid shut, and I caught sight of my reflection in the mirrored surface. The Grunglass Necklace glimmered around my neck, and each emerald and diamond seemed to sparkle in time to the wild theories and paranoid suspicions jangling through my mind.

After fifteen years of wondering what had really happened to my father, Henrika had given me a few more pieces to the puzzle, but I still had far more questions than answers.

TWENTY-SIX

DESMOND

Gabriel and I trudged down to the shore and heaved the guard's body out into the lake. Given his heavy winter clothes and boots, Floyd sank like a stone. The water rippled for a few seconds, then smoothed out.

"We can hope no one will find him until spring," I said. "Let's go."

Gabriel and I hiked through the woods, around the golf course, and back to the hotel. We hunkered down behind the same evergreen hedges I'd used earlier and waited for the guards to stroll past us. The ballroom lights were still burning brightly, but the conversation, laughter, and music had died down. It was a few minutes before midnight, and the casino party was wrapping up.

Given the gusty wind and continued snowfall, I didn't feel like climbing back up the side of the hotel, even with my spiked gloves and boots, so I tugged my winter hat off my head and stuffed it into my pocket. I also took off my jacket and turned it inside out, so that the light blue interior showed, then put it back on. The left sleeve was ripped, and blood stained the fabric from where the bullet had grazed my arm earlier, but I was hoping no one would notice the imperfections.

Gabriel arched an eyebrow. "A reversible jacket? What good is that going to do you?"

"Make it look a little less like I was dressed in black from head to toe and skulking around places I wasn't supposed to be." I gestured at his outfit. "Unlike some people."

"I don't care if Bryce and his goons realize I was skulking around." Gabriel popped up the collar on his black leather jacket. "Besides, I look amazing in this jacket."

I snorted, but the two of us slipped out from behind the hedges, crossed the terrace, and stepped inside the hotel. Lots of partygoers were still clustered in the lobby, doing a final bit of drinking and socializing before retiring to their rooms. Gabriel and I attached ourselves to the back of a large group of people and walked past the guards stationed close to the ballroom. The guards gave the guests bored looks, and their gazes passed right over Gabriel and me. None of the men looked upset, which meant they hadn't realized their buddy Floyd was missing yet. Good.

Gabriel and I were about halfway across the lobby when a flutter of movement caught my eye. Joan was hovering beside a column, pretending to check her phone. She tilted her head to the side, then walked into a corridor.

Gabriel spotted her too. "Looks like your friend wants to chat."

We followed Joan down the corridor and into the same public library Charlotte and I had ducked into earlier. A faint hum of magic crackled around Joan's body, and her head swiveled back and forth as though she was searching for something.

A few seconds later, she stopped in the back of the library. Joan glanced around, then nodded in satisfaction. With her transmuter power, she could sense the energy emanating off cameras and listening devices just like I could, and she knew this area was a security dead zone.

Joan spun around on her heel, crossed her arms over her chest, and glared at Gabriel. "What is *he* doing here?"

"Gabriel decided to tag along on my reconnaissance mission," I replied.

The former cleaner grinned at Joan. "What can I say? I just can't quit the spy business no matter how hard I try."

She scoffed and turned to me. "Did you find Henrika's lab?"

I shook my head. "No. If the lab is in the woods, it's too well hidden for me to detect, even with my galvanism. How is Charlotte?"

"She's fine," Joan replied. "Diego was finally able to hack into the hotel's security cameras. Charlotte left Henrika's penthouse about fifteen minutes ago and went back to your suite."

Relief coursed through me. Charlotte was a skilled spy, but that didn't mean I wasn't going to worry about her.

I quickly filled Joan in on Gabriel's and my search, my killing the guard, and the two of us dumping the body in the lake. "What's been happening here?"

Joan shrugged. "I've been trailing the other paramortals around the hotel. Steig hit on one woman after another before finally giving up and returning to his room, bitter, drunk, and alone. Oriana and Niles have both been roaming around the lobby, the common areas, and the terraces with various gadgets. They're obviously searching for Henrika's lab, although they haven't had any more luck than you two had in the woods."

"Maybe the resort is just a giant smokescreen," Gabriel chimed in. "Maybe Henrika's lab isn't here at all. Maybe it's back in D.C."

Joan nodded. "I had a similar thought, so I asked Diego to check topographical maps of the area around the resort, as well as thermal imaging, although he hasn't found anything unusual yet."

Gabriel gave her an appreciative look. "Smart and beautiful.

If you'd been my liaison, I might have stayed on as a Section cleaner."

He winked at Joan, who rolled her eyes. But the most curious thing was that both their auras flickered, his with obvious interest and hers with something I couldn't quite decipher.

Gabriel clapped me on the shoulder. "Well, Slick, this is where I leave you. I've got my own missions to check on. Try not to get yourself and Charlotte killed before morning. Okay?"

Gabriel strutted around a bookshelf and vanished from view.

"All the reports about him were right," Joan muttered. "Gabriel Chase is one of the most arrogant cleaners I've ever met."

She glared at the spot where he had disappeared, then focused on me again. "Gia texted me right before you entered the lobby. General Percy wants an update. Apparently, he's frustrated with our lack of progress and wants to send the strike teams in tonight in hopes of catching Henrika and the other paramortals off guard."

I shook my head. "He can't send strike teams into a hotel full of innocent guests and workers. Henrika has probably rigged the whole structure with explosives, just like she and Adrian Anatoly rigged the lawn at the Halstead Hotel to blow up Charlotte and me. If she has enough Redburn on-site, Henrika could kill everyone in the hotel and turn the entire mountain into a giant smoking crater. We can't risk creating a mass-casualty event."

Joan nodded. "That's what Gia told Percy, but she doesn't know how much longer he's going to wait. He outranks her, so he can assume tactical control anytime he wants."

It wasn't a question of *if* the General would take control but *when*. My father wasn't known for his patience, and sooner or later, he would decide that eliminating Henrika was worth any risk, even endangering civilian lives.

"We're still supposed to meet Henrika at eight a.m. in the lobby. Supposedly, that's when we'll get down to business, and she'll finally show us a sample of Redburn. After that, maybe we'll at least know where the lab is."

Joan nodded again. "I'll tell Gia and the others. Be careful, Dez."

"You too."

She slipped out of the library. I had started to follow her when my phone vibrated. I pulled it out of my pocket and grimaced. The General was demanding a video call.

I sighed and accepted the call, and my father's face appeared on the screen.

"Mission update," he barked.

I told him everything that had happened, from our first meeting with Henrika and the other paramortals in the penthouse to the poker game in the ballroom to my searching the woods. I edited out a lot of details, though, including Charlotte using the Grunglass Necklace as a bargaining chip and Gabriel accompanying me into the woods. When I finished, my father shook his head in a slow, disappointed motion I knew all too well.

"How hard can it be to find a weapons lab?" the General said, fixing his steely blue gaze on me. "It has to be on that mountain somewhere."

"Well, wherever it is, it's extremely well hidden. I'm hoping the Redburn demonstration tomorrow morning will give Charlotte and me some more hints about where the lab might be."

My father's lips puckered, and I could hear the steady drumming of his fingers. "Maybe you're right. Maybe Henrika will take you to the lab in the morning. Surely she won't risk demonstrating the explosive out in the open where all the guests could see it."

I didn't think there was anything Henrika Hyde wouldn't risk, especially if it meant keeping herself out of a Section black site, but I held my tongue.

"We have made some progress," I said, trying to put a positive spin on things. "Charlotte got Henrika to gamble away the UC list."

Instead of being pleased, the General let out a derisive snort. "I don't care about the list. We can always pull our undercover agents out of harm's way if needed. Getting our hands on the Redburn formula and eliminating Henrika are the two most important things. Those are still your primary objectives, Desmond. Everything else is secondary."

"I *know* that," I snapped.

"Then get it *done*," the General snapped right back. "Or I'll send in the strike teams and take care of matters myself just like I should have years ago."

I frowned. "What does that mean?"

My father hesitated, then cleared his throat. "Henrika has been a thorn in Section's side for far too long. She needs to be eliminated, no matter what. Do you understand me?"

"Yes, sir." I'd learned a long time ago there was no use arguing with the General when he was in one of his moods.

My father cleared his throat again. "Be careful, and stay safe, son."

"Yes, sir." Once again, that was all I could say.

My father hit a button and ended the video call. I stared at my phone, wondering at the General's cryptic words—and exactly why he wanted Henrika Hyde dead so badly.

TWENTY-SEVEN

CHARLOTTE

After my meeting with Henrika, I returned to the honeymoon suite.

The first thing I did was kick off my stilettoes, fish my laptop out of my suitcase, and check the flash drive. Henrika had kept her word, and the drive contained the list of undercover Section agents. Even better, the files were still encrypted and hadn't been copied, as far as I could tell. I sighed with relief and sagged back against the couch cushions. At least something had gone right tonight.

I basked in my relief for a few seconds, then prowled around the suite, opening one cabinet after another, until I discovered a printer tucked away in a credenza. I flipped it on and printed out several documents related to the Mexico mission, along with dozens of maps and satellite images of the Glittertop Resort.

Even though I'd reviewed the information at Section headquarters, I wanted to look at everything again. Now that I'd seen the resort grounds in person, maybe I would have a better idea of where Henrika might be hiding her lab. Plus, I could always absorb, understand, analyze, and retain information much better if I looked at paper printouts rather than surfing through electronic documents.

I'd been looking through the files, maps, and photos for about ten minutes when an electronic beep sounded, and the door opened. I scrambled to my feet and whirled around, and Desmond stepped into the living room.

I hurried around the end of the couch, went over to him, and hugged him. Desmond wrapped his arms around me and buried his face in my neck, his stubble tickling my skin. We held on to each other for the better part of a minute, just soaking up the comfort of each other's presence.

I shuddered out a breath, then drew back and pushed a rumpled lock of dark blond hair back over his forehead. "What did you find in the woods?"

"Nothing," Desmond muttered. "No buildings, no structures, not even the smallest hint about where Henrika's lab might be located. Please tell me you had better luck with the UC list."

I gestured over at my laptop on the low table in front of the couch. "Henrika honored our bet and gave me the list. She said she hadn't even opened the files or tried to make any copies."

"Do you believe her?"

"I do. According to my synesthesia, she wasn't lying or parsing her words."

Desmond frowned. "Why would Henrika just hand over the list? Especially when she went to so much trouble to hire Bryce to steal it in the first place?"

The same questions had been rattling around my mind ever since I'd left Henrika's penthouse, and I kept coming back to the same alarming answers. "I think she just used the UC list as bait. To get us to show up in person at the resort."

His frown deepened. "Why would she do that? Henrika knows how much you despise her. Me too."

"I haven't figured out her motives yet, but Henrika doled out a few more clues."

I told Desmond everything Henrika had said in her library, including her business arrangement and personal relationship with Feliciano Salvador.

"That's how she knows so much about the Mexico mission," I said. "She was *there*, on-site, when it all went down."

Desmond crossed his arms over his chest, his right index finger tapping on his left elbow. "Maybe that's why the General wants her dead. Maybe Henrika knows something about the Mexico mission that would reflect badly on Section, on him."

"The General doesn't strike me as someone who cares about a little spy scandal. Besides, everyone at Section 47 knows the Mexico mission was a disaster. The General survived the initial fallout back then, so why would he suddenly be worried about it fifteen years later?"

Desmond shrugged, neither agreeing nor disagreeing.

I gestured over at the papers I'd printed out. "I've been going back through all the files related to the Mexico mission. We know that Henrika has sold weapons to General Percy and Section 47 over the years."

That's what Henrika had claimed when Desmond and I confronted her at the Halstead Hotel a few months ago, and I had no reason to doubt her. Section 47 might ostensibly be the good guys, but the higher-ups did some pretty dark things from time to time, like buy weapons from criminals and use them to eliminate even more dangerous criminals.

"Sounds like there's a *but* coming," Desmond said.

I sighed. "But according to all my research, Henrika and General Percy have never crossed paths. So why his sudden interest in neutralizing her?"

Relief flickered across Desmond's face, although his index finger started tapping against his elbow again. "Maybe this mission is a preemptive strike. Maybe my father has finally realized how dangerous Henrika truly is and wants to take her out before she creates any more biomagical weapons. Something even worse than Redburn."

"Or maybe the General wants the Redburn formula for himself and doesn't want Henrika alive to make it for someone else," I countered.

Desmond shrugged a second time, once again neither agreeing nor disagreeing. Then he sighed and scrubbed his hands over his face, as if trying to slough off all the mysterious motives and unanswered questions. "Well, whatever my father is up to, I'm just glad he is finally considering Henrika a serious threat. I'm going to take a shower and go to bed."

"I'll be there soon. I want to look through a few more files first."

Desmond nodded, gave me a quick kiss on the lips, and stepped into the bedroom. A few seconds later, the steady hiss of water sounded.

I looked back out over the sea of papers, maps, and photos scattered across the table. Desmond knew exactly what kind of man the General was, but Percy was still his father, and he didn't want to think the General was guilty of being involved with Henrika. I didn't want Percy to be involved with Henrika either, for Desmond's sake, but I had my doubts.

General Jethro Percy was up to something, Henrika too, and I had a funny feeling that Desmond's and my survival depended on figuring out the answers.

An hour later, I had reviewed dozens of documents and had nothing to show for it but a raging migraine. Disgusted, I followed Desmond's lead, took a hot shower, and crawled into bed next to him.

Desmond slept soundly for a change, free from his usual nightmares about the Blacksea mission, and I was the one who tossed and turned. I finally drifted off a few hours before dawn, but my dreams were filled with disjointed images of everything that had happened over the past few days.

Bryce Finkley lobbing a smoke grenade at me after he'd stolen the UC list. General Percy examining me like a bug under a microscope during the Vault mission debriefing. Steig, Niles, and Oriana clearly calculating how they could kill Desmond and me and each other and seize the Redburn formula. The Grunglass Necklace glittering on the green felt of the poker table. Henrika staring at the photo of her cousin Meg, genuine anguish creasing her face . . .

I woke with a start, the image of Henrika's and Meg's smiling faces still filling my mind. Desmond murmured something and snuggled closer, throwing his arm across my chest as though he was protecting me, even in his sleep.

I started to get up, but then I thought better of it, and I lay there, warm, safe, and secure in Desmond's embrace, until my phone alarm went off.

Desmond grumbled, me too, but we both got up. We checked in with Gia, Joan, and Diego, along with Gabriel, but everything had been quiet overnight, and no one had any new information. Desmond also texted back and forth with his father. He didn't tell me what Percy said, but I imagined the General was giving him the same orders as before: kill Henrika and get the Redburn formula.

I donned a fuzzy pale blue sweater, thick black pants, and a pair of black boots with explosive-filled pom-poms dangling off the sides. I also put on a matching blue jacket and slid a pair of gloves into my pocket, along with a winter hat, both featuring the explosive pom-poms. I didn't know where Henrika would show us the formula, but I wanted to be prepared and warm in case the demonstration was outside.

I hesitated, then fastened the Grunglass Necklace around my throat. I didn't dare leave the necklace in the suite for fear that Henrika would send someone to steal it. I fished a thick blue wool scarf out of my suitcase and wrapped it around my throat to hide the glittering jewels.

Desmond dressed in a black sweater, cargo pants, and boots, although his were pom-pom-free. He strapped a knife to his left forearm and tucked his silver watch into a pocket on the front of his jacket. We both slid guns into our jacket pockets.

"You ready for this?" Desmond asked.

"Not really. Are you?"

"No, but going into the unknown is a spy's job." He grinned. "I kind of love not knowing what's going to happen next."

The excitement in his voice teased a laugh out of me. "Well, that makes one of us, because I *hate* the unknown."

"Don't think of it as the unknown. Think of it as another chance to get answers."

I grinned back at him. "I'll try my best. Even if answers have been in short supply lately."

His grin faded away. Mine too, and a tense, uneasy silence dropped over us.

Desmond smoothed a lock of my hair back over my shoulder. "No matter what happens, I'm glad you're my partner, Numbers."

I tugged his zipper a little higher up on his jacket. "Right back at you, Dundee."

We stared at each other a heartbeat longer. Then I threaded my arm through Desmond's, and we left the honeymoon suite, got into the elevator, and went down to the ground floor.

The other paramortals were already gathered in the lobby. Niles and Oriana were bundled up from head to toe in scarves, jackets, gloves, and boots, but Steig wore only a dark green hunter's vest over a green plaid shirt, and his hands were bare.

Niles and Oriana had on so many layers I couldn't tell if

they were carrying any weapons. Steig was sporting his usual hunting knife on his belt, and my synesthesia painted the long blade a brighter, bloodier red than usual.

No one spoke, and tension thickened the air. We'd played a few games at the poker table last night, and now it was time to get down to our real, deadly business.

The elevator in the far corner dinged out its arrival, the door slid back, and Henrika strutted into the lobby. She was dressed in a light green jacket, sweater, and pants, and she looked sleek and stylish, whereas I felt like a puffed-up blue marshmallow.

Bryce followed Henrika out of the elevator. He was dressed all in black, as were the guards who crossed the lobby and fell in step behind him. All the men had their jackets unzipped and open, showing off the guns holstered to their belts.

Henrika didn't break stride as she walked past us. "Come along, children. Time to see the toy you're all so desperate to acquire."

Oriana rolled her eyes, and Niles glared at Henrika's back, but the two of them followed her. Steig ambled along behind them.

Bryce gave Desmond a thin smile and held out his hand. "After you, Dez."

Desmond spun around on his heel and followed the other paramortals. I fell in step beside him, while Bryce and the guards closed ranks behind us.

My gaze flicked around the lobby. Joan was perched on a stool in the corner, checking her phone and sipping a hot chocolate, while Gabriel was leaning against a column, reading a newspaper. Neither one of them looked at Desmond and me. Our friends would do their best to keep an eye on us, as would Gia, Diego, and even General Percy through the resort's security cameras. But for the most part, Desmond and I were on our own.

We left the warm confines of the lobby and stepped outside.

The winter wind slapped me across the face and knifed through my heavy clothes, making me shiver. A couple of inches of snow had fallen overnight, crusting everything in a blanket of sparkling white. Dark gray clouds cloaked the skies, indicating that a massive storm was on the way.

Niles and Oriana grumbled about the cold, and even some of the guards stomped their feet and muttered their displeasure.

Steig drew in a deep, appreciative breath and held his arms out wide. "Ahhh! This sort of weather reminds me of home."

"Yeah, if your home is an iceberg," Oriana muttered.

Niles snorted out a laugh. So did Bryce, but Steig ignored them both.

Henrika strode over to the nearest set of stairs and headed down to the lawn, where several black snowmobiles were waiting with small red winter sleighs attached to them.

Henrika climbed into a sleigh, along with Bryce. Niles, Oriana, and Steig got into another sleigh, and Desmond and I claimed a third sleigh.

A guard hopped onto each snowmobile, cranked the engine, and took off. The snowmobiles easily pulled the passenger sleighs along behind them, and the smooth sensation reminded me of flying.

"If we weren't going to a weapons demonstration, being tucked in a sleigh with you would be an excellent way to spend the morning," Desmond murmured in my ear.

I laughed and rested my head on his shoulder. He was right. It was pleasant, and I was going to enjoy the journey, even as my stomach tied itself into knots about the destination.

The snowmobiles and sleighs sped across the golf course, then slowed down and stopped at the edge of the woods. We all got out of our sleighs, while the guards grabbed long coils of ropes that were attached to the backs of the snowmobiles. What were they going to do with the ropes?

"We walk from here," Henrika said.

Steig strode forward with no hesitation. Oriana and Niles grumbled again, but they too followed Henrika. Desmond and I fell in step behind them, and Bryce and the guards once again brought up the rear.

We went deep into the woods, so deep that I couldn't see or hear any noise from the hotel. According to the maps I'd studied, there were no buildings on this side of the resort grounds where Henrika might possibly have a hidden lab. I raised my eyebrows at Desmond in a silent question, and he nodded in return. This was the same area he'd searched with Gabriel last night, and he didn't know where Henrika was taking us either.

The trees thinned out, and we stepped into a large clearing with a lone spotlight at one end. It was still glowing, given the dark clouds gathering overhead. I recognized the area from Desmond's description. What were we doing way out here?

Henrika nodded at Bryce, who disappeared into the trees on the far side of the clearing. Then she faced the rest of us. "And now, what you've all been waiting for. A demonstration of my Redburn formula."

"What are you going to do? Blow up some trees?" Niles asked in a snide voice.

Henrika smiled, but it was a sharp, thin expression. "I promised a formula that will kill even the strongest paramortals, and that's exactly what I'm going to deliver."

Footsteps crunched through the snow, and a man stumbled into the clearing. He was wearing a long white lab coat, as though he was a scientist. One of his eyes was blackened, his lower lip was split and bloody, and his hands were bound in front of him with black plastic ties. Bryce followed the man, a gun in one hand and a small black briefcase in the other.

"Please, please! You don't have to do this!" the man pleaded. "I'm a scientist, not a spy! I don't even know what Section 47 is!"

Lie, my synesthesia muttered.

Even though no one was threatening me, a sick, sick feeling flooded my stomach. Desmond's hands clenched into fists, but Steig, Niles, and Oriana looked more curious than concerned.

The other guards forced the scientist up against a tree at the edge of the clearing and tied him to the trunk with the thick ropes they'd grabbed from the snowmobiles. The man kept begging, but no one else said a word, not even Henrika.

One of the guards produced a cloth from his pocket and shoved it into the scientist's mouth, although he kept trying to yell through the makeshift gag. His muffled pleas reminded me of a wounded animal keening, and the sounds ground against my heart like a dentist's drill.

Henrika studied the scientist with a cold expression. "You should have known better, Ethan. Did you really think I wouldn't find out you were taking photos of Redburn and offering to sell a sample to the highest bidder?"

Surprise spiked through me. Ethan had to be the person who'd sent General Percy a photo confirming Henrika was storing Redburn at the resort, although it sounded like the scientist had been interested in a quick payday more than anything else. Desmond glanced at me, the same uneasy realization on his face.

Bryce passed the black briefcase to Henrika, who opened it and plucked something out of the dark depths. She passed the briefcase to a guard, then turned around and held up an auto-injector where we all could see it. Red liquid shimmered inside the clear plastic, and the thick fluid matched what had been in the vials that Desmond had found at Tannenbaum Castle.

"And this is my Redburn formula," Henrika said, pride rippling through her voice.

For a moment, everyone was silent. Then Niles let out a derisive snort. "You promised us an explosive. Not some jelly in a jar."

Oriana and Steig murmured their agreement.

Henrika's lips flattened out into a thin line, and anger shimmered in her gaze.

Danger-danger-danger, my synesthesia warned.

Henrika whipped around and stabbed the injector into Ethan's upper left arm.

Desmond cursed and started forward. Red flared in the corner of my eye, and I saw Bryce snap up his gun. I grabbed Desmond's arm, stopping him.

Desmond tensed like he was going to pull away, but I tightened my grip in warning. If he tried to interfere, Bryce would shoot him, and my synesthesia was muttering that it was already too late to save the scientist anyway.

Desmond's gaze flicked over to Bryce, who smirked in return. A haunted look filled Desmond's face, and his shoulders slumped in resignation. I slid my hand down and gripped his cold fingers. Desmond didn't look at me, but he clung to my hand like it was a life raft keeping him from drowning in a sea of miserable memories.

Ethan's dark eyes bulged. The scientist shouted and shouted, although the cloth stuffed in his mouth muffled his cries. He also jerked and struggled against his bonds, although the thick ropes held him tightly to the tree.

Suddenly, Ethan stopped struggling. His eyes bulged even wider, and his muffled shouts morphed into sharp, shrieking screams that even the makeshift gag couldn't fully silence. Sweat beaded on his forehead and streamed down his face, as though he was standing in a too-hot sauna instead of the cold, open air.

A large red blister erupted on his left cheek like a volcanic pimple jutting up out of his skin. Then another blister on his right cheek. His nose. His chin. His neck . . .

Within seconds, every inch of Ethan's exposed skin was covered with ugly blisters, which puffed and puffed and puffed . . . until they popped. But instead of oozing fluid, the blisters disintegrated, and fresh ones formed, puffing up and popping just like the first wave. That happened over and over again, and the scientist's skin quickly turned a bright, shiny neon red.

Shock knifed through my heart. Not blisters—*burns*. The Redburn formula was literally burning through one layer of Ethan's skin after another.

The scientist's head snapped back, and he flailed and thrashed against the ropes as though he was having a violent seizure and couldn't control his own body. Blood poured out of his eyes and nose, like rivers of scarlet lava flowing down his skin.

I sucked in a breath, and a strange scent flooded my nose—harsh, acrid sulfur mixed with a lighter, gooey note, like burned sugar. The aroma slithered down my throat, and the foul smoky-sweetness made me want to vomit. Even though Desmond had described Redburn to me, what it did and how it felt, seeing the formula in action, hearing Ethan's screams, smelling his skin burning . . .

It was one of the most horrific things I'd ever witnessed.

Less than a minute later, it was over. Ethan slumped forward, his body covered with those ugly, ugly burns and his eyes still bulging, this time in death.

Desmond remained tall and rigid beside me, as though his body was made of glass and he would shatter if he so much as breathed. I tightened my grip on his hand, trying to comfort him in whatever small way I could. After a few seconds, he shuddered out a breath, and his face hardened with the same determination that was pumping through my own body.

Shock filled the faces of the other paramortals, although it quickly morphed into a mixture of grudging admiration and cold calculation.

"*This* is my Redburn formula," Henrika said, even more pride rippling through her voice as though she hadn't just dished out a brutal, agonizing death to another person. "I've been developing it for years, and I have conducted extensive tests, both in and out of the lab. Redburn has a ninety-nine-percent success rate, whether it is used as an explosive or as a poison, like you just witnessed. To date, only one person has ever managed to survive being exposed to it."

Henrika's gaze flicked over to Desmond. A muscle twitched an angry rhythm in his clenched jaw, like the timer on a bomb counting down to a massive explosion.

Niles crossed his arms over his chest. "Ninety-nine percent? You told us the formula was one-hundred-percent effective." He scoffed. "Any scientist would tell you those are *not* the same. You promised us something strong enough to kill *every* paramortal, no matter their powers or abilities."

Henrika nodded. "I did, and I've been wrestling with that problem for the last several months. I've run one experiment and simulation after another, but no matter what I do or what variables I input, I can't quite make my formula one-hundred-perfect effective."

"Who cares if it's not one-hundred-percent effective?" Oriana gestured at the dead scientist still tied to the tree. "Ninety-nine percent is good enough for me."

"Me too," Steig chimed in.

"It matters to *me*," Henrika hissed, anger creeping into her voice. "Because it's *my* formula, and it is *brilliant*. Except for one tiny, unforeseen, unexpected outlier."

Once again, her gaze flicked over to Desmond, and a cruel smile slowly curved her red lips. "But luckily, I've finally found a way to rectify this flaw."

"Flaw? What flaw?" Oriana asked. "You just said your formula was foolproof!"

"No, it's not," Niles argued.

"I don't care what the two of you are going on about," Steig cut in. "I want to see another demonstration . . ."

The three of them kept arguing with each other, but I tuned out their chatter. Instead, I thought about everything Henrika had just said about her formula, along with everything that had happened over the past few days.

During the Vault mission, Iris Berriston and Bryce Finkley had both had chances to kill me, but Iris claimed that she'd been ordered to let me live, and Bryce had only tossed a smoke grenade at me instead of a real bomb. Then Henrika had sent a personal invitation to me and a video to General Percy, basically forcing him to let me come to the resort. More than once, I'd wondered why Henrika now wanted me alive, instead of trying to orchestrate my death like she had before.

For the first time, I realized her seeming benevolence hid a sinister purpose: to make sure I ended up right here, right now.

Henrika kept staring at Desmond, and the greedy look on her face was like a key opening a lock in my mind. Henrika hadn't just fooled the two of us. She had been pulling the wool over everyone's eyes this entire time. This had never been about a weapons auction. Henrika had *never* intended to sell her Redburn formula to any of the paramortals—at least, not until it was *foolproof*. Her pride, ego, and arrogance wouldn't let her sell a weapon that wasn't one-hundred-percent effective, and there was only one way she could perfect her gruesome formula.

Henrika inviting us to her resort hadn't been about me or my father or the Mexico mission. At least, not directly, although I got the sense that was among her list of priorities, along with thumbing her nose at General Percy. Even stealing the undercover list had just been a feint to hide what—or rather whom—Henrika was really after.

My plus-one, as her invitation had said.

Desmond.

TWENTY-EIGHT

DESMOND

esmond." Charlotte whispered my name like it was a password that had just unlocked all the secrets of the universe.

She dropped my hand, whipped around to me, and drew in a breath, as though she was going to shout a warning. What was she suddenly so worried about?

"Execute!" Bryce yelled.

The guard closest to Charlotte drew his gun. I lunged in that direction, but the guard stepped forward and aimed his weapon at Charlotte's head before I could tackle him. The other guards also drew their guns and aimed them at Charlotte.

"I would stop right there if I were you, Dez," Bryce called out in a mocking voice. "Unless you want to see your girlfriend's brains splattered all over the snow."

I swallowed a frustrated growl, but I had no choice but to do as he commanded. Bryce grinned, drew his own gun, and pointed the weapon at me. He jerked his head. Another guard stepped forward and searched Charlotte. He removed the gun she'd had stuffed in her jacket pocket and tossed it aside.

"What is going on?" Niles asked, his gaze darting from one guard and gun to another.

"Desmond and Charlotte haven't been entirely truthful with the rest of us," Henrika replied. "They aren't arms dealers. They're spies for Section 47."

I muttered a curse, as did Charlotte. We had known Henrika could blow our cover at any time, but I'd been hoping we could take her down before that happened. Once again, though, she was three steps ahead, and she had just put Charlotte and me in even more danger.

Steig curled his hand around the hilt of his hunting knife, while Oriana cracked her knuckles, sparks of golden, caustic combusto magic flickering around her fingers. Niles pushed his glasses farther up his nose, but his lips curled back in a disgusted sneer, as though he was plotting the best way to kill us both.

Oriana's dark, angry gaze swung over to Henrika. "Wait a second. You *knew* they were Section spies? And invited us here anyway?"

Henrika held her hands out wide. "Guilty as charged."

"Why would you do that?" Steig bellowed. "We came here to buy your weapon! Not get captured by Section 47!"

Henrika shrugged. "If you want to walk away just because a couple of spies turned up, go ahead. I can always find other buyers for my formula."

"*After* you perfect it," Charlotte snarled. "Right? Isn't that what this is *really* about? Making your precious formula the deadliest it can be?"

Confusion filled me. What was Charlotte talking about?

Henrika let out a laugh and clapped her hands together in delight. "You really are too clever for your own good, Charlotte. It's too bad General Percy can't see the big picture like you can. He might have prevented this whole thing from happening."

"What does the General have to do with any of this?" I asked.

Henrika looked at me, fury sparking like matches in her green eyes. "He has *everything* to do with this, dear Desmond. And now Jethro is finally going to pay the price for his arrogance and treachery." She paused. "Or, rather, you are."

I opened my mouth to ask her another question and give myself a few more seconds to figure a way out of this mess—

Crack!

Crack! Crack!

Crack!

In the distance, gunshots zipped through the air.

Bryce checked the smartwatch on his wrist and nodded, as if he'd been expecting the commotion. "And that would be the Section strike teams swarming the golf course and firing on my men. Right on schedule."

"Jethro is nothing if not predictable in his impatience," Henrika replied.

"What do you want?" I asked, my hands balling into fists.

"*You*," Charlotte said in a soft, strangled voice. "She wants *you*, Desmond. This was never about leaking the UC list or any weapons auction. This was all about luring you into her trap."

I frowned. "Why would she want me? I'm just a Section cleaner."

Charlotte gave me a grim smile. "You're a Section cleaner who survived a Redburn explosion. You're Henrika's *flaw*."

My gaze flicked over to the dead scientist and locked on the horrific burns that had decimated his skin. The clearing melted away, and I was back on that blackened beach, the explosion blasting over me just as it had done countless times in my nightmares. The chemical fire of the Redburn formula just kept eating, eating, eating away at my skin like a red-hot monster that wouldn't be satisfied until it had devoured me completely . . .

"You also happen to be Jethro's son," Henrika added, her voice snapping me back to the here and now. "Which is an unexpected but delightful bonus."

She jerked her head at Bryce. "Let's move. Now. Before the strike teams reach the woods."

Bryce stepped forward and aimed his gun at Charlotte's head. She tensed, although she glared at the former cleaner. There was nothing I could do. Bryce could pull the trigger before I could take one step toward him, and I didn't know if I could use my galvanism to grab hold of the bullet's kinetic energy and send it spinning away from Charlotte. Not when he was that close to her.

"Your choice, Desmond," Henrika purred. "Come with me and save Charlotte. Or stay here, try to fight your way through my men, and watch her die."

My gaze zipped from one person to another. The dead scientist sagging against the tree. Henrika smirking at me. Bryce and the guards aiming their guns at Charlotte. Steig, Oriana, and Niles glaring at me, Charlotte, and Henrika in turn.

As a Section cleaner, I'd been in a lot of dangerous situations. Faced a lot of long odds and had to make a lot of tough choices, most of which involved picking the lesser of two evils. But these odds weren't merely long, they were bloody *impossible*, and really, it wasn't a tough choice at all.

Not when Charlotte was involved.

I stared at Charlotte, memorizing the way the winter sun brought out the highlights in her auburn hair. How her eyes crinkled and her heart-shaped lips quirked with worry. And most of all, I breathed in the cool, soothing blue of her aura, knowing I would need it for what was coming next.

Then, when I had that all locked away in my mind and especially in my heart, I looked away from Charlotte and walked over to Henrika.

"Good boy," she purred again.

"Desmond, no!" Charlotte yelled. "Don't do it! We can find a way out of this! Together!"

She lunged forward, but one of the guards grabbed her arm and dragged her back.

Fury roared through me. "You want me to go with you? Tell your men not to hurt Charlotte," I growled. "Right now. Or your guards will have to pump me so full of bullets to take me down you'll *never* figure out how I survived your monstrous formula."

Henrika arched a chiding eyebrow. "Temper, temper, Desmond. But very well. Although for the record, I never had any intention of killing Charlotte. Ms. Locke still has her part to play in this little drama, just like you do, Mr. Percy."

My gut twisted. I had no idea what Henrika was planning to do to me or how Charlotte fit into any of this, but it wouldn't be anything good.

"Give them the order," I growled again.

Henrika jerked her head at Bryce and the other guards. "You heard him. No one shoots or otherwise harms Ms. Locke. Am I understood?"

The guards all nodded, even Bryce, although he did so quite reluctantly.

Henrika snapped her fingers. "It's time for Desmond to go nighty-night."

"With pleasure," Bryce said. "I've waited a long time for this."

The former cleaner slid his gun into its holster, stepped in front of me, and flexed his fingers. Bryce grinned, then snapped up his fist and punched me in the jaw.

Thwack-thwack-thwack.

Bryce followed up that first punch with three more in rapid succession. He put the full force of his enduro strength into each blow, and pain exploded in my face like grenades detonating one after another. My galvanism surged up, trying to turn the jarring force into usable energy, but the pain quickly overwhelmed my power. A strange, numb sensation also spread through my body, and everything took on a dull, fuzzy haze, as though the entire clearing had somehow been plunged deep underwater . . .

Thwack.

Bryce plowed his fist into my ribs. This blow was harder and sharper than the others, and another, larger grenade of pain exploded in my chest.

I didn't even feel my legs buckle or my body hit the ground, but they must have, because suddenly, I was lying in the snow, trying to move my head so I could stare up at Charlotte. But it didn't work, and my eyes slowly slid shut, despite my best efforts to keep them open . . .

"Desmond! Desmond, wake up!"

The last thing I heard before the world went black was Charlotte screaming my name.

TWENTY-NINE

CHARLOTTE

"**D**esmond!" I yelled again. "Wake up!"

The guard tightened his viselike grip on my arm and shoved his gun into my side. "Shut up!" he growled. "Or I'll ignore the boss's orders and shoot you in the gut!"

Truth, my synesthesia whispered, as if I needed the magical confirmation that the man would make good on his threat. I bit my tongue and swallowed my screams.

Henrika made a circular motion with her index finger, and two guards stepped forward and took hold of Desmond. The two men must have been enduros with extra strength, because they maneuvered the cleaner around like he was as light as feather. The first guard removed all of Desmond's weapons, including his silver pocket watch, and tossed them aside. Then the second man bent down and hefted the unconscious cleaner over his shoulders in a fireman's carry.

In the distance, more gunshots sounded, louder and closer than before.

"Get him into the woods!" Henrika hissed. "Now!"

The second guard hefted Desmond a little higher onto his shoulders and vanished into the woods. The first guard followed him, and Henrika also headed in that direction. Bryce trailed after her, although he kept his gun trained on the three paramortals still standing in the clearing.

"What do you think you're doing?" Steig demanded. "Tell your men to lower their weapons!"

Henrika shook her head. "You still don't get it, do you, Steig? You were *never* here to bid on my formula. You and the others were just bait so I could lure Desmond and Charlotte to the resort. Spies like them will never pass up a chance to track down villains like you. And now? You're just a distraction, something for the Section agents to focus on and chase after, so I can escape."

The assassin's hands clenched into fists, and his handsome features twisted into something dark and ugly. "You duplicitous bitch! I'll kill you for this!"

Henrika backed toward the trees, with Bryce still by her side. "You'll be far too busy running from Section 47 to worry about me."

Fury stained Steig's face a mottled red. Oriana and Niles were just as pissed, and they also glared at Henrika.

"Anyone who tries to follow us will get shot. Let's go!" Henrika called out. "Move! Move! Move!"

The other guards dropped their guns and darted into the woods. Henrika smirked at me again, then she too vanished, with Bryce still right beside her.

The guard who'd been hanging on to my arm shoved me away. I stumbled back a few steps. He snapped up his gun, ready to fire if I moved toward him. I didn't care about the guard, so I held my hands up, wondering how I could get past him and get to Desmond—

"Gurp!" The guard let out a loud, strangled noise.

Steig's face appeared over the guard's shoulder, and he

yanked his hunting knife out of the man's back, then shoved it right back in again. Blood bubbled up out of the guard's lips, and he let out another strangled sound, as if asking for mercy.

But Steig wasn't in the mercy business. The assassin yanked the knife out of the guard's body, then wrenched the other man's head back and cut his throat. Blood sprayed everywhere, looking like a ruby fountain gushing down onto the snow. The guard thrashed around, but he was already more dead than alive, and Steig casually tossed him aside like a piece of trash.

The assassin's pale blue eyes fixed on me, and his lips drew back into a feral snarl. "Henrika might have escaped, but you won't be so lucky, spy bitch," he hissed.

Steig jumped over the guard's body and lunged at me. His hand clamped onto my shoulder, and his knife headed straight toward my throat—

Tink.

The tip of the blade cut through my thick scarf, but instead of stabbing into my body, it skittered away.

Steig growled and tried again and again.

Tink. Tink.

"What the fuck?" he growled.

He ripped the scarf off my neck, revealing the Grunglass Necklace. I had never been so glad to be wearing it as right now, as it was the only reason I was still alive.

Steig growled and raised his knife again, but I shoved him back and spun away. My gaze snapped left and right. All the weapons the guards had taken from Desmond and me were still lying in the snow, but I couldn't reach any of them.

Desperate, I bent down and yanked the two pom-poms off the side of my right boot. I dug my fingers through one fluffy piece of fabric until I found the hard plastic knot in the center. I hit the embedded button, arming the small hidden explosive. Then I whirled around and tossed it at Steig, who stopped in his tracks.

I was actually pretty good with ranged weapons, since my synesthesia usually told me exactly where to aim a gun, throw a knife, or hurl an axe. But the fuzzy pom-pom was no balanced blade, and the fluffy ball hit Steig's chest, bounced off, and plopped into the snow.

I backed away from him and started counting off the seconds in my mind. *Ten . . . nine . . . eight . . .*

Steig bent down, picked up the pom-pom, and waggled it at me. "What were you going to do with this? Tickle me to death?"

I backed up a few more steps. *Seven . . . six . . . five . . .*

"Quit messing around and kill her, you idiot!" Oriana snapped.

Four . . . three . . . two . . .

Steig ignored her and frowned down at the pom-pom. "Why does it feel like something is hidden inside this—"

Boom!

The pom-pom exploded. A bright burst of flame erupted in Steig's hand, as though he was a combusto clutching a fireball in his palm. The assassin screamed and screamed, his eyes bulging as he stared down at the mass of burned skin and bloody, stubby fingers that used to be his hand.

Steig screamed again and clutched his mangled hand to his chest. I tried to dart around him, but the assassin was blinded by pain, and he kept staggering back and forth, blocking my path. A frustrated growl tumbled out of my lips.

Crack!

A shot rang out, and a bullet punched into Steig's back. He staggered forward a few more steps, then his eyes rolled up into the back of his head, and he crumpled to the ground, landing right on top of the guard whose throat he'd cut.

Niles stepped forward, the gun in his hand still pointed at the other paramortal's body. He must have grabbed the weapon while I'd been blowing up Steig.

"Arrogant idiot," Niles muttered. "He squealed like a stuck pig."

I sidled to the left, hoping I could make it to the trees before Niles regrouped, but he leveled his gun at me.

"If you really are a Section spy, then you'll make an excellent hostage."

A bitter laugh spewed out of my lips. A few months ago, Miriam Lancaster had taken me hostage in the third-level bullpen at Section headquarters after I'd exposed her as a mole. Desmond had shot Miriam to save me, and the fact that he wasn't here to help me again was not lost on me.

"Why are you laughing?" Niles asked.

I swallowed the rest of my crazy chuckles. "Because Section 47 doesn't negotiate with anyone. And you're not taking me anywhere."

Niles's eyes narrowed behind his glasses. "In case you've forgotten, *I'm* the one with the gun."

I was still clutching the second pom-pom, and I hit the hidden button and tossed the fuzzy ball at Niles just like I had done with Steig. The chemist yelped and swatted it away with his free hand. The second pom-pom landed on the ground.

Boom!

The pom-pom exploded, sending up a large spray of snow and dirt.

Niles cursed, turned in my direction, and aimed his gun at my chest. I surged forward, lowered my shoulder, and rammed into him, sending us both tumbling to the ground.

The gun flew out of Niles's hand and flipped end over end through the snow. I got up onto my hands and knees and scrambled after it. The instant my fingers closed around the weapon, I snapped it up and spun around.

Niles was towering over me, a long, thick tree branch clutched in his hand. He yelled and drew the branch back like a baseball bat.

I pulled the trigger.

Crack!

My aim wasn't the best, given my low, awkward position, but I hit him in the shoulder. Niles yelped, and the tree branch slipped through his fingers and dropped to the ground.

I scrambled to my feet. Niles was clutching his shoulder and staggering in the opposite direction. Oriana had vanished without a trace.

No one was left to stop me, so I clutched the gun a little tighter and sprinted into the woods. I had to save Desmond.

I ran through the woods as fast as I could. My boots slipped on the snow and the loose rocks and fallen tree branches underneath, but I powered through the awkward slides, maintained my balance, and kept going.

Henrika and her men had left a trail of footprints, which made them easy to follow. I sprinted forward, my breath steaming out in thick clouds of frost and a dagger of pain slowly knifing its way deeper and deeper into my side. Right now, I would have given anything to be an enduro with enough stamina to run for miles and miles and never tire.

I wasn't an enduro, but my worry for Desmond drove me onward, and I forced myself to ignore my aches and pains and move faster.

Slowly but surely, the trees thinned out, and the sandy shore appeared in the distance. I quickened my pace yet again, even though my legs quivered like warm gelatin and my lungs burned as though I'd swallowed one of the pom-pom bombs.

A few seconds later, I burst through the tree line and skidded to a stop in the sand. My head snapped left, then right, and I spotted a long, wide dock that stretched out over the lake like an accusing finger. Henrika, Bryce, and the guards were already on board a boat at the end of the dock. So was Desmond, who had been slung down into a seat like a lifeless mannequin.

My heart wrenched, but I sucked down a breath and ran toward the dock.

DANGER! DANGER! DANGER!

My synesthesia screamed a warning out of nowhere. Even though I didn't see anything threatening, my instincts took over, and I veered sharply to the right, away from the dock.

BOOM!

A massive explosion ripped through the air, and the shock wave lifted me off my feet and tossed my body through the air like a leaf caught in a hurricane.

One second, I was racing along the lakeshore. The next, I was face down in the ice-crusted sand, wondering how I had gotten there. The back of my body felt like it had been used as a punching bag, and a dull ringing filled my ears, like someone was pressing a doorbell over and over inside my skull.

I spit out a mouthful of sand, pushed the pain away, and scrambled to my feet. Somehow I'd managed to hang on to the gun, although I staggered back and forth, my balance completely thrown off by the force of the explosion.

White stars exploded in my eyes, but I ruthlessly blinked them away. The buzzing in my ears died down, and my vision slowly sharpened.

Most of the dock was burning, and the red-orange flames licked at the wood like an overeager puppy and spewed out clouds of noxious black smoke at the same time. I staggered to my right a few steps and peered past the destroyed dock.

The boat had pulled away from the dock and was picking up speed. Henrika shoved her brown hair off her face, lifted her hands to her lips, and blew me a cheeky kiss, while Bryce raised his gun to his forehead and snapped off a mocking salute. The guard driving the boat revved the engine, and the vessel picked up speed, skimming across the lake.

I stood on the shore, completely helpless, and watched while the boat became a smaller and smaller speck before vanishing altogether. Worry spiked through my heart, pounding in time to my still-ringing ears.

Henrika was gone—and so was Desmond.

THIRTY

CHARLOTTE

"How did this happen?" General Percy demanded, pacing back and forth.

No one responded, and he kept pacing, his footsteps quick and heavy enough to rattle the shelves in Henrika's library.

Two hours had passed since Henrika, Bryce, and their men had kidnapped Desmond. Joan and the members of the strike team had found me standing on the shore, the gun still in my hand, staring out over the lake as if I could magically rewind time and save Desmond, instead of letting him slip through my fingers.

Joan had demanded to know what happened, so I'd told her everything Henrika had said and done in the clearing. A Section medic had injected me with something that finally stopped the ringing in my ears and soothed my other injuries. Joan had walked me back to the clearing, where I'd fished Desmond's pocket watch out of the snow. Then she'd escorted me back to the hotel, although I didn't really remember the journey.

Now I was slumped in a chair in Henrika's library, which had already been searched by the Section techs. Gia was standing by the fireplace, her arms crossed over her chest, while Joan was ensconced at the desk, poking around on Henrika's laptop.

And then there was General Percy, who had been pacing for the last ten minutes, alternately receiving updates on and barking orders into his phone.

"Anything?" Percy snapped.

Diego shook his head. The tech expert was sitting at a table in the corner, a couple of laptops spread out in front of him. "Nothing yet, sir. According to the Section agents stationed on the far side of the lake, Henrika set off a series of explosives buried in the sand when her boat landed, making it impossible for them to immediately follow. Henrika, Bryce, and their men got into some SUVs and drove up a neighboring mountain. They detonated several more explosives behind them, making the terrain impassable for other vehicles. After that, Henrika and the others boarded a helicopter hidden on top of the mountain and took off."

Diego shifted in his seat. "They also deactivated all the comms equipment and trackers Desmond was wearing."

General Percy muttered a curse, then raised the phone to his ear and barked out some more orders. "I want drone and satellite surveillance of the entire area. Find out where that chopper went *right now*."

"They won't find Henrika," I said, slowly sitting up in my chair. "This was her plan all along. Lure us to the resort, kidnap Desmond, and escape with him."

General Percy spun around on his heel and stabbed his finger at me. "This is *your* fault, Ms. Locke. *You* were the one Henrika drew into her web, and now my son is missing as a result."

He was right. Henrika had gotten the better of me, and now Desmond was going to suffer because of my mistakes and miscalculations. Henrika could already have Desmond in a lab. She could already have him strapped down to a table. She could already be poking, prodding, and experimenting on Desmond like he was a rat she could torture however she liked . . .

Bile rose in my throat, but I choked it down. "I'm not the only one she's playing a game with. Henrika took Desmond to send a message to *you*."

Percy's eyes grew even colder. "Be very careful what you say next, Ms. Locke."

Gia, Diego, and Joan all looked at me, as did the General. I got to my feet, even though the motion reignited my dull, throbbing headache.

"Back in the clearing, Henrika said she wanted to figure out how Desmond survived the Redburn explosions during the Blacksea mission. But she also said Desmond being your son was a bonus, which means she wants to hurt *you*. This is *personal* to her. Personal to *both* of you. Why?"

General Percy drew himself up to his full height, towering over me, but I lifted my chin, squared my shoulders, and stared right back at him. "Two things, Ms. Locke. I am your superior officer. You will address me as sir."

"And the second thing . . . *sir*?" I said, a mocking tone creeping into my voice.

"Henrika Hyde is a liar and a master manipulator," he snapped. "Maybe if you had been more concerned with those facts rather than listening to her spin stories, my son might still be here."

My hands balled into fists, but I wasn't about to back down. Not when Desmond's life was on the line. "You and Henrika obviously have some sort of feud, but right now I don't give a damn about that. All I want is information. Anything you can tell me about Henrika might help me figure out where she's taking Desmond. So please, *please* tell me everything you know about her."

The General stared at me, emotions flickering across his face. Worry. Dread. Unease. And something that looked a lot like guilt. But just as quickly as they appeared, the emotions vanished. His face hardened, and he peered down his nose at me again.

"As of this moment, you are off the mission," General Percy snapped. "Find your own way back to D.C., and clean out your desk, Ms. Locke. You are officially suspended from duty, pending a full investigation."

Disbelief shot through me, along with growing fury. Percy was hiding something, and instead of coming clean, he was doubling down on his treachery, even when his son's life was at stake. What was *wrong* with him? What was he hiding that was more important than saving Desmond?

Gia cleared her throat, and Percy swung his angry gaze over to the cleaner leader. "Sir, I think that's a bit extreme, given the circumstances. Charlotte is one of our best analysts, and if anyone can find Desmond, it's her."

General Percy stabbed his finger at me again. "Ms. Locke is the reason my son is missing. I don't want her anywhere *near* the search for Desmond. All she'll do is fuck it up just like she's done with everything else related to this mission."

I grimaced, but I held my tongue. I *had* fucked up this mission. If only I had figured out what Henrika had wanted sooner, Desmond might still be here with me instead of in her clutches.

Percy sneered at me. "But I shouldn't be surprised. That's what Lockes do. They ruin missions and leave the rest of us to pick up the bloody pieces."

Joan let out a soft gasp. Diego's fingers froze on his keyboard, and even Gia grimaced.

I bit back my angry retort. There was no use arguing. If I sniped at Percy again, he just might fire me outright. Being suspended wasn't much better, but at least I still had one foot in the door at Section 47.

General Percy stared at me, and I looked right back at him, doing my best to hide my fury, disgust, and worry. After several seconds, when it became apparent that I wasn't going to mouth off again, he snapped his fingers at Joan and then at Diego.

"There's nothing here," he growled. "Pack it up. I want an update from the strike teams by the time we get downstairs."

General Percy stormed out of the library. Gia gave me a sympathetic look and followed him. Joan helped Diego pack up the laptops, and the two of them also left. Neither one of them met my gaze on their way out.

I stared out over the library. The Section techs had swept through the space like a swarm of locusts. They'd focused on the scientist's worktable in the corner, handling the beakers, vials, and equipment with thick gloves and extreme caution, just in case Henrika had left a nasty surprise behind. But nothing had blown up, so the techs had turned their attention to the rest of the library.

The Section agents had taken everything of value, from the cases of jewelry on the shelves to the stained-glass lamps on the end tables to the antique fountain pens in the desk drawers. Even the liquor decanters had been bagged up and hauled away for testing, just in case the crystal held more than brandies and bourbons.

Right now, I felt very much like the ransacked library. Everything that mattered to me had been taken away—my confidence in my abilities as an analyst, my career at Section 47, and, most important of all, Desmond.

Worry shot through my heart at what Henrika might do to Desmond, but I squared my shoulders. Worrying never did anyone any good, as Grandma Jane would say, and it certainly wouldn't help me figure out where Henrika had taken Desmond.

I moved from one side of the library to the other, hoping the Section techs had missed something and Henrika had left a clue behind, but I didn't find anything useful. A stray paper clip that had fallen under the desk. A grape that had somehow escaped the refreshment tables and rolled into the corner. A fountain pen someone had crushed underfoot and shoved aside, leaving streaks of dark blue ink on the hardwood floor.

I was just about to admit defeat when a glimmer of glass caught my eye. The photo of Henrika and her cousin Meg had been knocked off its shelf and hit the floor. I crouched down, flicked away the pieces of broken glass, and slipped the worn photo out of its now-dented silver frame.

I studied the picture again, but it was the same as before. Henrika and Meg both smiling, despite the fact that Meg was terribly sick. I turned the photo over, expecting the back to be blank, but to my surprise, a small doodle had been drawn in the top-right corner. I frowned at the blue scribble. Was that . . . a clamshell?

Yes, it was a clamshell with a tiny pearl inside, and the strangest sense of déjà vu swept over me, as though I'd seen the mark somewhere before. I kept studying the symbol, but the answer didn't come to me.

Next, I picked up the silver frame that held the photo of Henrika and Feliciano. It too had been knocked to the floor, and I plucked the picture out of the broken glass. I flipped it over, but the back was blank. A frustrated sigh escaped my lips, but I studied the image again.

Despite their many sins, Henrika and Feliciano had looked very much in love, although their story had been cut short. A few weeks after the Mexico mission, some Section cleaners had finally caught up to Feliciano and eliminated him.

How had Henrika felt about her lover's death? Had that started the feud between Henrika and the General? And how did my father factor into whatever had happened between Henrika and Percy?

More questions crowded into my mind, but I only needed to solve one puzzle right now: Where was Desmond?

General Percy had said Henrika hadn't left anything behind, but I thought he was wrong about that. Either way, the two photos were the only clues I had, so I tucked them into my pocket and left the ransacked library.

I rode the elevator down to the lobby. Dozens of guests and hotel workers were milling around, talking on their phones or chattering to each other. Even Section 47 couldn't cover up squads of armed agents storming the resort grounds, but damned if they weren't trying.

The same agent who'd soothed the crowd at the Vault building was on the scene. The charmer held her hands up and starting speaking, projecting her calm, placating voice across the lobby.

". . . misunderstanding . . . false alarm . . . seems to be a juvenile prank . . . set off some firecrackers . . . no danger to anyone . . . the weekend's activities can proceed as planned . . ."

Her words drifted over to me, along with the warm glow of her charisma. The woman was using her paramortal abilities to their fullest effect, and everyone started nodding their heads in agreement.

Gia was standing in the corner, talking to one of the strike team leaders. I went over to them. The strike team leader gave me a disgusted look, as did several of her colleagues. Word had already spread about just how wrong the mission had gone and that Desmond was missing, but the other agents' disdain was nothing compared to my own anger for letting Henrika play me for a fool.

A flicker of movement caught my eye. Gabriel was standing at a display rack in front of the gift shop, trying on a pair of sunglasses. His back was to me, but his eyes met mine in the mirror on the rack. I shook my head the tiniest bit, warning him away. Gabriel returned the sunglasses to the rack, headed into the shop, and disappeared.

Gia finished her conversation with the strike team leader, then strode down a corridor. She didn't look at or speak to me, but I followed her anyway.

I didn't have anywhere else to go.

Gia stepped into the same library where Desmond and I had talked after the poker game. My heart gave a painful squeeze. Had that only been last night? It seemed like a lifetime ago. I stood just outside the door and watched the other agents.

The room had been turned into a mobile command center, and several techs were sitting at the reading tables, pounding away on laptops, and reviewing all the footage that had been recorded during the strike team raid, both from the agents' body cameras and from the hotel's security feeds.

To my surprise, Evelyn was here. I didn't know when she had arrived or how she had gotten to the resort so quickly from D.C., but she was standing behind Diego, along with Joan, and scribbling down notes on a legal pad, still playing the part of the unassuming assistant.

"Any updates?" General Percy demanded, pacing in front of the fireplace.

Gia shook her head. "No. Henrika's pilot didn't file a flight plan, so we haven't been able to track the helicopter yet, but I have people working on it."

A couple of the techs typed even faster on their laptops, as if they could make the helicopter location appear just by stabbing the keys quickly enough.

"What about Niles Perran and Oriana Luzzo?" Percy asked.

Gia shook her head again. "There's no sign of them. We've sent agents into the woods, but so far we haven't picked up their trail. We did capture several of Henrika's guards, but so far, none of them knows anything useful."

Percy pinched the bridge of his nose. "Well, keep looking. I want Niles Perran and Oriana Luzzo found, although right now the priority is Henrika Hyde and Bryce Finkley. Desmond will be wherever they are."

"Oh, no," Diego said.

His voice was barely above a whisper, but his fingers stuttered to a stop on his laptop, and the sudden silence was deafening.

General Percy zeroed in on him like a hawk diving for a mouse. "What's wrong?"

Diego swallowed. "We've just received an email and a video message from Henrika."

General Percy blinked at Diego for several seconds, as though he wasn't sure whether he'd heard the tech guru correctly. Then he stabbed his finger at a large monitor that had been set up in the corner. "Put it up there," he barked. "Now!"

Diego started typing again, and Henrika's face appeared on the monitor. Everyone stopped what they were doing to stare at it, and an expectant silence filled the library. Diego hit another key, and the video started playing.

Henrika grinned at the camera. "Hello, Jethro," she purred in a low, silky, satisfied voice. "Are you also experiencing a sense of déjà vu, or is it just me?"

A muscle twitched in the General's jaw, and his hands curled around the back of a chair like he wanted to rip the wood to pieces.

Henrika's grin faded away, and she leaned closer, her green eyes staring straight into the camera. "My demands are simple. In return for your son, I want a full Section pardon and immunity for all my crimes."

Gia was already shaking her head *no-no-no*, while Diego was chewing on a fingernail. Evelyn's face remained smooth, but Joan glanced in my direction, anger flaring in her pale eyes, although I wasn't sure whether the emotion was directed at me or Henrika or the whole messy situation. General Percy remained stone-faced.

Henrika leaned back and shrugged a shoulder. "I think my offer is more than generous. I'll give you a few hours to think it over. You'll receive further instructions then."

She stared at the camera again, a cold look on her face. "Any attempt to locate me in the meantime will result in Desmond's immediate execution."

Lie, my synesthesia whispered.

I tilted my head to the side and stretched out with my magic, but my inner voice remained steady and certain. Henrika wasn't going to kill Desmond. Not until she unlocked the secret of his galvanism. How much she might hurt him in the meantime . . . well, I didn't want to think about that. I *couldn't* think about it, or I wouldn't be able to function.

"I do hope we understand each other, Jethro. Next time, your agents won't be so lucky when they storm one of my properties, and I'll blow up more than just a dock and part of a mountain. And I will make sure that dear Desmond suffers the worst of all," Henrika continued. "And none of us wants that, do we?"

She smirked at the camera a moment longer, then slashed her hand across her throat. The video cut off.

General Percy stared at the dark screen. His hands dug into the back of the chair again, and the wood creaked in protest. After several long, tense seconds, the General released his grip and stabbed his finger at Diego.

"Find out where that video came from," he barked. "Now!"

Diego hunched over his laptop, his fingers flying across the keys. Joan took a seat next to him, cracked open her own laptop, and got to work. Gia and Evelyn glanced at each other, then Gia stepped forward.

"I shouldn't have to say this, but I will anyway," she said.

"Section 47 policy is not to negotiate with anyone, no matter the hostages taken or the circumstances."

"We are not *negotiating*," Percy growled. "We're going to find Henrika, eliminate her, and rescue my son. Do you understand me?"

"Yes, sir," Gia replied in a reluctant voice. She might be the head of the cleaners, but Percy still outranked her.

Gia also sat down at the table, dragged over a laptop, and got to work. Evelyn took a seat beside Gia, still clutching a pad. Evelyn glanced toward me, her face blank, then started taking notes again.

My heart sank. Even though Desmond was missing, Evelyn was sticking to her assistant role instead of revealing her true identity and authority as Maestro. For a moment, I considered outing Evelyn and forcing her to confront General Percy, but making an enemy out of her wouldn't do me—or, more importantly, Desmond—any good.

"We're wasting time here," Percy growled again. "Have one of the strike teams keep searching the woods for Niles Perran and Oriana Luzzo, but I want everyone else packed up and on their way back to Section headquarters in ten minutes."

Everyone bobbed their heads in agreement. General Percy spun around, and he finally noticed me hovering outside the library. That muscle twitched in his jaw again, and he strode forward. He stopped and looked at me for a moment, then slammed the door right in my face.

The sharp *bang* made me flinch.

I resisted the urge to pound my fist on the wood. General Percy had made his decision, and he was repeating the same mistakes he'd made on the Mexico mission all those years ago. Back then, Percy had ignored Grandma Jane's attempts to rescue her son, just like he was ignoring my help now. Well, I would be damned if I let Desmond suffer the same awful fate as my father.

I might be on the outside looking in, but that was nothing new at Section 47. For years, my supervisors and coworkers had overlooked and underestimated me, but I was the one who'd discovered Henrika's moles, and I knew that I could track her down now.

I spun around and strode away from the closed door. Jethro Percy could suspend me, fire me, and threaten me all he wanted. But one way or another, I *was* going to find Desmond.

THIRTY-ONE

DESMOND

For a long time, I floated in a black void of unconsciousness. But things slowly began to intrude on that peace and quiet.

The murmur of voices, one high and soft, the other low and deep. Cool air wafting across my skin. A hint of dampness tickling my nose. Callused hands clamping around my arms and legs. A rock-hard surface pressing against my back . . .

I knew that I needed to wake up instead of falling back down into the darkness, but I couldn't quite remember why it was so important. The nagging sensation wouldn't dissipate, so I cracked my eyes open. A dark gray ceiling swam into view. I frowned. This wasn't the honeymoon suite I was sharing with Charlotte—

Charlotte.

Memories erupted in my mind. The guards aiming their guns at Charlotte. Henrika telling the other paramortals that Charlotte and I were spies. Henrika demanding that I surrender. Bryce punching me over and over. Charlotte screaming my name. And then . . . and then . . . *nothing*.

The last thing I remembered was staring up at Charlotte

and watching her blue aura explode with worry. That same worry squeezed my chest tight right now. What had happened to Charlotte?

I rolled to the side, swung my legs down, sat up, and put my feet on the floor. My head spun at the motion, and fresh pain exploded in my face. Nausea sloshed in my stomach, and cold sweat broke out on my forehead.

I leaned forward, staring at the floor and trying not to vomit. The nausea slowly receded, and I gently probed my injuries. Sore, puffy bruises dotted my face, and I was willing to bet at least one of my eyes was blackened. My nose was broken, my lips were split and crusted with dried blood, and I had some cracked ribs, given how much my chest ached with every breath. Bryce hadn't pulled his punches, and I was lucky the vindictive former cleaner hadn't beaten me to death.

The last of the nausea faded away, and I raised my head. I was sitting on a paper-thin mattress stretched out over a slab of concrete to create a crude bed. The jacket I'd been wearing in the clearing had been stripped off my body and wadded up to form a makeshift pillow. The wall at my back was also concrete, as was the low ceiling. A metal toilet jutted out from the wall, along with a sink.

The other three walls were made of glass that looked at least two inches thick. A security camera was nestled in the corner of the ceiling, and the lone red light on it blinked like an all-seeing eye.

I slowly got to my feet. The aches in my skull, face, and ribs intensified, and my mouth felt like it had been stuffed with dry, bloody cotton, but I ignored the pain and staggered over to the door. It too was glass, with a metal knob. I twisted the knob, but it didn't move. Locked. I bit back a curse and tried again and again, twisting and rattling the knob and the glass door in its frame, but neither one budged an inch.

Trapped, I peered through the glass. Unlike my sparse cell, the area beyond was filled with scientific equipment. Microscopes, beakers, burners, test tubes, petri dishes, and more perched on long gray plastic tables that filled the center of the room. Metal counters studded with sinks lined one wall, while large industrial refrigerators with clear glass doors fronted another wall. The recycled air was unnaturally cool, and the faint lemony scent of disinfectant tickled my nose.

As a Section cleaner, I'd broken into dozens of places like this, so I knew exactly what it was: a lab.

Boots scuffed on the gray tile floor outside my cell, and Henrika strode into view. She was still wearing the same pale green sweater and pants she'd had on in the woods, but she'd traded in her winter jacket for a white lab coat. A chill slithered down my spine, but I squared my shoulders.

Henrika peered at me through the glass. "Oh, good. You're finally awake. I was starting to worry Bryce had hit you too hard and scrambled your brains for good."

"What are you going to do to me?"

She arched an eyebrow. "No blustering demands? No threats about how you're going to escape? No witty quips about how much you're going to enjoy killing me?"

"I'm not much for blustering demands."

Henrika nodded. "Blustering demands are definitely more your father's department. You're just the tool Jethro uses to carry out his dirty deeds, instead of doing them himself like he used to when he was a Section cleaner."

As much as I hated to admit it, she was right. I *was* a tool my father used to accomplish his objectives, whether it was thwarting a thief's heist, taking down a criminal conglomerate, or eliminating a terrorist.

But the way Henrika talked about my father . . . it sounded like she *knew* him, as though they'd had some personal interactions in the past. But how could that be? Sure, Henrika had said that the General had bought weapons from her, but the

General bought weapons from *everyone*, friend and foe alike. Charlotte hadn't found any other connections between Henrika and my father, but I still felt like the two of them were playing some game. Only I didn't know the rules, and they were both using me as their bloody pawn.

"What did my father do to you?" I asked, weary resignation creeping into my voice.

Henrika tilted her head to the side. "You're not even going to *try* to defend him? Protest that Jethro couldn't have possibly done anything wrong? After all, he is one of your commanding officers at Section 47. Even more important, he's your father."

A low, bitter laugh tumbled out of my lips. "Doing shady things is part of the job for everyone in Section 47, myself included, so we can serve the greater good and all those platitudes. And the General might be my father, but I have no illusions about what kind of man he is."

"Then you're a lot smarter and more perceptive than I expected. You not believing in your father's innocence is going to make this a lot less fun." Henrika pouted. "Oh, well. Fun doesn't matter to me nearly as much as science does."

I frowned. "What does that mean?"

Henrika smiled, and anticipation burned in her aura. She looked me up and down the way a scientist would view an exciting new discovery they were eager to explore—or a frog they were about to dissect.

"It means you're an anomaly, Desmond. And I *despise* anomalies, especially when it comes to my creations."

"You mean your *weapons*."

Henrika shrugged off my accusation. She strode over to a table near the center of the lab and hit some buttons on a laptop, making a display pop up on a monitor bolted to a wall.

I read through the information, my stomach sinking a little more with every word. "How did you get my Section personnel file?"

Henrika gave an airy wave of her hand. "Oh, this was one of the many things Miriam Lancaster slipped me. She gave me Charlotte's file too, although it's not *nearly* as interesting as yours, Desmond."

"Why is that?"

Henrika went over to the monitor and pointed to an area that detailed my paramortal abilities. "Your Section file claims that you have above-average stamina, speed, strength, and pain tolerance. All the basic enduro traits. Normally, I wouldn't think much of that, since Section is littered with enduros, and they are the most common type of paramortal."

"But?" I asked the obvious question.

"But Section 47 is known for meticulously documenting the powers and abilities of all its agents, right down to synth analysts like Charlotte who rarely leave their cubicles." Henrika's lips puckered in thought. "Your file seems rather . . . thin in comparison."

My hands clenched into fists. My file was thin because my galvanism was a rare ability, even among paramortals. To my knowledge, no other Section 47 agent was a galvanist, and I'd given more than one blood and tissue sample so the scientists could try to figure out how my magic worked and potentially replicate my power in other cleaners. But they had never been successful, and my father had buried all the research.

It was one of the few things he'd ever done to protect me.

But the General had his own reasons for that kindness. If other paramortals found out about my power, they could take measures to protect themselves, not to mention the fact that they would try to capture me, just like Henrika had. A galvanist could be useful in all sorts of criminal enterprises.

"So my file is thin. So what? Like you said, Section is littered with enduros. Just like Bryce Finkley and Trevor Donnelly and a dozen others I could name."

Henrika looked at me. "So someone with only a moderate

level of enduro magic shouldn't have been able to survive a single blast of Redburn. Much less an entire beach loaded with bombs all packed to the brim with my formula. And yet somehow you managed to do just that. Care to tell me how, Desmond?"

I pressed my hands flat against the cell wall. Fury spiked through me, and if I could have, I would have clawed my way through the glass to get to her. "Because my partner threw his body over mine and shoved me down into the sand. Graham took the brunt of the blasts, not me. He sacrificed himself to save me."

I swallowed the hard knots of guilt, regret, and shame lodged in my throat. "*I* should have been the one who died, not him."

Henrika nodded. "Yes, you should have. That's how I planned it."

I froze, my mind struggling to process her words. "You *planned* it? What does that mean?"

She gave me a look that was almost pitying. "I wanted *you* to die on the beach, Desmond. Your friend Graham was just collateral damage."

"What did you do?" I asked, my voice coming out as a low, harsh whisper.

Henrika clasped her hands behind her back and started pacing back and forth, eerily like my father would do.

"I was still testing Redburn. My results had been promising, but I needed data from a real-world situation. Adrian Anatoly wanted proof the explosive could kill any paramortal, no matter their powers or abilities, so he tasked me with rigging the beach in Australia to eliminate some Section cleaners who'd been authorized to kill him. You being sent on the Blacksea mission was just a happy coincidence, Desmond."

Understanding flashed through me. "You wanted to kill me to hurt my father. To get back at him for whatever he did to you."

Anger flared in Henrika's eyes, and her aura burned a dark, dangerous green over her heart. "You're damn right I did. But unfortunately, you survived my experiment. Then you and Charlotte escaped the trap Adrian Anatoly set for you both at the Halstead Hotel."

The anger dimmed in her eyes, and another thoughtful look creased her face. "I had cameras recording the lawn. It was quite ingenious of Charlotte to use her synesthesia to figure out where the bombs were buried. I'm still not quite sure how she did that. Care to share?"

I remained silent. Like me, Charlotte often downplayed her magic, and I wasn't about to reveal that Charlotte's synesthesia whispered about all the dangers around her. The less Henrika knew about Charlotte, the better.

"Cat got your tongue? Pity." Henrika clucked her own tongue in mock sympathy. "Maybe this will make you a bit more forth-coming."

She went over and hit a button on the laptop. Several loud hydraulic hisses sounded, and a chair moved away from a wall, rolled forward, and stopped in an open space near the center of the lab. The light gray chair looked like something in a dentist's office but with a few unwanted accessories, like thick plastic straps around the arms and the footrest.

Another chill slithered down my spine. "What is that?"

Henrika smiled. "Oh, just a little something to help me study my subjects up close."

I shook my head. "If you think I'm getting in that thing—"

She waved her hand, cutting me off. "I know, I know. I'll have to kill you before you get in that chair, much less tell me any Section secrets. But here's the thing, Desmond. You don't *have* to tell me anything. All the lovely data I'm about to collect will reveal everything I need to know."

Henrika hit another button. A second, louder hiss sounded, but this time, the noise was inside the cell.

I whirled around. A metal vent was embedded about halfway up the concrete wall in the back. White gas streamed out of the vent, quickly filling up the space.

I put my forearm up against my nose and mouth and backed into the corner, but I couldn't escape the gas. In less than ten seconds, it flowed over me like a cool, misty fog. The gas slithered down my throat, tasting of vanilla, strangely enough. A sudden, intense wave of drowsiness crashed over me, my legs buckled, and I slid down to the floor.

A sharp knock sounded on the glass, drawing my attention, and I lolled my head to the side. Henrika stood right outside the cell, staring down at me with a dispassionate expression.

"Sweet dreams, Desmond," she purred.

Another cloud of gas misted over me. The drowsiness in my body increased, and I didn't have the strength to hold myself upright. I pitched over onto my side, and the last thing I saw before I lost consciousness was Henrika's thin, malicious smile.

THIRTY-TWO

CHARLOTTE

Since I had been banished from the makeshift command center, I got into the elevator and returned to the honeymoon suite. I opened the door cautiously, but my synesthesia didn't signal any hazards. Of course not. Henrika and Bryce were long gone, and they'd taken all the danger with them, along with Desmond.

My heart squeezed at the thought of Desmond, of how Henrika could be hurting—*torturing*—him right this very moment, but I shoved my emotions down and buried them under a layer of ice. The only way to find Desmond was to think like Henrika, and to do that, I needed to be cold, calm, and ruthless.

I made sure the suite door locked behind me, then strode into the living room, sat down on the couch, cracked open my laptop, and logged into the Section system.

Access denied.

I frowned and tried my usual *CLocke* login and password again, making sure everything was spelled correctly.

Access denied.

I smacked the screen, but the message didn't change. Dammit. General Percy must have told Diego to revoke my access. I'd been hoping my suspension would have been an afterthought while everyone was searching for Desmond, but I should have known I wasn't that lucky. Not given the General's attention to detail and his intense dislike of me.

A sharp knock sounded on the suite door. Warily, I got to my feet, tiptoed to the door, and peered through the peephole. General Percy's bodyguards were standing outside with Joan. I muttered a curse, but if I didn't answer, they'd just come back with some of the strike team members, along with a battering ram.

I opened the door and crossed my arms over my chest. "What do you want?"

"General Percy has ordered you to turn over all Section weapons and accessories," Joan said in a bland, neutral voice. "Step aside, Charlotte."

I had no choice but to do as she commanded. Joan swept past me, as did the two bodyguards.

"Get the suitcases," Joan ordered.

The two men headed into the bedroom. A few thumps and bumps sounded, and a minute later, the guards rolled Desmond's and my suitcases into the living room.

"I wouldn't want you to have to buy a tacky T-shirt and flip-flops from the gift shop, so I'll let you keep the clothes you're wearing," Joan said.

"How kind of you," I sniped back.

Joan ignored my sarcasm and gestured at the bodyguards. "Get the rest of it."

The two men swept through the suite, grabbing all the guns and knives and stuffing them into their pockets. The first man also closed my laptop and tucked it under his arm.

I started to protest, but Joan shook her head. "That laptop is Section property. It doesn't belong to you while you're suspended from duty, Charlotte."

"What about the necklace?" one of the guards asked, stabbing his finger at the Grunglass Necklace, which was still hooked around my throat.

"It's a fake," Joan replied. "Ignore it."

Lie, my synesthesia muttered.

My eyes narrowed. Joan had told the same lie in the Section armory when she'd given me the necklace to take on the mission. The liaison *knew* this was the real necklace, so why was she letting me keep it?

One of the bodyguards reached for Desmond's pocket watch, which was also on the table, along with all the files, maps, and photos I'd printed out. I darted forward, snatched up the watch, and clutched it to my chest. It was the only piece of Desmond I had left, and I wasn't giving it up.

"This doesn't belong to Section," I growled.

The guard looked at Joan, who shook her head. "Leave it. The papers too. They're useless without access to the Section servers."

The guard nodded and continued his search. The two men went through every part of the suite and collected every piece of Section gear and clothing.

Five minutes later, the guards were ready to go.

Joan held out her hand. "I need your keycards too. The one for Section headquarters and the one for this suite."

Not only was the General kicking me out of the spy organization, but he was also making sure I couldn't stay in the suite either. I fished the keycards out of my pocket and slapped them into Joan's outstretched hand.

"You know this is wrong," I said, trying to reason with her. "I know more about Henrika Hyde than anyone else. I should be going back to Section headquarters and working with everyone else to find Desmond. Not getting kicked to the curb like an unwanted kitten."

"Then maybe you should have thought about that before

you led Desmond straight into Henrika's trap," Joan snapped in a cold voice. "I thought you were smarter than that, Charlotte."

"And I thought you were more than just an automaton," I snapped right back at her. "But even more important, I thought Desmond was your *friend*, that you truly *cared* about him."

Anger sparked in Joan's pale eyes, and the temperature in the suite dropped ten degrees. I got the sense the liaison was one more insult away from using her transmuter power to turn all the water in my body to ice.

"Unlike you, Charlotte, I know how to follow orders," Joan said, her voice even colder than before. "General Percy was right. You ruin everything you touch, just like your father did. You really are Jack Locke's daughter."

I used to be embarrassed by my father's death, by his supposedly flawed legacy inside Section 47 and all the financial problems he'd left behind for my grandmother. But not anymore. Jack Locke hadn't been perfect by any stretch of the imagination, not even close, but he had loved me in his own way, and he had given his life in service to others. Which was more than General Jethro Percy had ever done for anyone, including his own son.

I lifted my chin and squared my shoulders. "Damn right I am. Now, get out of my sight before I punch you in your pretty face, just the way my father would have."

Joan arched an eyebrow, not at all concerned by my threat. She stared at me a heartbeat longer, then whirled around and stalked out of the suite. The bodyguards followed her.

The door banged shut behind them, ringing out like a death knell for my time at Section 47.

I glared at the door, but it remained closed. Joan and the two guards had humiliated me, but they weren't coming back to physically remove me from the suite—yet.

The first thing I did was check the suite, just in case the bodyguards had left anything behind, but the two men had confiscated every single Section weapon and gadget, and they hadn't left me so much as an explosive pom-pom to work with.

It was just a matter of time before someone came to make sure I had vacated the premises, so I gathered up the papers, maps, and other information about Henrika, the Mexico mission, and the Glittertop Resort. I stuffed them all into a complimentary tote bag I found in the bathroom, then grabbed my purse, along with Desmond's pocket watch.

I rubbed my fingers over the silver case. "I'm going to find you, Dundee."

The walls soaked up my whispered promise, but just saying the words made me feel a little better. I slid the watch into my pocket, then hoisted the tote bag and my purse onto my shoulder and left the suite.

Down in the lobby, the strike team members had vanished, and the chattering crowd of guests and workers had also dissipated. Looked like everyone had believed the charmer's cover story, and things had already returned to normal.

I went down the corridor and poked my head into the library General Percy had commandeered earlier, but all the Section techs were gone, along with their equipment. Everyone had already left to return to headquarters. Well, if they weren't going to use the area, then I would.

I shut and locked the door behind me, then dumped the papers, maps, and other info out of my tote bag and onto a table. My gaze darted over to the spot where Desmond had calmed my nerves and kissed me after the poker game. A pang of longing twisted my heart. If only I could rewind time to that night, I would have done so many things differently, including telling Desmond how much I cared about him.

I blinked back the hot tears stinging my eyes. I still had a chance to tell Desmond all that and more. I just had to find him first.

Desmond had already been gone roughly three hours, and General Percy kicking me out of Section had wasted even more time—time that Desmond might not have. Henrika was smart, and it wouldn't be long before she figured out that Desmond's galvanism had helped him survive the Redburn explosions. After that . . . well, I didn't know what she would do. Release him, torture him, kill him.

Either way, Desmond didn't have time for me to waste.

I half expected a knock to sound on the door and for Joan, a strike team member, or a hotel worker to demand that I leave the library, but it didn't happen. Of course not. Henrika already had what she wanted in Desmond, and General Percy thought I was helpless without Section resources. Well, I was going to prove him wrong.

The first thing I did was go over to a lone, hotel-issued laptop left in the library and jiggle the mouse. The screen flared to life, asking if I wanted to check my flight or rent a car. The laptop was the definition of bare bones, but it had an Internet connection, which was all I needed.

The laptop had a surprisingly long cord, so I dragged it over to the table where I'd spread out my papers. I quickly accessed the main Section system, but this time, instead of using my *CLocke* login, I entered the Mockingbird login and password.

The screen went dark for several seconds, and I held my breath, hoping General Percy hadn't discovered my back door into the servers—and wondering what I would do if it didn't work . . .

A bright white light flared, and lines of black code filled the screen, forming the distinctive shape of a mockingbird, complete with the creature's jaunty tail. The screen abruptly went dark again, then the main Section home page appeared, with a message: *Welcome, Mockingbird.*

I hissed out a relieved breath, flexed my fingers, and started typing.

First, I looked at the reports and updates that chronicled the search for Desmond and Henrika. The Section agents were following several leads, but none were promising. No surprise there. Henrika was quite clever, and she would love nothing more than to lead the agents on a merry chase while she thumbed her nose at General Percy.

Next, I reviewed the photos and videos Section agents had taken in and around the hotel, as well as their reports about Henrika fleeing across the lake, driving up the mountain, and taking off in a helicopter.

I drummed my fingers on the tabletop, even as my mind whirred with possibilities. Depending on the helicopter, Henrika could have taken Desmond anywhere in the eastern U.S. Since I couldn't figure out the route, I turned to the second part of the equation: the destination.

If Henrika wanted to discover how Desmond had survived the Redburn explosions, then she would need supplies and equipment for blood tests, imaging scans, and other medical procedures. She must have taken him to a lab, maybe even the same lab where she was storing the Redburn formula. I just needed to figure out where it was.

I pulled up all the information I'd collected over the last several months about Henrika's production plants, office buildings, and other properties, including the Glittertop Resort. Then I sat back in my chair, reached for my synesthesia, and let the laptop monitor fill my field of vision.

I went through everything again, document by document, line by line, word by word. Every time a glimmer of gray or a pop of pink caught my eye, I stopped and studied the information, but they all turned out to be typos and addition errors. Nothing nefarious or sinister appeared, and I didn't learn anything I didn't already know.

Frustrated, I rocked back in my chair, making the wood groan in protest. Henrika was smart and dangerous, but she was a creature of habit, just like we all were. Out of all the rooms in the hotel, I'd come to the library because I had always loved being surrounded by books and Desmond had comforted me in here last night. Henrika was no different. She would go someplace she felt safe, someplace she thought no one would find her.

But *where*? Where was that?

Out of the corner of my eye, I spotted several curls of dark gray smoke sliding along the wall. Familiar footsteps sounded, and a shadow fell over me.

"It's about time you got here," I groused.

Gabriel slid into the chair across the table from me. "You're the one who warned me off in the lobby earlier. I would have been happy to confront Jethro Percy and give him a piece of my mind."

"As much as I would have enjoyed seeing that, it wouldn't have helped anything. Besides, I didn't want you to get caught up in my mess any more than you already are." I sighed. "I'm sorry for snapping at you. What I should have said was thank you for coming."

Gabriel tipped his head, accepting my apology. "No worries, Char. You always get cranky when you're concerned."

He fell silent, but his eyes darkened with worry. Gabriel had been a cleaner for a long time, and he knew exactly what someone like Henrika was capable of and just how much she could hurt Desmond.

I jerked my chin at the closed library door. "What's been happening out there?"

He waved his hand. "General Percy stormed out through the front door about thirty minutes ago. Most of the Section agents and techs followed him, and so did Gia, Evelyn, and

Diego. A strike team is still searching the woods for Niles Perran and Oriana Luzzo, but they'll probably stop soon. It's clear the other paramortals are long gone." He gestured at the papers spread out in front of me. "Find anything?"

I shook my head. "Nothing new. According to the Section agents, Henrika set off a bunch of bombs to cover her tracks. By the time they got across the lake and followed her up the mountain, she had boarded a helicopter and flown away. The agents are trying to track the chopper, with no luck so far."

Gabriel arched an eyebrow. "I hear a *but* in your voice."

"But . . . something about this whole situation doesn't feel right. Henrika's escape seems too . . . *easy*."

"You think planting bombs on two sides of a lake and decimating half a mountain to cover your escape route seems *easy*?" His eyebrow arched a little higher. "I would hate to hear your definition of *hard*."

"No, not easy for Henrika—easy for *us*, for Section. It's like Henrika laid out a trail of breadcrumbs, only those breadcrumbs ended in explosions." I rubbed my aching head. "I feel like this is all part of Henrika's plan and that she is leading General Percy *exactly* where she wants him to go."

"Through the woods to Grandma's house?" Gabriel quipped.

I snorted. "More like away from her super-secret weapons lab."

"Well, I'm sure you'll figure it out, Char. You always do."

I flashed him a grateful smile. "Thanks for the vote of confidence."

Gabriel stared at me, his gaze steady on mine. "It's not a vote of confidence. It's the *truth*. I believe in you, and so does Desmond. Wherever he is, Slick knows you won't stop searching until you find him. I've been in similar situations, and knowing someone is looking for you . . ." His voice trailed off, and he shifted in his chair. "Well, it helps more than you know. With all sorts of things."

Once again, hot tears stung my eyes, but I blinked them back. Gabriel's calm, unwavering belief made me feel like I could find Desmond after all. I grabbed his hand and squeezed his fingers. "You're a good friend."

Gabriel squeezed my hand back and flashed me a grin. "Correction. I'm a *terrific* friend." He pulled out his phone. "Speaking of friends, I have a pilot buddy who owes me a favor. Let me see what she says about flying choppers in this area."

"Thanks, Gabriel."

He winked at me. "Anytime, Char."

Gabriel murmured into his phone, calling one person after another, while I went through all the information on Henrika yet again. And once again, I didn't see anything different. Even with my synesthesia, I didn't find any typos, errors, mistakes, or outright lies that told me where she had taken Desmond.

Frustrated and more than a little desperate, I pushed the laptop aside and studied the maps of the resort grounds and surveillance photos of the surrounding area. I looked at one building, then another, then another, but the maps and photos didn't change, and they all showed the same things as before.

Think, Charlotte, think!

I swallowed a growl, leaned back in my chair, and glared at the ceiling. After a few seconds, I closed my eyes and drew in several deep breaths, cleansing the anger from my system, just like I would do on my yoga mat. Calmer, I opened my eyes, sat up straight, and went back to the beginning, reviewing all the facts yet again.

Bryce had knocked out Desmond, then a guard had carried Desmond to the dock, where he'd been put on a boat. Henrika, Bryce, and their men had used the boat to cross the lake and land on the opposite shore. After that, Henrika had set off several bombs to keep the Section agents from immediately following her up the mountain. Henrika, Bryce, and their men had abandoned their SUVs at the top of the mountain, gotten into a helicopter, and flown away.

Gabriel was still murmuring into his phone, so I sighed and clicked through the photos again, going through them one by one and reviewing the accompanying reports by the Section agents . . .

A photo of a dirt road leading up the mountain appeared. I started to click past it, but then I remembered something Diego had said during the briefing before the mission: *The resort covers several thousand acres . . . Not much else is around it . . . Lots of dirt roads and hiking trails . . .*

Henrika had used one of those dirt roads to reach the top of the mountain, but something about the information nagged at me. I sat back and stared at the screen, letting my synesthesia flare to life, but no telltale grays, pinks, or reds appeared on the photo or any of the other information. It was all true, correct, exact, and didn't contain any typos, mistakes, or outright lies.

My frustration bubbled up yet again, but I pushed it down and called up the video Henrika had sent demanding a full pardon in exchange for Desmond's return. I hadn't noticed it before, but the video jostled ever so slightly. A moment later, I realized why: Henrika had shot the video in the SUV that had hauled her up the mountain.

I frowned. Why would she have made the video while she was driving up the mountain? Why not do it in the helicopter when she was flying away? Or after she had reached a secure location?

My eyes narrowed, and I focused on the photo of the dirt road again. That was the last place any of the Section agents had actually *seen* Henrika. Just because the agents *thought* she had flown away didn't make it a *fact*. No one had witnessed Henrika actually *boarding* the helicopter. She might have used another form of transportation to escape . . . or she might not have gone anywhere at all.

As soon as the idea popped into my mind, everything tilted on its axis, and all the disparate pieces of the puzzle rearranged themselves into an entirely new pattern. My heart pounded, and I leaned forward and started typing, my fingers flying over the laptop keys like I was playing a piano concerto.

Gabriel noticed the sudden burst of noise and motion and lowered his phone. "Charlotte? You find something?"

I ignored him and kept typing and clicking, scrolling through one document and photo after another after another, until I found what I wanted.

There—*there* it was.

"Coal mines," I whispered.

Gabriel frowned. "What? What are you talking about?"

I spun the laptop around so he could see the topographical map on the screen. "In our briefing before the mission, Diego mentioned that this area is riddled with abandoned coal mines. That's one of the reasons Henrika was able to buy so much land so cheaply. No one else wanted it."

Gabriel shrugged. "Okay. So what?"

I clicked over to a spreadsheet listing the expenses for the construction companies that had worked on the resort. "Henrika spent a fortune upgrading the hotel and the resort grounds. This is all the money she doled out to bring everything up to code."

Gabriel frowned again, still not seeing it, so I tapped on a couple of the lines on the screen.

"But these building materials didn't come here to the hotel. See the delivery address? It's on the same road as the resort, but the materials were delivered to *another* spot—an address with a number that comes *before* the resort."

"You think Henrika had the construction crews work on something else in the area." Gabriel shook his head. "But there aren't any other buildings around for miles. At least, none that Section hasn't already checked out."

"There aren't any other buildings we can *see*," I replied.

"Henrika has to have a secret lab on the resort grounds, but Desmond and I couldn't find it, and neither could the other paramortals. That's because we've all been looking for the wrong kind of space. Henrika didn't need a giant warehouse out in the open. She has other labs that fit that bill. She just needed a private place away from prying eyes where she could brew up Redburn and her other biomagical weapons."

Understanding dawned on Gabriel's face. "Like an abandoned coal mine."

I shot my thumb and forefinger at him. "Exactly. Henrika didn't fly away on a helicopter. She ducked into her abandoned coal mine hidey-hole and waited for the Section agents to move past her location. Henrika has been on the neighboring mountain this whole time."

THIRTY-THREE

CHARLOTTE

Gabriel's eyes flicked over all the information. I held my breath, hoping he would see what I saw, because I couldn't do this without him.

After a few seconds, he nodded. "You're right. Clever of her. To literally go underground right under Section's nose."

I slapped my hand on the table. "Exactly! An abandoned mine is the perfect place for a secret lab, especially for someone like Henrika who has such a public profile. Her legitimate workers would notice her coming and going in a regular lab, and someone might get curious about what she was working on. But something like this? Henrika would have complete privacy. Since the lab is so close to the hotel, no one would think twice about her sailing off to enjoy a day on the lake and then sailing back later, after she finished working in the lab. All she would need to do to sell the illusion would be to take a few photos on the lake with the hotel in the background and then post them online."

I let out a bitter laugh. "And that's *exactly* what she's done. I've looked at dozens of photos of Henrika in a boat on the lake over the past few months, and I never suspected a thing."

Gabriel held up his hands. "You don't have to convince me, Char. I know how smart you are and especially how good your instincts are. The real question is, are you going to share the intel with General Percy?"

I thought of the disgust and fury in the General's icy gaze after Desmond had been taken. "No, I'm not going to tell Percy. He won't listen to a word I say. Even if by some miracle he did listen, he'd want to send a strike team into Henrika's lab. The more people who are involved, the greater the risk to Desmond."

"What about Gia Chan?"

I shook my head. "Gia believes in me, but General Percy has operational control of the mission. She can't go against his orders."

"And Evelyn Hawkes?" Gabriel asked.

A few weeks ago, I'd told him about Evelyn really being Maestro, so he knew how powerful she really was—and not to annoy her.

I thought about it for a few seconds, then shook my head again. "No. If I went to Evelyn and she acted on the intel, then General Percy would realize she is Maestro. I'm not going to blow her secret identity as Maestro unless absolutely necessary."

I blew out a tense breath. "Besides, Henrika set this whole thing up to play out *exactly* like the Mexico mission. She has a hostage, and we have no leverage. If she sees a strike team, she might just go ahead and execute Desmond."

My heart squeezed tight. "I can't risk that. I can't risk Desmond dying in the crossfire like my father did."

My heart squeezed tight again, but I breathed through the sharp spikes of pain. I needed to focus on saving Desmond right now, not on all the specters of spies past that were haunting me.

"Okay," Gabriel said. "Let's see what the two of us can do. First things first. We need to find exactly where Henrika is hiding."

Using the reports from the Section agents about where they'd last seen Henrika and where Bryce and the guards had abandoned their vehicles, I reviewed all the topographical maps of the area, along with drone and satellite surveillance photos. It didn't take me long to find an old coal mine about a mile away from the clearing on top of the mountain where the helicopter had taken off. I kept digging, and eventually, I found a map of the mine, although it was dated several years ago.

I printed out copies, then Gabriel and I bent our heads, poring over the information.

Several minutes later, Gabriel sat back and crossed his arms over his chest. "The mine entrance should be easy enough to find, but we don't know how many men Bryce might have inside or what other security measures he might have rigged up. This is at least a three-person job. One person to run point and navigate through the mine, one person to provide security and deal with any threats, and one person to help Desmond." He cleared his throat as though he didn't like what he was about to say next. "Slick is probably going to be in . . . rough shape."

I grimaced, and another spike of worry slammed into my chest. Gabriel shifted in his chair, clearly uncomfortable, but he was just laying out the facts. We didn't know what Henrika might have done to Desmond, how badly she might have hurt him, and we needed at least one more person for the mission.

Gabriel picked up his phone from the tabletop. "I could call in some folks from my crew, but they're all on other assignments, and it will take them a few hours to get here."

"Desmond might not have a few hours left."

Gabriel gave me a helpless shrug. The phaser might be able to walk through walls, but even he couldn't make an ally magically appear, someone who would help rescue Desmond no matter the consequences.

I looked out over the maps and surveillance images again, trying to conjure a solution. My gaze landed on the photo of

Henrika and Feliciano Salvador smiling with the beautiful sunset and glimmering ocean behind them . . .

My eyes narrowed, and I remembered another photo of a beautiful sunset and a glimmering ocean I had seen recently. My mind whirred, and a few pieces of a different puzzle clicked into place. I leaned forward and hit some keys on the laptop, searching for a new topic. It was ridiculously easy to find, and a rueful laugh escaped my lips.

"What are you looking at now?" Gabriel asked.

I stared at him over the screen. "I know someone who can help us rescue Desmond."

"Who?"

"Nemesis."

Gabriel jerked back in his chair. "*Nemesis?* Why would you think *she* would help *us*? She hasn't contacted me since the Tannenbaum mission. It's been radio silence since her last call on Christmas Day, and I don't have any way to reach her. The number she gave me was disconnected, and it was burner phone, so there was no way to trace it. She's a ghost, Char."

I gave him a grim smile. "Then it's a good thing I'm in the business of tracking down ghosts, even the Ghost of Christmas Past."

I picked up my phone and sent a text, along with my current location at the hotel. Then I laid the device on the table. Nothing to do now but wait and see if I was right about who Nemesis really was—

My phone lit up, and a grin curved on my face as I read the message. "She's on her way."

Twenty minutes later, the pale blue glow of magic sparked and shimmered around the library door. The lock turned, the door opened, and a woman stepped inside. She was wearing a long black trench coat that made her look exactly like the spy she was.

Joan Samson's sharp, searching gaze landed on me and Gabriel, and her lips flattened out into a thin line. She stalked in our direction, her coat flapping around her legs in time to her quick, angry strides.

"*She's* Nemesis?" Gabriel muttered. "Seriously? Ms. By-the-Book Section Liaison?"

"We need her help, so maybe don't call her juvenile names?"

Gabriel shot me a dark glower, which I ignored.

Joan yanked out the chair at the far end of the table and sat down. Gabriel eyed her, as if mentally comparing her to his idea of Nemesis, but he didn't say a word.

"Hello, Joan," I drawled. "So nice to see you again. Neat trick, using your transmuter magic to manipulate the metal lock and open the door."

Joan arched a dark eyebrow at my snide tone.

"It's been, what, two hours since you upbraided me in the honeymoon suite? That was a nice touch. A very convincing performance for General Percy's bodyguards. Brava."

"It wasn't a performance," she replied. "Everything I said was the truth."

I winced and clutched my heart, as though she had wounded me. "Ouch. Tell me, did General Percy order you to stay behind at the hotel to keep an eye on me? Or did you volunteer?"

"I volunteered," she replied in a tart tone. "Someone had to make sure you didn't screw things up any more than you already have."

I winced again, this time for real. She was right. I had screwed things up, and now Desmond was paying the price for my mistakes.

Joan's pale blue eyes frosted over even more, and she leaned back in her chair. "I got your rather cryptic text. What do you want, Charlotte? I'm busy overseeing the strike team while they hunt for Niles Perran and Oriana Luzzo."

"If my message was truly cryptic, you would have ignored it." I held my hands out wide. "Yet here you are."

Joan pulled her phone out and held the screen out where Gabriel and I could see it.

Love the photo of your Greek vacation. You should visit Germany next. Hope we can work together again soon. XOXO Charlotte.

"That is the very definition of cryptic," Joan muttered.

"Still going to play dumb?" I shook my head. "We're both too smart for that."

Agreement flickered across her face before she could hide it. Gabriel kept glaring at Joan, but she ignored him and kept staring at me. She wasn't going to crack unless I made her crack.

I leaned back in my own chair. "Don't you want to know how I figured out you're Nemesis?"

Joan's face remained calm and smooth, and she didn't move, fidget, blink, or twitch. The liaison should have gone to Casino Night with the other paramortals, because she had an excellent poker face, and I couldn't tell what she was thinking or feeling.

"I figured out you were Nemesis the same way I figured out Miriam Lancaster and Trevor Donnelly were moles—by adding up lots of little things."

Joan scoffed. "What things?"

I pointed at her suit jacket, which was visible underneath her trench coat. Once again, she was wearing the small sword brooch, and the white diamonds glittered like stars against the dark blue fabric. "Every time I've seen you over the past few days, you've been wearing that brooch."

Joan's fingers crept up to the brooch. "So what?"

"So people often wear a piece of jewelry over and over

because they have a deep sentimental attachment to it." I paused. "Usually because someone special gave it to them."

Once again, Joan's face remained calm, but her fingers curled a little more tightly around the brooch as if it was a scarlet *N* marking her as Nemesis and she wanted to hide it from sight.

"There were other clues. Your relationship with Graham Walker. Your insistence that you should be Desmond's liaison instead of me. And especially your burning desire to hurt Henrika Hyde however you could."

Joan dropped her hand from the brooch. "So what? Everyone in Section knows that."

"Yes, they do. It's all common knowledge. But then I saw the photo on your desk of your Greek vacation." I paused. "The photo Graham took of you, right?"

"So I took a vacation." Joan scoffed again, sidestepping my question about Graham. "So what?"

I stabbed my finger at the brooch on her jacket. "So I'm guessing Graham bought you that brooch as a memento of your trip. Diamonds are a popular gift among lovers, and wearing that brooch, well, it's like having a piece of Graham right next to your heart. Isn't it?"

Joan remained silent, and once again, she didn't move, fidget, blink, or twitch. If I didn't know better, I would have thought she didn't care about Graham Walker at all.

"Speaking of jewelry . . ." I tapped my finger on the Grunglass Necklace, which was still ringing my throat. "You *know* this is the real necklace. You can tell how old something is and the quality of materials used just by touching it. You said that when we were at my Section desk looking at the crystal mockingbird figurine, remember? You got the real Grunglass Necklace out of the armory for me to bring to the resort. Then, earlier today, you lied and told Percy's bodyguards it was a fake. Why would you take so many risks with Section property? Especially a necklace worth millions of dollars?"

Joan maintained her still silence. I admired her eerie calm, but it also annoyed me. Desmond didn't have time for us to sit around and play spy games.

I gestured at Gabriel. "A few days ago, Gabriel told me how a mysterious woman calling herself Nemesis had sent him an invitation to Elsa Eisen's holiday party. Desmond and I going to Germany wasn't common knowledge, but you're smart, Joan, and you could have accessed enough information in the Section servers to figure it out."

She shrugged, neither confirming nor denying my accusation.

I gestured at the laptop on the table. "Code names mean things to people too, just like jewelry does, and I've been researching the word *Nemesis*. Of course, the literal meaning is a long-standing enemy or archrival. But there's also another meaning that ties in with that one and connects everything back to you. The Greek vacation photo, the sword brooch, Gabriel's invitation to the holiday party."

Joan scoffed. "And what would that be?"

"Nemesis is the Greek goddess of revenge."

A tense, heavy silence dropped over the table. Joan looked at me, then at Gabriel, then back at me. The corner of her mouth quirked up, cracking her calm, detached façade, and a bit of grudging respect filled her eyes.

"I didn't think you would figure it out so quickly," she muttered. "I thought I had been more careful."

"You were careful, but this is what I do for a living, what Section trained me to do, and I am very, very good at it."

Joan clapped her hands together a few times in mocking applause. "Well, brava to the great Charlotte Locke."

"How did you disguise your voice?" Gabriel asked. "I talked to you on the phone after the Tannenbaum mission. You don't sound like Nemesis."

Joan gave him a disgusted look. "I'm a transmuter. I can turn water into ice and crack concrete with my bare hands. You really think I can't disguise *my own voice*?"

Her voice dropped on the last few words, turning into a low, husky purr that seemed to belong to an entirely different person. If I hadn't heard Joan say the words, I never would have guessed that was her talking.

Gabriel arched an eyebrow. "Cute party trick."

"It was good enough to fool you." Joan smirked at him. "Then again, we both know you aren't the brains of this operation."

"Never said I was," Gabriel drawled. "I'm just the muscle."

"And what does that make me?" Joan asked.

"A friend," I replied in a soft voice. "Desmond's friend, I hope."

Her gaze swung back around to me, then skimmed over the documents, maps, and photos spread across the table. "You found him, didn't you? You found Desmond and Henrika's secret lab."

"Isn't that what you were counting on?"

Once again, Joan shrugged off my accusation. "Like you said in the honeymoon suite, you know Henrika Hyde better than anyone."

"And you decided to use me to get your revenge by proxy."

She shook her head. "Not revenge. Not today. Right now, all I care about is saving Desmond."

Finally, something we agreed on.

Joan picked up her phone. "Tell me where Desmond is. I'll text Gia, and she can start assembling the strike teams."

"No," I said in a sharp voice. "We're not telling Gia anything."

Joan frowned. "Why not? Desmond has already been gone for hours. Henrika won't keep him alive any longer than necessary."

"If you tell Gia, General Percy will seize control of the mission. Henrika will cut her losses and kill Desmond as soon as she gets wind of any strike teams closing in on her."

Joan threw a hand up in the air. "Then what are we supposed to do?"

Gabriel pointed at himself, then me, and finally Joan. "Cleaner, analyst, liaison. We've got the Section trifecta right here. And of course, I can also double as a charmer if need be."

He flashed her a smile. Joan rolled her eyes, then looked at me again.

"Let me get this straight," she said. "You want me to help you infiltrate Henrika's secret lab, find and rescue Desmond, and then somehow escape, all without being captured or killed? Oh, and without any Section intel, support, or backup?"

Gabriel's smile widened. "When you say it like that, you make it sound even more fun."

Joan rolled her eyes again.

"That's exactly what I'm asking you to do." I paused, and it took me a few seconds to swallow the hard knot of worry in my throat. "It's the only chance Desmond has. *We're* the only chance Desmond has."

Joan looked at me, her face smooth, her eyes frosty. Once again, I couldn't tell what she was thinking or feeling, and I had to bite my tongue to keep from begging her to help us. Gabriel was right. This was a three-person job, and I didn't know what I would do if Joan turned us down.

No, that wasn't true. I knew *exactly* what I would do: try to rescue Desmond anyway and probably get myself and Gabriel killed in the process.

Joan stood up. My heart sank. She was going to leave.

She sighed, shrugged out of her trench coat, and sat back down. "All right," she muttered. "Tell me your crazy plan."

THIRTY-FOUR

DESMOND

Once again, I drifted along in the black void of unconsciousness for quite some time. And once again, sensations slowly intruded on that peaceful bubble.

Low voices talking. Rough hands grabbing my arms and
legs. Air flowing over my body. My back hitting a hard cushion.
Tight bands cinching around my wrists and ankles.

That last one finally roused me to wakefulness. My eyes
cracked open, and this time, I found myself staring up at a gray
tile ceiling. I tried to roll to the side, but I couldn't move. The
fog dissipated from my mind, the world snapped into focus,
and my gut twisted with dread.

I was strapped down to the chair in Henrika's lab.

Thick, wide plastic bands anchored my wrists to the chair
arms, while matching bands lashed my ankles to the metal
footrest. I jerked forward, but my bonds were tight, and all I
could do was wiggle around in the chair like a rabbit caught in
a snare, going nowhere fast.

The sound of clicking keys caught my attention, and I
stopped struggling and looked to my left. Henrika was standing

at a worktable, typing away on a laptop.

"Don't worry, darling," she said, grinning at me. "We're going to start with the easy stuff first."

Footsteps scuffed on the tile, and Bryce came into view, now wearing blue medical gloves and a white lab coat that matched Henrika's garment.

"Since when did you become a scientist?" I groused.

"I do whatever is necessary to get the job done, Dez," Bryce replied. "Unlike you."

He rolled a metal cart over to my left elbow. Instead of hammers, pliers, and other torture tools, some disinfectant wipes, a roll of gauze, and a long piece of rubber tubing covered the surface, along with several empty glass vials and a syringe with an alarmingly large needle.

"Bryce is going to collect some blood samples," Henrika said. "Nothing too painful. According to your file, Section medics take your blood all the time, so you should be used to it."

She was right. Section medics did take my blood all the time. Standard operating procedure for cleaners, especially if we were exposed to toxic gases, chemicals, or other hazardous materials on missions. Although given my galvanism, most of the time all I had to do to make myself better was grab the nearest source of electricity and channel it through my body, speeding up my own natural healing process. But I didn't dare do that right now, which was why my jaw and ribs were still aching from Bryce's punches.

Bryce grabbed a pair of scissors, cut through the left sleeve of my sweater, and shoved the fabric aside. Next, he swabbed my skin with a disinfectant wipe, tied the rubber tubing around my upper arm, and shoved the needle into the bulging vein in the crook of my elbow. He was none too gentle about it, but I didn't give him the satisfaction of wincing.

He filled the vials with my blood and handed them to

Henrika. Bryce plucked out the needle, stuck a cotton ball against my skin, and wrapped some gauze around the wound.

"What? No superhero bandage?" I asked in a snarky voice.

"Not today, tough guy," Bryce sniped back.

I growled and struggled against my bonds again, but they remained as tight as before. I couldn't lay a single finger on the former cleaner. Bryce laughed and moved away.

Next, Bryce dragged over portable X-ray and ultrasound machines and scanned my body from head to toe. The resulting images appeared on monitors around the lab, and Henrika paced back and forth, tapping a pen against her lips and studying them all in turn.

"You're in remarkably good shape for a cleaner," she said. "No broken bones, no torn ligaments, no major internal damage. Of course, your face is a mess, and your ribs are cracked from where Bryce hit you earlier, but those wounds are already healing."

"You know enduros heal faster than other paramortals," I lied. "Plus, Section 47 has excellent doctors and access to advanced biomagical medicines just like you do. Say what you will about Section, but they take care of their agents."

Bryce snorted. "Yeah, they patch us up so we can go right back out and get hurt all over again."

Henrika kept studying the scans. "Maybe Desmond's good health is due to Section's benevolence and his own enduro power, or maybe it's something else." She jerked her head at Bryce. "Let's move on to the next test."

Bryce went over to the industrial refrigerators along the wall. He put on a fresh pair of gloves, opened a refrigerator door, and carefully drew out a syringe filled with a red liquid. Bryce brought the syringe over to Henrika, who took it from him with her bare hand. I frowned. Why wasn't she wearing gloves? Was she immune to whatever hazardous thing was in the syringe?

Henrika held the syringe up to the light and shook it, as if checking the liquid's viscosity. My nose twitched, and a faint, familiar scent wafted over to me—sweet, sticky honey mixed with the stench of rotten eggs.

My hands clenched into fists, and sweat beaded on my forehead, despite the cool, recycled air. That syringe was filled with Redburn.

Henrika noticed my unease and let out a delighted laugh. "Well, at least you fear my formula."

This time, I couldn't hold back a shudder. "You're a brilliant scientist. You could have invented anything you wanted. Why not come up with a way to help people instead of hurting them?"

Henrika let out another laugh, but this sound was more bitter than mocking. "I had a similar conversation with Charlotte last night. But you already know that."

Yes, I did, but I would have the exact same conversation with her a dozen times over if it would keep her from jabbing that syringe into me.

Henrika sighed, as though suddenly weary, and her green aura flickered with the same dull emotion. "I did try, you know."

"Try what?"

"To be good. To make some great medical breakthrough that would help people. I tried—for years, I *tried*."

"What changed?" I needed to keep her talking, but I was also genuinely curious.

Henrika shrugged. "Someone approached me with a special project, and I discovered I had a knack for dreaming up ways to destroy things. Poisons to wreck internal organs. Acids strong enough to dissolve bones." She waggled the syringe of Redburn at me. "Explosives that will reduce even the strongest paramortal to a pile of messy parts."

I ground my teeth to hold back another shudder.

Henrika placed a drop of Redburn on a glass slide, then added a drop of my blood. I tensed, but nothing happened. No bangs, no booms, no explosions of any kind.

"Curious," Henrika murmured, staring at the slide through a microscope. "Normally, when Redburn comes into contact with blood, skin, muscles, and bones, paramortal or otherwise, it immediately starts burning through and disintegrating the tissue. But your blood seems to be stronger than most . . ."

She kept talking, muttering scientific ideas and theories to herself that I didn't understand and frankly didn't want to. While Henrika and Bryce worked, I glanced around, searching for a way to free myself from the chair, but my wrists and ankles were securely fastened. I didn't see any guns. No knives or other obvious weapons. I would have been more than happy to break a glass vial and cut Henrika's and Bryce's throats with a shard, but all the vials were out of my reach, like everything else.

But I was a cleaner, and I was good at making my own weapons, so I quit looking at the objects around me and focused on my own supplies, such as they were.

My clothes and boots were still intact, except my left sleeve, which Bryce had cut to draw my blood. The gun and knife I'd had in the clearing were gone, and my pocket watch was also missing. I had no weapons, and I was well and truly stuck, like a fly in a spider's web, and Henrika could do whatever she wanted to me . . .

Unless I used my galvanism.

I might be in the middle of the lab, but I could still sense the electricity humming down through the walls, along the floor, and up into the thick cables that hooked into the back of the chair so it could be raised and lowered and tilted up and down. Thanks to the knockout gas Henrika had dosed me with earlier, the current felt much weaker than usual, which was my first problem.

My second and most pressing problem was that I just didn't see a way to use my power to escape. The thick plastic bands around my wrists and ankles were manual, not electronic, which meant I couldn't use the chair's current to open them like I could do with a door locked with a keypad.

And then, of course, my third problem was the instant I used my galvanism, Henrika would realize *that* was how I had survived being blown to bits by her bombs. I wasn't about to give the sadistic bitch any information she could use to make her monstrous formula even deadlier. Not after suffering through all those explosions on the beach. Not after watching my best friend die in my arms. Not after taking what little energy Graham had left to save myself.

I would rather die in this chair than help Henrika hurt anyone else.

Henrika stopped muttering and snapped her fingers at Bryce, who went back over to the refrigerator and drew out another syringe. This one contained a bright, shimmering pink liquid that looked like the color of cotton candy, strangely enough.

Bryce gave the syringe to Henrika, who nodded with satisfaction. She also handled this syringe with her bare hands, as though she wasn't afraid of the contents at all.

"What is that?" I asked.

Henrika walked over and held the syringe up where I could see it. "I've been tinkering with my Redburn formula. Explosives are loud and messy, and sometimes my clients want a cleaner, quieter, and more discreet method of eliminating their enemies. So I've been working on a way to condense my formula down into a poison. You saw my first test earlier today."

She was talking about the scientist she'd injected with Redburn and killed in the woods. A disgusted, angry snarl rumbled out of my throat.

"Don't worry. This is a mild, modified dose, unlike what I

gave Ethan. Designed to test a paramortal's reaction to Redburn without killing them." Henrika flashed me a wicked grin. "And since you seem to be so very durable, Desmond, you are the perfect test subject."

More cold sweat beaded on my forehead. I jerked on my restraints yet again, but they remained as tight as before. Henrika ignored my flailing, rammed the syringe into my upper left arm, and pushed the plunger down.

Henrika jerked her head at Bryce. "Start recording. Now."

He hit some buttons on the laptop. A camera dropped down from the ceiling, the lens swiveled in my direction, and a light on the side turned green. I struggled against my bonds yet again, but I was as secure and helpless as before.

"I wouldn't do that if I were you," Henrika advised. "Any activity increases your heart rate, thus pumping the poison through your body even faster."

She was right, so I stopped struggling.

Henrika and Bryce watched me closely. For several seconds, nothing happened, and the only sound in the lab was my harsh, raspy breathing.

A strange, warm sensation erupted in my arm at the injection site. The odd, unnatural warmth spread across my chest and zipped down into my legs, even as it slithered up into my neck. With a sudden surge, the warmth reached my brain, making it hard to concentrate on anything else. Sweat beaded on my forehead and trickled down my face, and my skin became hot, clammy, and unbearably tight.

"Fascinating," Henrika murmured. "Most people would have been burning up by now, but Desmond's temperature has only shot up a few degrees."

A few degrees? I felt like a lobster being boiled alive in a pot of scalding water.

"It seems you were right, and I was wrong, Desmond," Henrika said, a thoughtful tone creeping into her voice. "You do have far more enduro magic than I expected, but we'll see how long your power lasts before the poison takes full effect . . ."

That was the last thing I heard before the slow burn ramped up into a raging inferno. Liquid fire rushed through my veins, and I screamed.

THIRTY-FIVE

CHARLOTTE

Joan, Gabriel, and I sketched out a plan of attack, then left the library. Joan returned to her room to get some supplies, while Gabriel and I headed outside to his SUV. While we'd been plotting, it had started snowing, and big, fat, fluffy flakes were tumbling down from the sky like icy confetti.

The storm had finally arrived, in more ways than one.

Gabriel opened the trunk and flipped back the cargo liner to reveal several black plastic crates. He removed the lids, and I let out a low whistle of appreciation. Guns and ammo glinted inside one of the crates, along with knives, grenades, and other weapons. Another case held heavy-duty winter gear, and I dug out a pair of ski bibs and put them on over my sweater and pants.

I also dug out a winter hat and peered at the pom-pom on the top. "Does this contain any explosives?"

Gabriel gave me a look like I was a couple of flakes short of a snow globe. "Why in the world would you wear an explosive pom-pom on your head?"

"Never mind," I muttered.

We'd just finished donning more layers when Joan strode into the parking lot wheeling two suitcases along behind her—the same two suitcases the guards had removed from the honeymoon suite earlier.

"Those look familiar," I replied in a wry voice.

Joan shrugged. "I packed all the gear, and I'm not letting it go to waste."

She set the suitcases on top of Gabriel's crates, and we rifled through the contents, slipping weapons and anything else we thought might be useful into our pockets. Then Gabriel shut the trunk, the three of us climbed into the SUV, and we left the hotel.

Three inches of snow had already covered the ground, and it was starting to stick to the road as well. Gabriel handled the SUV with expert precision, going as fast as he dared on the slick pavement, while Joan and I looked at maps and photos, double-checking our route.

Every few minutes, Joan's phone beeped, and she finally looked at the screen and grimaced. "Diego wants to know where I am. He says the strike team members at the hotel are looking for me."

"Are you going to tell him where you are?" I asked.

She slid her phone back into her pocket. "I don't have to. Sooner or later, he'll get the bright idea to track my phone. Even if I turn it off, Diego can still track it. And then, well, we all know what will happen."

Gabriel nodded, his eyes still on the road. "Old man Percy will realize we have a lead on Desmond and send a strike team to our location."

I didn't care what the General would do to me as long as we rescued Desmond, although I worried about the consequences for Joan and Gabriel.

We rode in silence for five more minutes before Gabriel

steered the SUV off the road and parked in a small lot that fronted a scenic overlook.

"This is as far up the mountain as I can drive in these conditions," he said.

"Then we go on foot from here," I replied.

Joan handed out some comms, which we all stuck in our ears. "Check," she said.

Gabriel and I checked back to her, making sure we could all hear one another. Then we got out of the SUV, crossed the parking lot, and plunged into the woods. Gabriel and Joan both had their guns drawn, but I had a map in one hand and my phone in the other.

We had to skirt around the enormous craters Henrika's explosives had left behind, but it didn't take us long to hike up the mountain. We didn't meet any resistance. No guards, no cameras, no booby traps. Not surprising, given the conditions. The storm was getting worse by the second. Hard bits of snow pelted my face, and the wind cut through my clothes like icy teeth.

I called a halt at the top of a small, rocky outcropping to orient myself. Despite the cold, I was sweating, thanks to the steep climb, my many layers of clothes, and the heavy gear tucked in my pockets. And for the first time, well, *ever*, I was glad my father had dragged me along on all those weekend training missions when I was a kid. I didn't know if I would have been able to keep going now without those harsh childhood lessons.

"According to the map, the mine entrance should be around here somewhere. Let's spread out."

Joan and Gabriel nodded, and the three of us set off in different directions, although we took care to stay in one another's line of sight. The last thing we needed was to get lost in the blowing, blinding snow.

"Over here." Joan's voice crackled in my earbud.

We weren't that far apart, but I couldn't hear her voice in the air over the howling wind.

Gabriel and I hurried in her direction, and Joan stabbed her finger to the right. A large pile of brush had been positioned in front of a rock wall, although the wind had blown some of it aside, revealing a rugged, cavelike entrance that was just wide enough for one person to duck into at a time.

I checked the map again. "This has to be it."

I slid the map and my phone into my pocket and drew my own gun. Joan and I kept watch while Gabriel cleared away the remaining brush. When he finished, we peered into the opening, but all I could see was darkness.

I looked at Joan and Gabriel. They both nodded and raised their weapons a little higher. I raised my own weapon, then stepped out of the raging storm and into the black unknown.

I activated a light in the top button on the front of my coat so we wouldn't stumble around in the dark. The narrow passage quickly opened into a wide cave with rough walls. We went in ten feet, twenty, thirty, fifty . . .

Nothing changed, and nothing moved or stirred in the darkness. On the bright side, being in the mine blocked out the howling wind and blowing snow, although my breath still frosted in the air.

"You sure this is the right place, Char?" Gabriel asked, his voice bouncing off the walls in an eerie echo.

"It has to be. One of the Section strike teams found Henrika's SUVs abandoned not far from here. Henrika, Bryce, and their goons would have had just enough time to cover their tracks, come here, hide the mine entrance, and disappear inside before the strike teams made it up the mountain."

We kept walking, our boots scraping against the uneven ground.

"This place gives me the creeps," Joan muttered.

"Not a fan of spelunking?" Gabriel drawled.

"Of willingly walking into a dark, dank hole in the ground? Nope, not a fan," she sniped back.

I tuned out their chatter and squinted. Was that a light up ahead?

I turned off the button flashlight on my coat. Yes, it was a light, although it was barely discernible. I quickened my steps. The light brightened, although it seemed like it was coming from somewhere below—

Instead of solid ground, my boot found nothing but empty air. I jerked my foot back and had to windmill my arms to keep my balance. When I was steady again, I cautiously tiptoed forward and peered down.

The cave floor abruptly dropped off and sloped downward, morphing into a set of crude stairs that had been carved into the rock. Gabriel and Joan stepped up beside me, shining their own coat-button flashlights down into the darkness. Small lights were set into the walls, offering a bit of illumination, but the space was largely dark.

"Okay, maybe this is the right place," Gabriel said.

"How far down do you think it goes?" Joan asked.

"No idea, but I'm guessing Desmond is at the bottom."

I tightened my grip on my gun and eased down the steps. I stopped every few feet to look and listen, as well as scan the next steps below for booby traps, but no flares of pink or red appeared, and my inner voice remained quiet.

"What are you doing?" Joan asked, stepping down beside me. "Why are your eyes glowing like that?"

"Don't you know? Charlotte is an expert at finding traps," Gabriel replied. "She hears lies too, so be careful what you say around her."

Joan gave me a thoughtful look. "So your synesthesia does more than just help you spot typos in reports."

"You have no idea," I muttered.

Joan followed me, with Gabriel bringing up the rear. The farther down we went, the brighter and warmer it got. By the time we reached the bottom, I was sweating again.

A tunnel stretched out before us. It looked like it had been part of the original mine, but steel beams had been added to support the low rock ceiling. The tunnel curved to the right, and I thought back to the maps and photos, trying to figure out where we were in relation to the resort. Unless I missed my guess, we had gone down the mountain to the shoreline and were about to start walking under the lake itself.

"Why aren't any guards posted down here?" Gabriel murmured.

"No idea, but we need to move," Joan replied.

She stepped forward, and my synesthesia screamed to life.

Danger-danger-danger!

"Stop!" I hissed.

Joan froze.

"Char?" Gabriel asked. "What do you see?"

I didn't actually *see* anything, but my synesthesia kept screaming out a warning. My magic had only acted up when Joan had moved forward, so I crouched down and studied the ground in front of her. A bright red glare filled my eyes, centered on a small pile of dirt about two feet in front of Joan's right boot.

I pointed it out. "See how the dirt is loose instead of hard-packed like the rest of the ground? I'm betting there's a pressure plate or some other explosive hidden there."

Joan hissed out a breath and eased away from it. "Thanks."

"You're welcome. Let me go first, and step *exactly* where I step. Bryce and his men probably left more booby traps behind."

I carefully maneuvered around the pile of dirt. Joan followed me, with Gabriel bringing up the rear. I was right, and we passed two more similar dirt bombs set about twenty-five feet apart from each other.

Shortly after that, the ground morphed from the natural stone and dirt of the old mining tunnel into smooth dark gray concrete. We walked ten feet, twenty, thirty, fifty, a hundred . . .

"How long is this tunnel?" Gabriel groused.

"At least a mile," I replied. "That would match the distance from this mountain and shoreline across the lake to the resort."

"So Henrika's lab *is* on the resort grounds," Joan murmured. "We just couldn't find it because it's so deep underground."

The farther we walked, the more doubt and dread crept into my heart. What if Henrika hadn't come here? What if she had already gotten the information she wanted from Desmond? What if she had already killed him?

No. I banished that thought from my mind. I would *not* consider that possibility.

Desmond was a trained spy and a strong paramortal. He could hold out—and hold his tongue—for a long, long time, especially about his own secrets. All I had to do was find him, and then we could escape from this place together, just like we had escaped from Tannenbaum Castle a few weeks ago.

The tunnel curved to the right again, and we rounded a corner and stopped. We'd come to a junction, and the tunnel branched off in three different directions.

"Eeny-meeny-miny-moe," Gabriel muttered. "Any idea which way we should go, Char?"

I pulled out the map of the old mine again, but I couldn't correlate the three tunnels with anything on the image. This must be a new section Henrika had constructed. I glanced into each of the three tunnels, but they all looked the same—long corridors with metal doors set into the walls.

"No clue," I replied, sliding the map back into my pocket. "We're going to have to split up."

Gabriel opened his mouth to protest, but Joan shook her

head. "Charlotte's right. If we all go down the same tunnel and choose the wrong one, we'll have to backtrack, and Desmond could be dead by the time we find him."

Gabriel shut his mouth. A grim look flickered across his face, and he nodded.

"We don't know how many men Henrika might have down here," I said. "If you run into any guards, let everyone know via comms, then fall back here, retreat up the old mine tunnel steps, and get back to the surface."

Joan nodded. Gabriel stared at me a moment before he also nodded.

"See you on the far side." He raised his gun to his forehead and snapped off a salute before stepping into the left tunnel.

"Good luck," Joan said, then moved toward the right tunnel.

"We're all going to need it," I replied.

I squared my shoulders, raised my gun, and entered the center tunnel.

THIRTY-SIX

DESMOND

I screamed for a long, long time.

Everything else dropped away. The tight plastic bands around my wrists and ankles. The hard chair cushion against the back of my body. Even Henrika intently studying my reactions while Bryce grinned with glee at my suffering.

All I was aware of was the Redburn poison burning through my veins, scorching every single part of me. Head, fingers, chest, toes. I half expected them all to erupt with actual flames, and yet that wouldn't have been as painful as the unending agony pumping through my body with every frantic, fluttering beat of my heart.

No flames appeared, but my skin grew redder and redder, as though I'd developed a sudden severe sunburn. My hands and fingers took on a bright sheen, and my skin grew tight, as though it was a too-small suit stitched onto my body. The tightness intensified, along with the redness, until blisters erupted on my skin. The blisters grew larger and larger, even as the neon-red burns spread across my body, eating through one layer of flesh after another.

I wasn't a lobster being boiled alive in a pot of water. I was in the center of an erupting volcano, caught in a geyser of lava that kept exploding over and over.

Through it all, I could feel my galvanism working overtime, right along with the rest of my body, trying to turn the poison into usable energy. I knew that I shouldn't reach for my power, shouldn't use it in any way, but the pain was so great I couldn't stop myself. I squeezed my eyes shut to hide the telltale glow of my power, but I was in such agony that I couldn't quite get a grip on my galvanism, and my magic dropped down into that erupting volcano of pain.

Eventually, my screams died down. The pain hadn't lessened, but I had lost my voice, and I barely had the strength to breathe.

Henrika watched through all my shrieking screams and raspy gurgles, scribbling notes on a pad. She kept the camera trained on me the whole time, while sensors embedded in the chair recorded my blood pressure, pulse rate, oxygen level, and more.

As a cleaner, I'd sustained my fair share of injuries, both during training and on missions. I'd been shot, stabbed, cut, hammered, and bludgeoned, but all those injuries had paled in comparison to the Redburn explosion, which was the worst pain I'd ever endured. The modified Redburn poison was a close second, though.

The torture, the agony, the relentless burning in my veins went on and on and on . . .

I must have finally blacked out, because sometime later, the soft, steady *beep-beep-beep* of a heart-rate monitor roused me back to consciousness. I cracked open my eyes, which were as dry and scratchy as sandpaper.

Henrika's face swam into view. I recoiled, but I was still strapped down to the chair so I couldn't go anywhere.

"Fascinating," she murmured, shining a penlight into my eyes. "You're already recovering from the poison."

I blinked dully at the bright light. I tried to speak, but my tongue was thick, numb, and heavy, and I couldn't form any words. That was probably for the best. My mind was spinning around and around, and I had no idea what secrets I might spill to stop her from injecting more poison into my body.

Henrika lowered the light and tilted her head to the side, studying me even more closely. "There's no way an enduro with a moderate level of power could have survived all those bombs on the beach in Australia or had such a mild reaction to the dose of poison I just gave him."

Mild reaction? I'd thought my bones were melting.

"So what?" Bryce asked, hovering behind her shoulder.

Henrika tapped the penlight on her lips. "So either Desmond is the most powerful enduro I've ever encountered . . ."

My gut clenched. Somehow I knew what she was going to say next.

Henrika dropped the penlight, her eyes narrowing in thought. "Or Mr. Percy has some *other* paramortal power that is keeping him alive."

Bryce blinked, as though the thought had never occurred to him that I might be more than what I said I was.

Henrika glanced over at the former cleaner. "Did Desmond ever show any unusual abilities on your missions? Did you ever hear any whispers at Section 47 that he was more than just an enduro?"

Bryce's face scrunched up, and my gut twisted again. But after several seconds, he shook his head. "Nothing that I remember."

Henrika turned around and leaned a little closer to me. "What are you hiding, Desmond? What other abilities do you have?"

An eager note crept into her voice, as though she had just made some wonderful scientific discovery. I had to grind my teeth to hold back a shudder of revulsion.

"What does the data say?" Henrika asked.

Bryce glanced at the monitors, then shrugged. "It all just looks like random numbers and gibberish. Come figure it out for yourself—"

Beep-beep-beep.

A series of sharp warning chimes sounded. I blinked. What was that?

Bryce hurried over to a laptop. His fingers flew over the keys, and he let out a vicious curse. "Charlotte Locke is in the main tunnel. How did she find us?"

He hit some more keys. The data on the monitors vanished, replaced by security feeds. I dragged my bleary gaze over to the screens. Sure enough, Charlotte was creeping down a corridor, a gun in her hand.

Charlotte was here.

My heart lifted with hope, but it crashed back down just as quickly. Worry surged up to take its place, burning through me just as swiftly and viciously as Henrika's cruel formula. Charlotte might have come here to save me, but she'd put herself in more danger than ever before. I couldn't let Bryce capture her. I couldn't let Henrika inject Charlotte with the Redburn poison.

I would *not* let that happen, no matter what it cost me.

Once again, I flexed my hands and feet, and once again, the plastic bands around my wrists and ankles didn't move an inch. I had to find some way to get out of this chair. I had to find some way to kill Henrika and Bryce before they could do to Charlotte what they had just done to me.

Henrika shrugged, as though the news was troubling but not unexpected. "Ms. Locke is quite brilliant, and perhaps even more tenacious. She must have realized we never left the mountain. After that, it wouldn't have taken her long to figure out we had literally gone underground."

"What do you want to do?" Bryce asked.

Henrika chewed on her lower lip. "How many intruders are in the facility?"

Bryce tapped a few more keys. "Looks like three so far. Locke, along with a man and a woman."

Henrika nodded, as if she had been expecting the information. "Charlotte only brought a few friends instead of an entire strike team. She doesn't trust Jethro Percy any more than I do. Maybe we can still salvage something out of this situation."

"What do you want to do?" Bryce repeated.

Henrika stood up, strode over to a shelf along the wall, and grabbed a silver briefcase. She snapped it open, revealing black foam padding inside, then pulled several syringes and vials out of the industrial refrigerators.

"I'll take the most important samples with me. The rest of it can burn. I'm not leaving anything behind for Jethro Percy to get his hands on. That arrogant bastard has already stolen enough of my work."

I frowned, my muddled mind trying to make sense of her words. When had my father stolen her work? And why?

Bryce nodded. "Understood. I'll alert the guards and start the evacuation and self-destruct procedures."

Henrika nodded back and closed the briefcase.

"What do you want to do about him?" Bryce jerked his thumb at me.

Henrika grabbed the briefcase, then walked over and stared down at me with a dispassionate expression. "We could take Desmond with us. I'd *love* to conduct more tests on him."

My breath seized in my throat. I wouldn't survive any more tests. My body would finally give out, or my mind, or both, and I'd start begging for mercy and spill every Section secret I knew.

"But we don't have time to knock him out again," Henrika continued in a regretful tone. "Leave him here. He can burn with everything else."

Henrika leaned down and grabbed my chin. Her fingers dug

into my burned skin, and she wrenched my head from side to side, still staring at me with that dispassionate expression. "It's a pity our time is being cut short, Desmond. You've been a marvelous test subject."

She leaned in a little closer, her voice dropping to a whisper only I could hear. "I do hope you figure out a way to escape and save Charlotte. Ms. Locke is a worthy adversary, and I don't have nearly enough of those. Call me a sentimental fool, but I'm rooting for you two crazy lovebirds."

I blinked, once again struggling to process her words. Why would Henrika want me to escape and save Charlotte? What game was she playing now?

Henrika winked at me, then released my chin. Still carrying the briefcase, she strode through the open door and left the lab.

I stared at the open door, but Henrika didn't return. Bryce kept tapping keys on the laptop. I studied the monitors, trying to learn everything I could about the layout and the number of guards.

Several men with guns ran through the corridors, but I couldn't tell whom they might be chasing. Charlotte was still moving through the main corridor, which seemed to run the length of the facility.

The sight of Charlotte cut through the rest of the dull fog cloaking my mind. Once again, I struggled against the wrist and ankle restraints, and once again, I went nowhere. I swallowed a frustrated growl and redoubled my efforts. I had to get out of this chair and help Charlotte.

Crack!
Crack! Crack!
Crack!
The distinctive sounds of gunfire zipped through the air. On

the monitor, Charlotte stopped. I flinched, thinking she'd been shot, but after a few long, tense seconds, she raised her gun a little higher and moved forward, her pace much quicker than before.

"Aw, are you concerned about your girlfriend? You should be. My men will kill her before she even gets close to the lab." Bryce looked at the monitor with an appreciative leer. "It's too bad we have to evacuate. I always enjoy having a little extra fun on my assignments."

White-hot rage roared through me at the thought of Bryce hurting Charlotte, and I jerked against my bonds even harder than before. Bryce laughed at my useless struggles, then started typing again.

I forced myself to stop moving. I simply didn't have the physical strength to snap the bonds, so I had to figure out some other way to get free. I focused on the chair itself, curled my fingers around the metal arms, and reached out with my galvanism.

An electrical current hummed through the chair, low and steady, just waiting for someone to press a button to activate it. Normally, I could have grabbed hold of that electricity with the smallest thought, but the Redburn poison had severely weakened me, and my power kept slipping out of my grasp like sparking grains of sand trickling through my fingers.

Bryce hit a final button on the laptop, then strutted over to me. "It's too bad Henrika didn't have more time to work on you, Dez. Watching you scream was the most fun I've had in a long, long time."

"Fuck off, you sadistic bastard." Admittedly, it wasn't the wittiest comeback, but I was more concerned about getting free than exchanging bons mots with the former cleaner.

"Although part of me is glad it's just you and me now," Bryce continued. "Because I still owe you for getting me kicked out of Section. And for this, of course."

He traced his index finger down the scar on his face, then reached around to the small of his back and drew out a long knife. The rogue cleaner wasn't going to leave me here to burn like Henrika had ordered. Bryce was going to carve me up and kill me right here and now.

"What? No gun?" I muttered.

Bryce admired the gleaming blade. "What can I say? Steig inspired me. Besides, guns are too quick and easy."

My gaze locked onto the weapon, and a hasty plan formed in my mind. I had to get the timing just right, or Bryce would filet me like a fish.

"Any last words, Dez?" Bryce crooned.

Instead of responding, I clutched the chair arms even tighter and tensed my muscles, getting ready for what I knew was coming next.

Bryce surged forward, lashing out with the knife and driving it straight toward my body. I jerked to the right as far as I could. Bryce wasn't expecting the move, and his blade punched into my upper left arm instead of my chest. A sharp, brutal spike of pain still erupted in my body, and I yelped at the stinging sensation.

"That's not going to save you," Bryce hissed.

I grunted with a combination of agony and agreement. He was probably right about that, but I still had to try.

Bryce twisted the knife deeper into my arm, and that pop of pain flared up into pure, raw power. I used the fresh burst of energy to reach out with my galvanism again, and I was finally able to grab the current running through the chair. I channeled all that power into my right arm, then forced my wrist up as hard and high as I could.

This time, it lifted half an inch. I did that over and over in rapid succession, channeling all the energy into that one sharp, short, jerking motion. Slowly but surely, the plastic restraint began to weaken and give.

"What are you doing?" Bryce asked. "Are you having a seizure?"

He leaned toward me, and I snapped forward, head-butting him in the nose. Bryce yelped and staggered away. The awkward angle of the blow made an answering spike of pain explode in my own skull, and I channeled that extra bit of strength and energy down into my right arm and jerked my wrist up again.

Snap!

The plastic band finally broke.

Bryce growled, lunged forward, and yanked the knife out of my left arm, making me scream. He twirled the knife around in his hand, and my blood dripped off the blade and splattered onto the floor.

"Time to die, Dez," he snarled.

Bryce lunged forward again, the knife flashing a wicked silver as it arced through the air. Once again, I jerked to the right, and the blade punched into my left upper arm in almost the same spot as before. More pain spiked through my body, bringing a fresh wave of energy along with it.

I gritted my teeth, reached up, and latched on to Bryce's arm with my right hand. My fingers dug into his wrist, and I grabbed hold of all the pain and energy pounding through my veins, along with the electrical current still humming through the chair.

And then I sent it all shooting from my body into his.

Bryce jerked as though he'd just touched a live wire. In a way, that was exactly what he was doing. Only I was the wire, and I was determined to give him much more than just a vicious shock.

I strained and clawed and used every single scrap of my galvanism to gather up as much of the chair's current as possible. The power poured into me, giving me even more strength and energy, and I reached out even farther with my galvanism, following the current through the floor and up the walls. The ceiling lights flickered, as did the monitors and the laptops. Even the industrial refrigerators moaned and groaned as I seized power from them and redirected it into my own body.

Bryce's eyes widened in surprise and disbelief, and his yellow aura crackled with fear and panic. He tried to wrench away, but I tightened my grip, my fingernails digging even deeper into his skin and drawing blood.

"Time to die, traitor!" I hissed.

I punched all that raw power and sparking electricity through my fingertips and into his body as though I was shooting a lightning bolt at him.

Bryce flailed and jerked, still trying to escape, but I tightened my grip yet again and sent even more power coursing through his body. The former cleaner might be a strong enduro, but the electricity overwhelmed his system and burned through him just like the Redburn poison had burned through me. He twitched once, twice, three times. When his heart stopped beating, I finally loosened my grip.

Bryce crumpled to the floor. He twitched a few more times, then stilled.

I released the electrical current, and all the energy snapped back into its rightful place. The lights, laptops, and monitors quit flickering, and the refrigerators' moans and groans smoothed out into steady hums.

I slumped back against the chair, breathing hard, my head spinning with adrenaline. But my galvanism turned the chemical into energy too, and my breathing quickly evened out.

I might have killed Bryce, but I was still mostly strapped to the chair, so I reached up and wrenched his knife out of my arm. Another scream rasped out of my throat, but I used the blade to cut through the restraint on my left wrist and the ones around my ankles.

Still clutching the bloody knife, I tried to stand up, but my head spun, and I had to sit back down in the chair to keep from vomiting. Sweat streamed down my face, and I gasped for air. My fight with Bryce had further weakened me

When my head stopped spinning, I tried again, forcing myself to move slowly but steadily to keep the nausea to a minimum. I got to my feet, then shuffled over and kicked my boot into Bryce's ribs, making sure he was dead.

Crack!

Crack! Crack!

Crack!

More gunshots sounded, louder and closer than before. I snapped my head up and listened, but no more shots broke the silence. Neither did any screams. Worry twisted my gut. I looked at the monitors again, but I didn't see Charlotte on the security feed anymore.

Still gripping the knife, I staggered over to the closest wall. I put my hand on the light switch and reached out with my galvanism again.

The current running through the wall was much easier to access than what had been in the chair, and electricity flowed into my body, clearing my head, healing some of my injuries, and giving me a much-needed burst of energy. The lights flickered again, even more violently than before, but I kept channeling more power.

Crack!

Crack! Crack!

Crack!

Another round of gunshots rang out. I released my grip on the electricity. The lights stopped flickering, and everything in the lab returned to normal.

I tightened my grip on the bloody knife, went over to the open lab door, and staggered out into the corridor beyond.

I had to find Charlotte.

THIRTY-SEVEN

CHARLOTTE

Gabriel and Joan disappeared down their respective corridors. I drew in a breath, then let it out and started exploring my own corridor.

I made my steps as soft as possible, although they rang out in my mind like gongs chiming one after another, announcing my presence to everyone in this cursed place. The corridor went on and on and on, making me feel like I was underwater, trudging through an unending tunnel of dull gray mud.

Even the metal doors with their small square glass windows didn't break up the monotony of the space. I glanced through all the windows, but most of the rooms were empty, as though I was walking through a giant prison and all the inmates had escaped from their cells. I shivered and hurried on.

"Gabriel? Joan?" I whispered. "Anything in your corridors?"

They didn't respond, and I didn't hear the faint buzz of our comms anymore. Bryce might have realized we were here and jammed the signal, or the concrete walls could simply be too thick for our comms to work this far underground. No way to tell for certain, so I kept going.

I reached another junction, where the corridor branched left and right, as well as continuing straight ahead. I stuck to my current position in the center tunnel. With any luck, Gabriel and Joan would clear their sections quickly and catch up with me.

Crack!

Crack! Crack!

Crack!

Gunshots came from the left. I whirled around, but no one was sneaking up behind me, and the center corridor remained empty. I listened, but there were no more gunshots, and I didn't hear the smallest whisper of sound. Whatever was happening was in a different part of the facility, and I just had to trust Gabriel and Joan to protect themselves.

I blew out a tense breath, turned around, and kept moving along the center corridor.

The metal doors vanished, replaced by smooth walls. More corridors and junctions appeared, and I stopped at each one, trying to figure out where I was and especially where Desmond might be. This place was a labyrinth, and I had no idea how much farther it went—or if Desmond was even here.

Once again, the corridor curved, so I followed it and stepped into a much larger, wider space. No one was visible, although a door was set into the wall a few feet away. I sidled in that direction, then tried the knob.

To my surprise, the door was open, so I slipped inside. Unlike the other rooms, which had been empty, this area was someone's office, although it was pretty spartan, with only a desk, a chair, and a couple of other pieces of furniture.

I hurried over to the laptop on the desk and hit the space bar, causing the screen to flicker to life. Unlike the laptop in Henrika's library, this one was locked. Excitement coursed through me. This had to be one of her work computers.

I fished a flash drive out of one of my zippered pockets

and stuck it into the laptop. Diego's handy-dandy decryption software went to work and automatically downloaded the laptop's contents.

I scanned the rest of the office, and my gaze landed on a small refrigerator in the back corner. Curious, I crouched down and opened the door to find . . . bags of blood nestled inside the cool space.

I blanched and drew back. Whose blood was this? And what was Henrika doing with it?

I fished out one of the bags, which had a barcode on it, along with several numbers. According to the information, the blood had been drawn a few hours ago, and it was type A-positive.

A relieved breath whooshed out of my mouth. Desmond was type O-negative, so this wasn't his blood. Although that didn't tell me whose blood it was or what Henrika was doing with it. I snapped a photo of the information on the plastic, then slid the blood bag back into the refrigerator with the others.

A soft chime sounded, indicating that Diego's software had finished its work. I yanked the flash drive out of the laptop and slid it back into my pocket. I didn't see anything else noteworthy, so I left the office and continued down the corridor.

I'd only gone about fifty feet before the corridor opened into a large square area filled with desks, tables, and chairs. A thick layer of dust coated the furniture, and it didn't look like anyone had touched the items in ages.

Crack!
Crack! Crack!
Crack!

Bullets zinged by my head. I darted forward and dove behind a thick wooden desk.

Crack!
Crack! Crack!
Crack!

Bullets thunked into the desk, shooting splinters of wood

in all directions. I peeked around the side. Three guards were standing at the opposite end of the square reloading their weapons. I swung my gun around the side of the desk, focused on the man closest to me, and pulled the trigger.

Crack! Crack!

He screamed and tumbled to the floor. I grimaced at both his screams and the sharp retort of the shots. I had never enjoyed killing, but I would do it to save myself, just like my father had taught me to. One man down, two to go—

Crack!

Crack! Crack!

Crack!

This time, bullets whizzed behind me, smacking into the concrete wall and knocking out small chunks of stone that stung my body like gray bees. I glanced back over my shoulder. Three more guards were rushing up the corridor from the opposite direction, all of them raising their guns to fire at me again.

My heart squeezed tight. I was pinned down and trapped.

THIRTY-EIGHT

DESMOND

I staggered from one corridor to the next, following the sounds of the gunshots. I kept one hand on the wall for balance, even as I greedily gobbled up all the electricity I could sense. The lights flickered as I passed underneath them, and several exploded as I poured their energy into my body, trying to heal myself as much as possible. The crash and tinkle of breaking glass trailed after me like a symphony announcing my presence, but I didn't care.

All that mattered was finding Charlotte.

I kept going, healing myself in spurts. It took several corridors, an ocean of electricity, and dozens of broken lights, but my breaths came easier, and my legs grew steadier.

Crack!

Crack! Crack!

Crack!

These gunshots were closer than before, and I quickened my pace and peered around a corner. Up ahead, two men were firing at a wooden desk that had been shoved up against a wall, slowly but surely shooting it to pieces.

Charlotte popped up from behind the desk, but instead of shooting at the two men in front of me, she whipped around and started firing at three more men running up the corridor behind her. The men stopped and scattered.

"Move!" one of the guards on my end of the corridor yelled. "Now! While she's distracted!"

The two men quickly reloaded and aimed their guns at Charlotte. I was still clutching the bloody knife Bryce had stabbed me with, and I threw it at the man closest to me.

The blade zipped through the air and sank into his back. The guard yelped, but he didn't go down, so I hurried forward and rammed my shoulder into his. Then I churned my feet, driving him across the corridor and into the other guard. The second man hit the wall, bounced off, and slammed into his buddy, who in turn ping-ponged back into me, and all three of us went down in a heap on the floor.

The second guard snarled and raised his gun to shoot me, but I yanked the knife out of the back of the first man and lashed out with it. The blade sliced across the second guard's forearm, and he hissed and dropped his weapon.

The first man tried to get up, but I threw myself forward and planted my knee into his back, knocking him back down to the floor. Then I used his body as a springboard to launch myself at the second guard, the bloody blade in my hand whistling through the air again.

The second guard tried to scoot out of the way, but I buried the knife in his chest. The man screamed, but I ignored his sharp cry and flailing fists and twisted the blade in deeper. He was not shooting at Charlotte again. The guard let out another scream, but it was softer and shorter than before, and his body went limp underneath mine—

A hand dug into my hair and wrenched my head back. My hand slipped off the knife that was still stuck in the dead guard's body. The first man yanked me back against his chest and locked his arm around my throat. He was an enduro with enhanced strength, and he was slowly but surely cutting off my air. Gray spots exploded like fireworks at the edges of my vision, and if I didn't find a way to break his grip, I would be unconscious in a minute and dead shortly thereafter.

Desperate, I stretched out with my hands, searching for a weapon. My fingers brushed up against the gun the other guard had dropped. I scooped it up, shoved it against the right thigh of the man behind me, and pulled the trigger.

Crack!

He yelped, and his arm fell away from my throat. Wheezing for air, I whirled around on my knees and shot him in the chest three times. He toppled onto his back, blood pooling underneath his body.

I crouched there a moment, still wheezing for air, then forced myself to hobble to my feet. I had to help Charlotte.

Crack! Crack!

Charlotte fired her gun, and one of the three guys rushing up the opposite end of the corridor dropped. Once again, the other men stopped and scattered. Charlotte scuttled around to the opposite side of the desk, putting it between her and the two guards. Her head whipped in my direction, and her eyes widened.

"Desmond! Behind you!"

I turned around. Two more guards were running toward me. Unlike Charlotte, I had no cover and was completely exposed in the middle of the corridor, but I lifted my gun. The guards might kill me, but they weren't going to hurt Charlotte.

Crack! Crack!
Crack! Crack!

The guard on the left dropped, quickly followed by the man on the right. Farther down the corridor, a smoky shadow detached itself from the wall and morphed into the form of a man. Gabriel winked at me. I whipped back around to

Charlotte and took aim at the two men once again advancing on her position.

Crack! Crack!

Crack! Crack!

Before I could fire, those men dropped as well, and Joan appeared in the distance, a gun clutched in her hand, hurrying in our direction. I hissed out a breath and glanced up and down the corridor, searching for more enemies.

Gabriel stepped up beside me, grinning wide. "That's twice now I've saved your life, Slick. And yes, I am totally keeping count—"

I leaned to the side, raised my gun, and pulled the trigger.

Crack!

A third guard farther down the corridor screamed and tumbled forward. Gabriel whirled around, but the man was already bleeding out on the floor.

"And that's twice now that I've repaid the favor," I rasped. "So I would say we're even—again."

"I suppose you're right. At least until the next time you get into trouble." Gabriel eyed the burns on my hands, arms, and face. "You look like death warmed over."

"Nice to see you too, Gaby," I drawled.

"Desmond! Desmond, are you okay?"

Charlotte sprinted over and skidded to a stop beside us. She reached for me, but at the last second, she bit her lip and lowered her arm, as if she didn't want to exacerbate my injuries by hugging me. I stepped forward and cupped her cheek with my hand, stroking my swollen, shiny red fingers over her smooth skin.

Charlotte shuddered out a breath and laid her fingers over mine, giving them a gentle squeeze. "What happened?" she asked in a low, strained voice. "What did Henrika do to you?"

"She injected me with her newest weapon—Redburn poison."

Horror flared in Charlotte's eyes, but it was quickly replaced by fury, and her sapphire aura spit, hissed, and crackled with the same emotion. "I'm going to kill Henrika for hurting you again."

"Not if I find her first," Joan chimed in.

Her voice was just as low and furious as Charlotte's, and even Gabriel looked angry and disgusted on my behalf.

Charlotte looked past me. "Where is she?"

"I don't know. I killed Bryce and escaped from the lab, but Henrika had already left. You didn't see her?"

All three of them shook their heads.

"Take us to the lab," Charlotte said. "Maybe she left some clue behind about where she's going."

"Or how we can get out of this maze," Gabriel muttered.

I jerked my head to the side. "It's back this way."

Gabriel and Joan moved in that direction, their guns up and ready to deal with any more guards.

Charlotte stepped closer to me. "Oh, Desmond, I'm so sorry we didn't get here sooner. If I had just realized Henrika had never left the area and that the whole point of inviting us to the resort was to kidnap you . . ." Her voice trailed off, guilt tightened her face, and tears gleamed in her eyes. "Maybe none of this would have happened."

I stroked my thumb over her cheek again. "There's no need to apologize. We both know how smart Henrika is." A crooked smile curved my lips. "Lucky for me, you're even smarter."

Charlotte returned my smile, but it quickly faded away, and her gaze swept over my burned skin again.

"Where is my father? And the strike teams?" I asked, looking past her. "They should have reached our position by now."

Charlotte winced. "They're not here."

"Why not?"

"Take me to the lab, and I'll tell you all about it."

I nodded. Charlotte put her arm around my waist. I leaned on her, and together we left the dead guards behind and headed toward Henrika's lab.

Charlotte told me the whole story, including how the General had blamed her for my kidnapping and suspended her from Section 47.

I sighed. "He's just pissed Henrika got the better of him again, and he took his anger out on you."

Charlotte shrugged. "He's not wrong. *I'm* the one Henrika baited into coming to the resort. I waltzed right into her trap, and I dragged you along with me."

I shook my head. "No, absolutely not. You didn't *drag* me into anything. Where you go, I go. Simple as that."

Now and for always. The words whispered through my mind, but I didn't say them out loud. Safety first, sentiment later.

Despite the electricity I'd used to heal the worst of my wounds, my fight with the guards had taken its toll. My steps slowed down, and I found myself leaning on Charlotte more and more the farther we walked. By the time we reached the lab, Gabriel and Joan were already exploring the space.

Gabriel turned around in a slow circle and let out a low whistle. "Being a supervillain pays better than I imagined. Henrika's got millions of dollars of equipment in here."

Joan's lips curled back in disgust. "Everything you would need to figure out the best and most painful ways to kill people."

I thought about what Henrika had said about how long she had tried to heal people instead of hurt them. Some genuine regret had been threaded through her words, and it raised a painful truth. Despite all the awful things she'd done to me,

I understood Henrika's point of view far better than she'd realized.

How many times had I been sent to kill someone on Section's orders when the General might have found another way, a more peaceful, diplomatic solution, if only he'd looked for it long and hard enough? And how many times had I carried out those orders without question because killing someone was the quickest and easiest thing to do?

My gaze flicked to Bryce's body on the floor. In my own way, I had just as much blood on my hands as Henrika Hyde.

"What are we going to do with all this stuff?" Charlotte asked.

Joan frowned. "What do you mean? Now that Desmond is safe, we can finally call in a strike team. After they clear the facility, the Section techs will analyze everything like usual."

Charlotte looked at me, and Joan glanced back and forth between the two of us.

"What's going on?" she asked, her voice growing sharper and more suspicious with every word. "Why are the two of you looking at each other like that?"

"You tell her," Charlotte said.

"Are you sure?" I asked.

She nodded. "Joan's come this far with us. She deserves to know the truth. So does Gabriel."

"What *truth*?" Joan snapped.

I faced her. "Charlotte and I found some vials of Redburn during the Tannenbaum mission. The mercenaries were going to use the explosives to blow up the castle."

Joan's eyes narrowed. "I reviewed all the after-action reports about the Tannenbaum mission. You didn't turn any explosives over to Section."

"No, we didn't."

All weapons, drugs, cash, and evidence, magical and otherwise, was supposed to be handed over to Section 47 to be analyzed, processed, and stored. Joan's eyes narrowed a little more, but she didn't ask why we had ignored protocol. She knew exactly what Section leaders did with the weapons agents recovered: studied them so the techs could create better, even deadlier versions of such weapons.

Joan's gaze traced over the burns on my skin. A shadow passed over her face, and her pale aura dimmed. I knew she was thinking about Graham and how his body had been burned even worse than mine.

"Screw it," Joan snarled, her voice vibrating with anger. "You're the one who was tortured, so you decide what to do, Dez."

"Thank you."

She nodded, and the gleam of tears filled her eyes. "No one deserves to suffer like you and Graham did. Not even our enemies."

Gabriel tilted his head to the side, as if he'd just learned something important about the liaison.

Beside me, Charlotte suddenly stiffened. I opened my mouth to ask what was wrong.

A clock showing fifteen minutes appeared on one of the monitors. It flashed red for several seconds—and then it started counting down.

THIRTY-NINE

CHARLOTTE

Everyone's eyes zipped over to the clock.

"Please tell me that is not some cliché self-destruct countdown ticking off the seconds until this place is blown to smithereens," Gabriel muttered.

No one responded. We all knew that was *exactly* what it was.

"We have to move," Joan said. "Desmond, which one of these laptops did Henrika use?"

He pointed out the laptop. Joan grabbed it off the table, tucked it under her arm, and ran over to the open lab door. I wrapped my arm around Desmond's waist again and helped him in that direction. Gabriel brought up the rear.

Joan veered to the left, back the way we had come, but I shook my head.

"No. It's too far. We'll never make it back to the stairs, much less all the way out of the mine. None of us has seen Henrika, which means she got out through some other exit on *this* side of the facility. We have to find it before the countdown ends. It's our only shot."

Joan nodded, a grim expression on her face. The four of us moved away from the lab, racing from one corridor to another. I helped Desmond as much as possible, but he was in a tremendous amount of pain, and I could tell it was all he could do to keep putting one foot in front of the other. He kept one hand on the wall, and the lights overhead flickered as we moved under them. Desmond was channeling the electricity into his own body, but he was still extremely weak and wobbly.

Gabriel took the lead, gun in hand, but no more guards appeared, and the entire facility was eerily quiet, except for the quick rhythm of our footsteps and Desmond's labored breathing.

"How much longer?" I asked.

Joan glanced at her smartwatch. "Twelve minutes."

"How big is this place?" Gabriel muttered.

He quickened his pace, and we all did the same, even Desmond, despite the sweat streaming down his face. A minute later, we reached another junction with three corridors splitting off in different directions.

Gabriel paced back and forth, peering down each corridor. "They all look the same," he growled. "I can't tell which way to go, and we don't have time to backtrack if we get it wrong. Any ideas?"

Joan shook her head, while Desmond braced a hand on the wall, his head hanging down and his chest heaving from exertion.

I also glanced down all three corridors, but I didn't see anything that would tell us which way to go. I reached out with my synesthesia, but for once, my inner voice didn't whisper, and no telltale flares of light appeared.

Frustrated, I prowled back and forth just like Gabriel was doing.

"We need to make a decision, Char," he warned. "I'd rather die trying to get out than just stand here and get blown to bits."

"I know, I know," I snapped back. "Let me think."

Gabriel fell quiet, but he kept staring at me, as did Joan. Desmond kept his head bowed, his hand on the wall, still pulling electricity into his body.

My eyes narrowed, and a thought sparked in my mind like the proverbial cartoon light bulb appearing over my head. "Desmond? Can you feel *all* the electricity in the facility?"

He lifted his head, a weary expression on his face. "Yeah. Why?"

I gestured up at the lights. "Can you separate the feel of the lights from something else? Something bigger that would require more energy?"

"Like what?"

"An elevator," I replied. "Henrika wouldn't have wanted to walk down rough stairs like we did every time she came to the lab. Plus, she had to have some way to get all that heavy equipment down here."

"Which means there has to be a freight elevator at this end of the facility." Joan gave me a look filled with grudging admiration. "Clever deduction."

I tipped my head, acknowledging the compliment. "Can you find it, Desmond?"

He nodded, but it was a slow, exhausted motion. "I can try."

Desmond closed his eyes and flattened his hand on the wall. The lights above us flickered, and an electrical charge filled the air, along with a faint stench of ozone, like a violent thunderstorm was about to blow through the corridor.

Joan held up her fingers where Gabriel and I could see them. Seven minutes and counting down. Gabriel opened his mouth, probably to urge Desmond to work faster, but I shook my head. He was injured, and rushing him wouldn't help anything.

We stood there and waited, the lights still flickering, the steady pulses keeping time with the mental countdown clock running in my mind . . .

Desmond dropped his hand, opened his eyes, and pointed to the right. "That way. Something at the end of that corridor is using more power than the surrounding lights."

"Good enough for me, Slick," Gabriel said. "Let's move."

He holstered his gun, stepped forward, bent down, and picked up Desmond, slinging the other cleaner into a fireman's carry across his shoulders. Desmond hissed with fresh pain, but it was a necessary evil. Gabriel headed down the right corridor, and Joan and I followed him.

Gabriel seemed to jog along with ease, but his face was twisted into a tight grimace, and the muscles in his neck stood out in stark relief from the strain of carrying Desmond so far so fast. Joan raised her eyebrows at me. She had noticed it too, but there was nothing we could do to help either one of them.

All we could do was run.

Finally, we turned a corner, and there it was—a large freight elevator. Even better, the car was on this level, as though it was waiting for us to arrive. Weird. Why would the car be down here? If I were Henrika, I would have left it up at the top and then disabled it so that no one else could escape.

Gabriel hustled inside, still carrying Desmond. I followed him, as did Joan, who punched a green button on the control panel. A metal grate rattled into place, and the car slowly started to rise.

"Time?" I asked.

Joan checked her watch. "Three minutes."

I willed the elevator to rise faster, but of course it didn't.

Five seconds . . . ten . . . twenty . . . forty-five . . .

At the sixty-second mark, the freight elevator finally floated to a stop, and the grate rattled back.

We raced through a short corridor and up a set of concrete stairs to a low ceiling. Joan punched another green button on the wall, and the ceiling slowly slid back, revealing the winter sky above. I drew in a breath. I had never been so glad to smell fresh air, no matter how cold and snowy it was.

"Ninety seconds," Joan called out.

"Go! Go! Go!" I yelled.

The instant the door was out of the way, Joan sprinted up the stairs, her gun in her hand, just in case any guards were stationed outside. "Clear!"

Gabriel went up the stairs next, still carrying Desmond, while I brought up the rear.

I cleared the last step and skidded to a stop. A spotlight burned over my head, and the unexpected glare made me blink in surprise. After being surrounded by gray walls for the last hour, it took me a moment to orient myself and realize where we were: the clearing where Henrika had conducted the Redburn demonstration.

Joan was already running toward the woods in the distance, along with Gabriel, who was still carrying Desmond. They stopped at the edge of the trees and turned around. Gabriel lowered Desmond to the ground, then gestured at me.

"Charlotte!" he yelled. "Run!"

But I couldn't run. Not without closing the door behind us. Henrika had probably packed her lab with enough explosives to blow it up ten times over, and I had to contain the blast as much as possible or we might still get fried to a crisp.

I whirled around, searching for a way to close the secret door, but it was embedded in the ground, and I didn't see a way to pull it shut. Henrika would have wanted to be able to access—and hide—the lab entrance on a moment's notice, which meant she had to have installed a way to open and close the door from this side.

I spun around in a circle, and my gaze landed on the spotlight. It was the only thing that didn't belong here. I raced over to the pole and ran my hands over the cold, slick surface. It had to have a hidden button or switch. Where was it? Where was it?

My hand brushed up against a tiny button, so small that it

blended in perfectly with the rest of the metal. *There.* I jabbed the button, and the door slowly started to slide shut.

"Fifteen seconds!" Joan screamed in the distance.

"Move, Charlotte!" Gabriel yelled.

I whirled around and sprinted in their direction, running as fast as possible, even as I counted down the remaining seconds in my mind.

Ten . . . nine . . . eight . . .

I was a quarter of the way across the clearing. My lungs burned, and my legs felt like jelly from our long run inside the facility.

Seven . . . six . . . five . . .

I forced myself to move faster, even though I was doing little more than plodding through the snow, which had piled up past my ankles.

Four . . . three . . . two . . . one . . .

I threw myself forward, trying to put a few more precious feet between me and the explosion—

BOOM!

FORTY

DESMOND

An explosion ripped through the clearing.

A massive fireball punched upward through the ground, blowing the hidden door to pieces and tossing the security light aside like a metal matchstick. The fireball boiled up and out like a mushroom cloud of red-hot death, and flames blasted through the clearing—heading straight for Charlotte.

She must have sensed the looming danger with her synesthesia, because her legs churned faster. At the last instant, right before the flames would have slammed into her back, Charlotte threw herself down into the snow. The fire zipped over her, and a muffled cry sounded.

"Charlotte!" I yelled.

I staggered to my feet and lunged forward, but Gabriel grabbed my arms and held me back. "There's nothing you can do!"

"Let me go!" I yelled at him. "Let me go!"

But I was injured, and Gabriel wasn't, and he clamped his arms tighter and held me still, despite my weak, flailing struggles. Helpless, all I could do was watch as the flames boiled up and out through the clearing, melting the snow, engulfing the nearby trees, and torching everything they touched . . .

A minute passed, maybe two, although it seemed much longer than that before the fire finally died down. Acrid black smoke spewed up from the massive hole in the ground, and bits of ash swirled through the air along with the snowflakes still falling from the sky.

Gabriel finally loosened his grip. I shoved him away and dashed straight for Charlotte, who was lying face down in the snow.

I dropped to my knees beside her. The explosion had scorched the back of Charlotte's coat, and I shoveled some icy slush onto the fabric to put out any hot patches. Then I gripped her shoulder and rolled her onto her back.

Her eyes were closed, but her skin was free of burns. The explosion hadn't scalded her. A relieved breath hissed out between my teeth, and I gently shook her shoulder.

"Charlotte? Charlotte!"

Her eyes cracked open, and she squinted up at me. "I'm sorry," she mumbled. "But I can't hear you right now. My ears are ringing from the explosion. Why are fireballs always so *loud*?"

A laugh spewed out of my lips, and relief rushed through me, stronger than any current I had ever channeled with my galvanism. I helped Charlotte sit up, then leaned forward and wrapped her up in my arms. Charlotte hugged me back just as tightly, shuddering against my body.

Behind me, I could hear Joan and Gabriel hurrying in our direction and asking if we were okay. I ignored them, buried my face in Charlotte's neck, and breathed in the blue of her while the trees burned, the snow melted, and the ground smoldered all around us.

A few minutes later, a Section strike team stormed into the clearing. Joan, Charlotte, and I all raised our hands, although the other agents lowered their weapons when they realized it was us. Gabriel had already vanished into the trees. I didn't blame the former cleaner for leaving, and I envied his freedom.

Joan took command, telling the strike team leader what had happened. A stretcher was brought into the clearing, and Joan ordered the agents to load me onto it and carry me out of the woods. I held out my hand, and Charlotte threaded her fingers through mine. She walked by my side all the way back to the hotel.

After that, things happened quickly. I was given a couple of bags of IV fluids, along with a host of biomagical medicines, and a healing cream was spread on the many burns on my body. Charlotte and Joan took me back to the honeymoon suite, where we could have some privacy, and I channeled just enough of the hotel's electricity to heal the deepest, most painful burns. Despite their protests that they were fine, I also channeled enough power to heal Charlotte's and Joan's bumps and bruises.

We were all still tired, dirty, and traumatized, but we would live.

Two hours later, Gia, Evelyn, and Diego arrived, along with my father.

Joan, Charlotte, and I were back in the first-floor library, which had once again been converted into a mobile command center by the strike team. Joan and Charlotte shot to their feet when Gia, Evelyn, Diego, and the General walked into the room, but I remained sprawled in a chair by the fireplace.

Gia, Evelyn, and Diego examined me from head to toe, their gazes lingering on the burns that remained on my hands and face. I could have used my galvanism to completely heal the ugly, shiny red marks, but I didn't want to reveal the full extent of my power, just in case Henrika had a spy stationed at the hotel or was watching us through a hidden camera.

My father also peered at me, his lips pressing into a thin, angry line. His gaze cut to Charlotte, who lifted her chin and stared right back at him, daring him to say something negative.

The General sighed, then reluctantly tipped his head. Charlotte returned the gesture, although she kept eyeing him, and I could practically see the wheels turning in her mind. I didn't know what questions or concerns she had about my father, and I was too tired to care.

"What happened?" Gia asked.

Charlotte explained how she had stayed at the resort, figured out where Henrika's lab was, and persuaded Joan to help rescue me. Joan picked up the story and told how the two of them had moved through the underground facility and killed several guards. And then I recounted my ordeal in the actual lab itself, although I glossed over a lot of the details, including just how much Henrika's Redburn poison had hurt. None of us mentioned Gabriel. No use dragging him into an already tense situation.

When we finished, Gia and my father looked at us, and then at each other, having a silent conversation I was too weary to interpret. Evelyn remained off to the side, her face neutral, but calculations filled her dark gaze, especially whenever she glanced at the General.

"Okay, that's all I need for now," Gia said, breaking the silence. "We'll do a full debrief when we return to headquarters. Right now, I need to handle the mortal authorities, as well as the hotel workers and guests. They're all asking questions about the explosion."

She gestured at the strike team members, who followed her out of the library. Evelyn gave me a small smile and also left, as did Diego.

"Give me a minute with my son," the General ordered.

Joan nodded and left the library, but Charlotte raised her eyebrows in a silent question.

"It's okay," I said.

Charlotte squeezed my hand, then shut the door behind her, leaving me alone with the General.

I slowly stood up, and the two of us faced each other. After a few seconds of uncomfortable silence, my father jerked forward and wrapped his arms around me in a surprisingly tight hug. I couldn't remember the last time he had done more than clap me on the shoulder. Emotion clogged my throat, and I lifted my arms and hugged him back.

We stayed like that for several seconds, then the General dropped his arms and stepped back. "I'm glad you're okay, son," he said, his voice rough and raw.

"You should be thanking Charlotte. She's the one who figured out where I was."

All the warmth and softness snuffed out of my father's eyes, and his face hardened into its usual icy mask. "Ms. Locke was suspended. She had no right to access the information she did, much less mount a rescue mission without alerting her superior officers. She will be severely disciplined for those actions, as will Ms. Samson."

"*No*," I growled. "You're not going to do anything to Charlotte or Joan. No suspensions, no reprimands, nothing. They saved my life. If not for Charlotte, I'd still be in Henrika's lab, being injected with who knows what and tortured to within an inch of my life."

"And because of Charlotte, Henrika's lab has been blown to kingdom come," the General snapped right back at me. "Henrika is gone, and she destroyed any chance we had of getting our hands on any Redburn samples."

"Is that really all you care about? Henrika's formula?"

The General shook his head. "Of course not. The most important thing is that you're safe, son."

"But?" I challenged, crossing my arms over my chest.

My father's face hardened again. "But I want Henrika's

formula. We need to stop it from falling into the wrong hands, and we especially need to study it, so we can find a way to protect ourselves from its devastating effects."

"And reverse engineer it, so you can start using Redburn against your enemies," I accused.

"Don't be a self-righteous fool. Of course I want to reverse engineer the formula," the General said, a chiding note in his voice. "One day, when you're the head of the board of directors, you'll understand all the hard choices I've had to make over the years."

My eyes narrowed. "What *choices*?"

"That's not important right now. Containing this mess is." He hesitated, then clapped me on the shoulder. "Get cleaned up, go home, and get some rest, son. That's an order."

My father tightened his grip for a moment, then spun around, opened the door, and marched out of the library. But the imprint of his hand lingered on my shoulder, and in some ways, it burned far worse than Henrika's poison had.

FORTY-ONE

CHARLOTTE

The next few days passed in a blur of meetings and debriefings.

All my actions during the Winterfest mission were put under the proverbial microscope, and I spent hours being interviewed and typing up reports. Joan was also grilled, although to a lesser extent, since I was the instigator and she was merely my reluctant accomplice.

I stayed quiet about Joan's alter ego as Nemesis and her interference in the Tannenbaum mission, and she kept her mouth shut about Gabriel helping us rescue Desmond. Between the two of us, we spun a plausible enough story to keep Gabriel out of the official reports.

Despite my going rogue, General Percy didn't fire me, although I knew that had more to do with Desmond's influence than any sudden benevolence on the General's part. My suspension was lifted, and I went back to my normal analyst duties on level three. Percy didn't return me to the hunts for Henrika Hyde, Niles Perran, and Oriana Luzzo, but I didn't need him to. One way or another, I was going to find Henrika and make her pay for everything she'd done to Desmond.

And so my life slowly returned to normal. Well, as normal as it could ever be at Section 47.

Two weeks after the lab explosion, I walked into the Moondust Diner to work my regular shift. I'd been so busy with Section meetings that Pablo had been stuck handling everything, and I wanted to give him a break.

It was another cold, snowy January night, and I was glad to leave the winter chill behind and step into the warm, bright diner. I shrugged out of my winter gear and hung it all on a hook. Then I tied a white apron on over my blue waitress uniform, went behind the counter, and peered through the open service window.

"Did you miss me?" I asked.

Pablo looked up from the burger and fries he was plating and gave me a wide smile. "Hey, stranger. Long time no see."

"I'm so sorry about my sudden vacation. A friend from out of town had to have knee surgery and needed some help. It took longer than I expected for her to get back on her feet."

The friend-in-need lie was an old Section standby which I'd used to explain my unexpected absence from the diner. Pablo had believed me, but I still felt terrible for deceiving him. Even if I'd told him the truth, I doubted he would have believed me. Supernatural spies, magical abilities, underground labs, daring rescues, massive explosions. I wouldn't have believed it myself, if I hadn't lived through it all.

Behind me, the front door opened, and the bell chimed. A gust of cold air blasted over my back, making me shiver.

"Be with you in a second," I called out, grabbing a notepad and pen from the back counter.

"Take your time, Charlotte. I'm in no rush."

My hands froze, and my entire body stiffened, as though someone had just shoved a knife into my back. That low, silky voice had echoed through more than a few of my nightmares over the past two weeks.

"Something wrong?" Pablo asked, frowning at my sudden silence and stillness.

I forced myself to smile at him, even as my fingers curled a little more tightly around the notepad and the pen. "I just need to see what this customer wants."

Pablo nodded and returned to his plating. I slowly turned around, knowing and dreading what I would find.

Henrika Hyde was standing at the dining counter wearing a stylish dark green coat. A smile spread across her face. "Hello, Charlotte."

Every muscle in my body tensed, and I had to resist the urge to leap across the counter and tackle her. Two men stepped into the diner behind Henrika, both wearing long dark coats over matching suits, and I didn't need my synesthesia to know they were armed.

Henrika tilted her head to the side. "Let's chat."

I had no choice but to step around the counter. Henrika sat down in the back corner booth that Gabriel, Desmond, and I always used. The two guards followed, although they plopped down in another booth a few feet away. All the customers kept eating, while the other waitresses saw to their needs. In the kitchen, Pablo and the other chefs continued cooking, and everyone was completely oblivious to the danger.

"What do you want?" I growled.

Henrika arced an eyebrow at my harsh tone. "I hear this place has excellent desserts. Let's start with that."

I whirled around, marched back behind the counter, and grabbed a blackberry cheesecake Pablo had made earlier. I put a slice on a plate, then carried it over to Henrika, who gestured for me to slide into the opposite side of the booth. My stomach clenched, but I did as commanded.

Henrika looked at me, and I looked right back at her. My heart thumped at a painful pace, and clammy sweat coated my palms. It took all my willpower *not* to look at the neon French fries sign burning in the window beside us—and the three vials of Redburn hidden inside it. I didn't know why Henrika was here, but if she realized I had samples of her formula, she would probably kill me and everyone else in the diner.

Henrika looked at me a moment longer, then stabbed a fork into the cheesecake and took a bite. "Mmm. Delicious."

She hadn't noticed the sign or the vials. I had to bite my tongue to keep from hissing with relief.

"What do you want?" I growled again. "If you're here to murder me, then take me out into the parking lot and put a bullet in my head. But leave these people out of it. Nobody here has done anything to you."

Henrika took another bite of cheesecake, set her fork down, and nudged her plate aside. "As amusing as it is to watch you plead for your customers' lives, mass murdering innocent civilians has never really been my style."

"You dream up biomagical weapons for *fun*. Mass murder is literally your *job*."

She waved off my accusation. "I just make the weapons. What the buyer does with those weapons is completely on their conscience, not mine." Henrika gave me a cool look. "I bet you'll reconsider your self-righteous stance when you realize what your Section superiors are *really* up to. Care to wager on it?"

I knew she was talking about General Percy, and I couldn't keep myself from asking the obvious question. "What would that be?"

Henrika shook her head. "I'm disappointed in you, Charlotte. I sent you everything you needed to find the answers you're so desperately searching for."

"What *answers*?"

She laughed, as though it should have been as clear as glass. "About your father, of course. And what really happened in Mexico."

Once again, my entire body stiffened, even as my heart gave a painful wrench. A dozen questions dangled on the tip of my tongue, but I swallowed them all down. Henrika was playing yet another game, and she wouldn't tell me anything she didn't want me to know.

She eyed me, but when it became apparent that I wasn't going to demand answers, her mouth puckered with disappointment. "Well, I'm sure you'll figure it out sooner or later. But in the meantime, I have another engagement."

Henrika delicately blotted her red lips with a napkin, slid out of the booth, and got to her feet. She pulled a hundred-dollar bill out of her coat pocket and laid it on the tabletop. She stared at me, a thoughtful look filling her face. "Come work for me, Charlotte."

Shock zinged through me. That was just about the last thing I'd expected her to say. "*What?*"

"Come work for me," she repeated. "We both know your talents are being wasted at Section 47. Jethro Percy is a duplicitous fool who will never appreciate your skills. I could use someone like you in my organization. Someone smart and dedicated. Someone who can see the big picture and isn't afraid to break the rules to get results."

Truth, my synesthesia whispered. As crazy as it seemed, Henrika's offer was genuine.

I slid out of the booth and climbed to my feet so that we were eye to eye. "I will *never* work for you," I growled. "And I will never stop trying to take you down for what you did to Desmond. You should just kill me now. Because sooner or later, one way or another, I *will* destroy you."

A mysterious smile played across her lips. "We'll see. Enjoy your evening, Charlotte. And please tell Pablo that cheesecake was *amazing*."

Henrika lifted her fingers to her mouth and blew a chef's kiss. She smirked at me a moment longer, then strolled away.

The two guards followed her, and all three of them left the diner.

Helpless and angry, I stood by the booth and watched through the windows as my greatest nemesis climbed into a waiting SUV and disappeared into the cold, snowy night.

I didn't call Gia or Evelyn and tell them what had happened. I didn't call Joan or Diego either. I didn't even alert Gabriel or Desmond. Instead, I finished my shift, closed the diner for the night, and went to my apartment.

Desmond was working late at Section headquarters, still caught up in his own mission debriefings and reports. I texted to let him know I was home, stripped off my waitress uniform, took a hot shower, and threw on some fuzzy fleece pajamas.

Then I got to work.

Over the past two weeks, I'd brought home copies of every single Section file relating to Henrika. All the initial research I'd done on her, all the reports about our confrontation at the Halstead Hotel, all the info from the Tannenbaum mission and the Vault heist, and every map, photo, and report relating to the Winterfest mission. Several towering piles of folders, binders, and papers covered the kitchen island counter, and I hadn't had a chance to put them in any kind of order yet.

No time like the present.

I grabbed the files, sat down on my yoga mat, and spread everything out on the floor. And then I went through them all again. Only this time, instead of trying to figure out where Henrika had gone, I scoured the files for anything connected to my father's doomed Mexico mission.

An hour passed, then two, then three. I didn't find anything I didn't already know, and I didn't see any report I hadn't already looked at a dozen times.

Frustration pounded through my body, igniting a dull ache in the back of my skull. I needed a break, so I left the papers behind, opened the to-go box Pablo had given me earlier, and shoved a big bite of cheesecake into my mouth. Summer-sweet blackberries floating in a rich, creamy vanilla-bean custard with a buttery graham-cracker crust and just a hint of cinnamon. So good.

I poured myself a glass of milk, then took my cheesecake and returned to the nest of papers and pictures on the floor. I stared out over the haphazard mess, and a tired sigh escaped my lips. As an analyst, I usually wanted more information, but right now I was drowning in facts, figures, and files. I knew the solution was here somewhere, but damned if I could see it right now.

I sent you everything you needed to find the answers you're so desperately searching for, Henrika's mocking words filled my mind.

"Sure you did, Henrika." I scoffed and shoved another bite of cheesecake into my mouth.

I sent you everything you needed to find the answers . . .

Sent you everything you needed . . .

Sent you . . .

My fork froze in midair. What had Henrika ever actually *sent* me?

As soon as I asked the question, the answer popped into my mind: the invitation to the Winterfest event at the Glittertop Resort.

Henrika had mailed the invitation, so I supposed that counted as sending me something. Either way, it had been one of the first dominoes to fall in this long, twisted chain of events, so I dug through the files until I found a Section report with a picture of the invitation.

I read through the invitation itself, but it was the same as it had been the day I received it, and no clues were hidden in Henrika's snarky words. According to the Section techs who had analyzed it, the invitation was exactly what it appeared to be—ink on paper, with no microdots, invisible messages, or anything else extra or suspicious. So why would Henrika boast about sending me everything I needed?

I huffed in annoyance and tossed the photo aside. It landed next to the brown envelope the invitation had arrived in. My eyes narrowed, and my head tilted to the side. Wait a second. Technically speaking, the invitation wasn't the *only* thing Henrika had sent me—she'd mailed it in a larger envelope.

Curious, I picked up the manila envelope. The mailroom had already scanned it for toxins and the like before it had reached my desk, so I'd never given it to the Section techs for further analysis. I carefully examined the envelope, but just like the invitation, it was exactly what it appeared to be—a plain brown mailing envelope with no microdots, invisible ink, or other hidden secrets.

Next, I reached out with my synesthesia, but the envelope wasn't hazardous or dangerous, so my magic didn't paint it in any bright warning colors. The envelope wasn't nearly as nice and fancy as the invitation was, and other than my name and the Section 47 address, the only other thing on it was the return address—

My eyes widened, and my gaze snapped over to the top left corner. *Seashell Imports* was printed on the envelope, along with a logo of an open clamshell with a pearl inside. A strange sense of déjà vu washed over me, and I remembered where else I'd seen the familiar symbol: drawn on the back of the photo of Henrika and her sick cousin Meg that had been in the penthouse library.

Henrika never did anything without a touch of treachery, and she hadn't put the name and logo on the envelope by accident. It had to be a clue, although to whom or what, I couldn't say—yet.

Excitement coursed through me. Desmond might like battling bad guys and stepping into the unknown, but deciphering clues and uncovering secrets was what I loved about being a spy.

I set the envelope aside, then dragged my laptop closer and typed *Seashell Imports* into the main Section database. To my surprise, I got a hit right away. It was a shell company, no pun intended, that had been created roughly seventeen years ago—two years *before* the Mexico mission. I frowned at the odd timing, but I kept digging.

Seashell Imports was the first of many such companies, all strung together like a daisy chain and all with offshore accounts, CEOs who didn't exist, and everything else you would need to hide money, including where it came from, whom you were sending it to, and what they were doing with it.

Eventually, one of the outlying companies led back to Seashell Imports, completing the circle of corruption. A frustrated growl rumbled in my throat. *Someone* had set up this elaborate paper trail, but who? Why? And why would Henrika point me in this direction? She wanted me to find something, although I still didn't know what it was.

I thought your mysterious benefactor took care of all your problems. Niles Perran's snide voice sounded in my mind. *You took full advantage of your big break.*

My eyes narrowed. The biomagical chemist had made those snide remarks when we were in Henrika's library, and Niles and Henrika's rivalry stretched back to graduate school.

Maybe I was looking at the wrong thing. Or, rather, at the wrong *time*.

From my months of research, I knew all the universities Henrika had attended, and I went to one website after another, clicking through their news stories, pictures, and archives.

Thirty minutes later, I found what I was looking for. It wasn't much, just a short article about grad students accepting medical research grants. Henrika's name wasn't mentioned in the news story, but Seashell Imports was among the companies that had doled out the money.

I *was going to be the one to do it—to finally cure cancer, leukemia, dementia, and every other horrible disease that robs people of their loved ones.* Henrika's voice whispered through my mind. She'd been telling the truth about her intentions being good, at least when she'd started out.

I skimmed the article, but it was little more than a press release. The truly interesting—and damning—thing was the accompanying photo. The image was a bit grainy, but it was easy to recognize Henrika smiling wide and holding up an oversize check, proudly showing off her grant money, along with her mysterious benefactor.

General Jethro Percy.

The General was clutching the other end of the check and scowling at the camera as if he could melt the lens with the sheer force of his icy gaze. Below the photo, a caption read: *Scientist receives grant money from Seashell Imports for cancer research project.*

For several seconds, I just sat there in shock, staring at the screen with wide eyes and a gaping mouth. I did one double take, then two, then three, but the image never changed or wavered. I couldn't believe this was right out in the open on the Internet for anyone to find. The story and photo weren't even protected by a paywall.

My shock wore off, and my mind started whirring again. Armed with this new information, I went back to Seashell Imports and its daisy chain of other shell companies. It took me another thirty minutes, but I finally found the magic number I was looking for: three million dollars.

The same amount as the ransom demand for my father all those years ago. That money had never been recovered, and now I knew why. It had been deposited into one of Seashell

Imports' many accounts and then transferred into an account that belonged to Henrika.

General Percy had used my father's ransom money to pay off Henrika Hyde.

As soon as I found the payment, more puzzle pieces clicked into place in my mind. I still didn't know exactly who had done what and when, but I had a pretty good idea how things had played out in Mexico—and how they were still playing out to this day.

I sat on my yoga mat for a long time, stunned, simply stunned, by what I'd discovered. In some ways, I couldn't quite believe it was real, but in other ways, it made perfect sense.

General Percy had ordered Desmond to eliminate Henrika because she was a threat, but not to Section 47, not really. No, Henrika was a threat to the General himself. Because if their past relationship ever came to light, it could spell the end of Percy's career.

This information could change *everything* at Section 47.

I never had any intention of killing Charlotte. Ms. Locke still has her part to play in this little drama. Henrika had said that in the clearing when she'd kidnapped Desmond, and now I knew exactly what she meant.

Henrika had hired Bryce because she knew the former cleaner would get under Desmond's skin. She'd also used Bryce to steal the Section undercover agent list to lure Desmond and me to the resort, but she'd never wanted either one of us dead. Henrika had wanted to capture Desmond and experiment on him in hopes of improving her Redburn formula, but she'd had something much more clever and subtle in mind for me.

Henrika wanted to use me to destroy Jethro Percy.

She'd put the Seashell Imports name and logo on the envelope because she wanted me to investigate the company and discover who had set it up and why. When we'd met in her penthouse library after Casino Night, Henrika had dropped all those tantalizing little hints about the Mexico mission to keep me engaged and on the hook. Then, last night, she'd visited the diner to remind me that I hadn't picked up on all the clues she'd dealt out like cards in a poker game.

Henrika could have leaked the info and tried to take down General Percy herself, but no one would have believed someone on Section 47's most-wanted list. No, the info had to come from someone else, someone who could follow elaborate electronic and paper trails, someone who could put all the puzzle pieces together, and maybe, most important of all, someone who wouldn't back down from Jethro Percy no matter what.

Me, Charlotte Locke, analyst extraordinaire.

A bitter laugh burst out of my lips. I'd known Henrika was smart, but the way she'd set all this up was nothing short of *spectacular*.

My mind whirred again as I considered the biggest question of all: What was I going to do with the information?

I scooped my phone up off the floor. First things first. I had to tell Desmond what I'd found . . . or did I?

My finger hovered over the call button, then wilted down to my side. Ever since the Winterfest mission, Desmond and his father had been getting along better. Oh, they weren't best friends by any stretch of the imagination, but Desmond didn't tense every time the General stepped into a room, and Percy didn't always take a superior *I-know-what's-best-for-you* tone with his son. The General had even been, well, not polite, but less hostile to me.

I didn't want to ruin Desmond's thawing relationship with his father. And more selfishly, I didn't want to drive a wedge between Desmond and myself by blowing the whistle about General Percy's past sins.

Could I do this? Could I really keep quiet about Percy's old partnership with Henrika? Could I really forget I'd finally figured out where the ransom money had gone? Money that had taken years for Grandma Jane and me to pay back to Gabriel and his father?

Those questions and a dozen others swirled through my mind. I reached out with my magic, trying to find a solution, the way I had so many times before, but my synesthesia was deathly quiet. This was one danger, one hazard, one minefield I would have to navigate on my own.

My gaze drifted over to the blue recliner by the windows. The chair had been an early Christmas present to myself as I slowly refurnished the apartment, although I'd been so busy working that I hadn't sat in it more than a dozen times.

But in my mind's eye, it was Grandma Jane's favorite recliner, and she was firmly ensconced in the seat, while I perched on the left arm. Grandma Jane was clutching a crystal mockingbird figurine and slowly rocking the two of us back and forth as we waited for news about my father and whether he was coming home from Mexico—or not.

For a moment, I could hear the soft, steady *creak-creak-creak* of the recliner, see the crystal glimmering in my grand-mother's wrinkled hands, even smell the faintest whiff of her rose perfume.

I blinked. The image, the memory, faded away, but my heart wrenched in my chest.

I knew what I had to do, no matter what it might cost me.

I drew in a deep breath, then let it out and set my phone aside. And then I leaned forward and started typing again, working on a brand-new report about Henrika Hyde—and General Jethro Percy.

FORTY-TWO

CHARLOTTE

A t eight o'clock the next morning, I walked into Section 47 headquarters just as I had so many times before.

I stopped in the lobby and turned around in a slow circle, looking at the shops and restaurants in the pedestrian mall, the Section 47 cafeteria off to the side, and everything in between. This might be the last time I was ever in this building, and I wanted to remember it.

Evelyn was sitting at her desk, although she got to her feet and scooped up some folders at my approach.

"Ready for the meeting?" I asked.

She nodded. "Yep. Care to tell me what it's about since you're the one who requested it?"

"You'll find out along with everyone else."

Evelyn's dark eyebrows lifted, but she didn't question me as we went through the turnstile and stepped into the elevator. I got off on level three, while Evelyn headed down to level five. I went to my cubicle, but it looked the same as always—a sterile functional space with only one personal touch.

I didn't know if I would be coming back here after the

meeting, so I plucked the crystal mockingbird figurine off my desk and slipped it into my pocket. Then I grabbed all the files and folders I needed, along with a flash drive, and went down to the fifth level.

A few cleaners and liaisons were typing on their laptops or murmuring into their phones. I went past them and stopped at Joan's desk.

"Where's Desmond?" I asked, eyeing his empty chair.

She shrugged. "I think he went up to level four looking for General Percy."

My stomach clenched. Even though I'd prepared myself for this moment, it was going to be even more difficult than I'd imagined.

Joan's forehead crinkled. "Are you okay? You look sick to your stomach."

I opened my mouth to spout some lie—

"Charlotte." Desmond's low voice slid against my skin like a delicate caress.

He stepped up beside me. He was dressed in a powder-blue suit jacket, tie, and shirt, and his silver watch gleamed in his vest pocket like usual. My heart clenched, right along with my stomach, but I forced myself to smile.

Desmond stared at me, his face calm. I couldn't tell what he was thinking, and I didn't know if that was good or bad. He leaned down and kissed me on the cheek, and I closed my eyes, savoring the moment. I was about to destroy my whole world—and his too.

"I'm so glad you're here," Desmond murmured.

I nodded, my throat too tight to croak out a response

Joan glanced back and forth between the two of us, her eyes narrowing with suspicion. "I'll see you two in the briefing."

The liaison scooped up some folders from her desk and headed into the conference room.

Desmond gestured with his hand. "After you, Numbers."

I ground my teeth to hold on to my smile. "Of course, Dundee."

I clutched my files and folders a little tighter to my chest and went to the conference room. Desmond fell in step beside me.

In addition to Joan and Evelyn, Diego and Gia were already inside. I passed Diego the flash drive with all the evidence I'd collected over the last several hours, and the tech guru slid it into his laptop and flashed me a thumbs-up, ready to rock 'n' roll. He also slid a black clicker across the table. I clutched the small piece of plastic like it was a life jacket that would keep me from drowning in the storm of secrets I was about to unleash.

I dropped into my chair like a stone, reminding myself that I was doing the right thing. That this was the *only* thing I could do if I wanted to clear my father's name and root out the last of Henrika Hyde's influence at Section 47.

More footsteps sounded, and General Percy strode into the room. The door shut behind him, and the familiar buzz of the soundproofing rang out. His two bodyguards took up positions outside.

General Percy sat down in his usual seat at the head of the table. "What's this update about Henrika that was so important it couldn't wait until the regular afternoon briefing?"

I drew in a breath and slowly got to my feet. For a moment, I wavered, but I couldn't ignore what I had learned and the ramifications it had for everyone in this room.

"I called the meeting. Henrika Hyde came to see me last night."

Evelyn, Gia, Diego, and Joan gasped in surprise. Desmond showed no reaction, but Percy's eyes narrowed.

"Henrika came to *see* you? When? Where?" the General demanded.

I hit the clicker. Footage of the interior of the Moondust Diner appeared on the film screen along the wall. When I'd bought the place a few months ago, one of the first things I'd done was install a state-of-the-art security system that covered every inch of the diner, as well as the surrounding parking lot and streets.

I hit the clicker again, and the footage began to play. The others watched my talk with Henrika, including her asking me to come work for her.

The video ended, and General Percy fixed his angry gaze on me. "Why didn't you report this immediately, Ms. Locke? If you had alerted us the moment Henrika arrived, we might have been able to capture her."

"And she would have killed everyone in the diner. I wasn't about to risk the lives of innocent people."

The General grunted, but for once, he didn't argue.

"Besides, I wanted to see if I could figure out what Henrika was talking about."

Joan frowned. "What do you mean?"

"A few months ago, when I first met Henrika at the Halstead Hotel, she claimed to have information about my father's death. Ever since then, I've been digging into the Mexico mission, although I probably never would have figured out what happened if not for Henrika's little clue last night."

"What clue?" Gia asked in a sharp voice.

"Seashell Imports."

I hit another button, and the clamshell logo from the mailing envelope appeared on the screen. Everyone stared at the logo, but I kept my gaze on General Percy. He blinked once, and his mouth puckered slightly, but those were his only visible reactions. If I hadn't known better, I would have chalked up the micro-expressions to his usual dislike of and perpetual annoyance with me.

But I did know better—about a lot of things.

"What's so special about Seashell Imports?" Diego asked in a confused voice.

"It's a shell company," I replied. "Used to funnel money to Henrika, starting about seventeen years ago, two years *before* the Mexico mission."

I hit some more buttons on the clicker, and financial documents filled the screen. "I kept thinking about something Niles Perran said at the Glittertop Resort. He claimed the reason Henrika was so much more successful than him was because a wealthy benefactor had given her a boost way back in grad school when she was first trying to get her business off the ground. And you know what? Niles was right."

I faced the others. "Last night, I finally figured out who Henrika's mysterious benefactor was: Jethro Percy."

Evelyn, Gia, Diego, and Joan all sucked in startled breaths. Desmond blinked a few times and looked at his father. A muscle twitched in the General's jaw, but other than that, he remained relaxed in his chair.

"I'm afraid you're mistaken, Ms. Locke," Percy replied in a cool voice. "My only interactions with Henrika have been to try to bring her to justice for her many crimes against Section 47."

"Bullshit," I countered. "You funded Henrika's research for *years*. I followed the money trail, and it leads straight back to you, General."

Percy waved his hand. "Documents can easily be faked. Maybe this is all just another scheme on Henrika's part. She plants some false documents in your path to try to incriminate me because she knows the noose is tightening around her neck and that Section will apprehend her soon."

I shook my head. "You don't want to apprehend her. You want to *kill* her so she can't ever point a finger back at you."

The General harrumphed and looked at Gia. "Clearly, Ms. Locke has issues. I suggest you put an end to this charade before she says something she can't walk back."

Gia crossed her arms over her chest. "Actually, I find Ms.

Locke's presentation to be extremely interesting. Please continue, Charlotte."

I let out a quiet exhale. Gia was going to back my play, which was half the battle. The other half would be Desmond's reaction. His face was blank, but he kept glancing back and forth between me and his father.

I hit another button, and a photo appeared on the screen: Henrika and the General hanging on to opposite ends of that oversize grant-money check.

General Percy blinked and blinked, and his face actually paled, as if he was seeing a ghost. "Where did you get that?"

"It ran in the university's student newspaper. You hid your tracks well, but no one can scrub away everything, especially once it hits the Internet."

The corner of the General's mouth twitched, as though he was agreeing with me, despite himself.

I gestured at the photo. "What was Henrika working on that first caught your attention? She started out doing cancer research, but I'm guessing somewhere along the way, Henrika discovered how to kill paramortals instead. And despite your best intentions, you just couldn't resist having such a powerful weapon for yourself. Right, General?"

"You don't know what you're talking about," Percy snapped.

"*Lie*," I hissed right back at him.

General Percy flinched at the venom in my voice.

"I don't have all the details, and most of them don't really matter. Here's what I think happened. You asked Henrika to veer away from her original cancer research and start building weapons for Section 47, to start building weapons for *you*. I have records of the money you funneled to her through your fake companies, including Seashell Imports."

"So I invested in some of Henrika's early research." Percy shrugged. "So what? Section 47 does things like that all the time. We're always trying to stay one step ahead of our enemies."

Anger flooded my chest at how he was trying to spin the story, but I tamped down my temper. "That's true. But somewhere along the way, you and Henrika had a falling-out. Maybe she wanted more money. Maybe she threatened to expose your arrangement. Or maybe she just wanted to be out from underneath your thumb. I don't know, and I don't really care. But eventually, you decided to get rid of her."

I drew in a breath and let it out. "That's when you ordered my father to go to Mexico, infiltrate Feliciano Salvador's compound, and kill Henrika. *She* was your true target, not Salvador."

Silence dropped over the conference room. Diego and Joan looked just as stunned as I had been when I finally put all the pieces together last night. Gia was staring at Percy like she'd never seen him before, while Evelyn tapped a finger on the table, deep in thought. Desmond kept looking back and forth between me and his father, and I still couldn't tell what he was thinking or feeling.

General Percy pushed his chair back from the table, stood up, and yanked at his jacket. "I would be very careful what you say next, Ms. Locke. So far, I've endured your conspiracy theories, but I'm growing tired of your baseless accusations."

He raised his bushy eyebrows in a clear challenge. Percy was giving me a final chance to back down, and we all knew it. I stared at the General a moment longer, then hit the clicker again. The sound was as loud as a gunshot in the tense silence.

A photo of my father filled the screen. Jack Locke was sprawled across the ground, his right arm underneath his head and his legs drawn up to his chest, almost as if he was sleeping in a fetal position. But the bullet hole in his stomach and the blood that had pooled under his body ruined the peaceful illusion. I had seen the photo countless times before, but the sight of it always punched the air out of my lungs.

"My father was taken hostage, and eventually, he was shot

in the stomach. He bled out before the Section medics could reach him," I said in a cold, clipped voice. "I'll probably never know who fired the fatal bullet. If it was Feliciano or one of his guards or Henrika or even a Section cleaner mistaking my father for an enemy. But I *do* know the three million dollars my grandmother paid in ransom money was never recovered."

I hit the clicker again, and another document appeared on the screen. The General grimaced.

"Six weeks after the Mexico mission, Seashell Imports wired three million dollars to one of Henrika's companies," I said, anger creeping into my voice. "Somehow you got your hands on the ransom money that was supposed to save my father's life and gave it to Henrika, probably to buy her silence about your plot to use Section agents to murder her."

My accusation hung in the air like a dark storm cloud about to shoot lightning at all of us.

"I didn't kill Jack Locke," General Percy snapped, his voice just as cold, harsh, and tight with anger as mine.

Truth, my inner voice whispered, although it didn't lessen my anger.

"You might not have killed my father, but you sure didn't help him either," I snarled. "Did my father figure out you were funding Henrika's research? And that you couldn't control her anymore? Is that why he didn't kill her? Or did my father refuse because he knew it was a shitty order from a man desperate to cover up his own crimes?"

General Percy slammed his hand down onto the table. "That is *enough!*"

Everyone else flinched, but I gave the General a cold look. He didn't scare me. Not anymore. In his own way, General Percy was even worse than Henrika. The weapons maker never pretended to be anything other than what she was, unlike Jethro Percy, who would smile to your face even while he stabbed you in the back.

"It's too late. I've uploaded the information to the Section servers, along with my report. You can't erase it now, and you can't get rid of me the same way you got rid of my father."

General Percy's fingers twitched as though he wanted to throw himself across the conference table and strangle me. "You bloody Lockes. You just can't let anything go, can you? And you're always so superior and self-righteous. Your father killed people for a living, Ms. Locke. Oh, we might pretty it up and call them cleaners at Section 47, but we all know they're really assassins, weapons to eliminate whatever target they are aimed at."

A muscle twitched in Desmond's jaw, and Gia's fingers clenched into fists on the tabletop.

The General straightened up to his full height and peered down his nose at me. "I've had enough of your theories. You're fired, Ms. Locke. Effective immediately."

"Don't bother," I countered. "Because I *quit*. I don't want to be part of an organization that would give you a free pass for turning on your own agents, the people you're supposed to support and protect. You failed my father. How many other people have you failed over the years? How many other people have died to keep your secrets?"

He shook his head, ignoring my accusations. "You're finished, Ms. Locke." General Percy waved his hand. "All I have to do is classify this briefing, and no one in this room will be able to breathe a word of your wild, baseless theories."

Another heavy silence dropped over the room. Then Evelyn slowly pushed her chair back from the table and stood up.

"Charlotte might not be able to do anything about you, Jethro," Evelyn said in a soft, dangerous voice. "But *I* certainly can."

The General blinked, but his surprise and confusion quickly morphed into disgust and annoyance. "So you're the mysterious Maestro. I should have known. You've always been a friend to the Lockes."

"I've always been a friend to loyal agents who serve Section 47 for the *right* reasons," she snapped back at him. "And I've known for a long time you were *not* one of those people."

He glared at her. "We'll see about that. The board of directors will back me on everything I did, then and now."

Evelyn shrugged. "Maybe they will, and maybe they won't. I have friends on the board of directors too, so I guess we'll find out."

General Percy looked from Evelyn to me and back again. Then his gaze flicked over everyone else in the conference room. Diego and Joan still looked stunned, but fury flashed in Gia's dark eyes. The General had gotten her fellow cleaners, her friends, killed, and she was just as pissed about it as I was about my father's death.

General Percy marched over to the door and threw it open. Then he jerked his head at Desmond. "Let's go, son. These people can't hurt me, no matter what they think."

Desmond slowly pushed his chair back from the table, stood up, and buttoned his suit jacket, a move I'd seen him do a hundred times. He dropped his hands to his sides and looked at me. Only a few feet separated us, but it might as well have been an ocean.

"Son?" General Percy said, a note of doubt creeping into his voice.

"You're right," Desmond replied. "We're done here."

He stared at me a moment longer, his face icy and unreadable. Then he spun around on his heel and left the conference room.

FORTY-THREE

DESMOND

My father trailed me through the level-five bullpen and into the elevator. The bodyguards started to follow us, but for once, he waved them off. The two of us rode in silence to the fourth level, then entered his office. The door shut behind me, and the familiar buzz of the soundproofing rang out.

The General marched over to the liquor bottles on a table, poured some whiskey into a crystal tumbler, and threw it back. His fingers curled around the empty glass as though he wanted to smash it against the wall, but he merely dropped it back onto the tray instead, making the other glasses rattle around.

"Fucking Lockes," he muttered. "That Legacy family has *always* been a thorn in my side. Always thinking *they* knew what was best for Section. What was good and just and right. As if there are such things as *good* and *just* and *right*. There's only evil and more evil and less evil."

"Finally, something we can agree on," I drawled.

The General snorted, then poured himself another glass of whiskey. He threw it back just like the first one, then looked at me. "For a moment there, I didn't think you were going to come with me."

"You're my father."

He eyed me. "Is that the only reason?"

I walked over and tapped the photo of my mother on his desk. "I came because of her."

My father stared at the photo. A shadow passed over his face, grief filled his eyes, and the same emotion flickered in his icy aura. For all his many faults, my father had truly loved my mother, and he still felt Iylena's loss as keenly as I did.

The General pulled his gaze away from my mother's photo and set his empty glass down on the desk. "I need to start working my sources and calling in favors to get ahead of this accusation."

"Is it true?" I asked, careful to keep my voice neutral. "Did you really fund Henrika's research? And give her the three-million-dollar ransom payment for Jack Locke to help start her company?"

My father looked at me, and I stared right back at him. After a few seconds of silent contemplation, he leaned down and hit a red button on the desk. A second, softer buzz sounded, and a telltale tingle of electricity swept across my skin.

"What's that?" I asked.

"A small electromagnetic pulse. One that temporarily disrupts cell phones, along with spy cameras and listening devices. Basically, anything electronic that could be used to record this conversation."

"You don't trust me?"

The General peered down his nose at me. "Verify, then trust. Especially since we both know you are emotionally compromised where Charlotte Locke is concerned."

I shrugged. My father could say whatever he wanted about my relationship with Charlotte. I knew the truth of what it was.

The General studied me, his eyes cold and assessing. Then

he jerked his head in agreement. "Yes, I did fund Henrika's research."

"Why?" Once again, I kept my voice neutral.

His gaze dropped to the photo of Iylena. "I did it for your mother," he replied in a soft voice.

Surprise shot through me. I hadn't expected that.

"When your mother first got sick, I reached out to all my contacts to make sure she would have the best treatment possible—the best chance possible to get well." He clasped his hands behind his back, his eyes dark and distant with memories.

"Okay, I can understand that. But how does Henrika fit into the equation?"

The General kept staring off into the distance. "We tried everything, but Iylena just kept getting sicker."

My heart twisted with memories. I remembered my mother's decline all too well. How she had stopped eating. How thin she had become. How her hair had fallen out in clumps. How pale and waxy her skin had become.

"One of my contacts came across an experiment Henrika had done. Something about using a specific formula tailored to an individual's DNA to target and kill cancerous cells and leave healthy ones behind." The General waved his hand. "I didn't understand it back then, and I still don't understand it now. But your mother was slipping away, and I was running out of options."

"So you set up Seashell Imports and gave Henrika a grant. I can understand that too. How did it all go so wrong?"

The General started pacing back and forth behind his desk. "At first, Henrika's research was extremely promising. But as time went on, it became less and less so. At least when it came to healing people. But eventually, I realized Henrika's formula could have other, more practical applications."

I did try, you know . . . to be good. To make some great

medical breakthrough that would help people. I tried—for years, I tried.

I hadn't known what Henrika had meant when she'd said that in the lab, but I did now. "Weapons. You saw the potential to turn Henrika's research into weapons that could kill paramortals."

The General shrugged. "Of course I did. Section 47 is always looking for advantages over our enemies. Henrika had already taken my money, so she was already on my payroll. Besides, if I hadn't approached her, someone else would have."

As much as I hated to admit it, he was right. Eventually, someone else would have found out about Henrika's research, seen its deadly potential, and sunk their hooks into her. The General had just beaten everyone to the punch.

"So what went wrong?"

My father's eyes narrowed in suspicion. "This is starting to sound like an interrogation."

I barked out a bitter laugh. "What? Do you think I'm wearing a wire?"

I yanked my shirt up so he could see my bare stomach and chest. I also pulled my phone out of my pocket and tossed it onto his desk, right next to the photo of my mother. A message on the screen warned that the device had malfunctioned and couldn't be used.

"Satisfied?" I demanded.

Some of the suspicion leaked out of my father's face, and he gestured for me to take a seat in front of the desk. This time, he poured us both a glass of whiskey, then dropped into his own chair. The General sipped his drink, but I didn't touch mine.

"Henrika produced several weapons for me. Pink sulfur smoke bombs, some poisons, a few truth serums." Anger crept into his face. "But she got greedy. Henrika wanted more money, more control over what she developed and when and how it was deployed. She actually had a sliver of a conscience, if you can believe that."

He shook his head, as though being worried about how her weapons were being used was a great failing on Henrika's part.

"She also wanted to branch out into other areas, like cosmetics and skin care, which would have invited much more attention and unwanted scrutiny. When I said no, she threatened to expose our arrangement."

"So you sent Jack Locke to Mexico to kill her."

The General scoffed. "Of course not. Jack Locke *never* would have taken such an assignment."

My heart lifted with a bit of unexpected hope. "So Charlotte is wrong, and you didn't try to kill Henrika."

My father barked out a laugh. "Don't be a fool. Of course I tried to kill her. I just sent someone else to do the job. Thomas, another cleaner on the Mexico mission. Thomas had orders to kill Henrika, while Jack Locke was supposed to eliminate Feliciano Salvador."

His mouth twisted. "But something went wrong. If I had to guess, I would say that Locke's conscience got the better of him the way it always did."

His nostrils flared, and his icy aura pulsed with anger and disgust. That tiny bit of hope crumbled to dust in my chest.

I'd been on similar missions where different cleaners had different targets and objectives, so I could guess what had happened. Jack Locke had been ready to do his job and eliminate Feliciano Salvador, but he had balked when the other cleaner had wanted to kill Henrika as well.

I would have balked at that too. I *had* balked at that, when Bryce Finkley had killed an innocent hostage to complete our mission.

"Whatever went wrong, Thomas was killed, along with all the other cleaners, except for Jack Locke. That stubborn bastard couldn't even do me the courtesy of dying."

My father glared into his whiskey glass for a moment before looking at me again. "Eventually, Section received a ransom demand for Locke. His mother, Jane, was still working here. Somehow she found out about the ransom demand, went behind my back, got the money, and sent it to Mexico."

Jane Locke, Charlotte's grandmother, had borrowed the money from Leon Chase, Gabriel's father and another Section cleaner. Leon had been the one to actually deliver the ransom, although the General didn't seem to know that, and I certainly wasn't going to tell him.

"Then what happened?" I asked.

My father shrugged again. "I sent another team of cleaners to eliminate Salvador once and for all, and I went with them to personally oversee the mission."

"And make sure Henrika was killed too."

My father arched an eyebrow at my snide tone, but I wasn't about to pull any punches now.

He harrumphed and continued his story. "Someone must have tipped off Salvador, because he knew we were coming. There was a massive firefight at his villa. When the dust settled, Henrika and Salvador were gone, and Jack Locke was dead. A few weeks later, another team of cleaners tracked down and eliminated Salvador, but I never did figure out who shot Locke."

I snorted in disbelief.

"It's the truth," the General snapped. "No matter what Charlotte thinks, I didn't kill her father. Someone else did. Probably Henrika, if I had to guess."

"And the ransom money?" I asked. "How did you wind up with it?"

"So many people were dead and injured. It was chaos. I picked up the briefcase with the ransom money and set it aside with the other evidence from the mission to turn in when I got back to headquarters." He sighed. "But then I got a message from Henrika. She wanted the money in exchange for her silence."

"So you gave it to her." Once again, I couldn't keep the snide note out of my voice. "Charlotte was right. You *did* pay off Henrika to keep quiet."

"It was mutually assured destruction," my father replied in a defensive tone. "Henrika had information that could derail my career at Section, but I could keep sending cleaners to kill her. So we called it a draw and went our separate ways."

"And you let Hyde Engineering grow and grow and sat by and watched while Henrika became even more dangerous and powerful."

The General waved his hand, dismissing my accusations yet again. "Henrika might be rich and powerful, but in the end, she's just another weapons maker. She didn't even create anything truly remarkable or revolutionary, except for Redburn." His eyes glittered with a cold light. "And that formula should have been mine all along."

I'm not leaving anything behind for Jethro Percy to get his hands on. That arrogant bastard has already stolen enough of my work. Once again, I heard Henrika's voice in my mind, and a sick, sinking sensation filled my stomach.

"Redburn is based on Henrika's original research," I said in a low, strained voice. "The cancer research she was working on when you first approached her. The formula you were hoping to use to save Mom."

The bright flare of bombs exploded in my eyes, and red-hot fire blasted over my body. My shoulders tensed, and my hands clenched into fists at my sides.

"Desmond? Are you okay?"

The General's voice broke through my memories. My vision cleared, although that phantom fire kept scorching my skin, and my own screams kept ringing in my ears, along with Graham's hoarse cries.

"Did you know Henrika was working with Adrian Anatoly?" I asked. "Before you sent me to kill Anatoly on the Blacksea mission?"

My father shook his head, and his face twisted with anger and a surprising amount of regret. "No, son. I had no idea Henrika was working with Anatoly, but she must have found out you'd been assigned to eliminate him."

"Trevor Donnelly told her," I muttered. "Graham mentioned the Blacksea mission to Trevor a few days before we left for Australia."

My father nodded. "That's what my sources have concluded too."

"So I went on the Blacksea mission, and Henrika finally saw a chance to get revenge on you."

Yet again, my father's pale aura pulsed with anger and disgust. "The bitch can certainly hold a grudge, I'll give her that."

"And Redburn?" I asked, my voice even lower and more strained than before. "Did you know Henrika was going to use Graham and me as her guinea pigs to test the explosive?"

Genuine surprise flickered across my father's face. "No! Of course not! I *never* would have sent you on the Blacksea mission if I had known what Henrika had planned. I know we haven't had the closest or easiest relationship, especially since your mother died, but I love you, Desmond."

My chest squeezed tight. I couldn't speak through the hard knot of emotion in my throat, so I nodded instead.

A relieved look flashed across my father's face, although it quickly vanished. He sank deeper into his chair and steepled his fingers together, once again morphing into the General I knew all too well. "Don't worry about what happened in the conference room. Despite Charlotte's accusations, this scandal will blow over soon."

"And Henrika?"

"I already have my best people searching for her. As soon as they find Henrika, they will eliminate her once and for all. I promise you that, son."

I got to my feet and buttoned my suit jacket. "You're not going to get Henrika. I am."

My father also got to his feet, and he grinned at me. "That's my boy."

I gave him a thin smile in return, then spun around on my heel, went over to the door, and opened it. "I think I got everything we need. Come on in."

I moved to the side, and Charlotte strode into the office. Evelyn was behind her with Gia. Joan and Diego were standing outside with several members of the strike team, who had already handcuffed the General's two bodyguards.

My father glanced back and forth between me and Charlotte. "What is this?"

"You're under arrest, Jethro," Evelyn said in a cold voice. "For working with Section enemies."

The General scoffed. "You have no real proof of that. All you have is an old photo and a few documents. Are you really going to believe a lowly analyst over me? A Locke? Someone with a tarnished family legacy inside Section?"

"Actually, they have all the proof they need," I cut in. "Thanks to your confession."

My father's startled gaze zipped over to me, and his eyes narrowed. "What did you do, Desmond?"

I went over to his desk and picked up the photo of my mother. I stared at her smiling face a moment, then opened the back of the silver frame, plucked out the tiny analog tape recorder hidden inside, and showed it to him.

My father's eyes widened. For a split second, he looked confused and uncertain, and his icy aura flickered with the tiniest bit of hurt. Then an angry flush swept up his neck. "Was that little tape recorder *her* idea?"

"No," I replied in a cold voice. "It was *mine*. You've always been paranoid about your security, so I knew I couldn't get any electronic surveillance in your office. Then I remembered seeing this recorder when we were in the armory prepping for the Winterfest mission, so I decided to go old school with my spy tech. Even you don't bother searching for analog devices anymore. Before I went to the conference room for Charlotte's briefing, I snuck in here and swapped out your picture frame for this one, which also serves as a makeshift Faraday cage that blocks electromagnetic pulses. Then, when we came into your office a few minutes ago, I tapped the top of the frame to activate the recorder hidden inside."

More fury and disgust filled the General's face. "You betrayed me for *her*? A *Locke*? Just because you're fucking her?"

I reached out, snatched my father's tie, and yanked him toward me. The General let out a startled grunt, and he had to brace his hands on the desk to keep from toppling over it.

"If you insult Charlotte again, I will stop your bloody heart," I growled in a low voice only he could hear. "And we both know I can do it."

I released his tie and shoved him away. My father staggered back, although he quickly regained his footing. Everyone else froze, except for Charlotte, who stepped up beside me. She didn't touch me, but just having her here steadied my nerves.

"And I didn't betray you for Charlotte. I did it for Graham," I growled again. "He was my best friend, and he died because of your bloody schemes. Me? I'm used to getting screwed over because of your crimes and manipulations, but Graham suffered unimaginable pain and agony just because Henrika wanted to get revenge on you through me. Graham didn't deserve that horrific fate, and neither did the other agents who died on the Blacksea mission. Neither did Jack Locke and the cleaners you sent to Mexico just so you could eliminate a personal threat."

I shook my head. "Mom would be so bloody ashamed of you."

My father jerked back as though I had punched him in the throat. His gaze flicked to my mother's photo, and longing creased his face. My own chest ached in response, but it was too late for him.

My father squared his shoulders and raised his eyes to mine, his face as cold as ice again. "You're going to regret this, son. You're too much like your mother, too tenderhearted, not to."

"You might be right about that, but you've been wrong about everything else." I jerked my head at the strike team members. "Take him away."

Two men stepped forward, but my father ignored them, stormed around his desk, and stopped in front of Evelyn.

"You might be Maestro, but we both know I have too many friends inside Section for you to hold me for long," he said.

A thin smile split her lips. "I'm looking forward to proving you wrong, Jethro."

Evelyn also jerked her head at the strike team members. "Put the General in an interrogation cell until I decide what to do with him."

The two men approached the General, but he spun toward Charlotte, fury shimmering in his icy eyes. "You're just like your father."

"I'll take that as a compliment," Charlotte replied.

"You have no idea the things Jack Locke did," the General snarled. "The people he killed. The deals he made. The devil's bargains he struck. Don't pretend he's some great *hero*."

Charlotte stepped forward, her face inches away from the General's, her eyes and aura even colder than his. "I know *exactly* what kind of man my father was. Jack Locke devoted his life to Section 47, while you lied to him and betrayed him not for any greater good but just because you wanted to cover your own ass. My father might not be a hero, but neither are you, General Percy. And now everyone at Section 47 will know it."

Again, my father recoiled as though someone had struck him, but again, he recovered quickly. "You're going to regret this, Ms. Locke. Even more than my son will. I'll make sure of that."

Anger spiked through me at his threat, but Charlotte stepped even closer to the General, still as cold as ice. "The only thing I regret is that Desmond was saddled with *you*. He deserves far better than the likes of you for a father."

My father glared at Charlotte a moment longer, and then the strike team members stepped in between them and led him away.

I followed the three men out of the office and to the elevators. My father got inside and turned around. His face was calm, but his eyes glittered with anger, as did his aura. His was the look of a man who was already planning to take his vengeance on those he thought had wronged him, including me.

Especially me.

The door slid shut, cutting off my view of the General, but a hard truth sliced through my gut.

I had just made an enemy out of my own father.

FORTY-FOUR

CHARLOTTE

We spent the rest of the day dealing with the fallout of General Percy's arrest. I showed Evelyn and Gia all the evidence I had collected connecting Percy to Henrika, while Desmond chimed in with his own memories of his father's actions during his mother's illness, along with the Mexico mission.

News of Percy's arrest quickly spread through headquarters, and everyone eyed Desmond and me with a combination of fear and wariness. Even at Section 47, spying and reporting on your own father was frowned upon, despite all the agents who had died because of the General's actions.

Jethro Percy might be in an interrogation cell, but his earlier words haunted me. He had a lot of friends in high places, and I doubted he would face any prolonged, severe punishment for his crimes.

It wasn't right, and it certainly wasn't perfect, but at least I'd gotten some small measure of justice for my father and cleared his name inside Section 47. No matter what happened with the General, I would be happy with that legacy, one that was free of the treachery that permeated Percy's actions.

Eventually, the meetings ended. Just before midnight, Desmond and I left Section headquarters and went to my apartment. We shrugged out of our coats and put our things down.

Desmond wandered over to the windows and stared out into the dark. I followed him. The calendar had flipped over to February, but this night was the coldest one yet, and only a few hard bits of snow drifted down from the sky.

As much as I wanted to hold him, comfort him, I kept my hands to myself. Desmond was the one who was hurting right now, not me, and I wanted to give him the time and space to deal with all the ugly events that had happened.

Desmond barked out a harsh laugh, breaking the silence. "I still can't believe you were right. Even though I've had hours for it to sink in, I still feel like I'm watching a horror movie, and this is all happening to someone else."

"I'm sorry it had to come to this," I replied in a soft voice.

"I know. I'm sorry too. I *hate* the things my father has done, to you and your father, to me and Graham, and to everyone else at Section."

"But?"

Desmond sighed. "But I still care about him. A small part of me always will."

I nodded, and we both stared out the window again, watching those hard bits of snow flutter down from the sky.

Desmond turned to me. "I'm surprised you came to me. That you told me your plan to take down my father and asked me to be a part of it."

After I'd written my report on General Percy's connection to Henrika, I'd packed up my laptop and folders and gone to Desmond's apartment. I'd shown him the evidence and laid out my theories.

Unlike General Percy, Desmond hadn't done anything wrong, and he didn't deserve to be blindsided. Even more than that, he was my partner, both inside and outside Section, and I didn't want to keep this secret from him. I *couldn't* keep it from him. Not if I wanted what we had to keep growing.

A touch of treachery had destroyed my father and General Percy, and I didn't want the same thing to happen to us.

"I'm surprised you agreed to help me. Whatever he's done, the General is still your father. I would have understood if you hadn't wanted any part in my plan."

Desmond nodded, his gaze searching mine. "So where do we go from here?"

That was the question I'd been asking myself all day, and I'd been bracing myself for this moment ever since I'd revealed the General's crimes. "I understand if you need some time."

Desmond's eyebrows drew together in a quizzical look. "Time?"

"Time away from Section." I swallowed, and my voice dropped to a ragged whisper. "Time away from *me*."

Desmond stared at me, his face once again blank and unreadable. I bit my lip, bracing myself for the worst.

My father had always chosen something else over me, whether it was a Section mission or hanging out with his cleaner friends or weekend training. I'd never felt like I was *enough* for the great Jack Locke, no matter how smart I was or how many good grades I got or how many logic puzzles I solved.

Desmond had never made me feel like I was inadequate or lacking or simply not important. Not for a single second. But I couldn't help wondering if General Percy was right. If Desmond would someday regret participating in my scheme to expose his father's crimes. If the storm of secrets that I'd unleashed would eventually doom us the way it had doomed our fathers.

A shadow passed over Desmond's face. I tensed. This was it. This was the moment he was going to agree and say he did need some time away from Section and especially from me.

This was the moment Desmond was going to break my heart.

Desmond stepped even closer, and I had to tip my head back to stare up into his eyes. "I don't have your synesthesia, but if there is one thing I know for certain, one absolute *truth*, it's that I will *never* need time away from you, Charlotte."

My heart soared, but I forced myself to remain calm. "Are you sure? After everything that's happened, no one would blame you for stepping away. *I* wouldn't blame you. I just destroyed your father's life, his career, his legacy inside Section 47."

Desmond stepped closer still, and his hands came up to cup my cheeks. "I don't care about the General's legacy inside Section. I don't even care about my own. All I care about is building a legacy with *you*." He hesitated. "If that's what you want too. I would understand if you needed some time as well. Especially since your father is dead because of mine."

I placed my hands over his and squeezed his fingers. "Building a legacy with you is *exactly* what I want."

We looked at each other a moment longer, then Desmond bent his head and kissed me. It was a soft kiss, a gentle brush of his lips against mine, but it made me tremble all the same. I dug my hands into the front of his vest as though the fabric was an anchor mooring him to my side and gave myself fully over to this moment. Here, right now, *this* was about the way we made each other feel, instead of all the awful things our fathers had done.

Maybe it was everything we'd been through over the past few days, all the death and danger and deception, but the kiss went from sweet and gentle to hard and demanding in an instant. Each press of his lips and stroke of his tongue against mine lit more and more fireworks of desire that exploded throughout my body

I pushed on Desmond's shoulders, walking him backward

away from the windows. He kissed me again, his tongue plunging into my mouth, then bent down and scooped me up. I wrapped my arms around his neck and locked my legs around his waist. The heat of his body blasted over me like a furnace, and I greedily squirmed closer to his warmth. His erection settled into the perfect spot between my thighs, and I hummed in appreciation and rocked forward.

Desmond groaned against my mouth. "You keep that up, and we're not even going to make it to the bedroom."

I rocked forward again and nuzzled my nose against the golden stubble along his jaw. I drank in his scent, a clean yet heady mix of pine and soap. "I guess you'd better hurry, then."

Desmond laughed, whirled around, and carried me into my bedroom. Like the rest of the apartment, it was sparsely furnished, with just a bed, but that was all we needed.

Desmond put my back against the wall. I slid my legs down his body and landed on my feet. He braced his hands on the wall beside me, then bent down and pressed a series of hot, hungry kisses against the sensitive skin of my neck.

I reached down, fumbling with his belt, then his zipper. As soon as I got his pants open, I plunged my hand down and wrapped my fingers around his hot, hard length.

Desmond jerked back. His gaze locked with mine, and his eyes burned a brilliant silver-blue. The overhead lights flickered in time to the quick, firm glide of my fingers as I stroked him.

"You . . . *ahhh* . . . Charlotte . . ." Desmond buried his face against my neck, his tongue lapping at the rapid pulse hammering in my throat.

He dropped his hands from the wall and went to work on my clothes, unzipping my pants and sliding his fingers down into my underwear. I gasped and spread my legs a little wider, giving him better access. Desmond caressed me with quick, firm motions, just as I had done to him.

My legs trembled again, and wave after wave of desire crashed through my body, each one stronger and faster, like a rip current dragging me out into an endless ocean of pleasure.

I surged forward and kissed him again, harder than before. We were both in a frenzy now, and we spun away from the wall, our lips, tongues, and hands all over each other, kissing, licking, and stripping off clothes. Desmond stopped long enough to grab a condom from his wallet and cover himself with it. I took birth-control pills, but we always used extra protection.

I pushed on his shoulders, and he sat down on the edge of the bed. His arm snaked around my waist. I straddled him, and he fell back onto the mattress, bringing my body down on top of his. I dug my fingers into his hair and kissed him again, long and hard and deep. Even though I was plastered against him, I couldn't feel enough of him, and I squirmed closer.

Desmond skimmed his hand down my chest and stomach, then teased me with his fingers again. Soft and slow, then fast and hard. I sucked in breath after breath as he stroked me, and every nerve ending in my body sparked, crackled, and vibrated in time to the movements of his nimble fingers.

Desmond kept teasing me, bringing me right to the edge of an orgasm. Then he removed his fingers and thrust inside me.

My hands dug into his shoulders, and I gasped at the heady sensations spiraling through me. Desmond let me adjust to the feel of him, then placed his hands on my hips. He drew me back, then forward, thrusting into me a little deeper than before. We both gasped.

"You feel so good," he growled against my neck.

"Not as good as you do," I rasped back.

We both lost all sense of control, and we rocked back and forth, each motion harder and quicker than the last. I threw my head back, fully engulfed in that rip current of motion and spine-tingling sensation. Desmond squeezed my hips and pulled me out into that ocean of heat and bright, sparking pleasure right along with him, until . . .

My body clenched around him, and an orgasm pulsed through me, intense and sharp and crackling. I cried out, and a moment later, so did he, each of us drowning in the other.

FORTY-FIVE

DESMOND

Charlotte shuddered out a breath and slumped forward, her chest resting against mine. We stayed like that for the better part of a minute. Then she drew back and opened her eyes, her dark blue gaze blazing just as brightly as her aura, which glowed like a sapphire sun.

It was—*she* was—the most beautiful thing I'd ever seen.

I gently kissed her, then slowly withdrew. Charlotte slid over onto her side. She nuzzled my neck, then sat up, got to her feet, and held out her hand. I took it, and she drew me up off the bed and into the bathroom. I got rid of the condom, and Charlotte tilted her head toward the shower, a wicked grin on her face.

"Want to get cleaned up, Dundee?"

"With you, Numbers?" I grinned. "Always."

We both shed the rest of our clothes. I grabbed another condom and laid it on a shelf in the shower. Charlotte turned on the faucet, and we stepped under the spray. The warm water beat down on my body, but it was nothing compared to the fire still raging through my veins. I'd just been as close to Charlotte as

I could be to another person, and I still wanted *more*.

My heart squeezed. Somehow I knew I would always want more of her.

Charlotte stepped forward and dug her hands into my hair. She massaged my scalp with her fingertips, then dragged her nails across it for good measure. My dick sprang to life again, and I was hard within seconds.

I groaned. "You have no idea how good that feels."

"Oh, I think I have some idea," Charlotte teased.

She kept massaging my scalp, and I gave myself over to the simple, sensual sensation.

The water continued to beat down on my back, but all I was aware of was Charlotte's magic touch. Not just on my body but on my soul too. Things had been so ugly with my father earlier that I thought I would never be clean again. But being here with her, I felt more like myself than I had in the whole time we'd been at headquarters today.

I dipped my head and nuzzled Charlotte's neck. I nipped at the pulse in the hollow of her throat, even as my hands snaked up between us. I cupped her breasts, and she sighed with pleasure. I nipped at her neck again, then kissed my way down her chest. I licked her right nipple, then her left one, then massaged both her breasts.

Charlotte's hands slid out of my hair and curled around my shoulders. Every one of her sighs, gasps, and moans heightened my own pleasure. Every part of me stiffened, throbbed, and burned with the need to plunge inside her, but I took my time and adjusted my touch to what she liked the best.

All I could see, feel, and taste was her silky skin, and her sugar-lime scent flooded my nose, making me hungry for even more. I never wanted to stop touching her and bringing her pleasure.

"Desmond . . ." Charlotte rasped.

I grabbed the condom from the shelf, tore the packet open,

and covered myself with it. Then I gave her a wicked grin, went down on my knees, and put my mouth on her, licking and sucking her as the hot water beat down on us both.

Charlotte moaned and squirmed against my tongue, and her aura crackled with her rapidly building pleasure. I kept going until she exploded, and her thighs clamped around my head.

Then, when she had started to come down, I stood up and positioned myself between her thighs again. Charlotte tangled her hands in my hair and hooked one of her legs around my hip. I eased closer, and she licked her lips in anticipation. I eased closer still, my dick poised at her entrance. Charlotte shifted toward me, and I slid into her.

People often say they see stars during sex. Well, with Charlotte, I saw a whole bloody galaxy.

I hoisted Charlotte's leg a little higher and slid even deeper into her warm, wet folds. More stars, more sensation, more pleasure . . .

She cupped my face in her hands, her lips crashing into mine. I kissed her back and pumped my hips hard and fast, until we were both moaning, squirming, and aching for more.

And then we found that more—together.

After it was over, I drew back and got rid of the condom. The water was still running, although it was lukewarm now, and we both cleaned up for real this time. Then I scooped up Charlotte, carried her back into the bedroom, laid her down, and stretched out beside her on the mattress.

Charlotte drew a blanket up over us and put her head on my chest. We didn't speak for a long time, both of us enjoying the afterglow.

"So where do we go from here?" she finally said, repeating

my earlier question, then raised her head to look at me. "Do you want to stay at Section? Go somewhere else? Forget all about being a spy? I'll support you no matter what, Desmond."

I knew she would, and it was one of the many things I adored about her. "Being part of a *we* with you is all I need, regardless of Section 47 or being a spy or anything else."

Charlotte's sapphire-blue aura pulsed with happiness. A wide smile split her face, although it quickly turned into a thoughtful look. "But?"

"But we still have an enemy to deal with."

"Henrika." Charlotte spat out the other woman's name. "She set us both up to get exactly what she wanted, and then she slipped away from us—*again*. I'm tired of her always being one step ahead."

"Me too. Which is why we're going to take her down." I hesitated. "If that's what you want?"

Charlotte nodded. "That's exactly what I want. And I have some ideas on how we can do that—together."

I nodded back, then rolled over so that she was beneath me. "We can talk all about your wonderful ideas, Numbers. Tomorrow."

"Tomorrow, eh?" Her hands started roaming over my body. "What did you have in mind for the rest of tonight, Dundee?"

A grin spread across my lips. "Let me show you."

And that's exactly what I did.

EPILOGUE

HENRIKA

"**S**he really did it," I murmured. "Good for you, Charlotte. Good for you."

I raised a mug of hot apple cider in a toast to the analyst, then kept scanning through the internal Section 47 report one of my sources had sent me. Charlotte had pieced it all together, just like I'd hoped, and she'd exposed Jethro Percy for the raging hypocrite he truly was. Even more stunning was the fact that Desmond had helped her do it.

I had no animus toward Desmond, and I hadn't blamed the son for the many, many sins of his father. But Desmond was one of the few things Jethro truly cared about, which made the cleaner a useful tool in getting my revenge.

However, the son was rapidly turning into just as much of a problem as his father. I still didn't understand how Desmond had survived both my original Redburn explosive *and* my new modified poison. None of the tests I'd done in my lab had yielded any unusual results, and I was no further along in perfecting my formula than before I'd captured Desmond. Pity.

But for the moment, I was going to bask in my victory, even if it was by proxy. Jethro Percy had been suspended from Section 47, pending a full investigation. In all likelihood, the other members of the board of directors, along with the station chiefs, would force him to quietly retire. It wasn't the brutal loss he deserved, but it was enough—for now.

Still clutching my mug of cider, I rolled my desk chair to the side and stared out through the window. Delicate flakes of snow fluttered down from the sky, adding a layer of fresh clean powder to the rugged Colorado landscape. In the distance, a few guards patrolled back and forth, looking like black ants trudging through the snow, but I wasn't worried. Section 47 would never find my mountain safe house, and I'd earned a few much-needed vacation days, which I planned to spend right here in my warm, comfortable library, curled up with a book by the fireplace.

A bit of disappointment flickered through me that Bryce wasn't here to appreciate the cozy scene. Bryce Finkley had been an amusing diversion, although I'd known as soon as I hired the former cleaner that he was no match for Desmond Percy. If Bryce had just followed my orders to leave Desmond behind in the lab instead of trying to kill the other cleaner, Bryce would have still been alive. Ah, well. These things happened.

I lifted my mug again, toasting Bryce this time, then rolled my chair back toward the desk. I took a sip of cider, enjoying the warm apple, cinnamon, and orange notes dancing on my tongue. Then I set the mug aside and grabbed another report to study.

Now that Jethro Percy was no longer an immediate threat, I could turn my attention to my other enemies.

A smile curved my lips. Charlotte had helped me take down one of my greatest rivals in Jethro Percy, and I saw no reason not to rely on her brilliance and tenacity again.

Charlotte Locke was going to help me destroy the Syndicate—whether she liked it or not.

Thank you for reading *A Touch of Treachery*. Charlotte and Desmond will return in another **Section 47** adventure.

BONUS CHAPTER

GABRIEL

'd been leaning my shoulder against the alley wall, waiting outside in the cold and snow for hours, but I didn't mind. Sometimes I thought that's all life really was—waiting for stuff to happen so you could finally react to it and move forward.

Shortly before midnight, Joan Samson pushed through the revolving doors of Section 47 headquarters. She glanced around a moment, then headed in the direction of her nearby apartment. She walked right past my position in the alley, and she didn't bat an eye as I sauntered out of the shadows and fell in step beside her on the sidewalk.

"What do you want?" she snapped.

Joan was a good six inches shorter than me, but I still had to lengthen my steps to keep up with her quick, angry strides.

"Charlotte texted me about everything that happened today. Just wanted to make sure the deed was done and there was no blowback on her."

Joan snorted. "For taking down Jethro Percy? The head of the board of directors? Please. We both know there's going to be some serious blowback. Especially since Evelyn had to out herself as Maestro, step in, and take charge. Your friend Charlotte just put a giant target on all our backs, including yours, Mr. Chase."

"I'm not a cleaner anymore."

Joan glanced at me out of the corner of her eye. "And yet you keep inserting yourself into Section business. Seems to me you just can't quit meddling in things that aren't supposed to concern you anymore."

"Says the woman who calls herself Nemesis," I countered. "Seems like someone else is a meddler too."

Joan rolled her eyes, but she finally stopped walking and faced me. The snow was falling all around us now, and several flakes landed in her long black hair, making her look like an ice queen come to life.

"Is that what this is about?" she asked. "My being Nemesis?"

I slid my hands into my jacket pockets and shrugged. "You hid your tracks well, but I warned you Charlotte would figure it out. She always does. I'm just wondering why you picked *me* for your scheme."

She shrugged right back at me. "Because you were already in Germany, and you're Charlotte's friend. I knew you wouldn't pass up an opportunity to help her."

"Just like you wouldn't pass up a chance to get your revenge on Henrika? I know all about you and Graham Walker. The two of you weren't nearly as discreet as you thought. All it took was a few phone calls to my old cleaner buddies, and I found out *exactly* how close the two of you were."

Joan shrugged again, but the motion was sharper and quicker than before, as though she was annoyed that I'd discovered one of her secrets for a change. "So Graham and I were involved. So what? So are lots of cleaners and liaisons."

"So why not reveal exactly who you were when you sent me to Tannenbaum Castle?"

"Because you didn't need to know, and I didn't feel like explaining myself to you," she snapped. "Now, if there's nothing else, it's late, and I'm tired."

"One more thing. You owe me a favor."

Joan blinked at the sudden change in topic, and a couple of snowflakes clung to her long, dark lashes. "Excuse me?"

I stepped forward, towering over her, but she didn't back away. Then again, with her transmuter power, all she had to do was touch me, and she could freeze my entire body and turn me into the world's biggest icicle. Which I found far more appealing than I should have. Then again, Section cleaners, even former ones, weren't known for shying away from danger—they were more likely to run straight toward it.

"You summoned me to Germany, and I helped Charlotte and Desmond when you couldn't, so now you owe me a favor in return."

Joan rolled her eyes again. "Let me guess. You're calling in your supposed favor right now?"

"Well, I do have some ideas for how you could make it up to me."

My voice came out lower and huskier than I'd intended. Joan's gaze snapped up to mine, and a rush of pink flooded her cheeks that had nothing to do with the cold. To my surprise, an answering spark of interest zinged through my own body.

Smart, strong, clever, capable, and utterly unattainable. Charlotte had been right back at the Glittertop Resort. Joan Samson was *exactly* the kind of woman I was attracted to, but something about her intrigued me more than most.

Joan's pale blue gaze traced over my shoulders and down my chest. The pink in her cheeks intensified, sending more sparks through me. The liaison wasn't nearly as disinterested as she pretended to be.

"You know I'm right," I said. "And aren't you all about doing the right thing?"

Joan let out an aggravated huff. "Fine. You win, Mr. Chase. You helped Charlotte and Desmond in Germany, so yes, I suppose I do owe you a favor in return. What do you want?"

"You."

Her eyes widened in shock, although she quickly schooled her face into a neutral expression. "For what?"

"I haven't decided yet." I leaned down so my mouth was close to her ear. "But when I do, you'll be the first to know."

She shivered, and I found myself wanting to lean into her warmth. But I knew better than to get involved with anyone at Section 47. I'd made that mistake once, and I wasn't about to make it again, so I forced myself to straighten up and step back.

I winked at her. "I'll be in touch, Ms. Samson."

"I will await your call with bated breath," she drawled.

I tipped an imaginary hat to her, then spun around on my heel and strolled away, whistling all the while. I was going to call in the favor Joan Samson owed me sooner than she might think—and I was going to enjoy every single minute of it.

BONUS CHAPTER

JOAN

Gabriel Chase strode away, whistling a loud, jaunty tune. He easily cut a path through the dark night, and even the snow seemed to swirl around him instead of slapping him in the face like it was doing to me.

Anger flickered in my chest. Gabriel Chase was everything I disliked in a cleaner, even a former cleaner—cocky. arrogant, deadly. He was also entirely too attractive for his own good. Well, more like for *my* own good.

I sighed, and my anger receded, replaced by more than a little uncomfortable guilt.

Ever since Graham had been killed on the Blacksea mission, I'd been going through the motions of life, walking around numb most of the time. But something about Gabriel Chase cut through the numbness and jolted me back to life whether I wanted it to or not.

More guilt filled me. I'd loved Graham, and he had loved me. We'd even been talking about leaving Section 47 and building a life together outside the spy world. Well, Graham had been talking about it. I had wanted to stay at Section, had wanted to keep being a liaison, which I loved.

But Graham was gone, and now I didn't know *what* I wanted, especially given all the disturbing secrets with General Percy that had come to light.

But try as I might, and despite my best intentions, I couldn't take my eyes off Gabriel as he walked away, rounded a corner, and disappeared into the dark night.

I didn't have synesthesia, so I didn't get warnings about danger or lies like Charlotte did, but I still had a funny feeling that Gabriel Chase's favor was going to cost me far more than I wanted to give.

ABOUT THE AUTHOR

Jennifer Estep is a *New York Times*, *USA Today*, and internationally bestselling author who prowls the streets of her imagination in search of her next fantasy idea.

Jennifer is the author of the **Galactic Bonds**, **Section 47**, **Elemental Assassin**, **Crown of Shards**, **Gargoyle Queen**, and other fantasy series. She has written more than fifty books, along with numerous novellas and stories.

In her spare time, Jennifer enjoys hanging out with friends and family, doing yoga, and reading fantasy and romance books. She also watches way too much TV and loves all things related to superheroes.

For more information on Jennifer and her books, visit her website at **www.jenniferestep.com** or follow her online on Facebook, Instagram, Threads, Bluesky, Amazon, BookBub, Goodreads, TikTok, and X (formerly Twitter).

Happy reading, everyone!

 To sign up for Jennifer's newsletter, scan the QR code or visit https://bit.ly/41AGJvn

OTHER BOOKS
BY JENNIFER ESTEP

THE SECTION 47 SERIES
A Sense of Danger
Sugar Plum Spies (holiday book)
A Touch of Treachery

THE GALACTIC BONDS SERIES
Only Bad Options
Only Good Enemies
Only Hard Problems (Zane Zimmer book)
Only Cold Depths
Only Rogue Actions

THE ELEMENTAL ASSASSIN SERIES
FEATURING GIN BLANCO

BOOKS
Spider's Bite
Web of Lies
Venom
Tangled Threads
Spider's Revenge
By a Thread
Widow's Web
Deadly Sting
Heart of Venom
The Spider

Poison Promise
Black Widow
Spider's Trap
Bitter Bite
Unraveled
Snared
Venom in the Veins
Sharpest Sting
Last Strand
Stings and Stones (short story collection)

E-NOVELLAS AND SHORT STORIES
Haints and Hobwebs
Thread of Death
Parlor Tricks
Kiss of Venom
Unwanted
Nice Guys Bite
Winter's Web
Heart Stings
Spider and Frost (crossover novella)

THE CROWN OF SHARDS SERIES
Kill the Queen
Protect the Prince
Crush the King

THE GARGOYLE QUEEN SERIES
Capture the Crown
Tear Down the Throne
Conquer the Kingdom

THE BLACK BLADE SERIES
Cold Burn of Magic
Dark Heart of Magic
Bright Blaze of Magic

www.ingramcontent.com/pod-product-compliance
Lightning Source LLC
Chambersburg PA
CBHW031435200726
48289CB00001BA/83